OMERTA

Also by Jack Weaver

Phantoms of the Woods—Copywright by Jack Weaver 1992
Hunting, Have Fun, Be Smart—Copywright by The Rosen Publishing
Group, Inc. 2000

Omerta
Code Of Silence

By

Jack Weaver

Order this book online at www.trafford.com
or email orders@trafford.com

Most Trafford titles are also available at major online book retailers.

Note for Librarians: A cataloguing record for this book is available from Library
and Archives Canada at www.collectionscanada.ca/amicus/index-e.html

Printed in Victoria, BC, Canada.

ISBN: 978-1-4269-1427-0 (Soft)
ISBN: 978-1-4269-1428-7 (Hard)

Library of Congress Control Number: 2009934473

*Our mission is to efficiently provide the world's finest, most comprehensive
book publishing service, enabling every author to experience success.
To find out how to publish your book, your way, and have it available
worldwide, visit us online at www.trafford.com*

Trafford rev. 01/07/2010

www.trafford.com

North America & international
toll-free: 1 888 232 4444 (USA & Canada)
phone: 250 383 6864 ♦ fax: 812 355 4082

Dedication

*To the one person in my life who has placed unshaken confidence in me—
my lovely wife Caroline. She is the light of my life and my greatest joy.*

Preface

Although this story is based on recorded facts it remains a work of historical fiction. Considerable literary license and no small amount of imagination needed to be invoked to bring it to life. It is through the venue of human emotion, passion and expression that we live life. Although these events took place over one hundred and ten years ago real people both good and bad, who loved, breathed and died, actually lived out this story. So while facts shape history—fiction puts flesh on their bones.

I drew upon many sources in an attempt to keep the storyline running in the right direction. These included copies of reports that were fearfully hand written by operative #89 in the woods around Hillsville. These reports were later typed by clerks at Pinkerton headquarters in Pittsburgh and a copy forwarded to the executive secretary of the old Board of Game Commissioners—known today as the Pennsylvania Game Commission. I ran across these copies in an old dusty file in Harrisburg while doing research for the agency's centennial. These reports read almost like a book but leave out much of the day to day dialogue that breathes life into history. However they did bring a vibrant, if not pungent, view of the plight of Italian laborers and their families. These were real people that were caught between their own sense of nationalism, the bigotry of the American community and the cruelty of the Black Hand. Not to mention the near poverty conditions under which immigrant laborers and their families were forced to live because of the depredations of the Black Hand.

Facts were also drawn from copies of the docket of the trial of Rocco Racca and other Black Hand trials of the period. Historical newspaper files of these trying times provided an American perspective on these issues. Actually there was such a fear on the part of the local American community that the local transit company, operating an interurban trolley service between New Castle and Youngstown, hired special armed detectives to provide safety for their passengers. Although even the most notorious members of the Society of Honor, as it was called by the Italian community, had little or no interest in bothering American citizens. The sole exception to this was Game Protector Seeley Houk who was hired to enforce the Commonwealth's new game laws, which were highly unpopular with almost everyone. High on the agenda of the relatively new wildlife agency was the protection of song birds. Unfortunately, many folks in the immigrant communities had a fondness for dining on wild birds—which were protected under the new game laws.

In defense of the law enforcement community of that day—they did what they had to do to uphold the laws of the land. 'It wasn't pretty and it might not work today. However, their methods were respected—as were their fathers. Be disrespectful to either and one might lose some teeth. Such were the times.

In order to protect the decedents of those who played active roles in this drama I chose, with a few exceptions, to create factitious names for the players. The exceptions were those few whose names were highlighted by history. These include District Attorney Charles H. Young, the Hon. William E. Porter, Creighton Logan, Rocco Racca, Clyde Duff and sons, and Seeley Houk. Many of us have skeletons in our closets but seldom do we choose to bring them out and shake them in people's faces. Therefore, you may embark on this adventure without being fearful of encountering a vengeful spirit on some dark and rainy night.

Jack Weaver

Acknowledgments

Without the help of dedicated people who believe passionately that stories such as this need to be told, this book would never have been written. Therefore, I wish to acknowledge those who made an impact with help and resources that contributed to its creation.

First is the late Dr. Ellis Hoffman, DO of New Castle who took the time to show my wife and I around the sites of the old Peanut Settlement and Hillsville. Together, along with the late Gene Beaumont who was the Wildlife Conservation Officer in Lawrence County at that time, we found and climbed the paths that Seeley Houk and the residents of the district used on a daily basis. We found the eddy in the Mohoning River where Seeley's body was disposed of and later found. And we fought the briars along the bluff to explore the old stone foundations of some of the immigrant shanties of Peanut. This gave me a personal feel of the land—enabling confidence in describing those wrinkled hollows along that section of the Mahoning River. But mostly Dr. Hoffman and his lovely wife became friends who threw open the resources of the Lawrence County Historical Society's collections of vintage photographs and documents, for which he was then the acting director.

Of course the Lawrence County Historical Society, New Castle, PA, deserves its own recognition for graciously allowing the publication of some of its historical photographs and for their encouragement to this author to publish Lawrence County's struggle with the Black Hand and the plight of immigrant laborers. Today Lawrence County, and specifically the New Castle area, has the greatest population of Italian/Americans in the United States. This is their story.

I should also like to thank the New Castle Public Library. With their help I was able to search and copy the period newspapers of 1906 through 1909 giving invaluable insight into those trying times.

Finally, I wish to thank my former superiors in the Game Commission, who were willing to turn one of their wildlife conservation officers loose to research the agency's rich and diversified history. Without this freedom, I would never have been able to tell this story.

Introduction

Perched on the bluffs above the Mahoning River, between New Castle, Pa. and Youngstown, Ohio a ramshackle collection of shantytowns provide cheap labor for quarries mining limestone for steel mills in nearby Pittsburgh. Between 1906 and 1909, the newspapers of the day call the place "Bloody Hillsville".

Omerta, follows Dominick Prugitore, a rookie Pinkerton detective, as he attempts to investigate the murder of his friend, Seeley Houk, one of Pennsylvania's first game wardens. What he found shocked the law enforcement community of his day and changed his life forever.

This is a world of secret codes, duels, vendettas, assassins, and bizarre initiation rights; of Mustachio Pete's and unbridled law enforcement. Of 60-mph interurban trolleys and horse drawn buggies, prejudice, bigotry, and the near slavery of immigrant labors. It is a dangerous world dominated by an organization known as The Black Hand. An organization held together by the Omerta, a code of silence. Breaking the Omerta is the key to solving the murder of the game warden. But to break the Omerta carries a sentence of death, and Dominick must take the oath knowing he is duty bound to break it.

Chapter 1

The game warden, his pin-striped pants tucked into the tops of tall boots, stepped easily over a low fence and struck a path that led along the north edge of the Johnson Quarry. Hunching his shoulders under a heavy slicker he pulled his slouch hat lower to protect a handlebar mustache already dripping from the March drizzle. Wood smoke from the settlement ahead pooled around piles of topsoil lining the cut like bumps on a dragon's tail.

The village of Peanut and its smaller quarry sat at the head of two hollows that ran steeply down a bluff to the Mahoning River, just east of Hillsville. Two young boys playing with a buggy hoop on the muddy street silently watched the tall man stride past. Nearby a young man leaned against a banister smoking a wrinkled black cigar. There were no greetings. As the game warden took a path leading to the Peanut quarry's stone crusher, he didn't notice another man step out of a house and speak quietly to the man leaning against the banister.

The warden glanced around the quarry as water dripped off his slicker onto the toes of high boots smeared with a grayish mixture of wet lime and mud. A steam shovel, shrouded in mist, sat sullenly in the distance. The gapping cut yawned before him quiet and empty. Dusk was settling. With an oath he turned back toward the settlement. At least the rain had stopped.

When the shanties of Peanut ghosted through the mist the game warden swung unto another path that cut along a ridge between the hollows. Just before the path dropped sharply toward the railroad, he spotted a young girl crouching behind a stump. Frightened dark eyes peered back as he strode past.

Jack Weaver

People often walked the railroad to Edinburg where they could cross the railroad trestle over the Mahoning River and catch the trolley into New Castle. The path to the railroad was steep and either side overgrown with brambles.

When the game warden reached the railroad and turned toward Edinburg, he heard the unmistakable report of a shotgun in some trees above the tracks. Hunting season was closed. Taking a pistol from his pocket, he climbed the bramble-covered bank above the tracks and peered into the darkening woods. He was near the trail when a man with a gun suddenly appeared around the side of a tree. There was a flash, and a tremendous force slammed into the warden's chest. Pinned to the ground like a beetle on a stick, he couldn't breathe. Something warm bubbled into his mouth. There were footsteps and a few excited words in a foreign language before something cold pressed against his face. As he looked into the twin muzzles of a double-barreled shotgun there was a sudden blast of flame, then darkness.

The body was still jerking when one of the men smashed his boot into the upper part of the game warden's face. The lower half had been blown into a bloody pulp.

"It's all right," the second man said. "He's dead."

"That's for Pauline," the other replied. Then he spit into the bloody remains of the dead man's face. They never noticed the girl scampering up the path toward the shanties.

Later that night the men returned and dragged the game warden's body over the railroad tracks. Wading into the swollen river, they filled the game warden's rain slicker with stones until the mutilated corpse sank into the muddy waters.

Chapter 2

Dominick Prugitore had a classical face, fine boned and handsome, except for the scars. A smallpox survivor from his native providence of Calabria in southern Italy, pockmarks ran from his chin to his thick, black hair. Pulling open one of the double oak doors, he was impressed, as always, with the ordered confusion he found at Pinkerton headquarters in downtown Pittsburgh. One place, however, stood in sharp contrast to this bustle of activity. At a small orderly desk, the office's only female employee sat poised before a stack of expense reports. Dominick shuffled uneasily in front of her desk.

"You're late, Mr. Pingatorie," she said without looking up.

"It's Prugitore, Miss Liptak."

"Have a seat then. I'll tell Superintendent Cafee you've finally arrived."

Rising, she walked to the middle one of three doors set in the back wall and, after rapping softly on the varnished oak, slipped quickly inside. A few minutes later she slipped back out looking unusually grave. "You may go right in, Mr. Prugitore," she said quickly.

Elmer Cafee sat dwarfed behind a highly polished desk in the middle of an immaculate room. An elaborate plaster framed portrait of Allen Pinkerton hung on the wall behind the desk. Cafee followed Dominick's approach through a pair of thick spectacles.

"You're late, Prugitore!" Cafee hurled the words like a javelin, his nasal sounding voice tearing the air between them.

"I'm sorry, sir. The train was late arriving in New Castle."

"A likely story. You Italians always have an excuse ready to cover your incompetence."

Dominick felt his neck flush but managed to remain impassive. "You can easily verify the story, sir."

Cafee's baldhead flushed as he rose to his feet. The little man leaned carefully forward over his desk supported by the tips of his fingers.

"You, impertinent young fool! Do you think I have time to trace all your lies?" When Dominick failed to reply he continued. "The case in Youngstown failed because you disobeyed orders."

"I...I beg your pardon, sir?"

"Don't play the innocent immigrant with me, Prugitore! Because you failed to keep me informed of your daily movements, we exposed the case there prematurely. That raid left the agency embarrassed, to say the least."

Dominick thrust his hands into his pockets to keep them from trembling. Slowly he began to recover from the shock of what Cafee was saying. He was being blamed for the debacle in Youngstown.

"Mr. Cafee, this was my first assignment. You knew I was living with those people. They watched me every minute. I couldn't write daily reports."

"So you took it upon yourself not to follow procedure, did you?"

"You could have trusted me, Mr. Cafee."

"My contacts told me you went over to their side. That's not surprising for an Italian, after all."

Dominick clenched his fists in his pockets. He wanted to grab the little man in the three-piece suit and shove the bow tie down his throat. "I see," Dominick replied slowly. "I am to take the blame for your own impetuous actions."

Elmer Cafee stuttered, then made a show of plucking off his spectacles and tossing them on the desk, however softly. "You're fired, Prugitore. You may collect your pay from Miss Liptak tomorrow. Now get out!"

Dominick inclined his head in a curt bow and, without a word, turned toward the door. Pausing half way through, he remarked casually, "Have a nice day, Mr. Cafee."

When the door shut, Dominick heard something shatter followed by a frustrated scream. A slight smile hinted at even white teeth and creased the pockmarks on his face when he realized Cafee must have hurled his spectacles at the varnished oak door.

Ambling through the crowded streets of Pittsburgh's Italian section, he felt strangely comforted. Snatches of Italian conversation pulled at his ears and his heart. The air was filled with the spicy aroma of Italian food mingled with the pungent odor of the wrinkled black Di Nobil cigars. Occasionally the soft strains of a mandolin, or violin, drifted from an open tenement. Eleven years I've been away from my countrymen. Tears filled his eyes unbidden. How I miss home. Then he thought of his Aunt Marie, who gave up her Italian heritage when she married Roland Gunther Winstead II. Uncle Roland, as he insisted on being called, was an Englishman who owned a large hotel in Philadelphia. Thinking of Uncle Roland and his hotel brought another wave of despair crashing over him. I couldn't bear that man's criticism if I returned, he thought, but I certainly can't keep roaming these streets.

Again he thought about Seeley Houk, and he had to lean against a streetlight as his stomach knotted. Yesterday's paper had carried the story. The game warden's body was found floating in the Mahoning River near a place called Hillsville. Dominick slapped the pole hard in frustration. Why didn't he take the warnings seriously?

Dominick had met the game warden on his way to his first assignment in Youngstown, and a warm friendship had formed. Seeley Houk was the first American to treat the young man as an equal rather than an unwanted foreigner. During dinner one evening Houk confided in Dominick that certain Italians had threatened his life. He warned Seeley to be careful, that Italians took such threats seriously. Now Houk was dead, and he was alone again.

By evening the young man realized he would have to eat despite the knots in his stomach. Three days had passed since he had been fired. Three days of wandering the streets, searching—for what, he wondered?

A small restaurant, with some particularly enticing odors drifting out an open window, pulled at him. At the jingling of the little bell on the door, two old men sipping wine at one of the four tables glanced at him. As Dominick sat down at a table by the door, a round, bald-headed man pushed through a curtain at the back of the room and hurried over.

"Buongiorno," the man said, eyeing him critically from under a pair of heavy brows.

"Buongiorno. Vino, please."

The bald-headed man inclined his head to one side and arched a lone brow slightly. "That will be five cents, young man."

Dominick handed the man a nickel, and when he returned with a glass of red wine the man's critical expression had softened. "You have a choice of spaghetti or tripe this evening."

"Spaghetti," Dominick replied. Thinking of the bitter tripe did little to settle his beleaguered stomach.

He was sipping a final glass of wine when the jingling bell drew his attention toward the door. Three men entered, and Dominick watched them out of the corner of his eye as he reflected on his problems. Two of the men took a table next to him, while the third and taller of the trio, strode toward the back of the room. As the waiter pushed through the curtains the stranger flashed a hand sign. The bald-headed man's eyes widened before he quickly stepped back, snapping the curtains shut between them. His curiosity aroused, Dominick watched intently as the taller man glared briefly at the old men sitting at the far table. They quit talking and peered sullenly at their wineglasses.

The stranger pulled out a chair from Dominick's table spun it around and straddled the seat before folding his arms over the rigid back facing him. He was clean-shaven with a derby hat and dark coat over a collarless shirt. An ugly scar slanted diagonally across his left cheek. One of the other men got up and stood with his arms folded by the door, glaring at Dominick. The man sitting at his table watched him a moment before speaking. "You are going to take a little walk with us, detective-man," he said finally.

A prickly sensation ran up Dominick's spine. He'd heard certain Italians hated authority, especially those who worked as policemen or even company foreman. "I'm sorry," he said, "you must be mistaken."

"No, I do not think so, detective-man." The stranger's face solidified like the statues in Rome.

As the man rose to his feet, Dominick could see the hand under his coat was clutching a pistol.

"And, now you will stand," the scared man said. "We are going to take a little walk. If you try to run..." The stranger nodded toward the next table. "Julio there is very quick with the knife."

Dominick glanced at Julio, a wiry young man in his late teens. Julio flashed an innocent smile and pulled back his shirtsleeve, revealing the handle of a stiletto under his left wrist.

Dominick felt the blood drain from his limbs, but managed, somehow, to keep his voice firm. "May I ask where we are going?"

"Someone wants to ask you some questions," the stranger said. "I suggest you tell him the truth. Then we shall see."

Dusk had fallen outside, and Dominick noticed that much of the street traffic had diminished. The man who stood by the door led the way toward an alley two blocks away. The scar-faced man was flanking him on the right, and the boy was walking with a loose- legged stride just behind his left side. When they reached the narrow alley cluttered with garbage and debris, the scar-faced man stepped aside to let the lad with the knife step behind Dominick. Dominick knew he couldn't outrun the boy. Even if he managed to knock him down the man with the gun would have him. Then there was always the third man, now several paces ahead. Dominick felt sure he carried something lethal.

Overhead, a spider web of wash lines stretched between tenement windows. The men made lewd remarks about a bloody sheet hanging from a windowsill which, in the custom of the old country, verified a bride's virginity. Soon they came to a pair of steps that led into a basement entry. The man up front knocked twice on a rough plank door before entering. When Dominick felt a hand grip his shoulder, he stopped on the top step and waited. No one spoke. A moment passed before the lead man opened the door and motioned for them to enter.

When Dominick felt the lad's hand prod him to move, he spun quickly, grabbed Julio's hand, and flipped him over his hip into the bottom of the entry. The boy, tumbling down the steps, crashed into the legs of the man by the door, causing him to fall with an oath.

Recovering quickly, Dominick spun and aimed a blow at the scar-faced man's stomach. Before it struck, sparks flashed across Dominick's left eye. He fell backwards, hard, into a pipe railing. The scar-faced man grabbed Dominick's shirt, jerking him upright, before slamming a heavy fist to his stomach. Dominick watched his dinner eject over the man's shoes. That sensation alone kept him from passing out while he gasped to catch his breath. Another blow drove him crashing into the bottom of the entry. As he struggled to rise, Dominick glimpsed a flash of steel, and then blackness engulfed him.

"Julio!" A loud voice shouted from the doorway. "Put that knife away, and get him inside!"

Dominick felt himself yanked across a rough wooden floor. He could see fuzzy shapes out of his right eye, and his head reeled with pain. Then the men dropped him in front of a crude table.

A wide-faced man sat behind the table. His dark eyes flashed with anger when he spoke. "I told you he was not to be injured, Tony!"

"You said you didn't want him killed, boss," the scar-faced man answered. "He's a clever one, and fast, too!"

"Get some water, and clean him up," the wide-faced man ordered. Dominick winced when one of the men sopped at his face with a wet cloth. There was a cut over his left eye that was bleeding freely, and his head thumped with pain.

"Easy, boy!" the man mopping at his face cautioned. "You might hurt some, but you're going to live."

Dominick took the wet cloth from the man and held it over his eye. His legs were weak when he tried to stand, but Dominick shoved a hand away when someone tried to help him up.

"I'm insulted, Prugitore," the man behind the table declared. "I go to all this trouble to invite you here, and you attack my men. What's the matter with you?"

He struggled to pull himself erect. There was a dull, lingering pain in his stomach. The sour reek of vomit lingered in the air. He tried to focus on the man at the table with his good eye. "I'm sorry; signore," he managed finally, "but you have the advantage of me. Do I know you?"

"No, Prugitore, but I know you to be a traitor to your people."

A chill ran down Dominick's spine. "What do you mean?" He asked weakly.

"When one of our people works for the authorities it is bad for us all. Especially when he works as a spy." The man stabbed a thick finger at him. "Like you do." The final phrase hung in the air like a death knell.

Dominick's mind raced. "What you say is true, signore. Yet, how are we to learn the ways of these Americans unless some of us join their organizations...even the polizia?"

Julio spit on the floor by his feet. "Let me kill the dog now." The boy growled.

"Yes!" Dominick shouted back. "Kill me now! But I tell you we must learn to play their game if we are to survive in America."

"What Toni said is true," the man behind the table said. "You are clever." Suddenly his voice turned chill as he pointed another accusing finger at Dominick. "In Ohio, you turned men over to the authorities."

Dominick shrugged, trying to keep his voice casual as he spoke, "They were only some dumb Irish." How could they know this? He wondered. Although he couldn't be sure, Dominick thought he detected an amused twinkle in the man's eye. "Do with me what you will, signore, but I am not a traitor to my people."

"We shall see," the man behind the table said. "Would you still work for the detectives if you could?"

He lowered his head. "I don't work for them. I was dismissed."

"That is not what I asked you! I asked if you would still work for them if you could."

Dominick raised a quizzical eyebrow. "Yes," he said softly, "I would."

The man slammed his fist on the table with a thud that echoed around the room. "Then you are condemned! Unless," he added slowly, "you follow my instructions exactly. Do you understand?"

"No, signore."

"Listen to me then, Dominick Prugitore, because your life depends upon it. You are to go to the detective agency tomorrow, at exactly one PM. You are to ask the lady there for Superintendent Dimuro. This you must do without fail. Do you understand?" He didn't wait for Dominick to answer before continuing. "These men will escort you back to your room. Now go!"

"I can find my own way," Dominick replied defiantly.

"Come along, lad." The scar-faced man said. "I hear there are ruffians on the streets this hour of the night."

Chapter 3

"The third door Mr. Prugitore, and you may go right in." Miss Liptak looked at him and smiled before adding softly, "I'm glad you came, Dominick."

"Thank you, madam." Surprised at her sudden informality, he moved slowly around her desk then walked quickly to the third door set along the rear wall. He noticed this door did not have a brass nameplate like the others, but he didn't have time to think about it.

"Come in!" Commanded a loud voice in response to his knock.

Dominick thought the voice sounded vaguely familiar. Opening the door he noticed this office was a sharp contrast to Cafee's. Stacks of papers and reports were piled everywhere. On the walls were pinned photographs and sketches of men with no discernible format. Notes, written in Italian, were tacked to many of them. Also, unlike the other office, there was a small door in the far corner that he presumed led to an alley. A thickset, obviously middle-aged, man was standing with his back to him tacking still another note to a photograph of a woman. All the photographs and sketches appeared to be Italians. A paper littered desk stood in one corner. When the man turned, Dominick's good eye widened in surprise.

"You!"

"Frank Dimuro," the man said, coming around the cluttered desk and extending a thick hand. "I see you're right on time." He spoke perfect English.

Dominick took the man's hand. "I was led to believe I had no other choice."

"Oh? I thought I made your choices perfectly clear. By the way, what are you doing for that eye? It looks terrible."

Before Dominick could reply the door in the far corner opened and the scar-faced man stepped into the room followed by a gust of wind that scattered papers across the floor. "Getting ready to storm any minute now," the man said.

"Dominick, I believe you met Tony Capizzi already."

"That eye looks pretty bad," Tony offered.

He ignored Tony's remark and addressed the older man. "Mr. Dimuro, I don't understand. What is it you want of me?"

The older man eyed him critically for a moment before replying. "Last evening you said you would work for the Pinkerton's again if you could. Do you still feel that way?"

"Yes, sir, I do but..."

"Then please allow me to explain myself. I have been commissioned by the company to start a special Italian undercover department here in Pittsburgh. It's an experiment to be sure, one fraught with its share of opposition. Like your former boss, the impetuous Mr. Cafee, for one."

"He doesn't like Italians much," Dominick replied.

With that, Tony let out a string of oaths, but Dimuro cut him off. "I apologize for the rough treatment, but you sort of interrupted our plans for a peaceful interrogation. I needed to know how you react under pressure, and if you have the wits to think fast under the same conditions."

"Did I pass?" he asked with a trace of sarcasm.

"You'll do," Dimuro replied before walking behind his desk and rummaging through some paraphernalia until he came up with the butt of a cigar. "You have a lot to learn, young man." The words tumbling out thick and rough around the cigar butt. "But the job's yours if you want it."

Tony came over and lit the cigar for his boss. Dimuro grunted his thanks from a cloud of brown smoke while they waited for Dominick's answer.

"What about Mr. Cafee? He fired me, you know."

Dimuro plucked the butt out of his mouth and poked it in Dominick's direction. "You let me worry about Cafee. He doesn't know who works for this department. If he finds out, I'll handle it. The question is will you work for me?"

"Yes, sir. I should like that very much."

"The kid has manners! How about that?" Tony exclaimed.

Frank Dimuro just shook his head. "OK, Tony here," he stabbed his cigar at the scar-faced man beside him, "is known as number 37. You will be..." he paused, rooting through more papers on his desk. "Yeah, here it is, number 89. Forget names, got that? This way we keep everyone's true identity a secret. Never sign your reports, just put your number on them. Now then..."

"Wait a minute, boss," Tony interrupted. "Before you get into this, I need to talk to you about my assignment in New Castle for the Board of Game Commissioners."

Dominick's face lit up. "You mean you're going to investigate the murder of Seeley Houk?"

Both of the other men looked at him with surprise.

"What do you know about it?" Dimuro snapped.

"I...I met him on the train while in route to Youngstown on assignment last month. We had dinner together at New Castle, and he spoke of threats by some of our people in Hillsville."

"What kind of threats?" Dimuro asked, and then rushed on before Dominick could answer. "And those kind of Italians are not our people. Remember that."

When Dominick finished relating Seeley's story he added, "I would also like to be assigned to this case, sir."

"Out of the question!" Dimuro snorted, stabbing what was left of his cigar into a heavy brass tray standing beside his desk. "You're far too inexperienced, and Hillsville is reported to be a dangerous place."

"But Seeley was my friend."

"Another good reason it's out of the question, son."

"Permesso, signore?" Tony's sudden change to Italian grabbed the attention of the others. "The boy has a point. I can't go into Hillsville for fear of being recognized. Dominick is a new face. Let him go into deep cover, as an immigrant labor looking for work. Perhaps he can get a job in the quarries and live among the people there." Tony gave Dimuro a sly glance. "He may even find what you are really looking for."

Dimuro flashed Tony a angry stare. "Absolutely not!"

"Permesso?" Tony asked again, raising a finger tentatively as if testing the air.

Superintendent Dimuro let out an impatient sigh, but allowed him to continue.

"Let me go to New Castle as planned. Perhaps I can learn something from the Italians there. Meanwhile, take Dominick, er 89, under your wing and teach him your crafty ways." There was a touch of irony in his voice now.

Dimuro flashed Tony another scowl. "Get out of here and go to work, Capizzi, but keep me informed." He turned to meet Dominick's intense gaze. "Meanwhile, I'll see if this upstart has the potential for such an assignment."

"Thank you, sir."

Frank Dimuro looked on Dominick's enthusiastic face, and slowly shook his head. "You may curse me before this is over, young man."

In the weeks that followed, Dominick stayed with Superintendent Dimuro and his wife. Meanwhile, Frank drilled the young detective on how to survive as an undercover agent.

"Don't trust no one," he told him, "and above all, don't allow yourself to become so personally involved you forget who you really are."

During one of his frequent after-dinner lectures, over a bottle of red wine, Frank confided in Dominick how he went to prison to infiltrate the New Orleans Mafia back in '90.

"The Americans think we broke up the Mafia in this country after that affair. But they are wrong, and I intend to prove it."

"Tell me about the Mafia," Dominick asked.

Frank Dimuro looked at him a long time before slowly shaking his head. "No. Safer, I think, if you go in as an innocent babe so-to-speak. If the Mafia is there it will rear its ugly head soon enough."

When Tony returned from New Castle he had only one suspect; a man named Rocco Racca.

Chapter 4

Y ou're the quiet one, my friend, but don't worry. No one will bother you, so long as you are with me."

Dana Carrello was well muscled. He had met the frail young man with the pockmarked face at the trolley stop in New Castle.

Dominick Prugitore flashed his new friend an apologetic smile as the interurban trolley sped along the north bank of the Mahoning River. "I am only worried about finding a job, Dana."

"Well, you have nothing to worry about. The quarries are always hiring, and the bed at the boarding house where I stay is big enough for two."

Dominick nodded and peered out the window at a freight train snaking its way along the opposite bank of the river. When he looked back Dana was frowning at him. "What's the matter?" he asked.

"You don't look like a laborer," Dana replied carefully.

"Perhaps I'm tougher than you think."

"Si, but the quarries are hard on a man and you look..." Dana stopped abruptly, stroked his thick crop of curly brown hair, then shrugged. "My boarding mistress is a good cook. She'll fatten you up."

They got off the car at Kennedy's Crossing where a wooden bridge spanned the river. The road immediately started up a steep grade that gave the town its name. Hillsville squatted atop bluffs overlooking the Mahoning River from the south. A gentle breeze mingled the scent of lilacs with the pungent reek of creosote from the rail ties. Two old quarries flanked the road as they climbed. The bluffs above the works hung thick with saplings and brambles.

"Not many big trees left, are there?" Dominick asked casually.

"There are a few down the tracks. Where the game warden's body was found."

"I heard that was a vendetta."

Dana stopped so suddenly Dominick became alarmed. "What's the matter?"

Dana's voice hushed from its usual bluster. "It is best not to talk about some things." He fixed Dominick with a serious expression before making a clumsy sign with his hand. When Dominick only looked confused, Dana suddenly broke into a wide grin. "Come along, compare." He laughed, giving the other a solid blow on the back. "We don't want to be late for supper."

They went a little further in silence before Dana touched Dominick's arm to stop him. "We are going to stay with the brother-in-law to a very bad man in this place. This man's name is Rocco Racca. You must not talk about this murder anymore, capeesh?"

Dominick did not trust himself to speak. He nodded in compliance, but Dana seemed to have made up his mind to talk.

"Rocco and I do not get along. He sent men to get money from me one day, and I beat them into the ground. Then I told Rocco the next time I would beat him, too. Now they leave me alone."

"I don't understand. Why then, do you stay at his brother-in-law's house?"

"Signora Carpellotti is a good cook, and Rocco can keep an eye on me." Dana shrugged. "It's a good arrangement, no?"

The men shared a small loft and a not so large a bed on the backside of the house. A wall-mounted kerosene light illuminated the room, and they shared an old immigrant trunk for their clothes. Dana pointed to a stained but lidded thunder mug in a corner by the bed. "Last one to use that has to empty it each morning," he stated solemnly.

The next morning Dana led the way down a rutted cart path toward the Peanut Settlement. Once, when they encountered a group of young men coming from Peanut, Dana only nodded and trudged past without further greeting. When Dominick asked about them, Dana mumbled something about bad men.

At the settlement a group of girls, under the direction of a stout woman, were pumping water from a hand pump on the street into copper boilers. Dana nodded at the woman and led Dominick to the only two-story house in Peanut. In what would have been the parlor were stacks of dry goods, work clothes, and boxes of tinned food.

Two men standing at the counter beside a curtained doorway stopped talking when they entered. One of the men was noticeably younger with penetrating eyes and a stern mouth set off by a well-trimmed mustache. The older man was shorter and stout with a bushy mustache that drooped over a pouting lower lip.

"What do you want, Carrello?" the shorter man demanded.

"I want you to meet a friend of mine, Rocco. He needs a spot in the quarry."

Rocco looked Dominick over without saying a word.

"How do you do, signore?" Dominick offered.

Rocco nodded stiffly. "What's your name?"

"Dominick Prugitore, signore."

"Where are you from?"

"Philadelphia, signore."

"When did you come over from the old country?"

"As a young boy, signore. After my father died."

The questions began to fly at him while the other man watched intently with cold eyes.

"What province are you from? What village? Where is the rest of your family?"

Dominick answered with a string of lies, shrugging, smiling, and hoping his fear didn't show. "I just brought my mother and sisters back from Italy three months ago," he lied.

Rocco raised his eyebrows. "Then why did you leave Philadelphia?"

Dominick felt his temper rise. "I love my mother and sisters more than anything in this world, signore. But there was some trouble and I had to leave."

"Are those parts of the problem?" Rocco pointed to a fading scar over the young man's eye and the remnants of the shiner Tony gave him.

When Dominick nodded, Rocco made a sign with his hand that Dominick didn't understand. After that Rocco relaxed. "Did you ever work in a quarry?"

"No, signore."

Rocco frowned at Dana. "What's the matter with you, Carrello? Do you want to get this boy killed? Let him work with you until he knows what to do. Then we will see about getting him a place."

On their way back to Hillsville, Dana explained how the quarries operated. "Each man works for himself. He is assigned a number and a place to work. Making those assignments is Rocco's job."

"I don't understand," Dominick interrupted.

The Americans at the quarry don't speak Italiano, so they hire Rocco to provide laborers. Because the dumb Americans can't pronounce our beautiful names, they assign us a number. You put the number on each car you fill with stone, and the bosses pay you from that. Simple, no?"

"But I speak American. Why don't we just go to the company office? I'll talk to them myself."

"Because this is our way," Dana explained patiently. "Besides, you must pay Rocco for your place to work. If Rocco doesn't get his money, something bad could happen."

"You must also pay for the dynamite and powder you use in the quarry," Dana grumbled. "In the end you will be lucky if you have enough to live on."

"Then why stay here?"

"This is the way for Italians all over this country." Dana's voice was getting louder, and he began waving his arms around. "Should I go back to Italy and starve?"

"I didn't know, Dana. I worked in a big city hotel before this."

"Is that where you learned to speak American?" Dana asked.

"Si," Dominick smiled. "I didn't get paid much, but the women were free."

Dana began to roar with laughter and pounded Dominick on the back nearly knocking him down. Suddenly the laughter broke into fits of coughing. "There are no women to be had here," he croaked, whenever he could catch his breath. "You will need to go to Lowellville." Another fit of laughter and coughing overtook him. "And compare, you will pay and pay."

Dana seized the young man's shoulder in a painful grip to steady himself until the spasms passed. "Dust from the quarries," he rasped when he could finally catch his breath. "Stuff gets in your lungs." Then he gave Dominick a huge grin. "You are going to kill me yet, compare."

The G.W. Johnson quarry was the largest operation in the area and hired the bulk of foreign laborers. A small and noisy steam engine sat puffing and hissing beside the crusher. One man yelled at Dana as they trudged past, but the muscular man just smiled and waved at him. Two other men working on the engine laughed loudly.

"He just called you a stinking fish-eater," Dominick told him.

"That's Bratton. He's the Dinky's engineer. Somebody will get him one of these days."

The two men followed the narrow gauge railroad into the cut as Dana led the way to his assigned work place. He carried an eight-pound sledge easily over his shoulder, while Dominick lugged a steel drill bit nearly as long as he was tall. Further on they encountered a red flag tied to a stick along the tracks.

"Hurry!" Dana yelled. "Get behind those stones."

He grabbed Dominick by the arm and dragged him toward a ledge. They had no sooner reached the shelter than a terrific explosion rocked the ground. When Dominick lifted his head to see, Dana yanked him off his feet. He fell to the ground as a cloud of dust and a shower of rock fragments enveloped them.

"That Ignazio Sebastianelli!" Dana scolded, rising like a vengeful wrath from the dust and debris. He jumped around Dominick and rushed into the cut, arms waving wildly. "You buried the tracks again!"

Dominick hurried after his friend. The air, heavy with dust and smoke, stung the young man's eyes and made him cough. He could hear Dana cursing and yelling ahead of him. When the air began to clear, he saw an old man materialize from behind some rocks grinning foolishly, and mopping a spot of blood from his head. The old man looked at Dominick with wide eyes. Brown, tobacco stained teeth leered through the coat of limestone dust covering his face.

"Make bigga' boom!" Ignazio declared in broken English, gesturing at the pile of rocks covering the tracks and spilling clear across the bottom of the cut.

Dana rushed over, his arms waving wildly. "You idiot! Won't you ever learn not to use so much dynamite? No one below here will be able to load stone for two days."

"Come," Ignazio answered, drifting smoothly back into Italian. "Help clear the tracks. Then the engine will come to you."

"Not this time," Dana replied.

Dana turned and began to climb over the pile of rocks. "Come on, Dominick, we have our own work to do."

They spent the next three days drilling blasting holes into the hard stone. They took turns, one of them holding and turning the drill bit while the other drove it into the rock with the sledge. Despite the gloves he wore, Dominick's hands blistered.

"You will get used to the work," Dana told him the next morning. "Then you will have muscles like me."

In the evenings Dominick wrote in a notebook he kept locked in a small leather trunk. Dana apparently mentioned this to the Carpellotti's because at breakfast one morning they wanted to know who he was writing to and why. The Italians, most of whom were illiterate, never sent letters unless it was absolutely necessary. They thought it very strange that he wrote every night, especially since he wrote in English. Dominick told them he promised to write his sister every day, and because she was trying to learn American he wrote to her in that language. They joked about it, saying she must be a very special sister indeed.

On the forth day, Dana showed Dominick how to attach wires to the primer caps and how to push the caps into the soft dynamite.

"We'll only shoot two holes at a time. That way we can control the amount of stone that comes down so we don't block the track like Ignazio did."

They packed clay into the holes behind the charges, set out their warning flags and then took shelter behind some boulders before Dana attached the wires to the plunger's box. The explosions weren't as violent as Ignazio's, but when the dust cleared, the rocks that separated from the cut were much larger. They had to spend the rest of the day breaking them into pieces small enough to load into the cars. By the end of the day, Dominick was so sore that he didn't come down for supper. When Dana came up to check on him, Dominick complained of a terrible headache.

"Nitroglycerine in the dynamite causes the headaches," Dana explained. "It is something you'll never get used to."

To make matters worse, strangers began hanging around the boarding house during the evenings. They usually came by after supper and joined in conversation, or just sat on the porch until Dominick left.

There was never any trouble, and whoever was there always seemed friendly enough. But Dominick sensed he was being watched.

The next evening, the young man took to the woods before supper to write his reports, striking out for the bluff between Hillsville and Peanut. He followed a narrow path that wound through the brambles and slashing toward a grove of oaks that somehow survived the woodcutter's axe. The path led down onto a wide bench that shouldered the steep bluff above the river. Inside the trees was a thick carpet of grass, covered with waves of blue and purple violets. He nearly completed four days worth of reports when he had the uncanny feeling he was being watched. Looking up, he was startled by a pretty young girl staring at him from across the glade. Dominick had the impression that if he moved she would bolt like a deer, and for some unexplainable reason, he didn't want her to.

Inclining her head slightly, she regarded him curiously. He noticed she was tiny featured, almost elf-like.

After an awkward moment he said. "My name is Dominick. Dominick Prugitore. Who are you?"

She stared at him. "Rosa Ciampanelli," she answered cautiously.

"Well, Rosa," Dominick said smiling, "if you're the princess of this glade I apologize for entering without your permission. At your command I shall ride off on my horse or fall upon my sword. What shall it be?"

Her giggle sounded like the trilling of a flute. A twinge of pain struck Dominick when he realized that his little sister would have been about this girl's age, had she lived. Rosa skipped a little closer.

"I'm not much of a princess with these clothes," she said sadly. "But you can stay, Sir Prince, if we can be friends."

"Friends we shall be till death, Princess Rosa," Dominick said, standing and bowing formally.

Her laughter trilled again.

"You must have a loving mother to keep that old dress patched and clean."

Rosa's eyes got big. "Mother will surely switch me if I'm late for supper. Perhaps, I will see you again, Dominick!" She turned and raced off before he could say anything more.

The glade seemed suddenly very empty.

Chapter 5

Two weeks later, Dominick sought out Rocco Racca. When he arrived at Rocco's store he found Romon Cerini and a wild-eyed young man conferring with Rocco at the counter. Once again the men stopped talking when he entered.

"I'm sorry, signore," he said to Rocco. "I'll come back if you're busy."

Rocco gave him a hard look. "Where is your friend, Carrello?"

Dominick shrugged. "I meet this man one day, and now he thinks he's my brother. Anyway, I need my own place at the quarry."

"Why don't you work with Saverino here? He's going to work on the steam shovel."

Dominick gestured broadly with his palms up, but shook his head. "Thank you, signore, but I'd rather have my own place. I need to make enough money to bring my mother and sister here from Philadelphia."

A lewd grin spread across Saverino's face. "We can always use a few more women around."

Dominick fixed him with such an intense stare that the young man stopped grinning.

"Maybe this one needs to learn a lesson," Saverino spat.

"Run along, Rolando," Rocco scolded. "I'll talk to you later."

Rolando swaggered out of the store, roughly shoving his shoulder into Dominick on his way by. When he was gone, Rocco turned to Cerini. "What do you think, Romon? Do you think he can keep from blowing himself to pieces?"

"Does it matter? So long as he pays?"

"Ten dollars," Rocco said.

Dominick looked perplexed. "I don't have ten dollars, but I can give you five this month and five next month."

"Work hard, Prugitore, then give me ten dollars this payday. Or you won't work next month, capeesh?"

Every other evening Dominick slipped away to write reports. One evening he met Rosa in the glade and helped her pick a bouquet of violets for her mamma.

"Well, Princess, your mother should be pleased with these flowers."

She pouted her lip. "Please, call me Rosa. I'm thirteen now. I'm not a child you know!"

"Of course not, but you remind me of the little sister I lost in Italy. Her name was Anna. She would be about your age, had she not died of smallpox."

Rosa's eyes grew round. "Oh, Dominick, I'm so sorry. I don't have any brothers." She wrinkled the side of her face in a mock look of disgust before adding, "Just two sisters."

Then her face brightened. "Perhaps, you could be my big brother."

He smiled slightly and inclined his head in a curt bow. "Whatever the princess commands."

Rosa laughed and grabbed his hand. "Come on! I want you to meet the rest of your family."

"Your folks will not like you dragging a strange man home."

"Oh, nonsense! They'll love you the minute they see you, just like I did."

"No, Rosa."

He said it firmly, maybe too firmly, for she regarded him with a pained look. Dominick placed his hands on her shoulders.

"Perhaps, the proper time will come to meet your family, but that time is not now." When Rosa continued to pout he added softly. "Your family's honor is at stake here, Rosa."

The next morning he and Dana were arguing as they walked to the quarry with a group of workers.

"You paid too much for your place!" Dana gestured wildly, and Dominick could tell he was working himself into another tirade about Rocco Racca.

"If I had been there you could have had it for eight, maybe five dollars."

One of the other labors in the group piped up. "Best this way, Dana. You know better than to argue with a headman."

Dana grew angrier. "This is America! We must learn to stand up for ourselves. I tell you. Rocco and his gang are no good."

Dominick saw the old argument coming and quietly intervened.

"Si, we must stand up for ourselves. That is why I needed to see Rocco myself. Besides, you told me I would pay and pay." With a wink he clapped Dana on the back, and the older man burst into laughter that ended in a fit of coughing.

When they arrived at Dana's work place, Dominick asked if he needed more help drilling holes.

"No compare, they are deep enough to hold the drill by itself now. But thanks for helping get them started yesterday."

They parted company, and Dominick continued deeper into the quarry with the other workers. He had almost reached his place when a loud report that sounded like the crack of a rifle reverberated down the quarry. Suddenly men were yelling behind him in the cut, and Dominick found himself running back up the track. As he neared Dana's work place he saw a group of men gesturing excitedly. Elbowing his way through the crowd, he was shocked at the site before him. Dana Carrello was thrashing about in the quarry dust. Dana's right hand was a mangled mess. His left hand clutched his face over his left eye. Dominick saw a mixture of blood and clear fluid seeping between his fingers.

Dominick knelt beside his stricken friend. "We're getting the doctor," he said finally. "You're going to be okay."

Eventually the Dinky engine arrived, and they loaded Dana in one of the ore cars and carried him to the quarry office. As was their custom, the men quit working for the day out of sympathy for the stricken man. Dominick, however, found himself wandering down the cut toward Dana's work place.

He found the drill hole fractured and strangely blackened. Stone fragments had blown off the rock around the hole, and the handle of Dana's sledgehammer lay shattered nearby. As he contemplated these things a wizened chirping startled him. He turned to see Ignazio Sebastianelli. The old man, wearing his usual gap-toothed grin, was holding the head of Dana's hammer and the battered drill.

"Looking for these?" When Dominick didn't answer right away, Ignazio chuckled crazily, emitting a sound much like a choking bird. "You can't have them. I find first."

"I don't want the tools, Ignazio." He nodded toward the blackened hole. "I just don't understand what happened here."

Ignazio ejected a stream of tobacco juice, the tail end of which dribbled down his chin. "You want the drill?" Ignazio paused looking over the equipment he found. "Nitro ruined the tip. Maybe it can be fixed." He held the long steel shaft out to Dominick.

"Nitro! What nitro?"

Ignazio ejected another stream of brown liquid over his lip and turned to leave, chuckling again.

"Un momento!" Dominick grabbed him roughly by the arm.

Rage flashed in Ignazio's eyes. The drill bar clattered on the ground as Ignazio grabbed Dominick's wrist to free his arm. His grip was surprisingly strong for an old man. Ignazio's thumb-nail jammed into the tender flesh at the juncture of Dominick's thumb and forefinger. A sharp pain spiked up Dominick's arm causing him to let loose of Ignazio.

"Dana is my friend," Dominick said, rubbing his arm. "I just want to know what happened here."

The chuckling sound started again then stopped abruptly as Ignazio's voice took on a higher pitch. "You are dumb boy!"

He gestured wildly at the blackened hole.

"Someone...," Ignazio paused a moment and peered cautiously around. "There was nitro in the drill hole."

"When Dana hit drill with the hammer," he suddenly threw his arms wide, "Boom!"

Dominick shook his head. "But, why?"

Ignazio's voice screeched back at him. "Silly boy! Bad men here!" He tossed the hammer's head at Dominick's feet making him jump to keep from getting his toes crushed. "You keep. No more questions." With that, the old man ambled quickly away mumbling and gesturing to himself.

The next day, Dominick heard Dana had lost a hand and one eye. On Saturday evening Mrs. Carpellotti told Dominick that Rocco Racca wanted to see him. When Dominick entered Rocco's store several men were playing scopa, a card game from the old country.

One of the men, with thick wavy hair parted almost in the middle, appeared to be about Dominick's age. Rocco introduced him as Salavatore Benedetti.

The young man laughed easily. "They call me Sam Bennett in American."

The stern looking Cerini was not around, and Rocco seemed to be in a good mood. "Will you play a game for cigars?" he asked.

Dominick consented and promptly lost.

Rocco blew a thick cloud of brownish smoke into the already foul air and looked hard at the young man. "I hear you speak good American. How is this so? I've been in this country six years and only speak but a little."

Trying to remember what he had told Rocco before, Dominick quickly explained some of his history. The older man nodded, seemingly satisfied with his answer. They played a couple more hands for drinks and Sam Bennett lost, buying a round for everyone.

"Dominick," Rocco said suddenly, putting the cards under the counter to signal the game was over. "We have collected some money for your friend Carrello. Tomorrow is Sunday. Will you go with Signore Benedetti and take this money to your friend?"

"But..." Dominick looked surprised.

"But what?" Rocco interrupted. "We take care of our own. You are his friend, and a friend should do this."

The next day was warm and sunny with a slight breeze blowing through the new summer leaves. Dominick found Sam Bennett to be good company as they trudged down the tracks toward Edinburg where they planned to catch a trolley into New Castle. Despite his friendly nature Sam wouldn't reveal exactly what he did, explaining only that he worked for Rocco and that he traveled a lot. The gift for Dana, Sam explained, had been collected by a special society headed by Rocco.

Dana was feverish and appeared to be in a great deal of pain. A nurse told them he would recover if his wounds didn't become infected. She cautioned them not to stay long. When they presented him with the money, Dana stirred suddenly and asked Sam if he would get some cigars. Sam looked questioningly at Dominick. On Sunday all the stores were closed. Dominick said he had a couple of cigars in his jacket pocket. The jacket hung on a rack outside the men's ward. When Sam left the room, Dana grabbed Dominick's shirt, yanking him close with surprising strength—his breath foul from sickness.

"Dominick," he hissed, "beware, La Mano Nera!"

Suddenly he was racked by a fit of coughing, and released his hold. A nurse hurried over and scolded Dominick, demanding he leave immediately. He backed away, shaken and confused. When the nurse left, Sam stuffed the cigars under Dana's pillow.

On the way back to Hillsville, Dominick puzzled silently. La Mano Nera, or The Black Hand as the American press called it, was supposed to be an organization of Italian criminals. But he didn't understand what such an organization had to do with Dana.

The following week he loaded five cars with stone for the Dinky engine to pull to the crusher. However, on payday he was only credited with loading four. By quietly inquiring with other laborers, Dominick found that someone was changing numbers on the cars they loaded. Their numbers were replaced with the numbers of men who seldom showed up for work. The other men only spoke of this in whispers or pretended it didn't happen. When Dominick came out of the paymaster's office, Romon Cerini called to him.

"You owe Rocco ten dollars," Romon reminded him. "I'll take it."

Dominick spread his hands. "After the company deducted the cost of caps and dynamite I only have eleven dollars left. Perhaps, I can pay part now and the rest next payday?"

Romon looked more stern than usual. "You will need to talk to Rocco about that. See him tonight."

That evening he found Rocco sitting on his porch smoking a cigar. Sam Bennett was there as well, along with several others including Rolando Saverino. The latter was just leaving with two others as Dominick approached. Two of his party carried shotguns.

"Bring us some birds, Rolando," Rocco called, "if you can hit them."

Saverino waved in return and the three men moved off joking among themselves.

"Ah, Dominick," Rocco greeted him as he approached the steps. "Did you bring the money you owe?"

"About that, signore..."

Rocco waved his hand to cut him off. "I know. Romon told me your wallet was a little thin today. But no matter, I will be your friend. You can pay me five dollars now and the rest next payday."

After he paid him, Rocco offered him a beer. "Sam tells me you were upset after seeing Carrello the other day. Put him out of your mind. We take care of our own."

"You mean Dana belonged to your society?"

Rocco shrugged. "Dana seldom paid his dues, but you should join as well. Then you need not fear any man."

"I must give this some thought, signore."

"Do so, but don't wait too long."

The next day a light drizzle kept most of the men at home. Dominick had to blast and, when he was finished, started toward the Dinky engine in order to have cars pulled down to load the next day. As he approached, he saw Saverino and some of his friends running away. Closer to the chugging engine he heard someone moaning, and hurried toward the Dinky's cab. Leaning against the ladder, a man was holding his face with blood soaked hands. It was Bratton, the Dinky's engineer, and Dominick could see blood running freely between the man's fingers and down his arms as he clutched his left cheek.

"What happened?" Dominick asked, rushing over and trying to pry the man's hands away from the wound so he could see how serious it was. He only got a glimpse before Bratton knocked his hands away, but it was enough to see the engineer's face was slashed from the corner of his mouth half way up his cheek.

"Dirty little wops!" Bratton exclaimed through clenched teeth. "They held me down and cut my face!"

"Come on," Dominick said, shoving his anger aside at Bratton's slur. "Let's get you up to the crusher."

Bratton nodded toward the engine's cab, and Dominick helped him up the ladder. With Dominick's help, Bratton backed the engine up to the crusher. When the doctor arrived he took one look at the wound and ordered the man taken to the hospital at once. Apparently the company's clerk didn't realize who Dominick was, because he started raving about the Italians cutting each other all the time.

"First time they cut someone that ain't a wop though," the clerk said. "Bratton was always gett'n on the fish eaters, so he was. Heard he filled the lunch pail of one of them dagos with sludge from the grease box. I swear, they find more dead bodies in the woods here 'bouts than on a battlefield."

"You mean the game warden?"

"Him too, but mostly they cut each other up. Got folks scared half to death around here, so they do."

Chapter 6

As Dominick slowly made his way back to the boarding house, his mind rebelled at the thought of joining these cutthroats and criminals. They went against everything; honesty, dignity, respect—everything his father taught him to believe in.

He stopped at the hand pump on the street and stripped off his shirt to soak the bloodstains so they wouldn't set. Julio Carpellotti, who owned the boarding house where he stayed, came up behind him. Julio couldn't help but notice the stains on the young man's clothes.

"Did you hurt yourself, Dominick? You shouldn't work at the quarry alone."

Dominick looked up at the older man as he wrung the excess water from his shirt. "This is not my blood, Signore Carpellotti. There was a fight, and that dog Bratton got cut." He smiled cunningly. "Perhaps he will show more respect for us now, no?"

Julio frowned somewhat. "Come along. My wife will clean your shirt. Let's have a beer before supper, and you can tell me of this fight."

Sitting on the porch steps, Dominick told Julio how he found Bratton with his face cut. He left out the part about seeing Saverino and the others running away. When he finished, Julio told him they must find Rocco and tell him what happened.

"This will bring the detectives," Julio added gravely.

They found Rocco and Romon Cerini at the store. Rolando Saverino was there as well, along with Sam Bennett.

"We have some problems," Julio announced, walking over to the men clustered around the counter.

Rocco slammed his fist on the counter. "Problems are all we get!" Rocco was about to say more but caught himself when he saw Dominick.

"Dominick found Bratton with his face cut," Julio said.

A hush fell while everyone focused on Dominick.

Romon Cerini broke the silence. "Tell us what you saw."

When he finished repeating the story, Romon asked if he saw who did it. Dominick replied that he didn't, which caused a murmur of discussion among the men at the counter.

Dominick glanced at Saverino. He was staring at Dominick with a puzzled expression, so Dominick chanced a wink. Saverino smiled faintly and winked back.

Rocco slammed his hand on the counter again. "This will bring la polizia!" He looked worried.

Saverino suddenly piped up, "If the detectives come, we will fight." The room settled into a tense hush.

"No, Saverino," Romon replied. "You will go to Buffalo for a couple of weeks. The rest of you go home. Drink some beer." He made a broad gesture with his arm. "Forget this thing."

The men began to shuffle toward the door. As Dominick turned to leave, Romon's voice stopped him cold. "Not you, Prugitore."

Romon fixed him with a flat stare. "We know you saw Saverino by the engine. You did a good thing not to mention it." Then in a calculated tone he added. "Perhaps you could do us a service."

Dominick shrugged. "How may I help, signore?"

Rocco, was watching him intently.

"I would like you to stay away from work for a few days." Dominick started to object, but Romon put up his hand. "We'll take care of your cars."

Dominick nodded.

"Read the American newspapers. See what they have to say about this thing. If detectives come here I want you to find Rocco and interpret for him. Will you do this?"

"Si, signore."

"Good. If detectives come, listen to what the Americans say among themselves and tell Rocco." Romon waved his hand in dismissal, and his voice grew a touch harder. "Nothing happened here, capeesh?"

Outside, Sam Bennett was waiting for him. "Come along, Dominick. I know where there is beer and singing."

Dominick liked this plain speaking young man. Sam dressed a cut above the others. Nothing fancy, just clean and well groomed.

"You did well," Sam said, looking at him and smiling. "For a while we weren't sure how you stood."

Dominick shrugged. "I have no love for the authorities."

Sam nodded in understanding. "You sound like you've had dealings with the American polizia?"

"A disagreement in Philadelphia caused me to leave in a hurry." Dominick glanced at his new friend, trying to determine if he should ask the next question. But Sam looked troubled about something.

"Cerini made all the decisions tonight," Sam said, almost as though he anticipated what was going through Dominick's mind. "Romon is supposed to be second to Rocco, but he seems to be taking over."

"He's shrewd, that one."

"Si, most of the young men, like Saverino, are behind him. I just hope there isn't trouble."

They walked down a muddy wagon road as thunder rumbled in the distance. Around a bend in the road, a cluster of shanties suddenly appeared. People gathered around one of the buildings and they heard the strumming of a guitar as they drew closer.

Sam began picking up the pace. "Come on! It is time for fun."

Standing on a small porch, beside some older men playing cards, was a beautiful young lady. Taken by the contrast between her fair complexion and the dark hair that tumbled over her shoulders, Dominick guessed she was in her late teens. When the girl saw Sam her face lit into a bright smile.

"Dominick, I want you to meet Maria," Sam declared, as they approached the porch. "We're engaged to be married," he added proudly.

The girl lowered her eyes. From out of the shadows an older woman materialized. She was trying to appear stern, but there was an amused twinkle in her eye. "Not unless you stop running from city to city long enough to find a house, Salvatore."

"Dominick, meet Signora Piccini. She is Maria's madre, and the protector of her virtue."

The older woman threw her arms in the air in mock agitation. She was trying hard not to laugh.

A deep voice rolled up from the table where the card game was in progress. "She is not the only protector of her virtue, Benedetti. You remember that."

Sam laughed in reply, and introduced Dominick to Maria's father, a slim, middle-aged man with a thick flowing mustache. Dominick accepted a beer and soon found himself playing cards while Sam and Maria strolled hand in hand down the street—her mother and another woman trailing behind.

That night Dominick lay awake as rain rattled against the tin roof, his mind filled with doubts about the Society and what part he was to play in it.

The next morning dawned fresh and clean. He was sitting on the porch reading a local newspaper when a boy, who obviously delighted in running bare foot through mud puddles, ran up and told him Signore Racca wanted him. When he arrived at the store, he found Rocco sitting on the porch with his dour wife.

"Good morning, Signora Racca," Dominick offered. "What a beautiful day."

"Perhaps, Signore Prugitore," Mrs Racca said, getting up and starting toward the door, "but we will first wait to see what this day brings."

Rocco waved him toward the chair vacated by his wife and offered him a cigar. "Don't mind her," Rocco said softly. "She worries about nothing. Now, tell me. What do the American newspapers have to say?"

"They say Bratton was injured in an accident yesterday at the quarry."

"That is strange." Rocco looked thoughtful for a while.

"Perhaps Bratton is too scared to talk," Dominick offered.

"And maybe this is a trick of the American authorities," Rocco countered. "They are always trying to get at me."

Dominick thought for a moment before deciding to take the plunge. "The Americans are upset about the murder of the game policeman. They believe some Italian did it."

He watched Rocco intently. The latter paled, then got up abruptly and stalked into the store. Dominick waited a few minutes to calm himself before following Rocco inside. The older man was making a pretense of looking over his accounting books.

"Unpaid bills?"

"Si," Rocco replied without looking up. He appeared shaken.

"I'll pay you fifty dollars for your books."

Rocco laughed. "You'll give me a hundred and fifty to collect these debts." Then he looked serious. "What do you know about this murder?"

Dominick shrugged. "Just what I read in the newspapers, signore."

"Yeah, and why is it you can read and write American so good? None of us can do this, except for some of the kids who go to the American school."

"Because, signore, when I was a kid, I too went to the American schools."

Rocco nodded soberly. "So, you know something about running a business?"

"Si, signore."

"I've been thinking about moving back to Italy after my wife is well. I may sell you this stuff cheap."

During the next week, Dominick read the newspapers to Rocco and Cerini, but there was nothing in the papers about the Dinky's engineer. After work, the young men in the Society took him from home to home where there was drinking and singing. Every now and then someone asked him to join the Association, but Dominick found himself making excuses. Twice he took the electric car into Youngstown to deliver his reports to Toni. He wanted Toni's advice about joining the Society, but the scar-faced detective was not to be found. Finally, he wrote to Superintendent Dimuro.

The following week Dominick went back to work at the quarry. That Wednesday the detectives arrived. He was breaking stones to load into one of the quarry cars when he saw Rocco hurrying toward him. With considerable excitement, the headman told him there were two detectives from New Castle waiting at the company's office to see him.

"I told you it was a trick of the American authorities to keep this out of the newspapers!"

Dominick tried to appear casual. "I don't think so. This is probably just a routine investigation." But he felt his stomach knot up. He had written a full account of the incident in his daily reports to the Pinkertons. Surely, they wouldn't have compromised his position over this incident.

When they arrived at the office, the clerk pointed to Dominick and exclaimed to the two men waiting there. "That's him! That's the fellah who brought Bratton in. Good Lord, I didn't know he was a Dago. He speaks perfect English."

Dominick flashed the clerk an angry glare and the little man wilted through a back door.

The older detective, with a face deeply etched from the rigors of a long life, took a step toward Dominick extending his hand. "I'm County Detective McFate," he announced. His voice seemed to rattle up from the loose skin around his neck.

Dominick stiffened. "You've taken me from my work, signore. What is it you want?"

Slouching in his chair, the younger man interrupted with a sneer. "I told you they were all the same, McFate."

McFate sighed, shaking his head sadly. "Please, Lloyd. Let me do the talking." Looking Dominick in the eyes, the older detective came directly to the point. "I understand you helped the Dinky engineer. Do you know how his face got cut?"

"No, signore."

The older man continued to stare at him. There was compassion in his face, and Dominick felt sorry because of what he must do.

"Would you tell me if it was otherwise, young man?"

Dominick curled his upper lip into a snarl. "No, signore! I will not help the American authorities." He punctuated his statement by spitting on the floor by McFate's feet before turning to leave.

Lloyd jumped to his feet, fists balled. "Just a minute, you greasy little dago!"

McFate held up his hand. "Let it go, Lloyd. Unless Bratton is willing to testify we don't have anything."

Rocco, who was watching the encounter with interest, hurried after Dominick. "In the name of all the Saints, you must be more careful when you talk to the Americans!"

"They know nothing, signore, and I don't have to put up with their insults."

The next day Dominick was feeling the ill effects from blasting and took the afternoon off. Lying on his bed, he heard some men asking Signora Carpellotti if he was home. One of the men was Rolando Saverino. With him was a young man named Mario Nardozi. Dominick recognized Mario as one of the men who helped cut the face of the engineer.

"I thought you went to Buffalo," he said to Saverino.

"That takes money, so I hid in the woods instead."

"We want to buy you a beer for being a friend," Mario explained.

They went to several houses that illegally sold beer, picking up more of their friends along the way. By the time they got to the last house it was getting late, and they were becoming loud and boisterous. Saverino was drunk, and the rest had to hold him up as they staggered down the road on their way home.

"You know," said Mario, "there is a secret association up here, but we can't tell who belongs to it."

"Why is that?"

"You must join first, compare, that's why."

Dominick liked the boy. He wasn't very bright, but he was cheerful. The rest of the crowd was more concerned with fighting, or bragging about what they were going to do to the American authorities. Suddenly he wheeled and shouted, "Who will buy a chicken?" The three stopped and looked at him curiously. "If someone will buy a chicken and have it cooked, I will buy a keg of beer. Tomorrow, we shall have some real fun."

The next afternoon Dominick left for the party. As he approached the cluster of shanties that comprised the Peanut settlement, he heard a commotion coming from a nearby spring. A girl was crying amid the shouts and laughter of several boys.

Dominick hurried down the path toward the spring in time to see three boys push a young girl into the mud. Another boy threw a large rock, splashing muddy water over her clothes. Finally, one of the boys yelled for the others to grab her so they could push her face into the mud. The girl began screaming and kicking when the boys grabbed her arms. They were so intent on their mischief they didn't see Dominick approach. He grabbed the two boys who held the girl's arms and knocked their heads together with a hollow thud. The third boy tore off through the brush; nearly skinning himself running through the briers.

Dominick shook the boys roughly as they rubbed their heads. "What are your names, and where do you live?" he demanded. When Dominick learned they came from one of the other settlements, he sent them running with a boot to their backsides.

The girl, who appeared to be about eight or nine, was sobbing softly. She had extracted herself from the mud and was picking up pieces of a broken crock lying on the ground beside the trail.

"Mother will surely spank me for this."

Dominick stooped down beside her and dug a blue bandanna from his pocket. "What is your name?" he asked, taking her chin in his hand and wiping some of the mud and tears from her face.

"Mary Ciampanelli," she sobbed.

"So, you're Rosa's sister?"

She stopped crying. "How do you know?" She was looking at him with new interest.

He suddenly worried about getting Rosa into trouble. "Oh, I talked to Rosa once or twice."

Mary gave him a funny look, then started crying again when she glanced down at the broken crock she had brought to carry water in. It was a gallon Weir, with a handle and a bail that held the lid in place.

"Don't worry, I'll go home with you and explain what happened. This wasn't your fault.

Besides," he added, "if you don't stop crying, those tears are going to turn all that mud on your face into a swamp."

She began to smile through the tears, and nodded bravely.

Mary's mother was a smoldering volcano after he explained what happened. She told her older daughters to watch Mary before rushing across the street to a neighbor's house. Soon a neighbor lady and Mary's mother, arms waving in tune to their agitation, were hurrying toward the community where the boys lived.

I sure would like to watch those fireworks, Dominick thought. A tugging at his sleeve caught his attention, and he turned to see Rosa smiling at him. "Hi, Sis," he said, returning the smile.

Rosa beamed, "Thank you for helping Mary."

"Well, I couldn't let those boys douse her in the mud, could I?"

Rosa looked serious, then troubled. "I waited for you in the woods this week," she said softly.

"This has been a busy week."

"Well, I'm going to ask mamma to invite you for dinner so we can thank you properly," she said cheerfully.

"Grazie, Rosa. I would like that."

After Rosa left, he went to where the party was being held. There he found the others cleaning a large rooster. When the chicken was ready they tapped the keg Dominick bought, spending the afternoon eating and drinking. He learned that Romon Cerini was now firmly in control of the secret association. Rocco Racca, however, was still the headman, if in name only.

That evening he picked up his mail, hoping it would contain a message from Superintendent Dimuro. Instead, there was a coded message from Superintendent Cafee ordering Dominick to meet him in Youngstown the next evening. For the life of him, he couldn't figure out what Cafee wanted, or how his former boss learned where he was.

The next afternoon he left early for Youngstown in the hope of finding Toni before meeting with Cafee. He couldn't understand what Cafee had to do with this case. Furthermore, he wasn't sure what authority, if any, Cafee held over him. Toni wasn't in his room, but he had left a message for Dominick to meet him there after 9 PM. Troubled, he left for the Excelsior Hotel.

Dominick approached a bespectacled clerk behind a marble-topped counter and asked for Cafee. The clerk glanced at his plain suit and, with a flick of his baldhead, curtly said his party was awaiting him in the dining room. He was relieved to see Cafee sitting alone at a small table by the wall. The little man was sipping a thick and creamy soup.

"Good evening, sir," he said, approaching the table.

When Cafee didn't acknowledge him, Dominick reached for a chair.

"Pray, don't sit, Prugitore. I couldn't bare the embarrassment of people thinking we were associates."

Dominick stiffened, fighting to control his rising temper. Cafee still hadn't looked up, but pulled off a linen napkin tucked into his celluloid collar and made a show of wiping his mouth. Then, snapping his head up, Cafee stared intently at the young man before speaking.

"I received your pathetic little note about this secret association, Prugitore. If you don't want to do your job as an undercover agent, please quit. We don't need your kind in our organization." Cafee's nasal voice rose several octaves as he spoke.

Dominick glanced hurriedly around the room. He had seen some Italian waiters, but fortunately no one was close by. In a low voice he addressed his superior, "That note was addressed to Superintendent Dimuro, sir."

"Dimuro is out of town, you impertinent fool! The note was passed to me as a matter of routine, and my orders to you are simple. Quit stalling, and join this association immediately. That's your job!" He turned his attention back to his soup and began tucking the napkin back into his collar. "Questions, Prugitore?"

"A comment, if I may, sir?"

Cafee paused with a spoonful of the creamy soup part way to his mouth. "What is it, Prugitore?" He waited until Cafee sipped and swallowed. He sounded very sincere. "There are bugs in your soup, sir."

Cafee's eyes bulged. He launched himself back from the table gagging and knocking the chair over in the process. Dominick, a thin smile creasing his lips, walked away amid the shouts of running waiters.

Toni Capazzi had rented a room at 223 E. Boardman Street. The room was far enough from the Italian section in Youngstown not to draw suspicion.

"Well, compare," Toni said, passing Dominick a bottle of wine. "How was your meeting with the strutting little rooster?"

They shared the bottle as he relayed what Cafee told him, and Toni roared when he told about the soup.

"Were there really bugs in his soup?"

Dominick shook his head. This time they both erupted in laughter. Then Toni grew serious. "Cafee is right about joining the Association. But when you do, be prepared to play the part."

"What do you mean?" Dominick was becoming excited. "Where is Superintendent Dimuro, and how does Cafee fit into this investigation?"

Toni held up his hands. "Slow down! One thing at a time." Toni stood, rubbing the scar on his face thoughtfully. "First, there is also an overt investigation of the Houk murder under Cafee's supervision. With Dimuro out of town, your note was bounced to him." He smiled devilishly. "There will be the devil to pay when the boss finds out Cafee met you in public."

"But must I listen to Cafee?"

"He's a boss, Dominick. A capo, capeesh?"

Dominick nodded.

"Good!" Toni placed his hand on the younger man's shoulder. "Now listen to me. When you join this association you must be as ruthless they are."

"How can I do that, Toni? They prey on our own people."

"That is why you must do this. The investigation into the murder of the game policeman is your excuse to be there. With your help, we will break the Black Hand."

Two days later, Dominick was invited to dinner at the Ciampanelli's. He learned that Rosa's father was not a member of this secret association. When it was time to leave, Rosa asked her mother if she could walk with him part way.

"Only to the end of the street," her mother said. "Then you come right back."

Rocco and his wife were sitting on the porch, talking with Sam Bennett. Dominick waved, and Sam came running over.

"There is going to be a meeting of the Association next week to take in new members," Sam said. "Rocco wants you to learn how to answer their questions."

He heard Rosa gasp, then saw her stiffen at Sam's announcement.

"I haven't decided to join for sure, Sam," he replied. He glanced at Rosa who was staring at him wide eyed.

Sam looked perplexed.

Dominick put his hand on the other man's shoulder. "I'll let you know in a couple of days, OK?"

After Sam left, they walked in silence for a while before Rosa spoke.

"Please, Dominick, don't join this society." There was an urgency to her voice, a serious tone she never heard him use before.

"I don't think I have a choice."

Stopping suddenly, Rosa took his hand and stared into his face. "Papa didn't join."

"You don't understand..."

Suddenly Rosa let go of his hand: her eyes filling with tears. "They're bad!" She exclaimed.

"What do you know about them?" he asked softly, smiling down at her. "Sam Bennett is okay."

Her hands made little twitching movements by her sides.

"Rosa, what are you afraid of?"

Suddenly, the girl raised balled fists as if to strike at him. Her wet face contorted in rage and fear. "They kill people!" she screamed, then took off down the street.

Chapter 7

On Friday, Dominick was having breakfast with Julio Carpellotti, when Sam Bennett stopped by with another man who appeared to be in his mid-twenties. After greeting Julio, Sam turned to Dominick. "This is Toni Santi, a good friend."

"Always a pleasure to meet a friend of Sam's, signore." As the two men shook hands, Dominick noticed Toni wore a wedding band, an unusual sight among the common laborers in the quarries.

"Toni's father owns the hotel here," Sam explained. "He wanted to meet you when he learned you worked in a big city hotel."

"We're going over to Romon Cerini's house," Toni said. "Why don't you come with us?"

Julio pushed himself away from the table. "Might as well. Ignazio blocked the track again."

Dominick shook his head then turned to Sam. "What is this meeting for?"

"Every so often we meet to decide who will be asked to join the Society. How about it? Are you going to join?"

A memory of Rosa, tears streaming down her face, drew back the reigns of caution. "I don't know. My brother wrote he might have a job for me in Pittsburgh," Dominick lied. "I would like to wait until I hear back from him."

"Come along anyway," Toni injected. "Maybe we'll have some fun."

They spent the day drinking and playing cards at Romon's house. Dominick learned they called their association The Society of Honor.

"There is safety in numbers," Romon explained. "We band together for protection. If anyone harms you, we punish him."

"I thought that is what the courts are for."

Romon slammed his cards on the table. "We take care of our own, Prugitore! Remember that."

Toni smiled at Romon. "Take it easy, signore. I don't think our friend understands." Then turning to Dominick he added, "We also collect money to help those who get injured."

"Si, that is what Rocco does," Romon said.

"Rocco is president of The St. Lucy Society," Sam explained. "He was the one who collected the money when Dana got hurt."

Throughout the day different members of the Society stopped by, and Romon took them inside to talk privately. On the way back to Hillsville, Toni explained that there were three classes in the Society. When one joined he became a member of the first class. Second class membership was limited to those with special ability, and headmen were of the third class.

Two days later, Dominick visited Jim Rossi, a second-class member in the Society. Jim sold beer at his store in Brierhill, a settlement the Americans called Little Italy. There he found Saverino, Fred Carnetti and Mario Nardozi arguing whether or not the policemen would try to stop them from selling beer. No one in the settlements had a license to sell alcoholic beverages.

Rolando Saverino was off on his usual tirade. "I do not care for policeman," he declared. "If they come, we will give them a good fight. We'll teach them we are not to be fooled with."

"The policemen will not come here," Dominick offered.

The others turned to look at him. He was standing with a bottle of beer in his hand, staring intently at Rolando.

Rolando's eyes grew wild. "How do you know?" he shouted, balling his fists. "You think you know so much! How do you know the polizia won't come?"

"Because they don't care. They know we sell beer, but they don't care."

Rolando's face was turning darker. "You know nothing! They will come, and we must fight!"

"The American authorities care nothing for Italians," Dominick said, allowing contempt to show in his voice. "We kill each other, and they don't care. But if we harm one of them, or even look at their women, our people are arrested." In a softer voice he added, "Like the game policeman or the Dinky's engineer."

Rolando choked, then his eyes rolled back in his head until only the whites showed. He fell to the floor thrashing around and shaking spasmodically. Those standing around crossed themselves or made the sign of horns, extending their index and little finger and bobbing them rabidly toward the ground three times. Others clutched amulets tied around their necks. Dominick watched as spittle frothed from the corners of Rolando's mouth. A wet stain spread across the front of his pants. Rolando continued to roll stiffly about for several moments before his body relaxed.

Jim Rossi, who was tall for an Italian, came barreling through the crowd. He grabbed Fred Carnetti by his coat. "Get him out of here!"

Fred and Mario helped the stricken man to sit up. Rolando was beginning to focus again.

"Go on! Get him out of here I said!" Jim began gesturing frantically.

The two men half-dragged, half-carried Rolando outside.

Jim turned on Dominick. "Stupido! Why did you get him so excited? Don't you know he takes fits?"

Dominick shrugged. "I only told the truth. His talk is dangerous."

Rocco Racca appeared behind Rossi, putting his hand on the man's shoulder. "He's right, Jim. Rolando was the one causing trouble."

"Maybe, but I don't want him having fits in my place."

Rocco looked at Dominick, and nodded toward the door. "Take Saverino a beer, and try to make peace. I don't want more trouble."

Rolando was sitting on the front step with his head in his hands as Dominick came out. Fred Carnetti had gone, but Mario was standing beside Rolando looking like a whipped pup. Dominick placed the beer on the step beside Saverino before stooping down in front of him. "I'm sorry," he said softly. "I wasn't trying to fight with you, compare. You'd beat me anyway." Saverino raised his head and blinked several times.

"We can't fight the Americans, Rolando. We're in their country. But we will stick up for ourselves when the time comes."

He nodded weakly.

"Right now, especially, we mustn't fight among ourselves. Okay?"

Saverino nodded again as Dominick stood up.

A voice came from the doorway. "Run along, Rolando. Get yourself cleaned up."

Dominick, looked up to see Jim Rossi and Rocco regarding him curiously.

"He's a peacemaker, this one." He heard Jim say on his way inside.

"Si," Rocco answered. "He is of value to the Association."

Later that evening Dominick found himself in company with Rocco and Sam Bennett. They had returned to Hillsville to await the announcement of midwives attending a woman in labor there. A throng of people had gathered.

Toni Santi came strolling over to them. A mandolin was hanging from a leather thong across his back and his arm around a pretty woman about Dominick's age. "Dominick," Toni exclaimed, "this is my wife, Carmine."

She acknowledged him with a nod and a smile.

Dominick bowed formally. "Such a pretty woman to have married a rogue like you," he said smiling.

A little curly headed boy came running over and grabbed his mother's hand. Toni smiled down at him. "My son, Guiseppe," he said proudly.

The child hid his face in the folds of his mother's skirt.

Laughing, Dominick pointed at the mandolin. "Is that just for decoration, or do you really play?"

"Si," Rocco exclaimed. "Give us a song!"

As Toni struck up a lively tune the crowd started clapping, and soon a circle formed on the street. Amid shouts and laughter, two middle-aged men stepped into the circle and began to dance the tarantella. Holding their shoulders and hips fixed, with their arms high over their heads, they kicked their feet and twisted their bodies in time to the music and clapping. Toni picked up the tempo and the dancers, much to the delight of the crowd, exaggerated their movements and rhythm.

Suddenly there was a shout from a nearby house. The music and dancing stopped immediately when a large hipped woman came out wiping her hands on a cloth. The crowd grew quiet as the woman spoke softly to some men waiting by the door. Then one of them turned toward the crowd and announced the arrival of a baby girl.

A cheer went up, and someone set off a string of firecrackers. Wine bottles passed from hand to hand as Roman candles screamed into the sky. Toni began to play again, and everyone started singing and dancing. A crimson streak rose over the eastern horizon as weary men and women carried their sleeping children back to the clapboard shanties of Hillsville.

A week later Dominick, Sam and Toni found themselves standing beside the railroad tracks, on the outskirts of Edinburg, critically surveying a small, one story house.

"I don't know, Sam," Toni said, "the place doesn't look so good."

"But it's not a shanty," Sam insisted. "The roof doesn't leak, and there's a big stove inside that will heat the whole place during the winter."

A section of picket fence that once ran around the front yard lay on the ground, nearly concealed by weeds and grass.

"Come on!" Sam exclaimed, starting toward the gate. "Let me show you inside." The gate fell over when he tried to open it. Sam stood it lovingly against a fence post. "There is even a well with a hand pump beside the back porch," he continued enthusiastically.

"Probably river water," Toni replied.

"No, the water's good. I tried it."

A garter snake slithered off a step and crawled under the porch as they approached.

"How much rent do they want?" Toni asked, looking about distastefully.

"Ten dollars a month," Sam said cheerfully.

"That's robbery! This dump isn't worth fifty cents!"

Sam turned toward his friend, his face clouding with anger. "Not everyone can live with his parents in a hotel."

"OK, you two!" Dominick said, stepping between them. He put his arm around Sam and turned toward the kitchen. "Let's have a look at this stove, compare."

Toni stomped out the back door, while Dominick and Sam examined a large Sears and Roebuck cook stove. A little later they could hear Toni working the hand pump outside. Soon he came back in. "The outhouse works," he said.

His two friends broke out laughing. "The only thing that has to work in an outhouse is you, compare," Dominick said.

Toni blushed. "No, I mean everything is solid out there."

Sam and Dominick began laughing all the harder. Then Toni broke into a broad smile. "Well, maybe not everything."

On their way back to Hillsville, Sam clapped Dominick on the back cutting into his thoughts. "I almost forgot. Romon wants to see you. He says it is time to join the Society."

Dominick nodded, suddenly feeling weak in his knees. "Si, I'll see Romon tomorrow after work."

The atmosphere in the room was somber. Men stood in groups of two's or three's talking in hushed tones. Except for one table and a chair, the usual furniture that filled Jim Rossi's parlor-saloon were shoved against the wall. The table stood in the middle of the room holding a pair of flickering candles on each side of the chair.

Dominick stood alone reflecting on the past two weeks. Almost every night, after he paid Romon the ten dollars required to join the Society, various members took him from house to house where they were treated to homemade wine or beer. On other nights he went to Vincenzo Cervica's house. Vic was charged with instructing new recruits.

He saw Vic limping towards him and steeled himself. Along with a leg injured in a quarry accident, Vic had rotten teeth and horrible breath.

Conspiratorially, the older man leaned within inches of Dominick's face before speaking in a harsh whisper. "Are you ready, compare?"

Dominick nodded, trying to hold his breath.

"Good! Good!"

Grabbing the young man by the arm, Vincenzo leaned even closer. "Now listen carefully. There have been some changes in the ceremony." His voice dropped to a sputtering whisper.

"What changes?"

Vic tightened his grip on Dominick's arm and leaned closer still.

"They want to use this ceremony to impress on everyone the importance of these vows. There will be a man standing behind you holding a knife at your throat."

Dominick shivered.

"Aye, do not hesitate to answer the questions. He has orders to kill should you fail!"

"But what if I forget the answers?"

Vic narrowed his eyebrows and glanced quickly around the room. "You must not," he whispered. "This one will look for the least excuse to cut you. Everyone fears Vito Siciliano."

"I never heard of him."

"He's an enforcer from Youngstown. He..." Vic stopped abruptly as the door opened.

Rocco and three others entered. One of the men was taller than the rest with black hair slick with oil. High, angular cheekbones framed eyes shaded under a prominent brow. A heavy jaw thrust his chin well beyond a protruding lower lip. Hanging under a sharply hooked nose was a waxed mustache; the tips twisted into sharp stiletto like points.

"Enough," Vincenzo whispered. He released Dominick's arm and patted his shoulder. "You'll do fine," he added out loud.

Rocco and the others walked toward the center of the room. When the crowd grew quiet, Rocco joined Romon Cerini at the table facing the chair. There was a knife thrust into Romon's belt. The other two men stood at the corners flanking the chair. The man Dominick took to be Vito Siciliano stood with large hands resting over the back of the chair like tentacles.

Rocco nodded solemnly toward an old man standing to the right. "Some of you know Don Cardi, from Pittsburgh."

A rustle of murmuring erupted in the room, and Rocco waited until everyone grew quiet before continuing.

Then he nodded toward the man standing to the left of the chair. "And most of you know Luca Caruzzi. They are here to witness this initiation." Again he nodded to Don Cardi.

The little man seemed to swell in stature as he peered around at the circle of men. Outside darkness gathered.

"I am here to impress on you all the importance the Society places on these vows." The Don had a voice that rattled like gravel. He looked up at the tall man standing behind the chair and paused a moment before going on.

Dominick saw other men follow the Don's gaze.

"Let whoever disobeys the Society," he paused for effect, "die like a dog!"

Dominick could feel fear grip the room. He began to sweat.

"Dominick Prugitore," Rocco announced, "come, sit before us."

Dominick brushed at an unruly lock of hair hanging over his forehead and forced his legs to carry him toward the chair. When he was seated, Rocco took a square of white cloth from his pocket and spread it on the table before him.

"White stands for purity." He paused to look at the young man. "For our society is, The Society of Honor."

Next he took a red cloth and spread it over the white one. "Red stands for the blood of our Lord, and the blood of our enemies." Again he paused and looked at Dominick. "Place your right hand in the center of the cloths."

As he did so, Rocco took a knife from under his coat and thrust it into the corner of the cloth nearest him. The other three did the same in rapid order, narrowly missing Dominick's hand.

These knives represent death," Rocco said, "death to those who break these vows!" He looked over Dominick's head and nodded gravely.

Dominick felt movement behind him, then felt a keen blade at his neck. Something warm began trickling toward his shoulder. He felt his skin crawl, but dared not flinch.

Don Cardi moved to the front. "Dominick Prugitore," the old man grated. "Do you pledge, with your eternal soul, to obey the rules of The Society of Honor above the laws of any land or government?"

Dominick swallowed, felt the blade slice another millimeter into his skin. "Si, signore. I do." He felt a bead of something warm running down his neck again and resisted the urge to wipe at it.

"Do you swear to obey, without question, the leaders of the Society? No matter what they may ask you to do?"

"Si, signore."

"And do you swear to obey the Omerta, the code of silence?"

He thought about his reports. "Si, signore," he lied.

"Do you swear never to testify before a judge or a court, even if you are the injured party?"

"Si, signore."

"To whom will you go, should someone wrong you in any way?"

"To the Society, signore."

The Don paused, and looked at Romon and Roco with raised eyebrows.

Unable to turn his head because of the knife at his throat, Dominick did not see these men nod in response.

The Don coughed to clear something in his throat. "Dominick, do you swear to kill anyone without question, upon the orders of your Capo Testa?"

He stared with wide eyes at Don Cardi. A murmur rose from those around the room. This was something new. Vincenzo had not told him this question would be asked. Suddenly he felt a hand grab his hair and yank his head back. The knife drew more blood. Men gasped.

Rocco raised his hand. "Let him answer, Vito."

He answered through teeth clenched against the pain. "Si, signore. Including this ugly whore behind me!"

Dominick felt the knife pull away from his throat, but not before slicing more skin. He tore the red cloth from the table and wiped at the blood running down his neck.

Don Cardi raised his eyebrows, looked at him questioningly.

"If red stands for blood. I'll give it blood!"

The old Don's voice rattled with the semblance of a chuckle, then announced gravely. "Gentlemen, may I present a new member of La Mano Nera."

Rocco motioned for Dominick to stand. Don Cardi stepped up to embrace him, kissing him on each cheek. "You did well, young man."

After he embraced each of those at the table, he turned to face Vito. The man was a head taller than he was. Vito curled his upper lip in a sneer, made more hideous by a missing upper tooth. Dominick stared at him defiantly a moment before he turned and walked stiffly away.

For the rest of the evening society members treated him to beers. The night had grown late when Sam and Toni helped him back to the rooming house. Sam was particularly happy since he and Maria had set the date for their wedding. The happy day was only two weeks away.

Dominick mentioned in his reports that he had joined the Society and related some of his ordeal to Toni Capizzi when he went to Youngstown to mail them.

"You'll have to watch your ass every minute now," Toni said.

However, it was Romon Cerini's statement that bothered him most. He was sitting on Rocco's porch, reading the American newspaper, when Romon stopped by. Romon asked him if there was anything in the papers recently about the Houk murder. Dominick noticed Rocco stiffen.

"The last I heard was in May. The *New Castle News* said the murderer of L. S. Houk is in a safe place. I suppose that means an Italian disappeared after the murder."

Rocco jumped to his feet. "The Americans are always quick to blame us for their troubles!"

Romon watched him stomp into the house, the trace of a smile on his lips. When he looked at Dominick, his face had hardened again. "You are with us now, Prugitore. Now you take orders from me. Capeesh?"

Dominick shrugged. "I thought Rocco was Capo Testa."

Romon rose to his feet, jaw muscles clenching. "We shall see. In the meantime, I am still your superior. This you will do well to remember."

"Si, signore."

"Good!" Romon turned to leave then stopped part way down the steps, twisting slightly, to face Dominick once again. "Oh, by the way. Vito sends his regards. He asks how your neck is healing."

Absently he touched the scab. "It is only a scratch, signore."

Romon turned with a wave of dismissal. "Ciao," he said cheerfully.

Dominick watched Romon stride down the street, then got up and entered the store. Rocco was standing behind the counter with his wife drinking a glass of wine. Dominick greeted her warmly. "Good evening, signora. How are you feeling?"

"Perhaps I will feel better after this game policeman is forgotten," she replied tartly.

Rocco gave her a hard look.

"Why is that, signora?" Dominick asked.

"The Americans blame my husband for everything," she replied bitterly. With that she disappeared behind the curtain. Rocco shoved the bottle toward Dominick.

After a swallow, he said. "Romon seems to think he is Capo Testa now."

"He knows I am planning to go back to the old country."

"When you do," Dominick replied, "we will have a big celebration."

Rocco was staring moodily into his glass of wine. "Oh, Si! We will have fifteen kegs of beer, one lamb and all the chickens in Hillsville."

"I shall miss you when you leave, compare."

Rocco looked up and blinked a couple of times. "Then we must drink to that," he replied somberly.

That night Dominick delivered his reports to Youngstown. In the morning he stopped at a barbershop for a shave. He had tossed and turned most of the night worrying about his position in the Society. Finally, he decided to stand with Rocco if trouble broke out between him and Romon. He was pondering this decision when he thought to board the car for Hillsville, but got on the Lowellville car by mistake.

Italians there were celebrating a patron saint, and two bands were playing. Walking back to the station after dinner he heard a familiar voice calling to him.

Sam Bennett stood with a small group of men from Hillsville. When Dominick trotted over he found Rocco in the center of the group.

The small Italian chieftain was in a foul mood. He grabbed the two men nearest him. "Go through the cigar stores." He punctuated each word by jabbing a finger into the nearest man's chest. "You find that traitor! Break into small groups. Search the bars and alleys. When you find him, kill him!"

As the crowd began to break into smaller groups, Rocco strode over to Dominick and Sam. "You two come with me. We're going to city hall."

"What happened?" Dominick asked.

"We have been betrayed." Rocco declared. "John Marsicano, that dog! He had some of our men arrested and now they are in jail." Rocco sliced his hand across his throat. "Now, Marsicano will die!" Rocco wheeled and started toward the center of town.

"Wait," Dominick yelled. "You can't do this! This is a celebration day. You will bring the authorities down on us all."

"Sometimes there are things we must do no matter what. Now come!" Rocco turned, striding toward city hall.

Dominick looked at Sam. Sam shrugged and turned away. There was a shiny gleam in his eyes. Suddenly Dominick realized. He likes this. They all do.

When they arrived at city hall, Dominick grabbed Rocco's arm. "Let me go in and find out what is needed. I speak American, and you are too upset to deal with the authorities."

Rocco nodded.

The bail was set at $300 for all three men. Rocco began cursing and swore that John Marsicano would die before nightfall. After Rocco and Sam signed the bail bond, they left with the bondsman to release the prisoners.

Dominick was left alone. Every so often he encountered groups of men searching the town. They were in a frenzy to kill. Somehow he had to find a way to stop this madness. He turned down a side street, passing a livery stable before turning into an alley. Then he saw that a wooden fence blocked the other end of the alley. Barrels and large wooden crates were stacked alongside an adjoining building, while bales of hay leaned haphazardly against the livery. He stopped and peered into the gloom behind some of the bails.

Suddenly he heard shouts on the street and the sound of running feet. A small man came pounding into the alley. When he saw Dominick and the fence, his eyes grew wild.

Dominick motioned for him to come near."Quickly!" he shouted.

He threw his body into the smaller man as he ran up; knocking him over a bail of hay into the hole he had been peering into. The blow knocked Dominick to the ground. He could hear the man stirring around in the hay.

"Lie still!" he barked.

The sound of pursuers poured into the alley behind him. Dominick got to his hands and knees, shaking his head to clear it just as three men ran up to him.

"Quick! He knocked me down and went over the fence."

The men didn't hesitate. Dominick waited until they climbed the fence before getting slowly to his feet. He sat heavily on a bail of hay in front of the hole and peered into the shadows. The man inside was covered with dried blood. His lip was cut. His eye and nose swollen.

"Grazie, signore," the man said weakly.

"Why did you do this?" Dominick asked. "Why did you go to the authorities?"

To his surprise the man began to sob. "Because I wanted to take my Virginia away from here," the man choked.

"What do you mean?"

John Marsicano took a deep breath. Then the battered, little man looked straight at Dominick, his one good eye smoldering with hatred.

"Rocco sent the men to beat me up because he is having an affair with my wife!"

Dominick felt a flood of despair wash over him. There was no honor here. Only treachery and lies. Worse, Rocco was an adulterer.

"You must wait until after dark," Dominick said standing up. "Crawl under some of these bails and stay hidden. Then you must leave town."

"But what about my wife?"

Dominick's voice hardened. "If you value your life, you will forget her."

Chapter 8

They're going to pay, Dominick thought when he awoke. His throbbing head and queasy stomach did little to suppress his growing anger. They're going to pay for what they did to John Marsicano, to Dana, to Seeley Houk, for what they're doing to my people. He crawled out of bed and used the slop jar to relieve his bladder rather than try to stagger down the narrow stairs and out to the shed. With a low ceiling the windowless loft was hot and stuffy. He laid back down, soaked in sweat and sick from too much beer. Just breathing was hard. Unbidden his thoughts drifted back to his boyhood in Italy.

His eyes grew moist despite his best effort to control his emotions. Eleven years, he thought. Eleven years since papa, mamma and Anna died. Why couldn't I have died, too? The empty pit inside gnawed at him. Trying hard to stifle a sob, he buried his face in the pillow, his lean frame shaking and convulsing as he gave into his emotions. It was nearly noon when he finally got up and washed his face in the basin. A long time ago his father told him a boy must be cunning like a fox.

By the time he struggled downstairs he had made up his mind. I'll be cunning, all right, he thought. I'll charm this snake then crush its head.

When Dominick couldn't work at the quarry he spent time with Rocco Racca. He learned an Italian was in the hospital in Youngstown with his throat cut open. A man from Hillsville was supposed to have committed the crime. He filed this information in his reports to the Pinkertons.

During the evenings he helped Sam repair his house. Occasionally Toni Santi went with them, wielding a scythe against the weeds and brush in the yard. On Friday a thundershower, sweeping in from the west, sent them scurrying for the porch. Sitting with their backs against the door, they shared a soggy cigar that Toni fished from his pocket.

"It won't be long now, compare," Dominick said, nudging Sam in the ribs, "before you fill this place with bambinos."

"Si," Sam replied, smiling. "But I'm worried."

Dominick and Toni looked at him.

"Worried about what?" Dominick asked.

"I'm afraid there's going to be trouble between Rocco and Romon. Vito Siciliano has been hanging around Romon's place recently, and he's gathered a group of trouble makers."

Dominick glanced at Sam. "You're Rocco's secretary. Are you in danger?"

Sam shrugged. "I'll work for whoever is capo and do whatever I must so me and Maria can have a good life."

Toni nodded solemnly. But Dominick wondered just how far he could trust the Society's secretary.

The next day Rocco invited Dominick to accompany him to Lowellville. The town was just across the Ohio line. A large building, its rough lumber walls weathered and worn, stood beside the track of the New Castle-Youngstown trolley. A sign hanging over the doorway announced in Italian and English that it was a hotel and saloon. Strains of a mandolin and guitar drifted through the open door. Inside, smoke from Italian cigars dulled the reek of vomit and stale beer.

The mandolin stopped playing when a girl plopped into the musician's lap. The man laughed as he ran a dirty hand under her skirt. She giggled, throwing bare arms around his neck. Dominick thought she couldn't be much older than Rosa. A woman smoking a small black cigar sat in a chair near the bar. When she noticed Dominick staring at her, she crossed her legs exposing a thigh marred with bruises.

Rocco led him toward a thickset man of middle age who was standing by the bar giving orders to a skinny man wearing an apron.

"Hello, Luca," Rocco said, when they arrived at the bar.

As the man turned Dominick recognized Luca Caruzzi, one of the men who attended his initiation into the Society. Luca was heavily mustached. His nose appeared to have been broken several times. A wide tie, stained with spots that looked suspiciously like dried blood, was tucked into a silk vest.

Thickly lidded eyes shifted to Rocco followed by a deep rumble of greeting.

Rocco nodded toward Dominick. "You remember Dominick Prugitore?"

Luca turned his gaze, knitting his brow and puckering his lips in a frown. Then he smiled, showing a chipped tooth in front.

"Of course, the man who was scratched by Siciliano." Luca extended a thick hand.

When Dominick took the hand, pain lanced up his arm. The man's grip was crushing. Luca held the grip looking coldly into Dominick's eyes. He managed to return the stare without flinching.

Suddenly Luca yanked him off balance, pulling the younger man close to him. Laughing, Luca threw an arm around Dominick's shoulders before releasing his hand.

"You'll do all right. Not many men can look Luca Caruzzi in the eyes like that." He gave Dominick's shoulders a painful squeeze before gesturing broadly around the saloon. "You need a woman?" He asked with a booming voice. "The first one is on me."

The woman sitting near the bar looked at Dominick with new interest.

Dominick's face flushed. He glanced at the floor. "Perhaps later, signore."

Luca roared with laughter. "Nicky!" He shouted. "Give my friends something to drink then."

After the drinks were served, Luca's face took on a serious expression. He reached into his vest and slid a brown envelope across the bar to Rocco. When Rocco opened the envelope, Dominick could see the corners of several greenbacks.

Rocco cast a puzzled expression at Luca.

"It's from Virginia." Luca's voice rumbled like distant thunder. "She's expecting you to come over."

"But," Rocco gestured with an open hand toward the envelope.

Luca shrugged. "Just be careful, Rocco. You know the rules." Rocco glanced at Dominick then tossed down the rest of his liquor. "Yeah," he gasped. "Take care of him will you? I'll be back later."

"Use the back door." Luca thundered.

After he left, Luca gestured for the bartender to come over. "Give Dominick whatever he wants. His drinks are on the house tonight."

"Grazie, signore."

Luca nodded. He seemed to be angry about something. The big man stared at the doorway Rocco went through. "The fool can be stubborn sometimes."

"I don't understand, signore."

Luca shook his head as though ridding himself of an unpleasant burden. "Best to leave it that way." Then his voice took on its usual bluster. "Look kid, if you need anything, just see Nicky, okay? I've got to tend to business."

As the afternoon wore on the saloon began to fill with a noisy crowd. Girls came down from up-stairs. They weren't down long before they were ushered back up by eager looking patrons. The woman who had been sitting by the bar flashed Dominick a defiant look before escorting two men, arm in arm, toward the stairs. Later he talked to some men from Hillsville before they drifted off in search of other diversions. By evening Dominick was getting a little sick from the beer and smoke. He thought about leaving but wasn't sure what Rocco would say.

At a nearby table, two men were suddenly on their feet facing each other.

A woman screamed.

Luca Caruzzi waded between the combatants, grabbing a man's wrist with a savage twist. A knife clattered to the floor as Luca's other fist crashed into the man's face with a cracking sound. The man flew backwards, smashing into a table and chair, blood spurting from his nose.

Luca motioned for some men to drag the stricken man out the back door. Then he turned to the other one. "Get out!" he snapped.

The man grabbed his hat and darted for the door.

Dominick noticed a young man standing near Caruzzi who was gawking around like a trapped rabbit.

Luca picked up the knife, and started toward the bar motioning for the young man to follow.

Nick was waiting for him as Luca slammed the knife down on the scared wood. "Put it with the rest of the collection, Nick. Someday we'll start a butcher shop."

"This is a butcher shop," Nick muttered.

Caruzzi ignored the bartender's remark and turned to Dominick, pulling some money from his pocket.

"I want you to do me a favor."

"Si, signore. My pleasure." Dominick was staring at the frightened young man who was dressed in rough clothes and wore a puffy short brimmed cap from the old country.

"Take this lad downtown and buy his supper. Then drop him at the train station. He has to be in Pittsburgh tomorrow morning."

Luca frowned at Dominick's puzzled expression. "Don't ask questions. Just go! And use the back door."

"What's your name?" Dominick asked once they were outside.

"Mario Palaone. I'm from Cleveland."

Mario seemed to be calming somewhat.

Dominick raised his eyebrows. "Why Pittsburgh?"

Mario looked at him for a long moment then shrugged. "I have to kill someone, that's why. Then I must go back to the old country."

Dominick stopped in his tracks. "Why?"

"I don't know."

"Then why do it?"

"Don't you know nothing!" The young man was getting angry. "If I don't, they kill me. Is that a good enough reason?"

"Are you married?" Dominick thought it might be a good idea to change the subject.

"No, that's why I was chosen to do this."

"Then why don't you just run away? Say, California or some place."

Mario stopped walking and flashed him a sign. This time Dominick recognized it.

"Monte Albano," he replied, with the password of the Society.

"You haven't been with the Society very long, have you?"

Dominick shook his head.

"Listen, you can't escape! The Society is everywhere our people live. If you're a member in the old country, you're in it here."

Dominick looked as though he'd been struck with a brick.

Mario grabbed him by the arm and started walking again. "Where do we go from here?" he asked roughly.

Dominick led him around the side of a building and up a dirt street that ran along the tracks toward the center of town.

Mario kept talking as they went. His voice tainted with bitterness. "They're well organized. They send me all the way from Cleveland to kill someone I don't even know. Then they pay my fare back to Italy. When I get there, they will pay me more."

When he got back to Luca's, Dominick found the swarthy saloon-keeper in a rage. "The stupid idiot!" Luca exclaimed, pointing to a table near the wall.

Rocco was slumped over the table. A pretty blonde woman was trying to rouse him.

"He's going to get himself killed," Luca said.

"What do you mean?" Dominick was becoming alarmed.

Luca ignored his question. "Look, I'll get him upstairs where he can sleep it off. See if you can get that slut out of here without trouble."

"But who is she?"

Luca grabbed him painfully by the shoulder. "She's John Marsicano's American-slut-of-a-wife, that's who!"

"OK, signore. But why is Rocco in trouble?"

"Because it's against the rules to dishonor a brother. Even a little turd like Marsicano."

Dominick nodded.

"That money was to help buy his way out of trouble. Now, the fool has flaunted the thing in public."

Dominick walked over to where Rocco and Virginia were. "Excuse me, Madam," he said.

She looked up. She had deep blue eyes.

"I'm a personal friend of Rocco's," he added, by way of introduction. "I'm afraid there may be some complications. May I talk to you privately for a moment."

She hesitated, looking at Rocco.

"Please." He moved behind her chair and helped her to stand. She didn't object.

"Allow me, Virginia." Taking her gently by the arm, Dominick led her toward the waiting door.

Under Caruzzi's supervision, two men moved in and grabbed Rocco under the arms.

Virginia put her hand to her mouth. "Where are they taking him?"

"He'll be all right. They're just taking him upstairs to sleep off the liquor."

"But he can go home with me!" She was almost crying.

"Please," he implored. "Rocco will be in more trouble if you make a scene here."

When they were outside, she dug in her purse and handed him the brown envelope with the money. "Rocco wouldn't take this," she said. "Please see that he gets the money. I understand he's going to need it."

She paused before turning to leave. "You must think we're terrible. But he isn't ashamed of me."

"I don't judge you, Madam."

She had started to walk away again, then whirled suddenly. "Don't you dare! Don't anyone dare!" Tears were running freely down her cheeks.

"I'll see he gets the money."

She turned abruptly and started down the dark alley swiping at the tears with the back of her hand.

Dominick managed to catch the last car to Youngstown. Once again, Toni wasn't at the room. Too tired to care, he fell across the bed with his clothes on. In the morning he wrote his reports and left them for Toni to convey to Pittsburgh. Then he went to the barbershop for a shave before heading back to the saloon to find Rocco.

Badly hung over, Rocco was in a foul mood. "Where the devil have you been?"

"Watching out for your butt, that's where!" Dominick came over to the table and flopped down in a wobbly chair. "Look, I'm as tired as you. So pardon my temper, signore."

Rocco held up his hand. "No more yelling, please." Wearily he buried his head in his hands.

After a while, Rocco's voice drifted up through his fingers and his misery. "You ready to go home?"

"Si, signore."

"Good, because I have to find Sam Bennett."

Luca had been smiling smugly at Rocco's plight. Now he looked at Dominick with a serious expression. "Did Mario get on the train last night?"

"Si, signore. He wasn't happy, but he got on the train."

Luca seemed relieved and nodded his head. "Unfortunately, another problem has developed."

"Now what?" Dominick asked wearily.

With a moan Rocco lifted his head. Bloodshot eyes swam in a puffy, pallid face. "Those dogs Sam and I got out of jail the other week have skipped bail."

"That's not the worst of it," Luca said.

"You tell him, Luca." With a moan, Rocco dropped his head back into his hands.

"They stole some money from one of my men before running away. Rocco wants to send Sam after them."

"But Sam is supposed to get married this week."

"Will you stop yelling!" Rocco lifted his head to stare angrily at Dominick. "What's the matter with you? Sam will have to wait."

If Maria wasn't happy about Sam going away, her father was furious. Only after Dominick took him down to see the house was Signore Piccini convinced his daughter's honor wasn't being trifled with. Meanwhile, Dominick was called upon more and more by Romon and Rocco to assist in the personal affairs of the community. When a fight broke out, he was asked to settle accounts between the beleaguered parties. When the Italian ship Sirio sunk off Carthagena, Spain, with appalling loss of life, he was asked to read the newspaper account to the residents of Peanut. That evening the three men sat on Rocco's porch discussing the tragedy.

"Maybe you better learn to swim before you leave for the old country, Rocco." Romon was not smiling, and Dominick had felt the tension building between them all evening. "Of course," Romon added, "I remember that water hurts your back."

Nodding toward Dominick, Rocco made a hasty sign with his hand.

"Oh don't worry. Your secret is safe with me."

Rocco cast Cerini a withering look before stalking stiffly into the house.

When he was gone Romon rose to leave, motioning for Dominick to walk with him.

They traveled a way in silence before Romon spoke. "I am arranging for a meeting to determine who is to be in charge here." His voice grew harder. "You must decide where you will stand."

"You mean a society meeting, then?"

"Perhaps. Meanwhile, I want you to stop working at the Johnson quarry. The stone is too hard there anyway. I'll arrange for you to get a job in the Peanut quarry. That way you will be closer when we need you."

"OK, signore. But I must have a job. I can't just quit."

"Don't worry. I'll take care of you. Just stick with me, understand?"

"Si, signore."

The next morning Dominick met Rocco on his way to work and told the older man about his conversation with Romon.

"You must listen to what Romon says. He is trying to drive me out."

"Can he do this thing?"

"He's welcome to it. My wife and I are going to leave soon anyway."

"When is that?"

"When Sam finds those dogs who skipped bail. Then he can get married, and I will be free to leave."

Dominick reached into his pocket and handed Rocco the brown envelope. "Virginia asked me to give this to you."

Rocco slipped the envelope into his pocket and the two men went on in silence. They passed several shanties. Women and children were tending tomato plants and beans tied neatly to tall stakes. Suddenly the ground trembled, followed by a deep rumble. Ahead of them a cloud of dust rose from the quarry. Rocco paused, looking at Dominick.

"You're a good friend. Some would have taken this money for themselves."

Dominick shrugged. "I would have given it to you sooner, but there was always someone around."

"Perhaps, if this murder of the game policeman is forgotten, I will stay here."

They were approaching the quarry offices before Dominick spoke again, his voice soft. "I hear the game policeman was a bad man."

"He shot my dog," Rocco replied bitterly. "Maybe, someday I will tell you about it. Now you must quit here. Go to the Peanut quarry with the others."

Dominick loaded stone for the rest of the day, placing his brass number on the cars. When he finished work he went to the office and told them he was going to quit. The timekeeper wasn't surprised. Workers came and went almost daily at the quarries.

The Society of Honor met on Wednesday evenings at the homes of its members. On this particular night the meeting was at Julio Carpellotti's house. Two strangers were present at the meeting. One man from Chicago had a baldhead set squarely over a barrel chest. His name was Joe Boggiano. The other man was younger, more expensively dressed, and came from New York. Both were emissaries for those yet to come.

Cerini warned everyone to behave. There was to be no vendettas, no fighting, nothing to attract the American authorities to Hillsville. Arrangements were made to lodge the arriving capos, and men were assigned to security. Overnight Hillsville became an armed camp.

On Sunday, lookouts and runners watched the railroad, paths and wagon roads. Mothers strove to keep their children quiet. Not a leaf stirred. Occasionally, the soft rumble of thunder sounded off to the northwest.

Dominick and Sam Bennett stood behind Rocco as he mopped his face and forehead with a blue bandanna. But what caused rivers of sweat to pour down his chest and back more then anything, was Romon Cerini's treachery.

Romon was still on his feet, talking in a slow, deliberate manner. "...and aside from becoming a guard at the Johnson quarry during last year's strike, Rocco Racca has broken the rules of the Society."

"Lies!" Rocco shouted. "I would never break the Society's rules!"

The Dons sat on chairs carried into the woods by the men standing behind them.

Don Filasto, from New York, had been fanning himself with a piece of wood he picked up along the trail. Now he stood slowly, motioning for silence. He stared angrily at Romon. "This is a serious charge, Cerini." His voice carried clearly around the glade. "I have known Rocco Racca in the old country. He stayed with me in New York, and I have always known him to be faithful to the Society."

Don Cardi, from Pittsburgh, nodded agreement.

Romon never took his eyes off the New York Don. "You are all honorable men," he continued. "I would not insult you by asking you to hear unsupported charges."

With a frown, the Don sank back onto his seat.

Romon turned and nodded to Vito Siciliano standing quietly beside him. Vito cast a mocking glance at Rocco before disappearing into the woods.

Romon continued talking. "The charge I bring against Rocco Racca is that of the lowest kind." He paused and looked sternly at Rocco. "This man," he said, raising his arm and pointing at Rocco, "...is having an affair with the wife of a member of this society."

Don Filasto rose angrily to his feet. He was about to speak when Vito reappeared, pushing two men ahead of him. One of the men was walking with a pronounced limp. The other was short and disheveled with a thick crop of curly black hair. Vito gave this man a shove, propelling him into the center of the group. The man looked nervously at the ground, fidgeting with a twig he had picked up in the woods.

Romon glanced at Rocco, and the briefest trace of a smile flickered across his lips.

"What is this?" Don Filasto demanded.

"Tell them who you are," Romon said to the little man.

"John Marsicano, signore." He began trembling violently. The twig broke in his hands, and the little man stared at it blankly.

"Tell them!" Romon demanded.

Tears began to flow down John Marsicano's face, and he began to sob, unable to talk.

"Come now, signore," Don Filasto said. "Hold up your head like a man." He gestured broadly with his hand. "Tell us your story."

Marsicano sighed deeply and wiped his face with a dirty hand. He couldn't bring himself to look at these men whom he had been taught to fear all his life.

"Rocco Racca is having an affair with my wife," he sobbed. Tears started flowing again.

"Tell them the rest," Romon demanded coldly.

"Rocco had some men beat me up in Lowellville. When I had these men put in jail, he tried to have me killed."

Don Filasto sat back down, shaking his head. "You went to the Americans over a fight?"

Marsicano stopped weeping and wiped at his face again. "I was scared, signore. And this man," he pointed at Rocco, lifting his chin for the first time as he did so, "wouldn't let me take my Virginia away from there."

Luca Caruzzi was standing behind the headman from Youngstown. His voice boomed through the glade. "His wife is an American slut! Rocco isn't the first man she's been unfaithful with."

Don Cardi got slowly to his feet. "Enough!"

He looked at each of the other Dons in succession. Then slashed his forefinger across his cheek. The others nodded.

The little man, who had been staring at his feet, didn't see the Don's gesture.

"Look at me, John Marsicano."

Marsicano, still trembling, looked up through swollen eyes.

"You dishonored the Society and broke the vow of silence by going to the American authorities. You are to be put out of the Society with the mark of disgrace." With that, he again slashed his forefinger across his cheek.

Marsicano's mouth fell open, then his eyes rolled back and he collapsed in a heap.

As Vito's men carried him away, Romon motioned for the other man to move forward. Frank Calvo dragged his crippled leg into the clearing. He appeared nervous but held his head high. "Tell them," Romon said.

Luca Caruzzi leaned forward and whispered something into the ear of the headman from Youngstown.

Frank told how they had beaten Marsicano on Rocco's orders, about being arrested and locked in the Lowellville jail.

Mariano Sochetti, slim and lithe, rose to his feet. Luca Caruzzi stood solidly behind him. "Luca tells me, Calvo, that you skipped the bail put up for you by Rocco Racca. Is this true?"

"Si, signore, but I am going to turn myself in tomorrow."

"Luca also tells me that you stole money from his men in Lowellville before you left."

"The other two men did that, signore."

"But you were with them, were you not?" Mariano's voice was soft as silk.

"Si, signore, but...I was going to pay it back." His voice was becoming squeaky. "Th...the others left me and took the money."

"Where are they, Calvo?"

"I...I don't know."

"Permesso, Don Sochetti," Romon interjected. "The point here is that Rocco Racca used these men to beat up Marsicano."

"I'm aware of what the point is, Cerini. We will deal with that after we clear up this little matter of the bail money." He turned to the other Dons. "Signores, may I take some liberty here? Aside from Rocco and Sam Bennett, it was my headman in Lowellville who was disgraced by this man."

The other men nodded in reply.

"Very well," he said. "Now, listen to me closely, Frank Calvo. You will turn yourself in to the authorities in Lowellville. I don't think Marsicano will testify against you, but you must answer for jumping bail. That will help Signore Racca and Signore Bennett somewhat. You will do this today! Do you understand?"

"Si, signore."

"Good! You will then assist Signore Bennett in finding the other two thieves, and repay double the money you owe. If you fail, you will be dead. Now go!"

Don Sochetti settled into his chair and, crossing his legs, watched Frank Calvo intently.

The crippled man looked blankly around at the other Dons, and sensing no support, shrugged before limping up the trail toward the Peanut settlement followed by one of Don Sochetti's henchmen.

Don Sochetti fixed his gaze on Romon once again. "Do you have anything further, signore?"

Romon told them about Rocco taking Virginia into Caruzzi's saloon and ended by demanding the death penalty for Rocco.

When he concluded, the Dons met alone. They deliberated for over an hour, finally calling Rocco and Romon back into the glade to hear their decision. The two men stood slightly apart facing a semi-circle where the four headmen sat. The Dons sat mopping their foreheads with handkerchiefs, or fanning themselves. Don Tripepi, from Chicago, spoke for them. He was an old man, older than Don Cardi, and Joe Boggiano helped him to his feet. His voice was deep and scratchy.

"I have been a member of The Society of Honor since I was a young man in Sicily," he began. "The Society will treat you well if you don't become greedy or overcome with passion. Some of us are growing old, and it is not easy to travel all this way to listen to the petty squabbles of children."

He paused and looked a long time at the men in front of him. The humidity became, suddenly, oppressive.

"I am here as a guest of Don Sochetti, Don Filasto and Don Cardi," Don Tripepi continued. "They have given to me the honor of passing judgement." He looked directly at Rocco. "Rocco Racca, your peers have judged you to be faithful to our society. For this reason you are to be spared the sentence of death. But in your lust, you have shamed us all. For this, you are to be put out.

You must pay $500 if you wish to be reinstated into the Society, and then you may never again be headman."

Slowly he turned to Romon. "Romon Cerini, you are to be headman in Hillsville temporally. However, we have decided it is in the best interest of the Society to send a new headman. And," he raised a finger, "perhaps not from the East."

He paused and stared hard at Romon. When he spoke again his voice took on an almost hissing quality.

"You must obey the one we send. Then perhaps, you may be second in command. Capeesh?"

Romon's jaw clenched and unclenched, causing his temples to flex spasmodically. "Si, signore."

"Good," Don Tripepi said before scanning his gaze over both men. "Understand this final thing. There is to be no vendetta here. No more bloodshed."

In the days that followed Romon warned Dominick twice to forsake Rocco, but since he felt Rocco might confide in him about the Houk murder, Dominick refused. Now the young man sat on Rocco's porch drinking a beer as a light summer rain rattled the tin roof overhead. Rocco had been unusually quiet lately. Eventually, the former headman cleared his throat. "You may be in danger sitting here, compare."

Dominick looked at Rocco for a moment. This was the first time the former Black Hand chieftain had used the term for friendship with him. He shrugged. "I thought there was to be no vendetta."

"No vendetta? What's the matter with you?" Rocco threw the empty beer bottle into the street. "Romon has already warned people not to buy from my store. You best be careful."

"What do you think will happen?"

"I think you better stay away from me for awhile. That's what I think!"

They sat in silence for a few moments before Dominick announced he should go. "My new roommate, Salvatori Tuttini has asked me to help him finish drilling at the Johnson quarry tomorrow. I must get some rest."

Rocco nodded and pointed a warning finger at him. "If you push Romon, his honor will demand a response."

The next morning dawned hot and sunny. Salvatori and Dominick walked together toward the quarry. Salvatori was nineteen and had only been in this country a year.

"I left the tools at the quarry yesterday, so they would be ready to go," he told Dominick. "Maybe we can blast today. I never did that before."

Dominick shook his head. "That was a dumb thing to do. Tools have a way of disappearing if you leave them unguarded."

"Oh, I told everyone you were going to help me today. People know you belong to the Society. It will be all right."

"What do you know about the Society?"

"Enough."

When they arrived at Salvatori's place in the quarry, the sledge and drill were propped against a stone where the lad had placed them the night before. A rusted tin can sat on top of the stone.

"I wonder who put this can here?" Salvatori said.

Dominick was busy examining the drill bit. "This drill is dull. Why didn't you leave it for the blacksmith to sharpen?"

The boy looked at the bit. "I thought it would be alright. Besides, I don't have the money to pay him."

Dominick shook his head in disgust. "We can't work with this, the stone is too hard here." He picked the drill up, balancing it carefully over his shoulder. "Look, the blacksmith owes me a favor. Why don't you start breaking some of these larger stones until I get back?"

As he started up the tracks toward the company's buildings something kept nagging at him. Something was wrong. When he tried to brush the feelings aside, he recalled Rocco's warning. Suddenly, Dominick remembered the rusty can and the silvery liquid spilled on the rock beside it. Contemplating what it could be, he turned to look back.

Salvatori had picked up the sledgehammer. The can was too tempting a target.

Dominick watched the boy raise the hammer over his head, saw it ark toward the rock and the rusty can. The warning shout was just forming on his lips when a blinding flash knocked him flat.

Dominick barely heard the explosion as he instinctively threw his arms over his face. Bits of stone and dirt came hurtling from the sky. Something warm and wet splattered across his shirt sleeve.

His eyes burned, and he held them tight shut for a while. The roaring sound in his head drowned everything. Choking and gasping for air he tried to get up, but it felt as though the earth tilted and he was falling. He forced his eyes open. Slowly objects begun to focus. He looked at the wet thing on his arm. A bloody piece of intestine clung jelly-like to his sleeve. Vomit filled his mouth and ran out his nose. Suddenly Dominick was on his knees, gagging and sobbing. He felt hands pulling at him, lifting him to his feet.

The men spent the rest of the morning picking up the few pieces of the boy that was left. Then, as was their custom, they took the rest of the day off.

Some men helped Dominick to his bed, while Mrs. Carpellotti fussed over him like a godmother. She tried to keep people away, but his friends, including Rocco, came to sit with him. He was unhurt, except for a persistent roaring and dizziness in his head plus cuts and bruises from falling debris.

When the others left, Dominick looked at Rocco and Julio Carpellotti. "There was nitro in the can, wasn't there?"

Rocco and Julio glanced at each other, and then nodded.

"We must tell the authorities."

Rocco glared at him a long moment. "It was you they were after," he said quietly.

Dominick's eyes filled with tears once again. "Si," he said, when he regained his composure, "but the next time it may be you or Julio."

When he went back to work at the Peanut quarry, the Society's members wouldn't talk to him. They nodded politely, showing they didn't hold any hard feelings against him, then walked away. The only person who did talk to him was Rosa's father.

"You're a good man, Dominick. I don't understand why you joined the Society, but I know you're not like the others."

"Grazie, signore, but how is your family?"

The older man looked at him carefully. "They are well. But since the explosion at the quarry, Rosa worries about you."

Casimo Ciampanelli paused for a moment, working on a chew, a habit he picked up from the Americans.

"I know you are somehow mixed up in this thing between Rocco and Romon. Be careful, both of these men are dangerous."

Dominick nodded. "I miss your kids," he said slowly.

Rosa's father sent a thick string of brown juice arcing over a nearby rock. "Well, why don't you come over for dinner? The family would like that."

He shook his head vigorously. "That might put your family in danger, signore. Perhaps after this business is over?"

Casimo got slowly to his feet. "You'd know best about that. Just be careful."

Finally, after a week of such treatment, Dominick had enough. After work one day he headed for Romon's house with every intention of confronting the acting headman. On the road he met a group of men coming toward him. One of the men was Vito Siciliano who appeared to be slightly drunk.

Vito staggered in front of him blocking his path. "So, if it isn't Prugitore. The cat with nine lives."

"Excuse me, signore." He tried to step around the leering Siciliano.

Vito shoved him backwards. "Don't ignore me when I talk to you, boy!"

Dominick looked at the taller man evenly. "I have no quarrel with you, signore."

Vito put his hands on his hips. "No? You think because you missed my little trap at the quarry, you are so lucky?"

A cold rage washed over Dominick. For a brief second, he saw pieces of Salvatori splattered in the dust around the quarry. Then he hit Vito as hard as he could. The blow glanced off the Sicilian's jaw.

Vito grabbed his hands so he couldn't move.

Still in a rage, Dominick spit in his face.

With a howl, Vito shoved him backwards. In one fluid movement, the Youngstown enforcer plucked a stiletto from his boot and took a step toward Dominick, who lay sprawled in the dirt.

"That will be enough, Vito!" The voice was cold and flat.

Vito stopped and looked behind him.

"What's the matter? Did he insult you?" Romon asked.

"He spit in my face!"

"Still, you can't just murder him in cold blood. This will have to be settled under the rules of the Society. With a duel."

The sneer crept back on Vito's face. "Si, somebody give him a knife."

"Not here. We'll go to Jim Rossi's saloon."

They cleared a space in the center of the room, stacking the tables and chairs by the walls. A number of men gathered to watch, forming a circle of bodies around the combatants. Once the thing was set everyone seemed eager to get on with it, everyone except Jim Rossi. Jim was arguing with Romon.

"This isn't according to the rules," Jim insisted. "Look at him, he doesn't even know how to hold a knife."

Dominick stood in the center of the circle. Someone had stripped his shirt off. He held a knife awkwardly in his right hand.

Romon seemed to be considering the situation with some amusement. "Okay, you have an hour. Teach him everything you know." With that, he and Vito left the room.

Jim whispered something to one of his boarders, and the latter quickly disappeared out the back. He sent the other men away while he tried to teach Dominick a few rudiments of knife fighting.

Jim taught him how to stand and how to hold the knife; explaining the rules of a duel as he went.

"There can be no slashing. You may only stab him in the stomach or chest, never in the back. There are to be no marks visible on the face. This way we can get a doctor to rule that the looser died from natural causes. If you fail in this, you will be taken outside and killed. Do you understand?"

Dominick nodded. He felt numb.

Jim showed him a few moves and then shook his head at the boy's obvious lack of coordination.

"Look, son," Jim said in exasperation. "Don't try to do anything fancy. Vito's an expert with a knife. Just wade in. When he strikes, take the blow in your hand or arm. The wound will hurt, but it may buy you a moment to strike back.

All too soon men began filing back into the room. Romon and Vito came in last. Vito casually took off his coat and shirt. Dominick saw a hairy torso scarred from previous battles.

As the men formed a circle, Dominick picked up the knife Jim had given him. His legs trembled, and he fought to keep from vomiting.

Vito was a picture of confidence. He smiled at Dominick like a cat playing with a mouse. "Come on, smart ass; let's see if your guts look the same as Salvatori's."

Dominick flushed with anger. One of Vito's tactics, Jim told him, was to get his opponent mad enough to make fatal mistakes.

Dominick didn't move. He maintained his crouched stance, holding the knife so tight it trembled in his hand.

Vito walked slowly around, feinting at him. Testing him. Teasing him.

Dominick turned as if in a trance, never moving or lunging in return. He was weak with fear. Absently, he lifted a hand to wipe at the sweat stinging his eyes.

Like a hawk, Vito saw his opportunity and lunged.

Suddenly the thundering blast of a shotgun shook the room. Dust and pieces of Jim's ceiling rained down on the combatants.

Vito stopped in mid-stride as a booming voice bellowed through the crowd. "Hold! Make way there, no!"

The crowd parted to let a short, round, baldheaded man through. Two serious looking men, carrying short double-barreled shotguns called luparas, or wolf guns, followed close behind.

"What's the meaning of this?" Romon asked in a cold voice.

The man's thick eyebrows bristled. "I'm Joe Boggiano, and I'm your new headman." Joe gestured toward the two men standing in the center of the room. "What is the meaning of this, huh?"

"This is a duel of honor. You have no right to interrupt."

Boggiano's eyes flashed. "There are rules for such a duel, no? And this one," he pointed to Dominick, "is not properly trained."

"This is a matter of honor." Romon insisted.

"There is no honor here!" Contempt leached into Joe's voice. "But perhaps there can be training and still satisfy your question of honor, no?"

Joe walked over to Romon, a razor uncoiling from his fist. Romon's eyebrows raised but he stood firm. Joe grabbed Romon's shirt and deftly sliced two buttons from the front. Then he walked to where Vito and Dominick stood, poised and facing each other. "Put these over the tips of your knives. The first one to draw blood wins."

The new headman stared at Vito for a moment. "Your honor will be satisfied with this, Siciliano. Capeesh?"

The taller man snarled an acknowledgement.

"Good! See that you don't break the button when you strike."

Again the combatants circled each other. This time there was no taunting. Vito feinted, exposing his mid-section to Dominick for an instant. Dominick staggered into a lunge, but Vito, staying just out of reach, caused him to over extend. Spinning on the balls of his feet, Vito grabbed Dominick's knife hand and jerked him off balance.

Dominick felt the tip of Vito's stiletto bite into his chest right over his heart, knocking him down, and knocking the wind out of him at the same time. Fortunately, the button held.

Without a word, Vito gathered his clothes and vanished into the night.

Chapter 9

The fight with Vito had won Dominick a balling out by Rocco, Jim Rossi and Joe Boggiano. Superintendent Dimuro wanted to take him off the case. That frightened him more than anything. Only by convincing Dimuro that he was winning the confidence of Rocco Racca, had kept the young detective in Hillsville.

Vito Siciliano disappeared after he walked out of Jim Rossi's saloon the night of the fight. Mario Sergio had disappeared as well. Rumors hinted that Boggiano was keeping Vito and Mario in Youngstown against the possibility of trouble later on. For the past week the settlement enjoyed a peaceful respite.

Friday afternoon the quarry shut down to repair equipment, and Dominick found himself at Rocco's store. Several men had just returned from hunting, and Rocco was annoyed with their scant bag of four small birds and a half-grown rabbit. Turning to Dominick, he put his arm around the younger man's shoulders. "Go to Ignazio Sebastianelli," Rocco declared. "Tell him I need the favor of some birds."

"Ignazio? What does that crazy old man have to do with birds?"

"Ignazio may be a little crazy but he keeps to the old ways. He'll have birds."

Ignazio's shanty looked like a ramshackle shed with a tin roof. A scrap of heavy canvas hung over the entrance in place of a door. Off to one side, a pile of rusting tins slumped beside a dilapidated outhouse. Pieces of junk and broken tools lay scattered about.

As Dominick walked slowly up the path, an old dog, sleeping on the shady side of the shanty, raised its head and growled. He went to one knee and held out his open hand as the shaggy mongrel wobbled to its feet and began a wheezing sort of bark. Scratching the dog behind its ear, Dominick heard the curious chirping he recognized as Ignazio's chuckle. He looked up to see the barefoot old man leaning on a hoe, regarding him intently.

"You come to steal my dog?" There was a look of amusement on the weathered old face.

"Rocco sent me for some birds."

Ignazio's eyes flashed. "You mean he sent you to ask the *favor* of some birds?"

"Si, signore. That is how he put it."

The old man's head popped up and the withered back straightened abruptly. "Young people have forgotten respect."

"Forgive me, signore. I did not mean to offend."

The leer washed back across the old man's face as Ignazio spit a stream of tobacco juice; his Adam's apple bobbing in rhythm to the sound emanating from his throat. "Si, si. Come see the peppers. Good ground for peppers, you know." Ignazio shuffled around the side of the shanty with the old dog wobbling along at his heels.

Among a people who took pride in their gardens, Ignazio's was, beyond a doubt, the finest garden in Hillsville. The old man picked a small red pepper and wiped off the lime dust that seemed to cover everything this close to the quarry before handing it to Dominick. The lad was familiar with the bite of peppers, but this one brought tears to his eyes.

Ignazio was smiling and chuckling as he chewed another. "That is the way of peppers," he said. "They talk to you going in, and talk to you coming out."

Dominick couldn't talk. He felt as though his windpipe was closing, and looked around wildly for water. Ignazio, emitting that curious chirping, motioned him toward the door of his shanty.

Inside, the room was cool and dark. Between his tearing eyes and dilating pupils, Dominick was momentarily blinded. He heard the old man pouring water into something, and then felt bony fingers press a damp tin cup into his hand. The water was cool and sweet, but for several minutes only seemed to stimulate the bite of the pepper. Slowly the burning sensation began to fade as his eyes adjusted to the darkened room. He blinked in surprise. The room was swept and orderly. Heavy cloths hung over two small windows. A bunk sat against the wall, neatly made with clean blankets. Wooden shelves along the walls held jars of home canned vegetables and fruit.

Ignazio picked up a cloth sack and pushed open the canvas flap over the doorway. A stream of sunlight flooded through the opening blinding Dominick again. "Come, boy. We'll get birds for your master."

Dominick stumbled outside, shielding his eyes from the glaring sun. "He's not my master!" Resentment and anger surfaced in his voice.

Suddenly the leer was gone from the old man's gaze. "No? We shall see who is master and who is not." He started off with a loose shuffle, leading down a path that led around his garden toward a stand of high brush.

Dominick followed the old man down a path that wound and twisted through gangling red maple and green briers. Sweat stung his eyes and soaked his shirt when Ignazio stopped suddenly, causing Dominick to bump roughly into his back.

"Clumsy, boy!" Ignazio scolded. Then he pointed toward the clearing. Again that chirping noise caused his Adam's apple to bob frantically.

A wide net, so fine it seemed to be only a mist, stretched across the opening. Birds of various sizes and colors struggled frantically in the net; others hung limply by their necks or broken wings.

Ignazio carefully removed the birds, ringing the necks of those still alive. When Dominick reached for a struggling bird, Ignazio's raspy voice stopped him.

"Don't touch net, silly boy! Net tears. Ignazio get birds." Dominick walked beside the old man holding the bag open as Ignazio dropped nearly a dozen birds into its folds. After they cleared the net, and Ignazio carefully repaired broken threads from a spool he carried in his pocket, they followed the path to other grassy openings hidden in the thick brush. A net, containing struggling birds, ran across the middle of each clearing. Dominick learned Ignazio brought the silk nets with him from Sicily. When they were done, they emerged on the trail leading back to the stone quarry. Dominick carried a sack nearly full of birds, some still flopping in their death throws.

"Tell your master, Ignazio will expect a favor some day."

"I told you, he is not my master!"

"We'll see, silly boy. We'll see." Turning abruptly, the old man ambled toward his shanty, still chirping like a strangled bird.

Dominick turned toward the quarry, wondering why the old man bothered him so much. The bag full of birds reminded him of a conversation with Game Warden Seeley Houk. Houk believed birds and wildlife were important, worth protecting. Worth dying for.

Monday morning found him working at the Johnson quarry again. The sun beat down unmercifully as he loaded broken stones into quarry cars. Dust and stone chips stuck to his sweating body. As he worked he thought about the party at Rocco's on Saturday. The bird's breasts were roasted on slender saplings and marinated with a spicy sauce. During the party Rocco had put his arm around Dominick and asked him to come back to work at the Johnson quarry. He said he wanted a friend to walk to work with.

Dominick paused to mop sweat from his eyes, and shook his head in disbelief. Since Rocco was kicked out of the Society, the former headman seemed to rely on him more and more. Rocco even offered him a place at the quarry for nothing, working as a sort of free agent wherever he was needed.

After work Dominick walked over to Ralph Fontanella's house to buy a beer. Ralph's house was near the Duff farm.

Before he finished drinking the beer, Dominick saw some men carrying a body on a plank. A cloud of excited people clamoring in Italian and English surrounded them. Pushing through the crowd, he saw that Walter Duff was carrying one end of the plank. Clyde and Walter Duff ran the Penaut quarry.

"What happened?" He asked.

Walter's face was a mixture of anxiety and fear. As he looked at Dominick, anger suddenly crowded out the fear. "A no-good wop shot grandfather! That's what happened!"

"How can I help?"

"Get these wop's outta' here, that's how!"

Clyde Duff touched his son's arm. "Calm down, Walter. That isn't helping." His voice held a slight tremor. "Just get Dad up to the house."

Dominick looked at the man on the plank. Squire Duff was an old man whose wisps of silver hair lay thick with matted blood. He had been shot in the face with a shotgun. As Dominick dropped back, Clyde Duff came over to him.

"You're the one who speaks English, aren't you?"

"Yes, sir." Dominick couldn't seem to take his eyes off the bloody old man bouncing along on the plank. He reminded him of a little bird hanging in one of Ignazio's nets.

"Please ask your people to go home. It wouldn't be good for them to come up to the house just now."

Dominick looked at the Peanut quarry's superintendent: at the war of emotions ragging across his face. "Who did this thing, Mr. Duff?"

Clyde Duff's face clouded suddenly. "That little dago who works on the steam shovel. Fred Carnetti!" Clyde turned and hurried to catch up with the plank carrying his injured father.

Dominick saw Ralph Fontanella standing with a crowd of Italians and walked over to him. "Signore Duff doesn't want our people to go any further," he said. Dominick knew Ralph carried some authority as a second class member in the Society.

Ralph looked at the men carrying the plank and flipped his wrist in the air, a sign of disrespect. "Americano swine!" He spat.

"Signore Duff claims one of our people shot his father."

"So? They blame us for everything."

Dominick looked pointedly into Ralph's stormy face. "He said it was Fred Carnetti."

Ralph looked as if he'd been struck with a brick. "Holy Mother!" he exclaimed, crossing himself. "Fred Carnetti, Rolando Saverino, and some others were drinking beer at my place before going hunting near the Duff farm."

Ralph ran after the small group of Italians following the make shift stretcher, shouting for them to come back.

After supper the next evening, Dominick went over to Rocco's house. The two men sat on the porch sipping homemade wine.

"It is a shame about the squire," Rocco declared, slowly shaking his head. "Do you know he died this morning?"

"Si. But because he was a squire and well respected by the Americans, there will be trouble." He looked over at Rocco, who was staring moodily into his wine, and tried to make his voice sound indifferent. "I wonder where they are now?"

"Who is that?" Rocco's voice sounded as though he was far away.

"Fred Carnetti and the others."

"Fred's probably over at Mahoningtown, at his brother Frank's place." Rocco seemed to shake himself. He looked at Dominick for a moment, and then shrugged. "Hard to tell where the others are."

Looking up, Dominick saw Sam Bennett hurrying down the dusty street.

Sam stopped at the edge of the porch. "Good evening, signores."

"What's the problem, Sam?" Rocco replied.

Sam looked embarrassed. "I'm sorry, Rocco, but I was sent to get Dominick. Boggiano called a special meeting of the Society."

Rocco's face hardened. "That's all right, Sam." His voice was tight. "But tell me. What's the trouble?"

Sam looked at Dominick and Rocco for a minute, then shrugged. "Some women, including Ralph Fontanella's wife, took fruit and baked goods over to the Duff farm this afternoon to show our sympathy and respect for the Squire." Sam frowned. "Someone threw the stuff in their faces and had them escorted off the property."

Rocco got to his feet and started pacing back and forth on the porch. "Better go, Dominick," he said. "I'm glad I don't have to handle this one."

The meeting was at Ralph Fontanella's house. Ralph was moving through the crowd, ranting about disrespectful Americans. To Dominick's surprise there were even some women present. The latter were displaying articles of clothing, splattered and stained with splotches of fruit.

Finally Boggiano stood and put his arm around Ralph Fontanella. Talking quietly, he led Ralph to a chair before facing the crowd and raising his arms for silence. Immediately the room grew quiet, and the women started to leave.

"No, no, signoras. Please stay."

A low murmur erupted again.

Joe raised a hand. "Signores, signoras. Please."

His voice carried a deep resonance that soothed the crowd. He put his arms down and looked around the room until it grew quiet.

"It is true," he declared, nodding his head. "The Americans have shown disrespect."

The new headman placed his hands on his hips. Almost as broad as he was tall, with black curly hair covering thick hands and bristling over a short neck and massive shoulders, Joe Boggiano presented a picture of immovable strength.

"Still, we are guests in this country. We are only a few. We cannot fight the Americans openly."

Joe paused, his thick eyebrows pinched together, daring someone to argue. No one did. "But!" A finger and one eyebrow shot up simultaneously. "We will not help them either."

He looked pointedly at Dominick.

"When the polizia come. Dominick will interpret for them." He allowed his finger to sweep the room. "You men will be polite, but you know nothing. Not where the men are hiding, nothing."

Suddenly, Joe smiled as he looked at the women standing in the back of the room. He opened his arms wide. "We will let the signoras vent our anger. It will be like in the old country, when the solders and polizia rode into your village."

The crowd broke out in laughter. They knew what this meant. No one on earth can deliver insults like an enraged Italian woman. Boggiano held up his hands once again.

"One more thing. We are going to increase enrollment in the Society."

Now Joe raised his voice, pounding a meaty fist into the open palm of his left hand.

"I want every Italian male in Hillsville to join The Society of Honor. Only then will we be La famiglia."

The crowd in the little house came to its feet shouting, "La famiglia! La famiglia!"

Standing in the center of the room, Dominick couldn't help but wonder if he would survive the storm that was coming. That night, he wrote his reports to the Pinkertons telling them to look for Carnetti in Mahoningtown.

The next day, he was working at the quarry when Docato Trevino came running through the dust."Dominick!" He gasped. He grabbed Dominick's arm for support as he coughed the dust out of his lungs and fought to catch his breath. He had a wild look in his eyes. "You must go to Jim Rossi's place at once. The detectives want you!"

"No, Docato. I am not going to quit work to please the American detectives."

Docato's eyes grew round, and he stammered. "B..but..Dominick! Rocco is there a..and he wants you, too."

Dominick put his hand on the boy's shoulder. "Si, for Rocco I'll go."

Nearby, one of the Society men nodded approvingly.

At Jim Rossi's house, he found two men sitting in a buggy. He recognized them as County Detective McFate and the tall, mouthy constable.

Rocco stood beside the buggy and exclaimed in broken English. "Whatta' you want? This man," he gestured toward Dominick, "musta' make a living."

McFate climbed down from the buggy and turned to face Rocco. "I already explained to you several times that I need this man to interpret. I don't intend to explain myself again."

Dominick allowed his eyes to narrow slightly then snapped at McFate. "Who is going to pay me for the time I lose?"

"Listen, young man, I'm not here to argue with you. You know I'm the county detective. I believe we met before." McFate glanced over at his younger companion who had finished tying the reins to the porch railing. "This is Constable Devin. We're officially demanding your help, not asking for it."

Dominick spit on the ground by McFate's feet. "Polizia don't scare me." His voice was low, almost a hiss. "I asked who is going to pay for my time."

Before he realized what was happening, Devin grabbed him by the shoulder and spun him around.

"You greasy little wop! I'll take you in the house myself, and you better do like you're told!"

Constable Devin lifted him onto the rough slab porch with one hand, yanked open the screen door with the other, and thrust him into Jim Rossi's saloon.

"Lloyd! Dadburn it, Lloyd!" McFate's short legs were working frantically to catch up.

A wildly gesticulating woman met the two men inside. "You dog!" She screamed into Lloyd's face. "You have the manners of a pig! This is my home, you ugly dog!"

Fortunately Lloyd couldn't understand what she was yelling, but he knew it wasn't complimentary. Without letting go of Dominick's shoulder, he raised his left hand to strike the woman. He was frozen by the coldness in Dominick's voice.

"Strike her, Lloyd, and you won't live two more seconds."

Jim Rossi and several others had pushed themselves deliberately away from a table and were moving toward them, faces tempered into hard lines. A glint of steel flashed briefly in a shaft of sunlight.

McFate burst into the room, out of breath and angry. "Dadburn it, Lloyd! Calm down!"

Devin's face drained of color. He let his arm drop to his side and released Dominick's shoulder.

Jim Rossi hurried over, scolding his wife and shooing her away. She went reluctantly, a string of curses aimed at Lloyd's ancestors lingering in her wake.

McFate pushed himself between the constable and Dominick. Although much shorter than Lloyd, the county detective glared up at the taller man and nodded toward the door. When the constable left, McFate turned to Dominick. "I'm sorry, son. Are you all right?"

Dominick instinctively liked this man who tried to go about his duty with an air of compassion. Still he refused to answer the county detective. Instead, he looked steadfastly at Rossi until Jim motioned for the others to back off.

"What is it you wish to ask these people, McFate?"

McFate sighed audibly. "Tell them there is a $1000 dollar reward for information leading to the arrest of Fred Carnetti. Tell them I would appreciate any information they might have."

Dominick looked pointedly at McFate for a second, raising his eyebrows in response to his last statement.

McFate left out a heavy sigh, "Just tell son."

When he repeated McFate's message in Italian it was met with an unsettled silence.

McFate glanced at him. "We know Fred Carnetti roomed here. Ask Mr. Rossi if he has a picture of him."

Jim made a lewd suggestion.

"Jim said he is sorry, but he doesn't have such a picture," Dominick replied.

When McFate and Constable Devin left, Jim Rossi gave everybody a bottle of beer. The men smiled shyly as feminine curses drifted in from the back room over the angry clanging of pots and pans.

The next morning's headlines read: *Italians In Hillsville Believed To Be Hiding Fred Carnetti, Murderer of Squire Duff.* That afternoon the vigilantes arrived.

Dominick was on his way home from the quarry when he saw two wagon teams tied up in the center of town. Small groups of men carrying rifles and shotguns were systematically entering each house. Groups of Italian men, some of them holding babies, stood on the street talking quietly among themselves. Posturing, spitting, and hissing the women of Hillsville followed the armed Americans from house to house like a cloud of gnats. Dominick didn't doubt for a moment that the Italian men hid knives, and even a few pistols, under their coats. He hoped the Americans didn't strike any of the women. Blood would flow for sure if they did.

When he got home, Dominick found Signora Carpellotti and a neighbor lady badgering three scruffy looking men who had just stepped out of her house. Julio was sitting on the porch watching the Americans with cold eyes. "What's going on, Signore Carpellotti," Dominick asked.

"The Americano pigs are looking for Carnetti." He smiled suddenly. "But they won't find him."

Dominick thought to ask Julio where Fred Carnetti might be hiding, but held his peace. Better not act too interested, he mused.

"Talk to these dogs," Julio said. "I'm not sure our people can take this disrespect much longer."

"Can I help you, gentlemen?" Dominick asked, walking over to the Americans.

Three heads snapped up at once. One appeared to be a farmer. He carried a double-barreled shotgun. Another might have been his son. The third was skinny with beady eyes. He reminded Dominick of a weasel in need of a shave. The weasel blinked rapidly at him before speaking. "Who the devil are you?"

"My name is, Dominick. How may I help you gentlemen?"

"You can call off these mouthy women fer starters," the weasel said.

Dominick smiled. "It's a custom in the old country. Italian women protect the home, and the men protect the women."

The farmer's voice rumbled. "Oh yeah! I don't take this off my own woman, and I sure ain't takin' much more off these greasers."

"I wouldn't lift a hand toward one of these ladies if I were you." He looked casually around. "Don't let on," he added conspiratorially, "but there's probably rifles pointed at you this very moment."

The three men began jerking their heads around like puppets. The weasel snapped the 45.70 Springfield off his shoulder and held it at port arms. He looked back at Dominick, blinking in time to a twitch that had developed in his cheek.

"How much longer do you plan to stay here," Dominick asked.

The farmer looked at the weasel. "I don't know about you, Ned, but Tim and I are leavin'."

The weasel bobbed his head. "Yep, lets go! This place is like a dad-blamed foreign country anyhow."

On Thursday morning, Dominick went to the quarry to load stones he had broken into small enough pieces to handle, only to find the Dinky's crew had broken up the tracks in order to reroute the engine. When he returned to his boarding house he saw Superintendent Cafee and Detective McFate walking toward the quarry. Before long, the two detectives returned from the quarry and stopped at the house where Docato Trevino lived. They began asking Docato questions and Dominick, sitting on the porch step next door, saw Docato wave for him to come over. After asking Docato a few questions about Carnetti, Cafee began asking the lad about the time he boarded with Rocco. Then he asked Docato if Seeley Houk had shot Rocco's dog. When Dominick translated, Docato's eyes grew round before he denied knowing anything about it.

Cafee's eyes narrowed and he pursed his lips.

Docato glanced from Dominick to Cafee, eyes wide with fear.

"I want to speak with Rocco Racca," Cafee announced.

"Rocco and his wife went to Sharon for a christening. They're not home," Dominick replied.

Cafee turned to the young detective abruptly, beady eyes flashing under a pair of thick spectacles. "I'll be back tomorrow, Prugitore. See to it that Rocco Racca is available for questioning."

Dominick shrugged. "Si, signore." He knew the little man hated being addressed in Italian.

Before Cafee could respond, he put his arm around Docato's shoulder and led him away. "You must warn Rocco that the detectives want to talk to him tomorrow."

That night Dominick didn't sleep well. When he did doze off he had nightmares about Rocco and Cerini finding out he was a detective. Dominick thought about going to New Castle in the morning and wiring Superintendent Dimuro for instructions, but there wasn't time. He would just have to be careful.

The next morning the track at the quarry was still broken and several of the men who worked with Dominick were standing around the boarding house talking when Superintendent Cafee and McFate drove up in a buggy. The men with Dominick started to leave, but McFate yelled for them to stay. Two hesitated. The others continued walking. With surprising agility McFate jumped down from the buggy and approached the men, showing them a badge.

Cafee sat in the buggy looking pointedly at Dominick, obviously expecting him to take the reins. Dominick continued to sit on the steps smoking a cigar. Finally Cafee cast him a disgusted look before climbing out of the buggy and tying off the reins to the porch banister.

"Come along, Prugitore," he said offhandedly, as he started toward where McFate was encountering shaking heads and comments of "No comprendere, signore."

Dominick sat where he was, his face impassive.

Cafee stopped and yelled for him to follow, his face red.

Still he didn't move.

One of the Italians was Londo Racca, Rocco's brother and a second class member of the Society. When Londo motioned for him to come over, Dominick got up and walked by Cafee as if the bald headed detective didn't exist. Dominick flipped the butt of his cigar between McFate's feet and looked at Londo.

"Ask these dogs what they want," Londo demanded.

Cafee hurried over, but before he could speak Dominick addressed McFate. "They ask what it is you want of them, signore."

"Tell them we're investigating the murders and cuttings around here."

"They know that."

"Just tell them, you impertinent fool!" Cafee interrupted.

When Dominick repeated McFate's statement the men just stood there, faces impassive.

"Well?" McFate asked.

Cafee started to speak when a familiar figure came around the back of the buggy with another man. "Hey! Whatta goes on here?"

The two detectives turned to face Rocco and a man named Nick Sparaio who was a bit thickheaded.

"This is Rocco Racca, Mr Cafee," McFate said. "I believe you wanted to question him?"

Cafee looked from Dominick to Rocco. "Tell him who I am, Prugitore."

"Who are you?"

A streak of red shot up Cafee's neck.

Rocco's eyebrows knitted together and he looked questionably at his brother. Londo shrugged his shoulders and nodded toward Dominick, shaking his head slightly.

"I'm sorry, Mr. Cafee," McFate Interrupted. "I believe, I forgot to introduce you when we arrived." The weathered old detective turned to Dominick. "This is Mr. Elmer Cafee of the Pinkerton National Detective Agency. He's investigating the murder of Game Warden Seeley Houk. I would thank you to inform Mr. Racca of this."

Dominick repeated McFate's statement to Rocco, and when he mentioned that Cafee was investigating the Houk murder Rocco paled.

Then Cafee seemed to forget about Dominick as he concentrated on firing questions at Rocco.

"Were you ever arrested by Houk?

Did the game warden shoot your dog?"

Rocco, growing more visibly agitated with each question, denied everything. Then Cafee focused on questions about Rocco's brother-in-law, Gus Mazzocco.

"Was Gus Mazzocco ever arrested by Houk?"

"I don't know, signore."

"When did Mazzocco leave for Italy?"

"It was sometime in March, signore."

Nick Sparaio suddenly chipped in, "No, No, Rocco! Remember? He left in April."

Rocco flashed a sign at Nick. "Shut up, you fool! Let me answer the questions."

Cafee was staring back and forth at the two men, his eyes bright with anticipation. "What are they saying, Prugitore?"

"They're not sure of the date, sir." Then he sensed a chance to redeem himself. He addressed Rocco, cutting into the argument. "Signore Racca, scusi."

Rocco looked blankly at him.

"You don't have to tell them everything you know, compare."

Rocco nodded, "Si. Grazie."

Cafee glanced at Dominick. "What's going on here?"

"They're not sure when he left, is all."

"Ask him why Mazzocco left."

When he repeated Cafee's question, Rocco just shook his head.

"He is not going to answer any more of your questions. He said you are too disrespectful."

Cafee ripped off his glasses and whirled on Dominick, but before he could speak McFate cut in.

"I believe we are finished for today, Mr. Cafee. Besides, we need to talk to this man Cerini."

Cafee could hardly speak. He shoved a finger at Dominick's nose. "I'm not through with you yet, Prugitore!"

When they left, Londo confronted Dominick.

"Why does this beady-eyed detective know you, Prugitore?"

Dominick shrugged.

"Leave him alone, Londo," Rocco said. "He helped me, not those rabid dogs."

"Si," Londo replied, "but there was something funny going on just the same!

Chapter 10

Rocco grabbed Dominick's shoulder and spun him around. "They're going to do what?"

The men were on their way to Rocco's for a drink of wine. "They're going to talk to Romon," Dominick replied.

Rocco turned to Nick Sparaio. "You must run to Romon's house. Tell him he must obey the Omerta!"

"Why? Romon knows this."

"Rocco's eyebrows furled over his nose. He shot out his finger, pointing down the road. Go!

Nick shrugged and picked up a faster gait, shuffling ahead of the others.

Rocco picked up a stone and threw it at him. "What's the matter with you? Run!"

"You better calm down, brother," Londo said. "Nick is right. Romon won't talk to the detectives."

"These Americans! They're always blaming me for the murder of the game policeman."

Londo gave Dominick a hard look. "Funny they always seem to know who to talk to."

Dominick's stomach lurched.

Sam Bennett was waiting at Rocco's store when they arrived. He pulled Dominick aside. "I need to ask a favor, compare," Sam whispered.

"What is that?" Dominick asked wearily.

"I bought furniture from some people who are leaving for the old country. I want you and Toni to go to New Castle and pick up my stuff."

"Why? Where are you off to now?"

Sam flicked his wrist in the air and scowled. "That dog Calvo. The cripple? He ran off again without paying the bondsman. Boggiano wants me to go after him."

"Why doesn't he send Siciliano? You're supposed to get married Saturday, remember?"

"Si, si. But I'll be back Friday. Will you do this for me, compare?"

Dominick placed his arm around his friend. "Sure, Sam. Now let's go have a drink of Rocco's wine."

Londo Racca didn't say anything further about Dominick. Instead he only cast suspicious glances in his direction. By the time Londo left, Dominick had a splitting headache and an upset stomach. *I've got to send a telegram to Superintendent Dimuro,* he thought. *But if I just leave they will become even more suspicious.*

After supper he borrowed Nick's shotgun and made a pretense of going hunting. He grabbed an old newspaper, crossed the bridge at Kennedy's Crossing and began walking toward a fading sunset. Once he was out of sight of the trolley stop, Dominick hid the shotgun and continued walking briskly down the track. Darkness had fallen by the time he saw the trolley's light coming towards him from the west. He rolled the newspaper into a funnel and set the large end on fire, then held the burning paper in the air as the car approached, stepping off the tracks as the trolley, bell clanging loudly in the night air, rolled to a stop beside him.

"Sure don't get many country stops around these parts anymore," the motorman said as Dominick climbed into the well-lighted interior. "You musta' got tired of walkn', young fella."

Dominick nodded and dropped a dime into the motorman's open palm.

"You go'n into New Castle?"

Dominick looked startled. "Yes, sir."

"Well then, that'll be fourteen cents. You're a mile this side of Kennedy's Crossing and it's six miles from there into town. Fare is two cents a mile, young fella." The motorman eased the controller ahead as he talked, and the heavy car began to sway as it picked up speed.

The next morning Dominick made his way over to the small hotel owned by Toni's father. Frank Santi's hotel was small by big city standards. Still it was one of the larger buildings in Hillsville, with a high-roofed porch that extended cross the front of the box-like, structure.

A little bell over the front door jingled happily as he entered. An open stairway on his right led to a landing that separated the Spartan lobby from the rooms upstairs.

A curtain behind the counter parted and Frank Santi emerged. He was a short, semi-bald man with a thin mustache. He frowned. "What do you want?"

"Buongiorno, signore. Is Toni around?"

"Toni has work to do, young man. He doesn't have time to loaf around with society members."

Dominick shuffled uncomfortably. He knew Toni's father didn't approve of his son belonging to The Society of Honor. He was about to leave when a voice from the stairs broke into his thoughts.

"Papa! This is no way to treat a friend."

Dominick looked up to see Toni standing on the landing, his arms full of dirty linen. "Perhaps, I could return when you are finished."

"Nonsense" Toni came quickly down the steps. "I was just helping mamma. Carmine isn't feeling well today."

Frank Santi cleared his throat. "You showed disrespect to your parents in joining this society, and now you show disrespect to your family by associating with these criminals."

Toni put the bundle of linen down by the counter. "Papa, Dominick and Sam Bennett are my friends. They are not criminals. You are old fashioned, Papa. This is America, and things are different here."

Frank threw his head back and waved his arm. "Si. La via nuova. The new way. Listen to me! There is an old Italian proverb that says, 'Whoever forsakes the old way for the new knows what he is losing...'"

"'...but not what he will find.'" Toni chipped in. "I know, Papa. I've heard it a hundred times."

"You hear it with your ears but not your heart," his father scolded.

Toni turned to Dominick. "Come on, compare. I'll finish this later."

When they were outside, Toni apologized to his friend.

"No, I am the one to apologize," Dominick replied. "I did not mean to cause trouble."

"Papa is old fashioned. He thinks the Society is evil."

He's right. Dominick thought. Why can't you and Sam see it?

When Dominick filled Toni in on what they had to do, Toni led the way to a barn behind the hotel where his father kept a horse and wagon. Soon they were on their way into New Castle to pick up Sam's furniture.

After loading the wagon they discovered they forgot to bring rope, and some of the pieces needed to be tied on. While Toni went to buy rope, Dominick darted into the nearby telegraph office. The reply to the telegram he sent came in early that morning. There was to be a meeting in Youngstown the following evening.

When Dominick walked into the room in Youngstown he found Frank Dimuro and Toni Capizzi waiting for him. Superintendent Dimuro was sitting on one of two beds in the room. His jacket lay on the bed beside him, and he had removed the collar from his shirt. On a stand between the beds were an open brief case and a bottle of wine. Toni was sprawled casually across the second bed smoking a cigar. The butt of a revolver protruded from the top of a holster, slung in a harness, under his left arm. Both men looked up when he entered the room.

"Well, if it isn't the rooster plucker," Toni said by way of greeting.

"What?" Dominick asked.

Capizzi smiled, "Heard you plucked some of Cafee's feathers the other day."

Dimuro got to his feet and grabbed the wine bottle before waving Dominick to a chair. Splashing some red liquid into the glass, Frank crossed the room and handed it to the younger man.

"Despite his dubious humor, Capizzi has a way of getting to the point." Dimuro's deep voice overrode the rhythmic clicking of a horse's hooves on the brick pavement outside. He glanced at the grinning detective sprawled on the other bed. "Shut the window, Toni. Voices have a way of carrying on an evening like this."

Dimuro turned to face Dominick, his stern expression softening somewhat as he studied the young detective. There were lines he hadn't noticed before. Then Frank noticed the faint twitching at the corner of Dominick's eye.

When Dominick finished telling about Cafee and Londo Racca, Dimuro poured himself a glass of wine and sat on the bed. "As Toni said, you ruffled Cafee's feathers. He wants you fired and has been causing quite a fuss about it, all the way to Philadelphia."

"But sir, Cafee almost compromised our whole operation."

"I know, son. But Cafee is still a superintendent in this agency. These matters have to be handled discreetly." He noticed Dominick's hand tremble slightly.

"But, sir, I..."

Dimuro held up his hand. "Listen. I've been on the phone with Robert Pinkerton about this. Bob understands undercover work. Tomorrow afternoon I have to be in Philadelphia for a meeting with him and Cafee. I suspect Mr. Pinkerton will explain to Cafee just how important your part in this investigation is. Meanwhile, you must understand this is both a covert and overt operation, and Cafee's office is handling the overt part."

Dominick began shaking his head. "He doesn't understand our people. All he's doing is alienating the witnesses."

Frank Dimuro got to his feet. "I know that." He poured some more wine.

Toni stretched and held his glass out to Dimuro. "How about sharing some of that, boss?"

Frank handed him the bottle and turned back to Dominick. "I'm trying to get this whole operation turned over to my office. Cafee will fail because it takes Italians to understand Italians. Mr. Pinkerton knows this, but because of internal politics the boss needs a good reason to take him off the case."

"Now," Dimuro continued, "you wrote some time ago that Rocco Racca was going to leave for the old country. Do you think that is still his plan?"

"He's scared, sir. I think he'll run if he gets the chance."

"Well then, maybe we can do something to move things along."

On Thursday evening Sam Bennett returned to Hillsville. Dominick was at Jim Rossi's saloon when Sam and Joe Boggiano stomped in. Sam looked despondent. Joe's face was a threating storm, and he immediately waved Jim Rossi into a back room. Sam bought a beer and slumped into a chair at Dominick's table.

"What's the matter, compare?"

Sam just shook his head. "I couldn't find Calvo. Now Joe is in a rage."

Dominick got to his feet. "Come on, Sam, let's get some fresh air."

Outside he turned to his friend. "Now, what happened?"

Sam let out a long sigh and flopped on the ground. "The cripple supposedly went to Chicago. I think Boggiano is going to send Siciliano after him. That is what he wants to talk to Jim about."

"Is this not good, compare? Now you will not be involved."

Sam looked at Dominick for a moment. "Don't you know what this means? Siciliano is an assassin. If he finds Calvo, the cripple is as good as dead. I will be stuck to pay the bondsman, and I don't have the money!"

"Surely the Society will help. Come on, compare, in two more days you'll be making love to Maria."

After dinner on Saturday, Dominick walked over to Peanut to meet Rocco before going to Sam and Maria's wedding. As he approached the little cluster of shanties, Dominick noticed a throng of people by Rocco's store. Sensing trouble, he picked up his stride. Even before he reached the house Dominick could hear Mrs. Racca wailing and screaming inside. Nick Sparaio and Romon Cerini were among those in the crowd.

"Rocco was just arrested," Romon said.

"Aye," Nick added, shaking his head. "Benedetti, too."

"What? Sam's supposed to get married in a couple of hours!"

Romon waved a hand in dismissal.

"Come on," Nick said. "Let's go see Boggiano about this."

Boggiano was mad about the arrests, but stated flatly that nothing could be done until Monday. Nobody seemed to know why Rocco and Sam were arrested.

"Dominick," Joe said, "would you do me the favor of informing Sam's fiance', and her family?"

"Si," he replied, "if Nick will go along."

Nick threw up his hands in protest, but Joe nodded for him to accompany the younger man.

"Come on, then," Nick said. "Let's get this over with."

As they approached Lou Piccini's shanty it was obvious that Maria had already learned of Sam's arrest. A girl was yelling inside, and they could hear her mother crying. Suddenly the door flew open, and Maria burst through carrying a bouquet of flowers. When she recognized Dominick she threw the flowers at the startled young man.

"The wedding's off!" she screamed. "I'll have no more of this!"

Maria's father came to the door, his face a mixture of sadness, frustration and anger. Wails and crying gathered behind him like the baying of wolves.

"This isn't Sam's fault, Signore Piccini," Dominick began. "You know how it is."

Signore Piccini motioned for them to follow him into the street. When they were safely away from the house, and the raging women, he stopped.

"Si, Dominick, I know how it is. But this is tearing my little girl apart." He shuttered as a fit of rage rippled through him. "And it is beginning to bear on my family's honor!"

"Signore Piccini, if you will try to help Maria see this is not Sam's fault, I will talk to Boggiano. But we must wait to see how this turns out. It will take time."

Lou Piccini balled his fists to control his emotions. "How much time?"

"I don't know, signore, but if Maria will still have Sam, I promise Boggiano will give them time to get married."

On Monday morning Dominick was pulling on his overalls when Docato Trevino knocked on his door. In the custom of the old country, Docato opened the door a few inches before cautiously inquiring if there was permission to come in.

Dominick laughed, "Of course, Docato. What can I do for you?"

"Signora Racca asked me to come for you."

"Oh? And what does Signora Racca want this morning?"

Docato glanced at his feet. "I..I don't know. She only asked me to bring you to her house. S..She isn't well, I think."

When they arrived at Rocco's store they found Mrs. Racca with a heavyset woman. Rocco's wife was pale, and there were dark circles under eyes red and swollen from crying.

"Please, Dominick." She fought to hold back the tears. "Go into New Castle and see what has become of my husband."

"Si, signora. I will do this for you. But tell me what is the matter with Rocco, that they put him in jail?"

"The bondsman for the crippled man had him arrested. He wants money we don't have." Finally she shook her head trying to fight the tears, but her face contorted with anguish. "I don't know what we are going to do!"

Dominick changed his clothes before catching an interurban trolley into New Castle. When he started in the direction of the courthouse, he saw Toni Santi sitting in his dad's wagon nearby. The wagon was loaded with goods for the hotel.

"Hello, compare," Dominick offered as he walked up to him, "where is Rocco?"

"He is coming. Boggiano and another man went up to the court house to get him."

"Signora Racca sent me to find him. What is going on?"

Toni reached into his pocket and produced a couple of cigars offering one to his friend. When they were lit he waved the cigar in the direction of the courthouse. "I know the other man. He is Signore D'Alessio. He owns a grocery business over in the eleventh ward. He looks very frightened."

"Si, but what does this man have to do with Rocco Racca?"

Toni shrugged. "I think Boggiano and Cerini got him to pay the bondsman so they could get Rocco out of jail."

Dominick shook his head. "I don't understand, Toni. Why are Joe and Romon concerned about Rocco? He was put out of the Society, remember?"

"Si, but Rocco paid Joe a large sum of money recently to be reinstated. That is why Rocco couldn't afford to pay the bondsman when Calvo ran away again."

A group of men came out of the courthouse. When they reached the sidewalk one of the men turned and hurried off in another direction. Soon Joe, Rocco and Sam Bennett walked up to the wagon.

"What are you doing here?" Rocco asked Dominick.

"Your wife sent me to find you."

"That woman is going to drive me crazy."

Sam looked worried. "I've got to find Maria. Maybe she won't even talk to me."

"You can have my woman," Rocco growled. "In a couple of days she'll have you crazy."

Sam didn't see the humor in Rocco's remark. "I'm going to have to sell my furniture to pay the bondsman. I don't know when we'll get married now." With that he hurried off.

"Yeah, well let's go," Rocco suggested. "We should be able to catch the trolley on the next block."

"Not me," Joe said, climbing onto the wagon beside Toni. "I don't trust those cars. Best to stick with the old ways."

"You guys are welcome to ride in the back," Toni offered.

"No thanks, compare," Dominick said. "Even if we have to wait a half hour for the car, we'll be in Hillsville long before you."

"Si," Rocco growled, "and without all the dust."

On the trip back, Dominick learned Sam was released after he promised to pay the bondsman with interest. Rocco, however, was released on $1000 bail. Dominick asked if they questioned him about the Houk and Duff cases.

"I've heard enough of that! Yesterday, that bald headed Pinkerton questioned me for over an hour. But he learned nothing."

The next day Julio Carpellotti informed Dominick that he would have to find another boarding house. Julio was moving to Ebinsburg to work as a foreman in a steel mill. Julio suggested he stay with Nick Sparaio. That afternoon he moved his stuff into a small curtained space containing two bunk beds. Two other men, besides Docato Trevino, slept in Nick's stuffy little space.

That evening Dominick sat at a table in Jim Rossi's saloon drinking beer with several other men. He couldn't help but notice an older man, a stranger, sitting alone by the wall. The stranger's face was like parched leather, with eyes that constantly roamed the room, missing nothing. When the man heard Dominick's name mentioned he made a hand sign. Those setting at Dominick's table suddenly grabbed their beer and left. Then the man sauntered over.

"Allow me buy you a beer." His voice seemed to wheeze out of his chest.

"No thank you, signore. I was just leaving."

"That is no way to treat a stranger, young man. I insist."

Dominick felt the cold edge of fear seep into his bowels. They discovered something, he thought, and this man is here to kill me! He wanted to bolt, to jump up and run from this place and never come back. He realized he was sweating.

The stranger casually set the beers down before pulling his chair close to Dominick. Leaning over, he dropped his voice and asked, "Are you Dominick, Dominick Prugitore?" His whispering sounded like a snake slithering through dry grass.

"Si."

Boggiano suddenly burst into the room with another man. Joe looked at the stranger, nodding to him curtly as he stomped by. Without saying a word he motioned Jim into the back room.

"Well, maybe they will get this mess fixed up," the man wheezed.

"What do you mean, signore?"

The older man studied him for a long moment, then shrugged. "I came here to slit Jim Rossi's throat."

Dominick's mouth popped open.

"But," the man continued, "Rossi is in the same society as I am, so I can't do the job."

"But why do you want to cut Jim?"

"It's not my business to know. When the man I work for wants someone tagged, I don't ask questions."

Then the stranger nudged Dominick. "Tell me," he whispered, "I hear you are acquainted with Signore Sebastianelli?"

"Crazy old Ignazio?"

The man frowned. "So! Crazy old Ignazio is it? No, young man. I mean Signore Ignazio Sebastianelli." The wheezing voice poured out like vapor.

Dominick realized he overstepped some boundary. Suddenly he feared for the old man. "You're not going to hurt him are you?"

The stranger straightened and raised both hands in the air in mock surrender. A broad smile flowed across his face turning wrinkles into canyons that reached to the bottom of his leathery ears.

"Hurt him? Me, hurt Signore Sebastianelli?" The older man got to his feet and clapped Dominick a heavy blow on his back. "Small chance of that happening boy, ever." He left his hand on Dominick's shoulder. "Now," the man said, suddenly serious again, "show me where he lives."

Darkness had fallen by the time Dominick led the way along a footpath toward the Johnson quarry. The path followed the black rim of the quarry's pit. Suddenly the man reached into his pocket and pulled something out. There was a metallic click and a silver blade flashed open in his hand. Dominick froze. Suddenly he realized his mistake. The man had tricked him into leading them to this place, alone.

The older man stopped and gave him a funny look. "What's the matter? Haven't you ever seen a switchblade before?"

Slowly Dominick shook his head.

The stranger glanced at the knife in his hand. "That's the problem with these things." He rolled his shoulders. "They're irresistible toys." A wrinkled face looked up at Dominick suddenly. "Tell me, boy. Do you like your crazy old Ignazio?"

"Si, signore. I do."

"Then consider yourself under his protection. Now can we continue? I would like to get there before it grows too late."

They continued around the quarry's edge, finally arriving at the path leading to Ignazio's cabin. They could see a shaft of yellow light spilling from under the canvas-covered entry when the stranger stopped.

"I will go alone from here, I think. Surely you don't want to listen while old men babble about the past."

Dominick felt a pang of disappointment. He wanted to learn more about this crazy old man who blew big charges, trapped songbirds and grew super hot peppers. But he knew this wasn't the time. Reluctantly he made his way back to Nick Sparaio's shanty and a stuffy upper bunk.

Rocco Racca remained subdued and quiet during the days that followed. Sensing a change was taking place; Dominick tried to stay close to Rocco. But the tough little man still remained aloof and moody.

"How is your case going?" Dominick asked one evening. They were sitting on the porch step smoking cigars.

Rocco shook his head. "Theft by bailee, or something they call it. My attorney has asked for a new trial, but they raised the bail to $2000."

"You would think you were charged with murder!" Dominick exclaimed.

Rocco got quickly to his feet. "Si! That is what the Americans think, too." He began pacing the floor. "Since the Houk and Duff killings the authorities want to hang someone. I think this someone is me!"

Rocco stormed back into the house, and Dominick heard Mrs. Racca ask him what was the matter, her voice high pitched and panicky. Rocco told her to shut up, and she began to cry. There was the sound of a sudden slap followed by a shrill wail.

Dominick wandered up the street toward the Ciampanelli's. He noticed Rosa was rounding out in places. Her older sister, Grace, picked on her constantly. Mary wanted to take a walk, so the three of them started along the path toward the railroad tracks. It was the same path

Seeley Houk took one rainy day in March. Mary skipped ahead of them, racing back occasionally to show them a flower or some other treasure she found.

"Do you still write letters in the glade?" Rosa asked during one of Mary's treasure hunts.

"I still go there occasionally."

"Papa won't allow me to go into the woods alone anymore. He says I'm getting too big."

The path suddenly began to drop sharply toward the tracks. Rosa stopped so suddenly Dominick became startled, and he glanced around for a sign of danger.

"Mary!" Rosa hollered with a tinge of panic in her voice. "Mary, come back this instant!" She seemed, suddenly, very frightened.

"Rosa?" Dominick asked. "What's the matter?"

"It's just that I saw....nothing. Mary!" she called again.

When Mary came running back, she was short of breath. "What's wrong, Rosa? I want to go down to the tracks."

"No!" she scolded. "This is a bad place." Rosa grabbed her sister's hand and started leading her back toward the settlement at a determined pace.

Dominick followed, wondering at the sudden fear that came over the girl.

Three days later, County Detective McFate stopped him on his way home from work.

"Excuse me, young man. I see you are alone, may I have a word with you?"

Dominick paused to look at the man whom he had always given such a hard time. "Of course, how may I help?"

McFate arched his eyebrows. "Have you seen Rocco Racca? I've been all around the quarry, and I can't find him anywhere."

"Rocco was at the quarry yesterday. What do you want with him?"

"Well, I'm supposed to check on him now and then. Make sure he doesn't skip out."

A group of workers coming from the quarry was drawing closer, so Dominick began to walk away. "I'll check around," he said softly.

That evening he went to Rocco's house, but nobody was home. Patrons at Jim Rossi's saloon didn't know where he was either. By the next day, however, it was apparent to the entire community that Rocco had left. At noon Dominick found Mrs. Racca sitting on her porch.

"How are you, signora?"

Her stern face still looked drawn and pale. "I'm getting better, Dominick."

"Since Rocco went away you have been half dead. Where has he gone?"

She looked at her feet a moment before answering. "He got a letter from West Virginia that said his brother was dead, so he went there." Her hand began to tremble as she stood up. "I...I've got to go in now, Dominick."

He noticed Cerini standing by the village pump and walked over. "Good day, signore."

Romon eyed him coldly. "What did the county detective ask you the other day?"

Dominick nervously brushed the lock of hair off his forehead. "He was looking for Fred Carnetti." He tried to sound casual.

Romon allowed a calculated smile to crease his face. "He was looking for Rocco Racca. Don't you know Rocco ran away from here?"

"I know he went to West Virginia because his brother died."

Romon cast a disgusted glance at him before turning away. "Yeah," he said over his shoulder, "but he won't be back."

Several days later Dominick stopped at the post office in Hillsville. There he occasionally received letters, supposedly from friends and relatives. People who worked for Superintendent Dimuro wrote the letters in Italian. Usually there was nothing official in them, just fictitious news from a fictitious home. Occasionally, however, they concealed coded orders or notices about meetings with his superiors. This time he had no mail of his own but noticed a letter in Rocco's box that he offered to deliver to Mrs. Racca. The postmaster gave him the letter with instructions to return it if it couldn't be delivered. Dominick's heart skipped when he saw the letter was addressed to Mrs. Racca from F. Filasto, 299 Mott Street, New York City. He instantly recognized the name of the headman of the New York City Society of Honor. The letter was folded and sealed with a stamp.

Carefully as he could, he peeled back the stamp. The letter directed Mrs. Racca to sell everything and get ready to leave. A ship departed for Italy within two weeks. It was signed Rocco Racca.

Dominick dropped the letter into a puddle, then plucked it out before the paper was completely soaked. When he went back to the post office, he shrugged and apologized to the frowning postmaster before catching a trolley into New Castle. He had to wire the Pinkerton's right away.

Several days later he found Mrs. Racca wearing a new dress. There were several bundles wrapped in sheets and a suitcase sitting by the door.

"I'm moving in with my sister for a while," she said. "Would you help carry this stuff over to her house?"

When they got to her sister's house, he found them waiting for a team to pick up the rest of her things. Dominick made his way down to Hillsville Station where he learned Mrs. Racca had bought a ticket for New York.

Boarding the trolley at Kennedy's Crossing, he dropped the coins into the motorman's palm and hoped the telegraph office in New Castle was still open.

It wasn't. The sheriff's office and the courthouse were also closed for the day. He thought about going to the jail to see if someone there could help him, but remembered Frank Dimuro's advice not to trust anyone. Dominick rang county detective McFate's house. An old woman answered. She said the detective was out of town. The railroad, he thought. The railroad uses a telegraph!

The clerk at the station office was dourly adamant. The telegraph there was strictly for railroad business. He started toward the trolley stop to catch an electric car back to Hillsville. He knew Toni Capizzi wasn't in Youngstown. Toni had left for New York several days ago.

A clean-shaven man wearing a coat and cream-colored vest was standing under the street lamp at the trolley stop. Dominick recognized him as the detective who worked on the cars between Youngstown and New Castle, supposedly to protect people traveling through the Italian section. He hesitated a moment while Superintendent Dimuro's warning echoed through his mind. "Don't trust no one!"

"Excuse me, sir," he said stepping up to the man. "I'm with the Pinkerton National Detective Agency. I wonder if you could help?"

Chapter 11

As the electric car sped toward Kennedy's Crossing Dominick stared at the bald spot on the back of Ruben Mehard's head and wondered for the hundredth time how the transit company's detective could have learned that Rosa witnessed the Houk murder. Was is Rosa? He wondered. He'd been pondering that possibility since Ruben told him about it earlier this evening. But what really bothered him was who else knew?

Ruben reacted to his request for help with surprising speed. When he told the trolley detective he needed to send an urgent telegram to the Pinkertons, Ruben grabbed his arm and started propelling him down the street toward the train station. Dominick jerked his arm away quickly explaining that he couldn't be seen with a detective.

"Of course." Ruben reached into his vest pocket and produced a note pad and pencil. "Here, write your message on this. I'll send it out."

After Dominick handed him the message, Ruben glanced up and down the street before asking if he was working on the Houk murder. When he nodded, Ruben pushed him into the shadows of a building.

"Seeley was a friend of mine," he whispered.

Then he told Dominick that an Italian girl, about twelve or thirteen years old, supposedly witnessed the murder. He said an American told him this on the trolley one night. Now, Ruben sat in his customary seat behind the motorman on the run toward Hillsville.

He hoped for the thousandth time Ruben was mistaken yet remembered Rosa's anxiety the night he that told her he was going to join the Society. "They kill people!" she had screamed. Then there was her evident panic just a few evenings ago, when they walked down the path toward where Houk was ambushed, she had started to say she saw...what?

A week later Docato Trevino burst into the little room Dominick shared with him and two other men.

"Dominick! D..Dominick, did you hear!"

"No, Docato. What is the matter?"

"They have R..Rocco Racca in the New Castle jail!"

Dominick pushed his legs over the edge of the bunk and eased himself down to the floor. There was a bloody bandage on his right leg below the knee.

Docato pointed to the bandage. "What h..happened?"

"I caught a sliver of steel in my leg. Nick Sparaio cut it out with his pocket knife."

"Steel? F..From where?"

"From the drill. It will be all right," Dominick said. "Now, tell me about Rocco."

"Th..they arrested Rocco Racca in New York and br..brought him back yesterday. R..Romon Cerini said the man who posted his bail...." he paused, looked at the floor, frowned, then raised his head suddenly." ...S..Signore D'Alessio, I think it is, h..had him arrested for running away."

Docato looked into Dominick's eyes. "W..What will happen to him, do you think?"

"I don't know," he replied shaking his head.

"R..Romon, said that the Americans want to h..hang Rocco for the Houk and Duff murders."

"They have nothing on him. Not even a motive."

Docato looked perplexed. "What is this m...motive? he asked."

Dominick was rubbing his sore leg. This talk of the Houk murder brought the problem of Rosa disturbingly back into focus, and he didn't know what to do about it.

"The Americans have to prove that Rocco had a reason to kill Houk. They call it a motive."

Docato looked at the floor again. "The g..game policeman killed P..Pauline." The lad spoke so softly that Dominick scarcely heard him.

"Wh...who?"

"The g..game policeman shot Rocco's dog, P..Pauline."

"How do you know this?"

"B..Because I was there."

Suddenly the import of what Docato was saying struck him. Dominick had heard stories about Docato and the dog before, but never first hand.

"P..Pauline and I were hunting…" The lad kept his voice low. "…when the g..game policeman began to chase us. I ran, b..but the stupid dog just stood there. I heard a shot, and thought the g..game policeman was s..shooting at me. I ran faster! T..That night I stayed in the woods, afraid to go home."

"You were staying with Rocco then, weren't you?"

"Si. He is my uncle, Dominick. The next day I found the dead dog. When I told Rocco what happened…" Docato paused to rub his face. "…h..he struck me. Then my uncle s..swore that the g..game policeman would die for this." The boy looked inquiringly at Dominick. "T..That is a motive, no?"

"You must not speak of this to anyone, unless I tell you it is okay."

"I..I know. But you are my friend, and I trust you. Besides, you belong to The S..Society of Honor. You won't tell."

Dominick glanced at the floor. "Si, this is true." Then his head came up. "But I don't understand why Rocco was so upset about a dumb dog?"

Docato's eyes brightened. "Because this d..dog was a gift from Rocco's aunt. The d..dog belonged to his uncle who had died. Rocco considered it a gift of honor."

Later that evening Dominick limped into the woods to write his reports. He was excited about what Docato had told him. He realized that it was the first break in the Houk murder case. He didn't mention anything in his reports about Rosa, however.

Later he went to see Boggiano about raising money for Rocco's bail. He knew that so long as Rocco was in jail the former Black Hand leader would never confide in him about the murder.

"You would think you are his brother," Joe said. "Rocco was stupid to run away. He should stay in jail."

"Rocco rejoined the society. We are supposed to take care of our own, are we not?"

"Si, perhaps you are right. A sly look crept into Joe's eyes. "Tomorrow we will go to New Castle and talk to Rocco's lawyer to see what can be done. You can start by collecting money from society members."

"Me?"

"You are his friend, no?" Joe knitted his bushy brow and tapped Dominick on the chest. "But you must bring the money to me. I will keep it until we have enough for his bail."

In the days that followed, Dominick's leg became infected. Nick Sparaio sent Docato for a doctor who lanced the wound to let it drain.

"You should have called me sooner, young man." The doctor frowned as he wrapped Dominick's leg with a clean bandage. "It will be a miracle if this poison doesn't spread. As it is, you'll have to stay off your feet for at least a week. Do you understand?"

"But I have work to do. I can't just lay here for a week!"

The doctor, a tall, skinny man who wore extremely thick glasses, rose to his feet. "If you wish to save your leg you will do as I say."

When the doctor stopped speaking there was only a pencil thin line under the beak of his nose.

"I want you to change the dressing everyday, and clean the wound with alcohol. It will burn, but it just might keep the infection from spreading."

The next day Boggiano came to see Dominick, knocking on the doorjamb before pushing the curtains aside and entering the small, stuffy room. "So, how are you feeling?"

"Not so good, signore. I fell this morning trying to get up."

"I thought you were supposed to stay in bed?"

"Si, but sometimes I must use the chamber pot," Dominick said shyly.

"What's the matter with that stupid Sparaio," Joe scolded. "He should have put you in the bottom bunk."

Joe grabbed some articles of clothing lying on the bottom bunk and tossed them on the top by Dominick's feet.

"Come on, you're switching bunks."

"But I don't want to cause trouble, signore."

"You let me worry about that. Now, sit up. I'll help you."

Dominick swung his legs over the edge of his bunk. He had to bend over to keep from hitting his head on the ceiling.

Joe reached out two hairy arms and grabbed his waist. "Grab hold of my shoulders."

When Dominick did as he was told, Joe lifted him easily off the bunk and stood him upon his good leg on the floor. Then he eased him into a sitting position on the edge of the lower bunk.

"How do you feel now?"

"A little dizzy."

"By the way," Joe added. I have Sam Bennett collecting Rocco's bail, so you needn't worry about it for now."

When the headman left, he could hear Joe telling Mrs. Sparaio that he had moved him to the bottom bunk. There would be no trouble. That evening Dominick noticed the wound was unusually red and very tender. When he poked at it, a foul smelling, greenish-yellow puss leaked out of the open wound.

The next day some Society men from Elwood City stopped to see him. They visited for over two hours before one of the men announced that he had something private to say to Dominick. The others left the room and he could hear them talking to Nick outside.

The man who stayed cleared his throat before reaching into his coat pocket. "How much money do you need, compare?"

"I don't need any," Dominick replied. "I got some money from a cousin of mine. Don't worry," he added when he saw the man's disappointed face, "when I need something I will ask for it."

"But, we have to help one another. Please, take this as a favor to me."

Dominick slowly shook his head. "I am fine, compare. I will let you know if I need anything. Grazie."

The man looked nervously toward the sound of his comrades talking outside before he shrugged and left.

I don't want your money, Dominick thought. If I take the money, I will owe a favor I may not be able to repay.

That evening Boggiano came storming through the curtains. "What is the matter with you?" he shouted, after he chased two of the other boarders outside. "I hear you refused to accept help from the Society."

"No, signore. I sold my block at the quarry for $25. I don't need the money just now."

"No, signore! No, signore!" Joe was pacing back and forth between the bunks, waving his arms in agitation. He stopped suddenly and stared at him. "Don't you know what you have done?"

Dominick shook his head wearily. This afternoon he noticed the red mark around the wound had begun creeping up his leg.

"Of course not, you are too sick to know what you are doing." Joe leaned against Dominick's bunk, extending his hand toward the young man with his thumb and index finger touching. He shook the fingers at Dominick to emphasize each phrase.

"You have brought shame on the Association here by not accepting this money from the Elwood City men. You are supposed to let the Association support you now."

"I do not need money at present, signore. When I do, I will ask for it."

"Bah," Joe exclaimed. "Between you and Cerini, I am going to go mad!"

"Cer...Cerini?" Dominick struggled to rise up on his elbow. "What of Cerini?"

Joe was pacing between the bunks again. "That dog eating worm has blackmailed D'Alessio, the man who had Rocco arrested." He stopped and threw his arms in the air. "And without my permission! Now he has disappeared. Run away! But I tell you this." Joe punched a finger toward the ceiling. "This association is going to know discipline. They will learn about honor."

Joe paused to look at Dominick. He could see the boy was struggling to focus on him. "Rest," he said. "I'll straighten out this little misunderstanding with the Elwood City men." Joe turned to leave then spun around and pointed to the chamber pot under the bunk. "And I'll have those other fools who stay here keep your pot empty. It reeks like an outhouse in here!"

Joe turned on his heel and stormed back through the curtains, mumbling about disrespect and discipline.

That night Dominick's fever broke somewhat. While the others were sleeping, he tried to write his reports that he kept hidden under the mattress. He didn't know when he would get to mail them to Toni in Youngstown, but he wanted to record what he could. A shaft of pale moonlight radiated through an open window. It would have to do. He noticed that the red streak had spread further, and it felt as though his whole leg was on fire. In the morning they found him draped over the edge of the bunk. Papers were scattered on the floor. Docato gathered up the papers, and Nick Sparaio summoned the doctor. By noon the doctor still hadn't arrived, and they could tell he was dying. That was when Casimo Ciampanelli burst into the room with his wife and two older daughters in tow.

Dominick would remember being lifted, remember a girl crying, and remember bouncing painfully on a homemade stretcher amid glaring patches of sunlight. Now and then he thought he heard a familiar chirping sound. A biting pain in his side brought him back into consciousness. The room was blurry, but he could tell his body was naked under the cool sheets. As he struggled to sit up a familiar high-pitched voice sliced into his mind.

"There, there silly boy."

Dominick focused on a bony, skeleton of a hand reaching for him.

"Ig..Ignazio?" His mouth felt as though it was full of dirty rags. His throat burned.

"Si, Ignazio here, silly boy. Ignazio take care of you, but now you must lay still."

He had to get up. "P..PP...Pee!"

The chirping sound trilled higher. He tried to focus, felt bony fingers move his bare legs over the edge of the bed, felt himself exposed.

"Go on, silly boy. Ignazio, will hold the pot."

Dominick's eyes focused on a grinning old man, as urine poured into the chamber pot splashing over a pair of stick-thin arms.

Drawn by the commotion Casimo stood in the doorway, his broad body blocking the view to those behind him. Casimo watched the young man, with a helpless, foolish grin on his face, pissing into a porcelain pot held by old Ignazio Sebastianelli.

"Un momentino!" he shouted over his shoulder at a chorus of excited feminine voices behind him.

In the days that followed, the Ciampanelli family took care of him. Rosa, particularly, fussed and fretted over his every need. Ignazio didn't return after Dominick awoke from the coma. However, he did send a supply of the black, oily potion that smelled like tar but seemed to be sucking the poison from his leg.

Although it was only a one floor dwelling, the Ciampanelli's house was larger than most of the neighboring shanties. Rosa's father had expanded the structure over the years so that Dominick occupied a small addition. The room was clean and smelled of fresh lumber. A small table held a kerosene lamp and washbasin. An open trunk sat in one corner. He could see it contained his clothes, all neatly folded. An old blanket, cut down the middle, and hanging from a rope strung over the doorway provided privacy.

Dominick instantly recognized a light knock on the doorpost. "Come in, Rosa."

He sat on the edge of the bed wearing one of Casimo's huge nightshirts. It billowed around him in a cloud of soft flannel. There had been a frost that night, and the air was chill in the room.

"Dominick! You shouldn't get out of bed." Rosa was carrying a bowl of steaming oatmeal.

"I can't lie here forever. Besides, I feel much better, thanks to you and your folks."

"And Signore Sebastianelli," Rosa added.

"Si, and old Ignazio."

She was regarding him with her hands clasped behind her back and her head slightly cocked to one side.

He looked at her suddenly. "What ever happened to your pig tails, sis?"

"Dominick!" Her eyes flashed. "Pig tails are for little girls."

He raised his hand. "I know, I know. You're not a little girl anymore."

She lowered her eyes. "No," she said softly, "I'm not."

Suddenly his face turned serious. Something had been bothering him for days.

"Rosa, I was writing some letters when I got sick, and..."

"Oh," she interrupted. "Un momentino." She came back a few moments later with several sheets of paper.

"Docato gave these to me the day we came for you."

When he reached for the papers, Rosa didn't let go. He cocked his head and raised his eyebrows slightly.

"Dominick, I...I know why you joined the Society. You're a spy aren't you?"

His heart sank. "Rosa, I..."

"Rosa!" It was her sister Grace's voice. "Rosa, you get out here this instant and help with the chores!"

Rosa ignored her sister. "We learn to read English in the public school, you know."

They could hear footsteps approaching. Rosa turned to leave, then glanced back at him and winked. "I won't tell," she whispered, "honest."

She had almost reached the curtain when Grace, frowning as usual, peered in.

"I'm coming, sister," she said sweetly.

Dominick couldn't trust his voice to speak. He was left with an overwhelming sense of sadness and fear.

That evening Sam Bennett came to see him. Sam had sold his household furniture to help pay the bondsman.

"Maria wants to call off the wedding again," he said. "Her father won't even let me talk to her now."

"I'm sorry, Sam. I don't know what to do."

"Me either. Joe has me collecting money for Rocco's bail, but no one around here wants to pay anything. Now, I'm afraid I will be sent out of town again."

The two friends continued talking until Mrs. Ciampanelli chased Sam out, insisting Dominick must rest.

In the days that followed, Dominick's strength grew until he was able to dress and be up long enough to take his meals with the family. At dinner one evening he brought up the subject of Sam and Maria's postponed wedding and about Sam having to sell the furniture.

"Oh Papa," Rosa said. "That's so sad."

Her father snorted, "The problems of society members are no affair of ours."

Mary, sitting beside her mother, reached out and touched Mrs. Ciampanelli's arm. "Mamma?" she asked quietly.

"What is it, dear?"

"Aren't Sam Bennett and Maria Italians like us?"

Mrs. Ciampanelli got to her feet in a rush and began gathering dishes from the table. "Your papa and I will discuss this later. For now we must clean the table and do the dishes."

Casimo pulled a black plug of tobacco from his shirt pocket and bit off a sizable chew, then extended the plug to Dominick. The younger man shook his head. "Are you able to sit on the front steps for a while?" Casimo asked.

"Si, I would speak with you alone, if I may?"

Casimo nodded solemnly as he stood.

They walked out on a small porch of rough lumber. "Signore Ciampanelli, I want you to know how much I appreciate what your family has done, but perhaps it is best if I move back to Nick's or even over with Jim Rossi if he has room."

Casimo spat a stream of dark juice. "That is not necessary. After all, you are not well yet."

"But, signore, the Society's problems will continue to barge through your door if I stay here."

"I will trust you to handle that discreetly. My family will not become involved with the Society. Meanwhile, you can pay for room and board as you have elsewhere. That will put us on a business footing, eh?"

Later that evening Docato stopped by to see Dominick. "Signora Racca sends her condolences, and hopes you are feeling better," he said.

"Has the signora come home from New York then?"

"She is staying in Lowellville with S..Signore Martino. She asks that you s..stop by when you're able."

"And what does the signora want from me?"

"I...I don't know. Perhaps, she w..wants you to help get her husband out of jail."

"I am not well enough to travel yet, Docato. Besides, Signore Boggiano and Sam Bennett are in charge of gathering Rocco's bail. I can do nothing without his permission. You know that."

"Si," Docato said, shaking his head. "B.. But this is n..not good! Signore B..Bo..Boggiano w..wants all the Italian men in Hillsville to join the S..Society. Everyone must pay Signore J..Joe ten dollars to join. This may cause t..trouble."

Dominick shrugged. "So what can I do about it, Docato?"

Docato lowered his eyes and fidgeted nervously. "You ca..can talk to Signore J..Joe. H..he listens to you."

Dominick threw his hands in the air. "Docato! I'm not a godfather you know!"

"Si," the boy said standing up. "B..But maybe you should be."

Dominick felt overwhelmed, his mind tumbling over a waterfall of despair. I don't know if I can keep doing this, he thought. Signora Racca expects me to get Rocco out of jail, Docato expects me to stop Boggiano's craziness, and somehow I'm supposed to help Sam and Maria get married. If they only knew the truth! When he thought of Rosa, Dominick shuttered. The idea of her knowing the truth about him was both frightening and yet strangely comforting. He fell asleep wondering how to deal with it all.

The next morning frost silvered the grass and tin roofs of the Peanut Settlement as the Ciampanelli family sat around the breakfast table in tense silence. Rosa's father was moody and quiet. When breakfast was consumed, Mrs. Ciampanelli made no move to clean the table. Instead, she sat back in her chair folding her hands in a spacious lap. When Casimo continued to sip his coffee in silence, Mrs. Ciampanelli cleared her throat.

"Well, Papa? Are you going to tell them, or should I?"

"It is your idea, woman. You tell them."

"Very well. Girls, your papa has decided that it might be good if we do something nice for Sam and Maria."

This extracted a snort from Casimo. The girls looked at their father then quickly back to their mother. The mood was changing from dreary to exciting. Mary, particularly, could hardly keep from jumping up and down in her chair.

"Papa is going to talk with some of the men at work about making furniture for Sam and Maria."

Rosa and Mary squealed with delight.

"The furniture will be rough at best," Casimo offered.

"It will be the finest furniture in the world for two people in love," Signora Ciampanelli declared.

The girls broke into laughter and fits of giggles. Finally even Grace cracked a smile.

"Meanwhile," Signora Ciampanelli continued, looking at the girls, "we are going to organize the women to make curtains and coverings for the furniture."

The thumping of the knife on the table brought the laughter and giggles to an abrupt halt. Casimo looked pointedly at Dominick before laying his knife down. "This all depends on whether Boggiano will allow Sam and Maria to get married."

Dominick looked at the expectant faces around the table. "I have already promised Maria's father that I would talk with Boggiano about this, but you will have to give me some time. As a matter of honor, the Society may not permit non-members to help its people. This has not happened before."

"I know you will get permission," Rosa said admiringly.

We'll see, Dominick mused. Given the Society's perverted sense of honor it could even cause bloodshed.

Chapter 12

A middle-aged man, his shirtsleeves rolled up, was raking leaves beside a sprawling two-story house. When he saw the young man open the front gate, he put the rake down and walked over to meet him.

"Frank Martino," he said, approaching Dominick with his hand extended in the American way. "What can I do for you?" He spoke good English, but with a strong accent.

Dominick noticed Frank Martino was well dressed. Tight waves of black hair, tinged with gray, flowed back from a high and sloping forehead like ripples on a pond. The creases on Frank's forehead matched the waves in his hair. Dominick introduced himself, explaining that Mrs. Racca asked him to stop by.

"Come inside," Frank said. "She will be helping my wife in the kitchen."

When they reached the porch, Martino turned to face Dominick. He looked perturbed. "I have been in this country for twenty years. How is it you speak such very good American for a young man?"

Dominick lowered his head. Among Italians it was taboo to marry outside their own race. "I was raised by my aunt and her American husband," he said with a tinge of bitterness in his voice.

"But that is good," Frank declared suddenly. "Our people have a lot to offer this country. We speak only American here because I want my children to become good American citizens.

Sometimes," he added, "we must put off the old ways." Frank put his arm around Dominick's shoulders and ushered him into the house, calling loudly for the ladies.

A lovely young woman, wiping her hands on an apron, strolled into the living room. She had fiery red hair with a splattering of freckles over the bridge of her nose. "Dominick, meet my wife Susan," Frank announced proudly. "She too, is American."

"Irish actually," Susan said, extending a hand that was moist from something in the kitchen.

"A good combination, is it not?" Frank declared.

"You'll stay for supper, won't you?" Susan asked.

"Uh...I don't know. Signo..er, Mrs. Racca asked me to stop by and..."

"Si, this one will stay for supper," Mrs. Racca announced, marching stiffly in from the kitchen. "You never had to be asked twice in Hillsville, young man."

Rocco's wife didn't speak much English, and her Italian speech contrasted sharply in this American household.

Dominick bowed stiffly from the waist. "Signora." He turned and bowed to Susan. "Mrs. Martino, I shall be honored to have dinner with your family."

"Well, I guess that settles that," Susan said. "I better peel a few more potatoes."

"We can talk after supper, Dominick," Mrs. Racca declared. "You men get acquainted while I help Susan."

The two men followed the women into the kitchen then out to a lattice-covered patio over-run with a network of grapevines. "Hard to keep the place clean this time of year," Frank said brushing some of the large yellow, and brown spotted, leaves from a chair. The sun was warm and the smell of burning leaves drifted with the breeze. "Indian summer, they call it," Frank added, indicating the moderate weather. "Best enjoy it while we can."

Mrs. Racca brought them a bottle of wine and two glasses. "My own grapes," Frank declared proudly. He poured Dominick a glass of wine and sat back to watch him taste it.

Dominick swirled the wine in his glass before inhaling deeply, then took a sip, swishing the red liquid around inside his mouth. "Very good," he declared. "Excellent!"

Frank, smiling contentedly, paused to fill his own glass. "So, tell me news of Hillsville."

A serious look clouded Dominick's face. "Permit me," he said before setting his glass on the table. "But I must ask first if you are a member of the Society?"

Frank made a crude sign with his hand and sighed. "It has been a long while, Dominick. I don't attend the meetings anymore, haven't for over ten years. Luca Caruzzi leaves me alone so long as I do a favor for him now and then."

Dominick nodded but thought better about sharing the Society's business with Frank. He wondered if this might be some sort of test, or a trap. Instead, he told him about Sam and Maria. "It's the strangest thing I've ever seen," he concluded. "There's a group of people up there who don't even belong to the Society making furniture so Sam and Maria can get married."

Frank was about to comment when two young boys came running onto the patio dressed in knickers with knee socks and matching caps.

Frank embraced both boys before the smallest one snuggled into his lap. "Boys, I want you to meet our guest."

They grew quiet then, staring at Dominick.

When he greeted the boys in Italian, Frank frowned somewhat. "I told you we only speak American here."

"That's English, father," the oldest chided. He was looking intently at Dominick. "Are you a Black Handler?" he asked suddenly.

"Nathan!"

"That's all right, Mr. Martino. I am the one who must apologize." Dominick looked directly at Nathan. "The Black Hand is a term the American newspapers invented to create bad feelings against Italians. There is no such thing." He was amazed how easy the lie rolled off his lips.

Nathan pinched his face together. "That's too bad," he said.

"What did you say?" his father asked.

"They call us wop and dago," the younger boy said.

"Yeah, so I tell them my dad belongs to the Black Hand," Nathan answered defiantly. "Then they leave us alone."

"Let me explain something, boys," Dominick said. "A wop is a term for someone who comes into this country illegally. Someone without papers. That's what W.O.P. means...without papers."

"Do we have papers, daddy?" the youngest asked.

"Papers? You don't need papers. I am American citizen!" He thumped his chest with an open hand. "Your mother is American citizen!" Frank's accent thickened with emotion. "You boys American citizen because you mamma and papa American citizen. You as much American as the damma' Iri...!" He caught himself. "Go now," he said after a moment. "Go. Wash for supper."

When the boys went back into the house, Dominick smiled at Frank and raised his eyebrows questionably.

"Yes," Frank said. "Why are they so accepted in this country when we must struggle?"

"I suspect it wasn't easy for them either."

Their conversation was interrupted when Susan announced supper was ready. Afterward Frank motioned Dominick into the parlor, while Mrs. Martino took the boys upstairs. When they were seated, Frank poured them each a glass of sherry before speaking. "Mrs. Racca asked me to talk with you about Rocco. She fears enough is not being done to gather his bail, and she cannot talk about it without crying. Did you know she is forced to sell her house in Hillsville?"

Dominick shook his head. "No, sir. Since I have been ill, Joe Boggiano put Sam Bennett in charge of collecting Rocco's bail, but I understand it isn't going very well."

"What seems to be the problem?"

"The people are poor. They can barely give but one or two dollars each."

Frank sat back in his chair and stared at the ceiling, then abruptly set his glass on the table. "I think I may have a way of killing two birds in the bushes, as the Americans say. We will have Sam and Maria's wedding here, in Lowellville. I will invite my business associates, and we will use the occasion of the wedding to collect Rocco's bail."

"But why...how?"

Frank spread his arms wide. "Why? Because Mrs. Racca is my cousin. I am..." Frank rolled his eyes toward the ceiling. "Ah, how do you say? I am obliged to help." He paused to smile at Dominick. "As to how? Well, unlike your friends in Hillsville, my business associates do have money. If each gives twenty, thirty or more dollars...he shrugged.

Frank got to his feet and began pacing the floor. "You must go into New Castle and find Rocco's attorney. Ask him how much money we will need. Then talk to Boggiano and Sam Bennett. See if they will agree to this." The little man stopped suddenly and looked at Dominick. " So! What do you think?"

Dominick got to his feet and approached Frank Martino, giving him a hug in the custom of the old country. "I think you are more Italian than you care to let on, compare."

Frank lowered his head somewhat. "Yes, I still miss the old country. Everything here is in such...turmoil."

Dominick nodded before clapping Frank on the shoulder. "But I must to talk to Boggiano first. We can do nothing in Hillsville without his blessing."

"I will talk to Luca Caruzzi," Frank said. "He is Rocco's friend, and Luca has ways of making sure my friends give generously."

The young man awoke in the morning to a steady drumming of rain on the tin roof. Although it was still dark outside, light spilled through cracks in the curtain and over the doorway. He could hear pans rattling in the kitchen, and Mary's cheerful voice talking to her father. Dominick dressed quickly and stepped into the warmth of the Ciampanelli's living room. The smell of frying sausage drifted from the small kitchen.

Mary came running over and took his hand. "Dominick! Guess what?"

He knelt down and gave the girl a playful hug. "What are you so excited about, little one?"

"Why, Dominick. Mr. Swanson, who runs the steam shovel, gave us beautiful furniture for Sam and Maria."

A grunt from across the room focused their attention on Casimo who was sitting at the table reading an Italian newspaper. "It's just an old sofa and chair."

"But, Papa, it will help when Sam and Maria get married."

Casimo put the paper down and looked at them. "Are they going to get married, Dominick?"

He got slowly to his feet. "I don't know, signore. I am going to talk to Boggiano today. Signore Martino has a proposal that he should like."

"And what is that?"

"He is going to ask Sam and Maria to be married at his home in Lowellville." Dominick hesitated. He didn't really want to get into this with Casimo, who disliked the Society. "Uh...well, he is going to invite his business associates and use the occasion to collect enough money for Rocco Racca's bail."

"Humph! That is just like the Society. This money should go to Sam and Maria. Not to a criminal like Rocco Racca."

"There will be gifts for Sam and Maria, too. All in all, it will be a good compromise, I think."

Casimo slowly shook his head. "Is not good," he said rattling his paper as he folded it in his lap. Then he looked intently at Dominick. "Siciliano is back."

Dominick felt a chill.

Casimo continued. "The men are scared nearly to death. Some talk about leaving. Others believe they will have to join the Society."

Later that morning, Dominick made his way along the path that led to Boggiano's house. The rain had stopped, but the path was slick with wet leaves. A cold wind whipped at the flanks of dark clouds, bringing the ominous promise of winter. At the little cluster of shanty's where Joe Boggiano lived, Dominick wasn't prepared for what he saw.

A small crowd gathered around two men lying on the ground. One of the men appeared to be unconscious and was bleeding profusely from his face. The other was trying to cover his head with his arms as Boggiano danced around him in a rage, raining blows, and kicking him repeatedly after he fell. Joe's wife was attached to his shirttail, crying and pleading and trying to pull her husband away from the stricken man.

"You, dogs! How dare you demand money from my men?"

There was a sharp crack as Joe smashed his foot into the man's ribs.

"No! Please, I beg you." Mrs. Boggiano was tugging furiously on her husband's shirt.

Joe leaned over and spit on the man's head. "Get up! Get up, you filthy dog!"

The man didn't move.

"Then you will die like a dog! I'm going to get my shotgun, and you are going to die right there in the dirt."

Mrs. Boggiano let out a loud wail. "No! Joe, no! Pleeease!"

As Dominick tried to run toward the Boggianos', he saw the man Joe was kicking crawl toward his unconscious partner who began to shake spasmodically.

"Somebody get my gun!" Joe roared. Then the door slammed shut cutting off another wail from his wife.

Dominick's leg throbbed as he hurried toward the house. He watched the crawling man reach his partner and try to help him stand. Dominick paused at the door. The men were on their feet now, leaning on each other as they tried to limp away.

Dominick knocked and then slowly opened the door. "Permesso, signore." Mrs. Boggiano was sitting in a chair, crying.

Joe began laughing when he saw Dominick's bewildered expression. "Tell me," he asked waving toward the window, "what are they doing now?"

Dominick walked over to the window and peered out. "They are trying to run away, but they are not moving so fast."

Joe doubled over with laughter. His wife got up and stomped into the kitchen, still crying.

Joe suddenly grew serious. His rising anger brought him to his feet. "Those swine!" he waved his arms. "Jim Rossi lost more money gambling in Youngstown. Instead of coming to me, those dogs go to Jim and demand the money with interest. Demand mind you! Jim doesn't have the money so he told them to meet him here and he would pay. They were going to cut him! Cut my man?" Joe stopped pacing and looked intently at Dominick. "I don't think so," he added softly.

Joe put his thick hands on Dominick's shoulders. "You look better, my boy. How is the leg?"

"Much better, signore. I...I came to seek your advice."

"Good, good. And, I must talk with you as well." He turned toward the kitchen. "Monna, for the love of the Blessed Virgin stop that crying and bring some wine." Joe turned and winked at Dominick. "Women just don't understand the politics of fighting. The headman in Youngstown will know we intend to defend our honor. This matter can now be settled peacefully."

Mrs. Boggiano came in carrying a bottle and two glasses, and Joe put his arm around her. "You're a good wife, Monna," he said giving her a squeeze.

Joe chuckled and poured the glasses full of thick red wine. "So," he said, handing Dominick a glass, "what can I do for you?"

"It would seem there is nothing simple, signore. I came to seek your advice about Sam and Maria, and about Rocco Racca."

"Si, this thing about Sam and Maria and the non-society people..." He got up suddenly, pacing and waving his arms. "At first, I am angry.

I think, how dare these people meddle in society business. I will teach Casimo Ciampanelli something about The Society of Honor."

Dominick's heart jumped, "Signore..."

Joe whirled, turning a fearfully frowning face on the startled young man. "I know Ciampanelli does not like the Society. Then I think of Dominick Prugitore. I was not happy when Ciampanelli moved you without my permission, but," Joe rolled his shoulders in a massive shrug, "I suppose he saved your life. Then came this thing with them and Sam Bennett. And I think, that sly Dominick. He has tricked Casimo into becoming involved with the Society's business. Now he will be obliged to join." Joe came back and sat in the chair facing Dominick. He was smiling. "Si," he added after taking another sip of wine. "A good tactic, my boy."

Dominick was stunned. When he got control of himself he said, "Vito is scaring these people. I am afraid some will run away."

Joe's face became intent. "Sometimes a little persuasion is necessary." Joe picked up his glass and swirled the red liquid around. "The Ciampanelli's are under your protection for now." His head came up. "You mentioned Rocco Racca?"

Dominick took a sip of wine. "I visited a Signore Martino, in Lowellville yesterday. Signora Racca is his cousin, and she is staying with him. Signora Racca is concerned about raising Rocco's bail."

Joe jumped to his feet again. His anger poured out in a torrent. "Rocco Racca deserves to be in jail! He was a bad headman, and stupid. There were too many murders and cuttings under him." Joe took a deep breath and shook himself before sitting back down. "Still, Rocco is one of us, and we need to help if we can."

He shook his baldhead. "I have never met such people as live here. They are stingy and make excuses. I don't think we can raise Rocco's bail money." His face grew dark again, brow bunched together over his nose. "I am sorry for Fred Carnetti. He is innocent, yet they are after him." Joe made a meaty fist and shook it in the air. "I would like to see the scum who shot an old man like Duff. I would cut his face!"

"Who is that, signore?"

"That man they used to call crazy around here. The one who took fits."

Saverino! Dominick thought. Yes, he worked on the steam shovel with Carnetti.

Dominick forced his mind back to the issue at hand. "There is, perhaps, a way to raise the money for Rocco's bail."

Joe Boggiano raised his eyebrows.

"If you will give permission for Sam and Maria to be married, Signore Martino has offered to hold the wedding at his home in Lowellville. Signore Martino said he would invite the area merchants to the wedding and use the occasion to collect money for Rocco's bail. He believes he could collect all the money there."

Now Joe was sitting on the edge of his seat. "This Martino, he is a member of the Society, no?"

"Si."

"And, these friends of his? They are rich, no?"

"Comfortable, I believe the Americans call it."

Boggiano's eyes were gleaming. "We must go to New Castle and talk with Rocco's attorney. He will tell us what we must do, then we will see about Sam Bennett's wedding."

"Si, but perhaps you could talk with Signore Piccini. Maria's father is very upset."

Joe pursed his lips and flipped his hand in the air. "You let me handle Piccini. The man thinks his family's honor is in question. I will talk with Lou Piccini, and he will talk sense to his daughter. Maria will do what her papa says and that will be the end of it." Joe pointed at Dominick. "Now we must talk about you."

Dominick took another sip of wine and steeled himself.

"The time has come for you to ask for your place in the Society," Joe said. "You must move up to a level where you can be more useful."

Dominick's mind recoiled at the thought. His only chance was to quit. To walk away and never return. But Rosa was in danger, and now the Ciampanelli's were under his protection.

"I...I am honored, signore. But, you must give me time. I am not working, and I don't have money for the initiation."

Joe waved his hand in dismissal. "Do not worry. Normally such a thing would cost twenty-five, but we all know you have been sick. This initiation will only cost you ten dollars, and you may pay it after you are working again."

Dominick stared moodily into the bottom of his glass.

Joe Boggiano got to his feet and put his arm around the younger man's shoulders. "I know you are overwhelmed with this honor." He gave Dominick a hearty squeeze. "You will come to the Society meeting at Jim Rossi's this Wednesday. You must stand up and demand your place in the Society. Then you must leave. We will discuss it, and the second-class members will vote. But, do not worry. You will pass."

On Friday morning, Dominick found himself in a livery wagon bouncing along the deeply rutted road into New Castle with Joe Boggiano and Nick Sparaio. The latter was trying to buy Rocco's house, and needed Rocco to sign off on the deed. Joe seemed moody and quiet.

"So, how did the meeting go after I left Wednesday night?"

Joe shrugged his massive shoulders. "You can't please everyone."

Dominick got a hollow feeling in the pit of his stomach. The young detective was afraid that calling for his place in the Society would focus too much attention on himself. "Well, I expected Vito to object."

"Vito, didn't say anything," Joe replied.

It was Nick who cleared the air. "Londo Racca, that fool, thinks you are working with the detectives somehow."

A flash of fear gripped Dominick's heart, especially after Joe cast Nick a menacing look. "That Judis pig!" he exploded. "I told him I didn't know that cocky, little detective."

Joe tuned to face him, his face as cold as the morning frost. "Then tell me, how is it this detective seems to know you?"

Dominick looked intently into Joe's eyes and forced himself to stay calm. "I don't know, signore. But ever since you and Rocco had me acting as an interpreter, all the detectives act as if they know me."

Joe's face softened. "Nick claims you saved Rocco."

Dominick shrugged. "The detective was pressing Rocco about the Houk murder. I was afraid Rocco was going to make a mistake, so I told him he didn't have to answer the man's questions."

For a while the headman seemed absorbed with the rhythm of the horse's flanks. Then Joe turned to face him again. "I believe Londo is wrong," he said evenly.

When they arrived at the jail they found Rocco in a melancholy mood. "If I can get the money," he said sadly, "I am going to send my wife back to Italy. Then I don't care what they do with me."

"You better concentrate on making bail," Joe growled.

"How am I supposed to collect such a sum from here?"

"We are doing what we can," Dominick said. "The people are poor, but perhaps we have found a way."

Joe flashed him a menacing look. "Sam Bennett is trying to collect the debts from your store. That is to go toward your bail."

"Give the book to Dominick," Rocco said. "The people trust him, and he understands these things."

"I will decide who does what in Hillsville!" Joe shouted.

Something banged loudly on the cell door behind them, causing the men to jerk around. An angry looking deputy with a short club was glaring at them. "All right," he shouted. "Time's up! Let's go."

Dominick got slowly to his feet. "Please," he said. "It is hard for our people to talk without getting excited. Just a few more minutes? We'll be quiet, I promise."

"I'll give you two more minutes, buster," the deputy growled. "That's all." He leaned back against the wall outside the cell and watched them warily.

When Dominick translated what the deputy said, Joe snorted loudly and stood up.

Nick looked worried and spread his hands. "Please, signore," he said to Rocco. "If I am to buy your house, you must sign this paper."

Rocco thrust out his hand. "Give me the bloody thing!"

When Rocco signed the deed, Nick got up and walked to the cell door with Joe. As Dominick stood to leave, Rocco grabbed his sleeve. "Before you go back to Hillsville, do me the favor of bringing some fruit and cigarettes."

Dominick nodded, but Rocco tugged at his sleeve again. "Also, twenty-five cents worth of sugar. They don't give us any sugar in this place," he added gruffly.

On the way out, Dominick asked the deputy if he could return with the requested items. "You may do so," the deputy said sternly, "but I don't want to see them fellahs again. They were just stirr'n up trouble."

As they walked along the street toward the Lawrence Trust Company building, where Rocco's attorney had his office, Dominick explained what the deputy had said. To his surprise, Boggiano slapped him roughly on the back. "See," Joe beamed, "already you are becoming more useful to the Society."

Dominick smiled faintly.

At the attorney's office, they learned that J. W. Boffitt was tied up in court for most of the afternoon. They were directed to return after three o'clock.

Joe put a thick arm around Dominick's shoulders. "You speak good American. Do me the favor of waiting to see this attorney about Rocco's bail, then come see me tonight."

"Si, but please do me the favor of talking with Signore Piccini about Sam and Maria," Dominick asked.

"I already have. Piccini is going to talk to those young people today. By tonight we should know whether or not we will have a wedding."

When Dominick returned to the jail, Rocco seemed to be in a better frame of mind. The sheriff's deputy checked the bag and told Dominick he could only stay for a few minutes. Rocco asked about his wife.

"She is in good health, compare," he said, "but she cries for you all the time."

Rocco shook his head. "I don't know if I will come out from here," he said softly. "After I was arrested in New York, the detectives took me to Philadelphia. They questioned me hard about the murder of the game policeman." Rocco paused and looked suspiciously toward the cell door. When he spoke again it was almost a whisper. "A less experienced man would have been caught."

Dominick was about to ask exactly what he meant, when he heard keys rattling.

"Time's up, young man," the deputy said.

Jason Warren Boffitt was built like a beer keg. He reeked of cigar smoke and cheap cologne.

"Look here," he puffed. The man seemed to run out of breath after speaking only a few words. "I can't give you any hope about Mr. Racca." He gasped for breath, his face and chins turning red with the effort. "The bail now is high. But it will probably go to $5000. They don't want him out."

"When is his trial?"

"First Monday in November." He waved a chubby hand at Dominick's startled look. "Don't worry." he gasped. "I'm going to file for a continuance. Maybe the trial won't come up for months after that."

On his way back to Hillsville, the young detective wondered if Rocco would see the light of day again. *He was about to tell me something,* he thought.

Dusk had fallen when Dominick returned to Boggiano's house. Several men were standing around outside. Joe, who was sitting on the porch, motioned him inside. The sparse furniture had been pushed back to make a large open area in the center of the room. A small table stood there. Dominick recognized what was happening immediately.

"I want you to stay for this." Joe said, gesturing toward the table.

Dominick nodded, and then told Joe what the attorney had said about Rocco's bail.

"Good, maybe he will get what he deserves. Maybe they will even hang him twice—once for Houk and once for Duff." Joe was smiling broadly.

"I don't think they have anything on him," Dominick said gravely. "But tell me, signore. What of Sam and Maria?"

"Looks like we are going to have a wedding." Joe rolled his shoulders. "Now come along," he added impatiently. "We have important things to do."

When they went back outside they saw a small group walking down the street with two dejected looking men in the middle. Vito Siciliano was leading them, grinning wolfishly, with Mario Nardozi swaggering along behind.

"Bring them inside," Boggiano roared.

As the men filed into Joe's house, they fanned out in a large circle around the room. Joe was standing behind the table facing the door. A large square of white cloth lay in the middle of the table before him. Jim Rossi and Sam Bennett took positions on either side of Boggiano. Dominick looked to see two men, escorted by Siciliano and Nardozi, enter the room. The circle parted to let the men in, then closed behind them.

Joe's deep voice echoed in the room. "Paolo and Angleo Vertanilo, come forward and prepare to take the sacred oath."

The men looked at each other and, with shoulders slumped, walked forward.

When the men reached the table, Joe raised a hand and suddenly each of the men in the circle pulled knives, one in each hand and clashed them together over their chests. Both of the men standing in front of the table gawked around wide-eyed.

Dominick stepped out of the circle, bumping into a hard muscled body behind him. He looked around into the sneering face of Siciliano. "What's the matter, boy?" Vito's fowl breath hissed into his face. "Afraid of knives?"

Dominick forced himself to turn calmly toward the center of the room. His heart was tearing at the underside of his rib cage as he listened to Siciliano's hissing laughter behind him.

Joe went through the ritual of the cloth and each time the bald headman finished telling what the colors stood for, the men encircling the room clashed their knives together. The Vertanilo brothers flinched with each clash of steel, then stood trembling, looking down at the white cloth overlaid with red on the table in front of them.

"Put your right hands on the cloth, one on top of the other. And for the love of the Blessed Virgin, don't move!" Boggiano whispered.

When the brothers placed their hands on the cloth, Joe pulled a dark handled stiletto from his belt and thrust it between their splayed fingers. Angleo moaned before Sam and Jim thrust knives into the table on each side of the brother's hands. As the circled men clashed their knives over their chests, Angleo's knees buckled and he slumped to the floor. Paolo reached up and clasped his brother's hand to keep it in place on top of his own; tears running freely down his cheeks.

"These knives represent death." Joe intoned, followed by another clash of steel. "Death to those who break the Omerta."

Clash!

Now Paolo slumped to his knees beside his brother.

"Look at me," Joe demanded.

But they knelt there, shaking their heads and crying.

"Look at me!"

Slowly the brothers raised their heads and looked into Joe's raging face.

"Do you swear, with your eternal soul, to obey the rules of The Society of Honor...?"

When it was over Joe was frowning. "Disgusting display of manhood," he grumbled.

"A bit melodramatic, wasn't it?" Dominick demanded flatly.

"What do you mean?"

"Dominick thinks it was a little overdone," Sam said.

Joe shrugged. "Sometimes we must put fear in their hearts." He tapped his chest with a stubby finger, eyes blazing. "Then we get respect!"

Outside, Dominick asked Sam if he had set a date for the wedding.

"Si, compare. November 10th, if I don't get arrested again."

"If tonight is any indication of where things are going," Dominick said dryly, "I wouldn't buy the flowers yet."

Sam looked at him a moment, his lips tight. "Sometimes, compare, I wonder if you have the stomach for this business."

Mug shot of Rocco Racca. Circa: 1905
Photo courtesy Lawrence County Historical Society.

Seeley Houk, PA. Game Protector, Badge No5
Lawrence County, PA. Circa: 1903
Photo courtesy Lawrence County Historical Society.

New Castle Trolley #116
Crew includes detective on board for safety of passangers
Photo courtesy Lawrence County Historical Society.

Grant Street Interurban Trolley
Circa: early 1900's
Photo courtesy Lawrence County Historical Society.

Quarry workers. Notice tip is bent on hand trill
due to exceptionally hard limestone Photo courtesy
Lawrence County Historical Society.

Labors at Johnson Quarry with new pneumatic drills. Circa 1907
Photo courtesy Lawrence County Historical Society.

District Attorney Charles H. Young Circa 1907
Photo courtesy Lawrence County Historical Society.

Hornable William E. Porter,
President Judge Lawrence County, PA Circa 1905
Photo courtesy Lawrence County Historical Society.

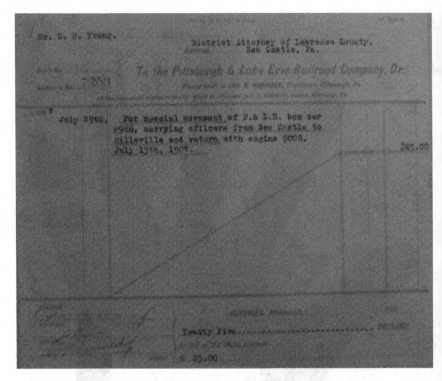

Mr. C. H. Young.   District Attorney of Lawrence County,
                                              New Castle, Pa.

                    To the Pittsburgh & Lake Erie Railroad Company, Dr.

July 29th.   For special movement of P.& L.E. box car
              #900, carrying officers from New Castle to
              Hillsville and return with engine 9008.
              July 15th, 1907. $25.00

                                    Twenty Five   DOLLARS

                                    $ 25.00

Invoice for use of engine and boxcar to conduct
raid on Black Hand in Hillsville July 1907
Photo courtesy Lawrence County Historical Society.

Black Hand warning sent to Dr. Joseph Kalbfus,
Executive Secretary and Chief Game Protector,
Pennsylvania Board of Game Commissioners.

Written in Italian "Beware La Mano Nera!" The Black Hand
Photo courtesy Pennsylvania Game Commission.

Chapter 13

"We won't be going to the wedding." Casimo, leaning against a porch post, spit a stream of tobacco into a cold rain that was knocking the most stubborn leaves to the ground. "The girls are upset, but we'll not involve ourselves with the Society anymore."

Dominick nodded, but he knew it was too late as far as Boggiano was concerned. "I have been informed, signore, that you are under my protection for as long as I stay here." He spoke softly, unsure how Casimo would take this.

Rosa's father grunted, spat, and then held up a beefy hand before slowly nodding his head. "I am grateful for that, I suppose." He glanced at Dominick. "Four more families left today."

An uneasy silence followed.

"I heard you moved up in the Society. I wish this were not so."

"I didn't have much choice, signore."

Again the older man nodded before shifting his feet uncomfortably. "Dominick, I must speak with you about Rosa. She cares more for you than for a brother I think."

Dominick's face flushed. "Signore, I..."

"Please hear me out. Believe me, this is not easy." He paused, reaching into his mouth and hooking the chew with a calloused finger before flinging it into the rain. Then he turned to face Dominick. "Rosa is growing up in some ways. Some girls even marry at fourteen. Still, she is very much the little girl."

Dominick fingered the silver watch fob hanging over his pocket. He could feel the words of endearment etched in Italian on the cold metal. The fob, his only keepsake from home, had been a gift from his mother to his father on some lost occasion. He wanted to tell Casimo that Rosa might be in danger—to take his family and flee from here. But that would require lengthy explanations. Besides he had a job to do. He had to find Houk's murderer, and he had to bring down The Society of Honor. Then, and only then, would Rosa and her family be safe. Instead, he told Casimo about the family he lost to smallpox. About the little sister he had loved so dearly.

"Rosa is like Anna to me, signore." Tears blurred his vision.

Casimo nodded solemnly. "Thank you for telling me this, Dominick. I will tell Rosa's mother not to worry. Now, tell me. How is your leg?"

"Much better, signore. I haven't needed to bandage it for several days now."

"Would you like me to speak to the quarry foreman for you?"

"Grazie, signore, but I start at the Johnson quarry on Friday."

Casimo looked surprised. "But, Sam is getting married on Saturday."

Dominick shrugged. "I should be able to get in a day and a half of work before the wedding."

That Saturday the wind howled through the quarry, causing little swirls of lime dust to whip and dance along the ledges. A greasy looking sky slid rapidly south on the heels of a northwester. Dominick leaned on the handle of his sledge for a breather, surveying the large stones that still needed breaking. He had been here since daybreak, his mind in a turmoil. He wasn't sure about this wedding or the collections. Then too, he felt bad for the girls because the Ciampanelli's weren't going. He glanced at his watch. It was nearly nine o'clock. After a minute Dominick raised the sledge, squinting his eyes shut just before the hammer struck. He decided to quit before noon.

Bathed and dressed, Dominick stopped by Boggiano's house before dinner. Joe was loading a block of ice into the chest on his porch with a heavy pair of iron tongs. "At least twenty cent's worth of ice will last longer now that it has turned colder," Joe said, hanging the heavy tongs on the wall beside the ice chest.

"Si, signore, before long you won't need ice."

"This is true. So, what can I do for you?"

Dominick spread his arms. "It's this wedding, signore. With non-society people, and even Americans going there, I don't know what to make of it." He shrugged as if confused.

Joe pursed his lips together. "I think I want you to go to this wedding, Dominick. You can keep an eye on things." Joe looked thoughtful. "Make sure there is no trouble, but don't talk about this business of Rocco's bail."

"I don't understand. Signore Martino is talking about it all over. Why such a secret?"

Joe stabbed a thick finger into Dominick's chest. "You tell Martino to give that money to me! I'm the headman around here!" He began pacing the porch, waving his arms. "Nick gave Signora Racca five hundred for his house, and Sam collected almost one hundred dollars on that worthless man's books. Rocco's gonna' get at least half of it."

"Only half, signore? He needs $2000."

Joe wheeled, his face red. "What do you think? Huh? Do you think Sam and I shouldn't get something for all the work we did?"

"I'm sorry, signore. I didn't know."

Joe stopped in front of the frustrated young man. His finger thudded repeatedly against Dominick's chest. "You think it doesn't cost money to run this Society?" He paused and shook his head. "No, you don't know. But you will. After this wedding you are going to go with Benedetti, and help collect money. Then you will see."

Dominick paled. He didn't want to commit extortion.

"Until then you will go to school twice each week. You must learn all the signs and the language of The Society of Honor." Joe placed his arm around the boy and smiled. "But for now, go to this wedding. Be my eyes and ears, no?"

Everything was a bustle of activity when Dominick arrived at the Martino's big house. A beer wagon was just leaving. A touring car and a roundabout had parked beside the road, and wagons and carriages were tied along the fence. Standing about the patio behind the house, a group of musicians hungrily watched Frank Martino supervise the tapping of a large wooden beer keg. A table beside the keg stood full of glasses and jugs and bottles of wine.

Dominick walked to the table, nodding to a couple of men talking nearby. Selecting a bottle of Frank's homemade wine, the young man poured some pale liquid into a glass before leaning against a pillar to think about what he should do. *How can I alert Signore Martino about Rocco's bail money without seeming to betray Boggiano?* He wondered. He held no illusions as to what would happen if Joe felt betrayed.

The heavy hand that suddenly clamped on the base of his neck caused him to jump. Dominick peered carefully over his shoulder at a crooked nose hanging over a hedge-like mustache and a mouth full of stained teeth with a gap in the center.

"Well, Dominick Prugitore!" The grip on his neck tightened painfully, then the booming voice dropped into a raspy growl. "You haven't been back to my place." There was a sudden flicker behind the heavily lidded eyes. "You remember Monica? Of course not! You wouldn't go upstairs with her. She always asks about the scar-faced boy." The battered face split into a wide grin. She thinks you like boys.

Dominick fought against the pain lancing through the cords of his neck and shoulder. Turning toward the inside caused the man's grip to loosen. It was a lesson he would remember. He extended his hand.

"Signore Caruzzi. It is good to see you."

When Luca Caruzzi offered his hand, Dominick gripped as hard as he could and pulled. Luca smiled wolfishly and yanked the younger man against his chest like a rag doll. "Nice try, kid. I see you still have guts. But you need to gain some weight if you ever hope to win that little tug-of-war."

Once he regained his composure, Dominick looked into Luca's battered face. "I am in need of a consigliere. Is there some place we can talk?"

"Always the serious one, are you? Well come on. Let's have a look at Martino's rose bushes, or something."

As Luca guided him toward a freshly raked lawn they noticed Frank Martino talking with two Americans wearing suits and Derby hats. Frank gestured toward the table filled with booze, but the men nervously shook their heads and handed Frank a brown envelope, which he quickly tucked inside his vest.

"Well, I see the donations for Rocco are coming in. One must handle the American's carefully, so I leave them to Martino."

"That is what I need to talk to you about, signore. I have been ordered by Joe Boggiano to bring him the money collected for Rocco's bail." There! It was out!

Luca gestured toward the open lawn. When they were safely away from the others he spoke with a lowered voice. "So? You have your orders. Why do you come to me?"

"You are the headman here, signore. Signore Boggiano does not wish to offend."

"The pompous fool already beat two of Don Sochetti's men into the ground just to protect that good-for-nothing Rossi." Luca stopped and shook his head solemnly. "No," he said. "I don't think you are telling everything." Luca raised his hand as Dominick started to speak, cutting him off. "Martino tells me you are Rocco's friend, and that you are trying to help him. Is this true?"

"Si, signore."

Luca nodded knowingly. "And you are afraid, maybe, that Boggiano will keep the money?"

"Signore, Joe Boggiano is my capo..."

The big man put his hand on Dominick's back and gently propelled him toward a rose garden. The bushes, devoid of their leaves and blooms, were cactus-like, green and brown stems brisling with thorns.

"Martino is good with roses," Luca said. "Too bad he is not a good Italian."

The two Americans were just leaving when a Model T truck pulled up at the front. Another American got out and nodded to the men who were leaving.

Luca gestured toward the scene. "Frank handles the Americans well, but I suspect they have about as much respect for him as we do." He looked at Dominick again. "A man should not be afraid of who he is." Luca nodded in Martino's direction. "A pity for his children."

"Signore, I..."

"No, I will tell you what we are going to do. You are right. I am the headman here." He tapped his chest. "I will keep the money for Rocco. Do not worry about Boggiano. I will get a message to your capo. He can do nothing."

As Luca and Dominick made their way back toward the house they could see more people coming, some walking and some in carriages. Many were carrying food and presents. Two men began lighting a string of kerosene lanterns strung around the patio. After pouring himself a beer, Luca ambled over to talk with some other people he knew. Rather than just stand around, Dominick entered the house.

Pandemonium reigned inside. The kitchen table was stacked with food and the rich odor of spices filled the air. Women hustled here and there with armloads of decorations, and presents. Furniture in the parlor had been removed and a wooden trellis, decorated with red and white ribbons, stood in one corner. A red runner ran from the trellis to a doorway that opened into Frank's study. The double doors were closed. Behind them Dominick could hear feminine voices and laughter. An old gentleman stood solemnly in front of the doors, arms folded across his chest. As Dominick looked around he noticed Lou Piccini coming toward him. Lou, as usual, didn't look happy.

"Where is that Judas pig, Benedetti? It's almost five thirty."

"I don't know, signore. But, the wedding isn't until seven. The priest isn't even here yet."

"You mark my words, Prugitore. If Benedetti lets my Maria stand this time, I'll kill him!"

Dominick got a hollow feeling in his stomach. He had no doubt Lou meant what he said.

Suddenly Frank Martino was there, his arm circling Lou Piccini's shoulders. "There, there, Lou. Sam went into Youngstown. He should be back anytime now."

"But he has to arrange for the carriage to take him and Maria back to Ellwood City after the wedding. I swear to you by the Blessed Virgin, I will kill him yet if he lets my daughter stand alone."

Frank smiled at Dominick. "Why don't you take my carriage and go down to the station to meet him?"

Frank swung Lou away, motioning behind his back for Dominick to leave. "Come now, Lou. We must see to the band. Toni Santi brought his mandolin and..."

Outside the wind picked up, turning colder with the coming of night. Frank's one horse carriage stood hitched by the little barn behind the house. Dominick turned the horse down a dirt alley that ran behind the expansive lawns and barns. Further up the hill were the mansions and servant's quarters of the local industrial barons.

Dominick knew Sam preferred to ride the interurban trolley and decided to check the trolley stop near Caruzzi's saloon. Soon the clanging of the gong announced the arrival of car 139 from Youngstown.

Sam was dragging a heavy cloth sack down the aisle. Dominick waited by the door and when Sam reached him they wrestled the sack down the ladder and hefted it into the carriage.

"That sack is heavy!" Dominick exclaimed. "Did you rob a bank?"

Sam smiled. "Hard candy. A hundred pounds of it."

"A hundred pounds?"

"It will be a sweet wedding, although, maybe we should throw rice like the Americans. Rice is lighter, at least." Sam reached in his pocket and pulled out a small velvet box. "Pull over by that light, compare. I want to show you something."

Sam opened the box reverently and extended it toward Dominick with both hands. Inside were two slim gold bands.

Sam looked serious. "I would like for you to present these rings at the ceremony, compare."

"Si," Dominick said. He clucked the horse into a trot and headed toward the livery stable. "But first you must arrange for the wedding carriage. Then I must get you to Martino's before Maria's father starts looking for a shotgun."

Frank Martino was waiting for them on the front porch. "Where is the wedding carriage?" He looked worried.

"There is a driver that goes with it," Sam replied. "I told him to come about eleven." Sam nodded toward Dominick. "My friend will present the rings during the ceremony," he added.

Frank nodded and put his arms around the shoulders of both young men, ushering them inside. "Si, that is fine. But now we must get you cleaned up. It is almost seven."

"There is a bag of candy in your carriage," Dominick said, as Frank swept them into the kitchen pantry and began brushing dust from their coats.

"I'll take care of it," Frank replied firmly. "Come on now. Wash your face and hands." He handed them a comb. "Use it. You don't want to look like a couple of country bumpkins, do you?"

"Like what?" Sam asked.

"An American saying," Dominick explained to his friend. "He means like a couple of fools."

When they were through, Frank ushered them into the parlor. Folks stood on either side of the red carpet. Sam and Dominick walked to the front of the room where Father DeMita, from New Castle, was waiting under the trellis.

Susan played softly on the piano. When she finished the piece, she glanced at her husband standing by the study. Frank nodded solemnly and swung open the doors while Susan began the wedding march.

Maria stood in the doorway holding her father's arm. She wore a simple floor length, white dress. A lace veil covered her face. Lou Piccini, back straight and looking straight ahead, slowly led his daughter down the aisle behind two little girls carrying bouquets of chrysanthemums. .

After the ceremonies the band moved inside and began playing snappy tunes from the old country, while Sam and Maria were kept busy on the dance floor. Those dancing with the bride were given a pin and expected to pin money on her dress.

The driver of the wedding carriage, wearing a silk top hat and tails, was surprised when the crowd began pelting them with hard candy. He wasted no time trotting the horses down the street toward the train station.

It was well after midnight before Dominick took the trolley back to Hillsville. He was tired and confused. Sam Bennett was Black Hand through and through. Yet Sam counted him a friend—enough of a friend to be the best man at his wedding.

Later that morning he went to church with the Ciampanelli's, but afternoon found him back in Lowellville. He was curious to learn how much money Frank Martino collected for Rocco's bail. The crowd of guests had gathered once again, and there was still plenty of food, drink and music.

Dominick couldn't catch Frank Martino alone long enough to ask about Rocco's bail until early evening. They were in the kitchen where Frank was wiping dust from jugs of wine just brought up from the cellar.

Frank paused briefly and patted Dominick's forearm. "We will be all right, I think. With the money Mrs. Racca got from selling their house we have almost enough."

"Is Luca Caruzzi holding the money, signore?"

"Si," Frank answered, grabbing two jugs of homemade wine. "No need to worry."

Frank nodded toward a third jug of wine setting on the floor. "Grab that for me, will you?" He smiled cunningly. "I like to follow the Bible when I can."

"Signore?"

"You remember the wedding feast? When Jesus turned water into wine?"

"Si, but I don't understand?"

"The master of the feast said that most people serve good wine until the guests are well drunk, then bring out the poor wine." Frank nodded toward the jugs as he started toward the music. "'Don't drink this stuff. If you want good wine there is a bottle in the cupboard!"

Chapter 14

Docato stood in the doorway, nervously wringing his hat as if it had just fallen into a mud puddle. "D...Dominick. Signore B..Bo..Boggiano w..wa..wants to see you right away!"

Dominick noticed the boy was stuttering more and more lately. "I'm on my way to work, Docato. Please tell Signore Boggiano that I will stop by this afternoon."

Docato shook his head frantically. "N..N..No! He s..said, I m..must catch you before you go to work. H..He said you must g..go to town with him."

"Docato, I must earn a living, you know."

"H..He is v..very upset, Dominick. He f..fr..frightens me!"

Dominick sighed. "Very well. Tell Signore Boggiano, I will be over after I change clothes."

As he stripped out of his bib's and into a sturdy pair of woolen trousers, Dominick thought about Boggiano. He had no doubt that the object of his frustration was Rocco's bail money. Could Joe know he had betrayed him? He pushed the thought away.

Dominick was about to turn off the wagon road onto a shortcut to Boggiano's, when he noticed a round figure approaching in a livery wagon. He waited by the side of the road trying to quell his rising fear.

"Dominick, my boy! Thought I might save you some steps."

Dominick walked around the back of the wagon. He wanted to see if Joe brought his shotgun. He didn't see it.

"What is the problem, signore?" he said, after he climbed onto the seat beside Joe. "Docato seemed very frightened."

"Everything frightens that one," Joe said, flipping the reins to get the team moving. "But sometimes fear buys respect. Remember that. Some day you may be a capo."

"Si." Dominick paused to choose his words carefully. "I am sorry I failed you, signore."

"Yeah, I heard he pushed you around."

Dominick tried to hide his surprise. Apparently, Luca Caruzzi made up a cover story to protect him. "I can take care of myself, signore."

"Si. But you did well to control yourself. We don't want trouble."

The wagon gave a terrific jolt as it bounced over some ruts, nearly throwing Dominick out of the seat.

"Don't you ever take a buggy, signore?"

"Too light and fluffy. Besides, this way I can get supplies while we are in New Castle."

"So, we are going into New Castle then?"

Joe nodded. "Si, apparently they have enough money for Rocco's bail. They want to bring him out today, and you are the only one around here that speaks such good American."

Despite their differences, Joe Boggiano and Luca Caruzzi greeted each other with polite indifference. Dominick greeted Frank Martino warmly.

"I am surprised to see you here, signore."

Frank shrugged. "Signore Caruzzi claims I am a good diplomat with the Americans."

Si, but you also speak English, Dominick thought. He glanced at the two headmen. Is it that you don't trust me, or that you don't trust each other? He pushed the former thought away. He had to.

"Come! Let us see what this American attorney can do now," Caruzzi declared, pulling a bulging envelope from his coat pocket and waving it at Boggiano.

J.W. Boffitt's cheeks bulged with short puffs of air after Dominick placed the money on the little man's desk and explained what they wanted.

"I told you before, young man; the court will not let him out."

Dominick slammed his fist on the bulging envelope and leaned over the desk. He kept his voice low. Deliberate. "The court set the bail at $2000." Uncoiling his fist, he grabbed the short pudgy fingers of the attorney and planted them over the envelope. "Here is your bail money. I suggest you get Mr. Racca out today."

There was a loud metallic click, and JW's eyes bulged even more when he saw the hard, battered face of Luca Caruzzi staring at him. Luca was cleaning his fingernails with a huge switchblade.

The brown envelope crinkled loudly as the pudgy fingers wrapped around the bundle of money. Then the fat man bobbed to his feet like a cork on a pond.

"Yes," he sputtered. "Of course. I'll see what I can do." He began stuffing the money into his coat pocket.

Caruzzi looked at Boggiano with raised eyebrows. Luca flicked his fingers toward Dominick, indicating that he should accompany the attorney. Boggiano glanced at Dominick and jerked his head in a brief nod.

"They wish me to accompany you, sir."

Boffitt shook his head and puffed his cheeks. "Impossible!" He sucked in another breath of air. "This is court business, and...they don't allow foreigners in the court house."

Luca Caruzzi, still cleaning his fingernails and smiling wolfishly, took a step toward the attorney.

Dominick held up his hand.

Caruzzi stopped.

"I'm afraid you don't understand, Mr. Boffitt." Dominick nodded toward the two headmen. "They think it would be best if I accompany you."

"Yes, but of course." The round little man was trying to squeeze between a wooden filing cabinet and the furthest corner of his desk.

An hour and a half later, Dominick returned and laid the envelope of money on the attorney's desk.

Luca reached the envelope before Joe and snatched it off the desk. "What is this?" he demanded, when he saw the money was still there.

"The judge wouldn't let him out. He said the bail is now five thousand dollars."

Luca exploded into a fit of cursing. With a backhand he scattered a sheaf of papers from the corner of Attorney Boffitt's desk. He would have done more damage had not Boggiano's harsh laughter brought him up on the balls of his feet.

"So, signore!" Joe exclaimed. "We must continue our collections. This should be profitable for all of us, no?" He rocked back on his heels, taken by another burst of laughter.

Luca fixed an angry glare on Dominick. "Where is that fat little attorney? I swear by all the saints, he will pay for this treachery."

Another peal of laughter erupted from Boggiano. Luca wheeled to glare at the bald headman from Hillsville.

Joe waved his arms in the air. "Si! Kill an American attorney and they will be hanging Italians from every tree they can find. That's why you'll never be anything but a saloon keeper, Caruzzi! You're only smart enough to lick Don Sochetti's boots!"

Luca's face turned purple. His hand slipped into his coat pocket and emerged with a metallic click. He took a step toward Boggiano, the knife gripped low in his right hand.

Joe's thick brow folded over the bridge of his nose, then with surprising agility for a man his size, bounced back and to the side. At the same time his hand came out of his pocket with a rolling action, the blade of a straight razor uncurling from his fingertips.

The two men crouched and began circling each other on the balls of their feet; spitting curses and insults in Italian. Dominick was too shocked to move. He couldn't believe this was happening. Suddenly, he caught a blur of movement out of the corner of his eye. He ducked as a wooden chair flew by and crashed into the attorney's desk between the two combatants.

Welding a coat rack like a club, Frank Martino rushed between Boggiano and Caruzzi. Luca ducked as Frank swung the coat rack. The momentum carried the little man around toward Boggiano, where Frank managed to bring it smashing down against the floor. Broken slivers of wood pelted the feet and shins of the headman from Hillsville. Frank picked up the broken coat rack and slammed it down again with a crash before raising both fists over his head like writhing snakes.

"What is the matter with you?" he screamed, his face bright red. "You'll get us all thrown in jail, and there won't be anyone to raise our bail!"

Dominick looked at the two combatants. They were both smiling sheepishly.

Boggiano, carefully folded his razor before stuffing it back into his pocket. He waved his hand, palm up, toward Caruzzi. "My apologies, signore. Sometimes my mouth gets in front of my brain."

"You both have brains in your, ur, er,…" Frank's slurring came to a stuttering halt as he slumped against the desk, his trembling hands gripping the edge tightly. Tears ran freely down his cheeks.

Both headmen glared at him.

Frank waved a trembling hand in front of his bowed head. "I don't know what I'm saying."

Luca walked over to the trembling man and put one arm around Frank's shoulders. "It's all right, Frank. You probably saved both our lives. His from my knife, and mine from a hangman's rope."

Boggiano snorted. "Come along, Dominick. I believe our work is finished here."

Two days later Dominick was summoned to a meeting in Pittsburgh and had time to reflect as a local of the Lake Erie and Pittsburgh chugged south along the Ohio River. Somewhere between Coraopolis and Pittsburgh, lulled by the slowly rocking coach and rhythmic clanking of the wheels, he fell asleep. His dreams were fitful. A collage of horrors chased themselves through his mind. There was Boggiano and Caruzzi cutting each other to pieces in Boffitt's office. Boffitt, lying in a pool of blood by the doorway with his throat slit. Dominick and Frank Martino were standing on a gallows with a hangman's noose around their necks. Frank's wife and children were among the crowd. He could hear Susan telling the children that their father was really an Irishman. As he plunged through the trap door, Dominick caught a glimpse of Rosa running wild-eyed through the woods, Siciliano loping through the shadows behind her with a knife in his hand.

His strangled shout and flailing arms startled the gray haired conductor shaking his shoulder. "Easy there, young fellow!"

Dominick ran a trembling hand through his thick hair. "I'm sorry. I guess I was dreaming." Folks in the seat across the isle were staring at him.

The conductor held out an envelope for him. "A man who got off at the last stop said I was to give this to you before we get into Pittsburgh."

Dominick took the envelope. "What did this man look like?"

"Rough looking character with a scar on his face," the trainman replied.

"Thank you, signore."

The conductor frowned at the unexpected use of Italian, then moved on through the car. "Last stop, Pittsburgh Station," he called in a rolling tone that carried over the clacking rail joints.

Dominick opened the envelope. Inside was a set of tickets from Pittsburgh to Philadelphia via the Pennsylvania Railroad. A note scribbled in Italian warned that a mutual friend would be waiting in a Pullman after the train left Harrisburg.

Union Station at Pittsburgh squatted on the ground floor of an imposing stone building that stacked the Pennsylvania Railroad Company offices six stories into the smog-laden sky. A large metal dome, almost four stories high and supported by a spider web of steel girders stretched over the passenger tracks in the main rail yard. It was a wet, steamy world under the dome with clanking journal boxes, puffing engines, clouds of hissing steam, the rattle of baggage carts and the shouts of busy trainmen. Over everything hung the permeating fumes of hot oil, steam and grease. Glancing across two sets of empty tracks, Dominick could see the magenta colored coaches of a waiting Pennsy train—its engine belching a periodic hollow sounding chug.

An elaborate system of wrought iron gateways guided debarking passengers into the bustle of the main station. A huge timetable behind the ticket counter announced the Pennsy's express to Altoona, Harrisburg and Philadelphia was scheduled to leave on track five. A wall clock beside the timetable showed he had twenty minutes until departure.

Dominick grabbed the handrail and pulled himself quickly onto the steel steps between a pair of waiting Pullmans before making his way forward. A haze of yellowish-brown smoke and the murmur of masculine voices greeted him when he opened the door of the smoking car. Reaching into his coat pocket for a cigar, he wondered who was to meet him at Harrisburg. He fervently hoped it wasn't Superintendent Cafee. He was surprised to discover he possessed a Pullman ticket for the last leg of his journey.

As the train pulled slowly out of the Harrisburg station, Dominick worked his way past passengers lounging in plush chairs under a mahogany headboard. Frank Dimuro sat in one of two chairs facing each other across a small wooden table, its top polished to a glistening sheen.

"Excuse me, sir. Is this seat taken?"

Superintendent Dimuro looked up from an open folder in his lap. "Stow that satchel will you. You're not riding in a coach now."

Dominick looked at his satchel as though it had suddenly turned into a rattlesnake.

Dimuro flicked his hand toward the rear of the car. "Give it to one of the porters at the galley. They have a small baggage compartment back there."

"I wasn't expecting a Pullman ticket," he challenged.

"Enjoy it. This doesn't happen often, signore." He surprised Dominick by his sudden lapse into Italian. "The people we are after normally don't travel by Pullman either."

"I see."

"No you don't. Speak Italiano, signore. It will afford us privacy in more ways than one."

As if in answer to his statement, a man sitting across the aisle noisily folded his newspaper and, with a mild curse, hurried toward the forward end of the car.

"Now you see!" Frank exclaimed.

Dominick noticed his boss was careful not to use his name.

"Could I fetch you gentlemens' a drink?"

Dominick looked into the dark face of a porter.

"Bring us each a glass of red wine, please." Frank answered. "Italian red wine," he added a bit louder.

As Dominick handed his satchel to the porter, another person moved away from their vicinity.

Superintendent Dimuro carefully tucked his papers into a leather portfolio before the waiter returned with their drinks. "Now, perhaps, we can get down to business."

Soon the train was racing along the river bottoms and valleys of Pennsylvania Deutschland at almost seventy-five miles per hour, the engine slowing occasionally to scoop water from special tanks lying between the rails.

"Can you tell me what this is all about, signore?"

"Actually, I was hoping you would be able to tell me," Frank replied.

"I'm afraid not." He paused a moment to glance moodily into his wine. "I was afraid I was to meet Superintendent Cafee. We don't usually get along very well."

"Humph! Well, I suspect he'll be at the meeting this evening." Frank shook a thick finger at Dominick. "You let me do the talking, unless Bob asks you a direct question, understand?"

"Do you mean Signore Pinkerton?"

Frank sipped at his wine and nodded. "Si, he is the one who called the meeting. I suspect the folks who hired us are getting nervous. We've spent a lot of money to date, and I understand the governor stuck his neck out to finance our mission in the first place. I imagine they've about reached the bottom of the barrel."

Dominick felt a pang of alarm. "Surely they won't cancel the operation?"

"We run a business, signore."

He sat up stiff in his chair, his heart racing.

"Best tell me where we stand with regard to the successful completion of our mission," Superintendent Dimuro added softly.

Dominick brought his boss up to date. At length, the train pulled into Market Street Station in Philadelphia.

"We'll leave separately," Frank stated. "Be at the company office within the hour."

Superintendent Gerald Tearce presided over the meeting. "I believe all of you gentlemen know each other, with the possible exception of Number 89 and Mr. Saville my superintendent." His hand swept back toward Dominick. "Jim, meet Dominick Prugitore, better known to us as Number 89."

"Now gentlemen," Mr Tearce continued, "let's cut right into the lean meat, shall we? Mr. Pinkerton sends his regrets. He would have been here except for pressing business in New York. As you know, Governor Pennypacker authorized Dr. Kalbfus, the Executive Secretary of The Board of Game Commissioners, to hire our agency to apprehend the murderer of the game warden in New Castle. Unfortunately, this is the governor's last term in office, and Dr. Kalbfus has written to me expressing concern about funding the operation into 1907. They are looking for results, gentlemen."

Mr. Tearce looked at Dominick. "That brings us to you, 89."

Frank Dimuro stood up. "Ah, perhaps I should clarify the situation in Hillsville first, sir. It's very explosive just now and..."

"Later, Frank." Mr. Tearce interrupted. "We didn't bring this young man here by Pullman just for fun."

Superintendent Cafee nearly jumped out of his seat. "Pullman! I came by coach."

"Please sit down, Elmer. Superintendent Dimuro needed to consult with his operative."

"That's preposterous."

"It was approved by Robert Pinkerton himself, Elmer. Now please, sit down."

Elmer Cafee sat, but the looks he cast at the young detective radiated pure hate.

Mr. Tearce glanced at Dominick. "It's your show, son."

Dominick detailed his actions. "So you see, sir," he concluded, "if it could be arranged for Rocco to be let out of jail, for a little while at least, I have reason to believe he would confide in me about his part in the Houk murder."

"Yes. Well, we shall see what might be done in that regard," Mr. Tearce declared eventually.

Elmer Cafee leaped to his feet again. His face and neck were crimson. The little man jerked his glasses off of his ears with shaking hands. "This is preposterous! Preposterous, I say!"

His voice shook with indignation.

"I have been with this company for ten years. Ten years mind you! And I was a police officer for seven years before that."

"Never, gentlemen, have I listened to such a preposterous statement that blatantly demands a known criminal, who has attempted to escape the country already, be allowed to go free because this..," he pointed a trembling finger at Dominick "...this brash, inexperienced foreigner thinks a criminal will fall down and confess to him. Gentlemen, he is one of them! Prugitore has fought us every step of the way. How do we know he isn't working with these criminals so Rocco Racca can make good his escape?"

Suddenly, Dominick was on his feet with Frank Dimuro right behind him. "Sit down," Frank whispered, putting pressure on his shoulder. "Sit down, now!"

Reluctantly, Dominick sank into his chair.

"I can not believe you are considering this man's statement for even one second," Cafee concluded.

"Elmer," Mr. Tearce replied, "it is obvious you don't understand undercover work."

"Undercover...undercover work?" Superintendent Cafee choked. "You put one of their own kind in with these...these foreigners and expect them to turn on their own countrymen? I tell you, sir. This is not good police work!"

Gerald Tearce sounded tired. "One more time, Elmer. Sit down." Mr. Tearce stood up as Elmer Cafee's arms dropped to his sides. "I said, sit down!"

Mr. Cafee sank heavily into the chair.

A spark of fire lit Gerald Tearce's eyes. "You forget, sir. We are not a police department. We are an investigating service and, from the beginning, covert operations has been a major factor in our success. From now on you will stay completely clear of Number 89 whenever you encounter him in the field. As far as you are concerned he does not exist, other than as another suspect of the investigation. Do you understand, sir?"

Cafee barely nodded his head. He seemed to be staring at his shoelaces.

"Number 89 is under the supervision of Mr. Dimuro, and his operation is separate from yours. Not only are you not to interfere with Dimuro's operation, but you are to cooperate in every way possible. Do you understand?"

"Quite."

Mr. Tearce studied Cafee for a moment. The little man was hooking his glasses back over his ears. "Very well then. I will meet with you supervisors at eight o'clock in the morning." Tearce turned to Dominick. "I am sorry, young man, but there is a train leaving for Pittsburgh at midnight. I want you back in Hillsville as soon as possible. Thank you for your fine effort to date."

Mr. Tearce produced an envelope bearing the monogram PRR within a keystone. "Here are your return tickets, 89."

On the way back to Broad Street Station, Dominick noticed that the tickets were for coach fare only. He would catch what sleep he could on the pitching seat of a railway car.

Chapter 15

When Dominick arrived in Hillsville the first snow had fallen. Flurries, whirling in from the Northwest through the night and following day, pilled up more until nearly eight inches blanketed the shanties and quarries of Hillsville. After supper Dominick sought out Boggiano. Second class members were required to inform the headman whenever they left or returned from a trip. He found him at Jim Rossi's saloon. The place was crowded and games of scopa were in progress at all of the tables, except one.

Vito Siciliano sat with his chair leaning against the wall and his feet propped on the table. Vito stared at the crowd like a mountain lion studying a herd of deer. Beside him Mario Nardozi peered sullenly into a half empty bottle of beer. When Dominick entered, Vito's face froze into razor sharp angles. The lion had found its prey.

Dominick forced himself to look into that frigid stare a moment before moving toward a booming voice he recognized as Boggiano's. He could feel Siciliano's gaze follow him across the room. As he reached Boggiano's table one of the men pushed back his chair.

"Hey!" Joe yelled, "What's the matter with you? You can't afford a few cigars?"

The man muttered some apologies and began to bow his way into the crowd.

Joe flipped his hand in the air. "Disgraziato!" With a scowl, he grabbed for the pile of cards to throw at the man.

Dominick laid his hand on the back of the vacated chair. "You wouldn't throw away those cards just when your luck is about to change, would you?"

"So, back from Pittsburgh, I see." Joe began to shuffle the cards as Dominick took his seat. Then he glanced at him from under a heavy brow. "So, how was your trip?"

Dominick shrugged. "A cousin of mine was afraid because he was asked to join the Society."

Joe stopped shuffling and stared at him. "And what did you tell him?"

"I said he was being foolish, that the Society would take care of him and protect him."

Joe nodded and began dealing. He paused when he got to Dominick. "You'll be glad to know Rocco Racca got out of jail this afternoon."

"So what is that to me?"

"Don't try to hide it." Joe growled. "You like that worthless dog." He continued dealing cards. "First you get in trouble with Cerini over him, and then very nearly get killed by Siciliano on top of that."

"Rocco was capo when I joined the Society, signore. Perhaps, I owed him something."

"You paid him back." Joe's voice fell into a low rumble. "What I want to know is where do you stand with me, huh?"

Dominick felt his blood pressure rise. He stood up slowly and made a flourishing bow, sweeping the table with his fingers and scattering cards. "I shall always remain your obedient servant, signore," he said solemnly.

Joe roared with laughter, turning heads. A few men at the table laughed nervously.

"Sit down, compare. Sometimes you're so serious, you're funny."

Dominick bent down to scoop cards from the floor. The move gave him a chance to calm himself. His hands were trembling when he took his seat.

"I suppose you will have to visit the little whore," Joe continued. "I hear he's staying in Lowellville, probably at Martino's." Then he paused, brow furled. "Horrible waste of money, that."

Dominick played several winning hands, piling up a small stack of cigars for him and Boggiano. When Joe got up to talk with some other society members, he excused himself from the game. He was still tired from his trip, and worried. Apparently the agency had pulled some strings in New Castle to get Rocco out on bail. The young detective knew it represented a last chance for him to extract a confession from the former headman. Yet, despite pressure to complete the case, he also knew he had to be careful. Rocco was no fool.

When Dominick stepped from Jim's ramshackled porch he was glad he had worn his rubber over-shoes. The early December snow was heavy with moisture. As he cut down the path that led back to the Peanut Settlement he scooped up a handful and absently packed a snowball. He wondered if he should rush over to see Rocco, or pretend indifference. Perhaps, it would be better to let Rocco come to him. Movement in the woods just in front of him brought his head up with a snap. Then fear gripped his soul.

Vito Siciliano stepped into a patch of pale moonlight only an arm length in front of him. Rustling in the brush behind him caused Dominick to slowly turn his head. Mario Nardozi stood beside the path to his rear. Dominick felt his knees begin to tremble.

"Where do you think you're going, boy?" Vito sounded like a growling dog talking. A mean growling dog.

I'm going to die here, he thought. Somehow the horrid realization calmed him a little. He realized he had stopped breathing and slowly let out a long stream of frosty vapor. "I had planned on going home, signore." There was only the faintest tremor in his voice.

Vito took a step closer. "Oh yeah? Well, I don't like you, boy." He seemed to spit the last word through his missing front tooth.

"You know how Boggiano feels about vendettas, especially without his permission." It sounded weak even in his own ears, but the leer disappeared off the ugly man's face.

"You don't have to kill him," Mario quipped.

Suddenly a knife appeared in Vito's hand. "Hold him, Nardozi, while I cut his face!"

Dominick reacted from instinct. He smashed the snowball into Vito's eyes. As the big man staggered back a step, flailing and sputtering, Dominick kicked his leg. More from luck than anything the blow struck Vito's knee and he went down with a curse.

Dominick started running down the slippery path but as he rushed by Vito he felt something burn across his hip. He knew without looking that Vito had slashed him as he ran by.

Mario started to help the bigger man up, but Vito pushed him away. "Get him!"

Mario spun around and took off after Dominick, but the lad was wearing shoes that slipped in the snow and slush. Soon Vito shoved Nardozi out of the way.

When he broke onto the snow packed street at Peanut, Dominick could sense that one of them was gaining on him. Lighted windows cast a warm homey glow about his feet as he ran by. Realizing he didn't have time to turn into one of the homes, he plunged into the woods and cut onto the trail that led down to the railroad. His lungs and hip felt like scalding fire. The pant-leg below his wounded hip was soaked.

Dominick's legs were weakening, each step becoming heavy and forced. Suddenly he felt fingers groping for his coat and then the path dropped away, plunging toward the railroad and the river beyond. Dominick threw himself into the air. He landed hard about four feet down the hill and began sliding like a toboggan down the packed trail. Sticks and twigs tore at his face, and stones slammed into his body as he rocketed down the snowy hill. Suddenly he spilled into a semi-frozen ditch beside the track. The rumbling of heavy ore cars, moving slowly along the rails above his head, shook the ground. He began scrambling up the bank toward the track bed. He heard a curse and a splash as Vito rolled into the ditch behind him. Then a vice-like grip clamped onto his ankle. He kicked frantically, heard another curse, and then he was free. The train was slowly working up speed as it pulled away from a siding. Dominick staggered to his feet and focused on a brakeman's ladder gliding by at the front end of an ore car. Grabbing for it, he felt his feet sweep out from under him then felt a heavy steel wheel brush against one foot. A rush of adrenaline kicked in and he scrambled up and under the car's overhang.

A cold wind whipped at his wet clothes as he balanced himself over a network of steel supports that slanted back toward the car's bed. There wasn't room to stand fully erect, and when he glanced back he saw Vito's hands grip the ladder.

A wave of panic and exhaustion almost made him give up. Then red-hot anger filled him. He started crabbing his way toward the center of the car. Looking out over the coupling he could see the top of the leading car about four feet away, too far to reach from where he stood. Glancing down, he could see the ties and snow covered gravel of the rail bed whipping past as the car rolled and rumbled over the rail joints. They were going faster than a man could walk and still picking up speed.

Dominick focused on the coupling, yawing and bucking between the rolling cars. With one hand clinging to the car's overhang, he cautiously slid one foot onto the coupling, each rail joint sending tremors through his body. Kicking at a patch of frozen snow, he eased his other foot out while reaching for one of the leading car's supports with his other hand. He still couldn't reach it. Inching forward, he allowed his knees to flex absorbing the coupling's energy while his body swayed with the rhythm of the rolling car. Now he was at the point where the couplings joined as both cars rolled and swayed over the tracks. Carefully, he slid his forward foot onto the other car's coupling, stepping over where they joined like clasp fists. Suddenly the full fury of their energy slammed into him. One coupling bounced up and the other down at the same instant, then one suddenly jerked right, the other left— small movements, but violent. Sensing motion by the latter, Dominick lunged for the other support, leaving go of the one behind as he caught it. Then his foot slipped, and he went down.

Momentum threw him forward, and fresh pain slammed into his arm and chest as he fell on the coupling stunning him momentarily. His legs straddled the pitching steel, gripping the cold hardness of it with the tenacity of life. Then he felt his pant leg catch in the maw where the couplings ground together; drawing his leg into the grinding steel. Instinctively he grabbed at the frame of the other car with numb hands and pulled. He felt the pant leg tear then slipped again and suddenly found he was hanging sideways off the pitching couplings, his open jacket slapping off rail ties rushing past inches below his shoulder. If he slipped further he knew he would be lost. Each shutter of the wheels rolling over a rail joint rippled painfully through his body. Pulling with the hand that gripped the back edge of the car in front of him and shinning with his legs, Dominick inched forward until he could again grasp the bottom edge of the lead car. Pulling with every ounce of his draining strength, he managed to get one arm over the car's edge. He felt the heavy wheel brushing his shoulder and realized if the open end of his jacket caught under the wheel he would be pulled under. With a final surge of adrenalin he heaved himself partly onto the car's frame then screamed as his right foot dropped down and slammed into a rail tie, ripping his boot and pealing it down over his heel. Somehow he managed to get his leg up and pull himself under the car's overhang. Glancing back he looked fearfully for Vito, but the Society's assassin was nowhere to be seen. Shivering, weeping and bleeding, Dominick huddled under the back of the oar car until the train pulled into the rail yard at New Castle.

When the train shuttered to a stop, he crawled painfully down from the car and limped away before the yardmen came looking for the hotbox that caused the train to be delayed on a siding near Hillsville. Cut and badly bruised, Dominick felt fortunate to be alive.

He spent the next couple of days recuperating and then sought out Boggiano. The burly headman flew into a rage when he learned of Vito's attempt on his life. "You are under my protection now," he declared finally, thumping his chest. "Vito will not bother you again."

"I don't know if it will do any good, Signore. Siciliano seems to fear no man."

Joe slammed a meaty finger painfully into Dominick's bruised chest. "Oh, yeah! Well, you can better well believe he fears the Society of Honor!"

When Superintendent Dimuro received his written report, Dominick was called into Pittsburgh to explain. Dimuro was satisfied only after Dominick told him he was now under Boggiano's protection. Frank confirmed that they had managed to get Rocco out on bail once again. "Some people put themselves on a limb to give you this final chance," he declared gruffly.

The following evening Dominick took the trolley over to Frank Martino's house in Lowellville, but no one was home. Alarm gripped him. What if Rocco had run away again? On the way home he stopped at Mrs. Firilli's store, which sat near the Catholic Church on the hill overlooking Kennedy's Crossing. She gave him a glass of wine, and told him Rocco was going to stop there in the morning.

By ten thirty the next morning Rocco arrived with a wagon and team, his breath clinging in small icicles to his bushy mustache. Mrs. Firilli came rushing through a curtain that separated their back rooms bellowing wails of welcome. Rocco and Dominick greeted each other with a nod, unable to get in more than a word around Mrs. Firilli's ministrations and questions about his wife. After she disappeared behind the curtain, the two men talked of work at the quarry. In between greetings from customers who visited the store, Rocco inquired as to whether certain people still lived in the area.

"Many have left," Dominick confided. "Boggiano has been trying to frighten everyone into joining the Society."

Rocco shook his head. "Better to have a few handpicked men than to sign up the whole town. But it is none of my affair."

Again well-wishers interrupted them. Finally, Dominick went to the counter and bought a handful of cigars.

"Let's take a ride, signore," he suggested, handing one of the cigars to Rocco.

"Si, I left my wife at her parent's house. Perhaps, they will have dinner ready."

After they got the team moving toward Peanut, Dominick was unsure how to start. Finally he took a deep breath and said, "When you were in jail, compare, you were mad at every one of us, although we were all working hard to get you out. One day, Lawyer Boffitt said to me, 'There is no use collecting money to get Rocco Racca out, because the court will not let him go with $2000 bail.'"

Rocco exhaled a cloud of smoke. "Why?"

Dominick glanced at Rocco. The older man still looked formidable.

"I did not tell you everything when you were in jail, compare, because it would have made you downhearted." He paused, watching Rocco carefully. "Boffitt said the court blames you for the Houk murder, also for all the cutting that has been done around here."

Rocco scowled, his face hard. "How can they blame me? They don't know who did it."

"That is what I told the lawyer, but you know more about the court than I do."

"That's right. They can't prove anything."

The rig rattled up to a neat looking shanty on the edge of town. Warm smells of Italian cooking swam invitingly in the cold air. "Come on, compare, Signora Soccisano knows how to cook. Too bad her daughter didn't pay attention when she was living at home."

After dinner, Rocco wanted Dominick to take him over to see the foreman at the Johnson quarry so he could collect money owed to men who had left the area. When he interpreted for Rocco, the foreman informed him that Rocco would have to get a paper signed by the squire saying he could collect for these men. On the way back to Signore Soccisano's house, Rocco sadly shook his head.

"You see what the world is coming to. I had their numbers put on those cars. That money should come to me. A good example of American justice, is it not?" Suddenly Rocco reached over and slapped Dominick on the knee. "I would like you to come to Ellwood City on Sunday. My brother-in-law is having a baby baptized, and there will be a party. We'll have a good time."

When Rocco and his wife left, Dominick watched them go with mixed feelings. He knew he would have to stay very close to Rocco if he hoped to glean a confession from him.

That evening, despite the cold, he went to Joe Boggiano's. Several people were there, including Sam Bennett. The men were crowded into a semi-circle in the parlor. With Siciliano standing behind him, Joe sat in a chair like a king holding court. One of the workers Dominick recognized from the Johnson quarry was standing in front of the headman. He was a thin man and stood with his back straight. Dominick noticed he had not removed his hat. He felt a pang of fear for the man.

"So," Joe was saying, "you not only refuse to join the Society, but you wouldn't allow one of my men to work in your block." Joe pointed at the man's head. "And get that hat off, you disrespectful dog!"

The man had a soft voice that quavered slightly, but he continued to hold his head erect and look directly at the headman while he spoke. "That is my block. I will hire whomever I choose, signore." He made no move to touch his hat.

Dominick expected Joe to jump up and pound the man through the floor. Instead the headman had a dangerously bemused look on his face. "Vito, give this dog a little lesson in respect."

Vito flowed around Joe's chair with deadly grace and snatched the hat from the man's head. With a leer, Vito produced a stiletto and cut the hat in two. He held the two halves out and when the man reached for them, Vito let them fall to the floor. The ugly assassin was grinning as he stepped behind Boggiano's chair.

The thin man began trembling, but Dominick suspected it was more with rage than fear. He made no move to retrieve the pieces of his hat, only continued to stare at Boggiano.

"I fine you twenty-five dollars for refusing to permit a member of this society to work in your block. This you will pay to Sam Bennett by next payday." Joe raised his voice slightly. "Fail in this, and I will have Vito pay you a visit." Joe drew his finger across his own cheek in a slashing motion. "If you still refuse to pay..." he shrugged, "...there may be a new widow in Hillsville."

The man's shoulders slumped before he slowly bent down to retrieve the pieces of his hat.

A profound silence reigned as the man turned to go. After the door closed, Joe stood to address the little crowd of society members that had gathered in his home.

"Let this be a lesson," he said. "I will not tolerate disobedience. I don't give a care if it is from a society member or not!" Joe glared around the room. "I want all the men in this community to become members of The Society of Honor." He banged a meaty fist into an equally meaty palm for emphasis. "I want each of you to bring in one new member each month. If you don't, you will be fined ten dollars. Is that clear?"

A man standing near Sam Bennett spoke up. "Permesso, signore?"

Joe nodded.

"But what about those who refuse to join? Ten American dollars is often a week's pay for us, and we have families to feed."

Joe's thick lips pouted thoughtfully as his head nodded in sympathy. "If someone refuses to give you an answer after a month, you will bring his name to me." He beckoned toward where Vito was standing. "Then Vito will be our ambassador to that man."

An evil leer slid up one side of Siciliano's face.

No one else smiled except Boggiano.

After the meeting, Dominick was talking with some men outside when Siciliano shoved his way through the crowd and grabbed him painfully by the shoulder. "I don't know how you survived that fall from the train, boy, and I don't care. But there will be another time. I'll be watching, and some dark night you just won't come home."

Dominick started to speak, to tell Vito he was under Boggiano's protection, but the assassin shook him into silence before jerking him so close their faces were almost touching.

"No one will know, boy," he hissed. "And even if they did no one would dare tell!" With that he shoved Dominick into the startled crowd before turning into the night.

Just past mid-December the weather turned bitter. Dominick was eating a lunch that Rosa and Mrs. Ciampanelli had packed for him when he heard a familiar voice.

"You are a sorry sight, compare."

Dominick looked up to see Rocco regarding him with amusement. Dominick's gloves and pant legs had frozen solid. "It's a living," he replied. A hearty sneeze caused his sandwich to drop into the mud. The young man seemed frozen to the rock he was sitting on.

"Come on," Rocco said, holding out his hand to help him stand. "I must go to New Castle to see about my trial, and I could use your services."

Dominick allowed Rocco to pull him up and began stomping to get the blood circulating in his feet again. "I am afraid I'm broke, compare. I won't have any money until payday." It was a lie, of course, but Dimuro had been complaining about his expenses lately.

"I'll pay." Rocco gestured with a hand at Dominick's muddy clothes. "Meet me at Nick Sparaio's store after you change. I want to see if he's doing any better there than I did."

Later they stopped at Mrs. Firilli's store where Rocco bought lunch. When they were finished, they caught the trolley into New Castle and went directly to Attorney Boffitt's office. They found the office locked, so they went over to the courthouse. No one was there either, but Dominick checked a posting of trial dates on the bulletin board. There was no mention of Rocco's trial. When Rocco led the way to an Italian restaurant for supper it was already getting dark. While they were waiting for their meal, Dominick tried to push Rocco once again into talking about the Houk murder. This time a dark cloud seemed to descend over the older man's face. He looked at Dominick. "I think maybe you ask too many questions about this thing."

Dominick reacted the way the Society taught him. He jumped to his feet and slammed his fist on the table, spilling some wine from his glass.

"You!" he said through clenched teeth. "I've been your friend when nobody else cares what happens. I spent my own money running around trying to get you out of jail, and now you accuse me of treachery?"

Rocco's eyes widened. "OK, OK! It's just this trial I guess. Come on, have some supper and forget this, no?"

Dominick settled slowly into his chair. "Fine," he said softly, "but I'm afraid you don't understand how serious this thing is to the American authorities."

Tension prevailed throughout the rest of the meal, and Dominick wondered if everything he worked for had just gone down the gutter.

The next morning he found that water seeping into the quarry bottom where he worked was over the tops of his boots. He decided to ask for a new place, or go back to the Peanut quarry.

Sam Bennett was just coming out of the company offices when he arrived. Sam grabbed him by the arm and pulled him a few steps away from the office. "They are going to pay me to bring in laborers," Sam whispered. "Will you help train them?"

"Si, I will help, but they will have to help me drill."

Sam smiled. "You won't need help to drill after the first of the year, compare. They will have steam drills by then. They also told me the company is going to supply explosives for free."

Sam told him the quarry's production of high-grade limestone was down. The stone was used as flux in the steel mills around Pittsburgh, and the mills were urging the quarry to increase production. The limiting factor, so far as limestone was concerned, was a shortage of laborers. Dominick understood why.

That evening he went to Jim Rossi's saloon. Sam was talking with Boggiano when Dominick came in behind a gust of frigid air. Joe called him over.

"What's it doing out there?" he asked.

"Nothing so far, but the air has a raw feel about it. I think it's going to snow."

Joe nodded a baldheaded affirmation. He looked thoughtful. "Are you going home for Christmas then?"

"If you have no objections, signore."

Joe shook his head. "A man should be with his family for the holidays." Then he stabbed a thick finger at Dominick's chest. "After the holidays, I want you to hang close to Sam here. He's second in command now, so I want you to travel with him. You must learn the ways of the Society."

"Si," Dominick answered cautiously. Somehow he didn't think that was the end of it.

Joe bobbed his head. "Good! I want you to go to classes again. You need more training." Then his thick brow folded over the bridge of his nose. "I also want you to move in with Nick Sparaio."

"But why, signore? I have a good arrangement with the Ciampanelli's."

"Si, too good perhaps."

"But, signore..."

Joe held up his hand for silence, then put his arm around Dominick's shoulders while motioning for Sam to get lost.

"Look, things are going to get a little rough before long. We will be drawing a line between society people and non-society people. You need to be where your loyalty isn't in question." Joe paused and shook his head. "Casimo Ciampanelli won't join the society, and I don't want you caught in the crossfire."

"But, signore. You promised the Ciampanelli's would be under my protection."

Joe's face turned red. He stabbed his finger into Dominick's chest —hard! "I'll tell you!" He bellowed.

Dominick noticed it was suddenly very quiet in the little room.

The headman clamped his mouth shut and wheeled around. Jim had frozen in the middle of handing someone a bottle of beer. Joe nodded toward Jim's back room. When Jim nodded soberly in return, Joe grabbed Dominick by the arm and pulled him through the curtains into the small kitchen.

"What do you want me to do, huh? I suppose you want special favors, no?"

"But they are like family to me, signore." It seemed weak even in his ears. "I couldn't bear to see them injured."

The redness in Joe's face spread in waves over his baldhead.

Slowly Dominick took a step back, spreading his hands out in front of him.

"No, signore. I don't expect special favors." The beginning of an idea formed in his mind. "You are right, of course, but may I make a suggestion?"

Joe snapped his head in a quick nod. Fists balled at his side.

"You are right. Signore Ciampanelli will never join the Society. Still, everyone who works at the Peanut quarry respects him. Even the Americans."

He paused a moment to let the last statement sink in.

"It might be wiser to let him stand alone. Don't even bother to ask Casimo Ciampanelli to join the Society. Eventually the others will wonder, and this will cause Signore Ciampanelli to lose respect."

He stared at Joe a moment. His head now looked like a baby's butt with a diaper rash.

Dominick pressed on. "If you challenge a man like Casimo, others may rally behind him. Clyde Duff might even get the American authorities to help. If the trouble effects production at the quarries, I guarantee this will happen. But leave him alone and, as others lose respect for him, he will be neutralized."

Joe's color returned to normal. There was a shrewd look on his face. He raised a meaty finger and shook it at Dominick. "I like the way you think. And you get what you want too, no?"

Suddenly Joe's face grew hard again, and he slammed his fist into the palm of his left hand. "But I tell you this. If Ciampanelli interferes or causes trouble, there will be no more neutrality! Capeesh?"

Dominick nodded. "With your permission, signore, I will talk with Casimo about this."

"We will try this plan of yours, but you must still move in with Nick Sparaio. I have already talked to Nick. He is expecting you."

"Si, but allow me to wait until after the holidays. This will give me time to talk with Signore Ciampanelli and help him understand that he must not interfere."

"Fair enough. Now come, you may buy me a beer, no?"

Dominick lay awake most of the night wondering how he was going to tell the Ciampanelli's he had to move out of their home. Worse, he had no idea how to approach Casimo about his agreement with Boggiano. He hated what he must do. Yet there was no other way to protect the Ciampanelli's from what he knew was coming. And if something happened to Rosa's father, Dominick knew the family would be left destitute.

He decided to spend Christmas in Pittsburgh. He could tell everyone he was going to visit his fictitious family in Philadelphia. In Pittsburgh, he would try to meet with Superintendent Dimuro. Dimuro would know what to do.

Telling the Ciampanelli's he wouldn't be there for Christmas was harder than he thought. For one thing, Dominick realized he couldn't tell them he was leaving to visit his family in Philadelphia. He had already told Casimo the truth about losing his family in Italy. For another, Rosa surprised him by leaving the room in tears. He decided to tell everyone that he must visit his cousin in Pittsburgh. That was supposedly why he had left the last time. The young detective wondered just how long the thin net of lies he had spun about his past would hold together, or would they trap him like a bird in one of Ignazio's nets?

The following day the trains were running late. It was almost 9 PM before he arrived in Pittsburgh. Dominick knew the company's offices were closed, so he bought dinner and spent the night in a cheap room at the Drum Hotel.

Early the next morning he made his way up the trash filled alley behind the Pinkerton office building. Dimuro had made it perfectly clear he was never to go near the front of the building. When he reached the rear entry to Frank's office he was surprised to find the door unlocked. Slowly he pushed the door open enough to peer into the darkness inside.

A gruff voice broke the silence. "Get in here before someone sees you, 89."

It was Toni.

After he slipped inside, Toni snapped the light on and eased his revolver back into the holster under his jacket. "Afraid you missed the boss," he said unceremoniously. "Where were you?"

"Merry Christmas to you, too."

"Bull!" Toni snapped, flopping into Dimuro's chair and propping his feet on the desk. "Anyway, it doesn't mean much to the likes of us. The boss now, he's a family man. Frank waited until late last night," he added accusingly.

"The trains were behind schedule. I didn't get in until late."

"Well, the boss went to West Virginia to check out another of those crazy sightings of Fred Carnetti." Toni shook his head. "Carnetti seems to be showing up all over the country. Last month the police in some North Carolina town held one of our countrymen in jail for three weeks because he looked like Carnetti."

Toni picked up a sheet of paper and waved it at Dominick. "Here. Boss said to look this over and see if it looks right before we make a batch of them."

Dominick looked into the likeness of Rolando Saverino. "Looks okay."

"We're trying to keep this one low key. Maybe he'll feel safe and make a mistake." Toni smiled suddenly. "So what's new in Hillsville?"

After Dominick told him, Toni let out a low whistle. "There's going to be trouble all right."

Dominick perched on the edge of the desk by Toni's feet. "The Campanelli's are good people, Toni. I don't want to see something bad happen to them."

Toni stood up suddenly and paced the floor. "Listen, Boggiano's right about one thing. You have to get away from the Campanelli's. You're getting too attached, and in this business that will get you killed quicker than anything."

"Si," Dominick said softly, "but we're still human."

"Not us, compare! We're spooks is all, just spooks."

"I was hoping to talk to Superintendent Dimuro about this."

Toni stopped pacing. "I wouldn't do that," he said slowly. "After that last incident with Siciliano, the boss will chew your ears if you're lucky. If not,..." he shrugged.

Toni offered him a cigar. When he saw the younger man struggling with a match, Toni scratched a barnburner on the side of the desk and held it up when it flared into flame.

"Look, I know how you feel. You done all you could. You have given Signore Ciampanelli and his family a chance. But I believe this thing is bigger than any of us can imagine. You are finally in the position all of us had hoped to be in." He paused and put his hand on Dominick's shoulder. "We owe it to our people, campare."

"Si, I know this, but it is still very hard."

Suddenly Toni reached into a desk drawer, pulled out a small manila envelope and tossed it on Dominick's lap. "You have another train to catch. They want you in Philadelphia this evening."

Dominick picked up the envelope containing a set of tickets. "But it's Christmas Eve!"

Toni shrugged. "So what is that to us? You'd just sit around in a hotel getting drunk anyway."

"What do you think the people in Philadelphia want?'" He was getting an unsettling feeling in the pit of his stomach already.

"Probably just a current report, who knows?" Toni shook his head and began rummaging through the desk drawers. "Here it is!" He pulled out a bottle. "Come on. Let's have a Christmas drink on the boss."

Chapter 16

Dominick sat in a straight-backed chair facing Superintendent James Saville of the Philadelphia Office. General Superintendent Tearce was busy looking for something on his desk, which gave Dominick a moment to reflect.

He had already met with both men the night before. They listened intently as he gave them a complete report covering his progress on the case and the recent developments in Hillsville. They scribbled some notes, especially when he mentioned the trouble the quarries were having keeping laborers. When he finished, they thanked him and requested he come back at two o'clock on Christmas Day.

"Ah, here it is." Tearce came around the corner of his desk waving a folder and took a seat facing Dominick.

"You've done a fine job with those reports, by the way."

"Are they going to keep the case open then, sir?"

The Pinkerton superintendents glanced at one another for an instant.

"For now at least," Tearce said. "But I want to make myself perfectly clear. Should..." He wagged his finger at Dominick. "...should, I say, you be called off the case. You must leave immediately. Do you understand?"

Dominick felt his hope failing. "But, sir, I..."

"No buts!" Should you choose to stay after you are recalled, I want you to understand that your position will be terminated. If you try to work on your own, you will do so without authorization and will not enjoy the sanction of our organization. We will not tolerate independent agents. Is that clear?"

"Yes, sir."

"Enough said then."

Mr. Tearce paused to clear his throat. "I am concerned about the situation in Hillsville. Especially in light of changes that are occurring on the American side of things, so to speak."

Dominick cocked his head to one side. "I don't understand, sir."

Leather squeeked as Tearce leaned forward in his chair. "There has been a change within the Lawrence County government. A new district attorney has been elected."

Mr. Tearce sat back and opened the file in his lap. "Yes, here it is. Mr. Charles H. Young will take over as the Lawrence County DA shortly after the first of the year." He leaned toward Dominick again. "Mr. Young is an ambitious young attorney who is determined to drive the Black Hand out of Lawrence County. Eliminating the Black Hand is the platform he was elected on, but that is not all. Judge Porter and Mr. Young are well acquainted with each other, and I assume of the same political persuasion."

"I've read the newspapers, sir. But what does this have to do with me?" Dominick was getting a sickening feeling in the pit of his stomach.

"Patience, young man," Mr. Tearce cautioned. "Mr. McFate is also retiring as county detective."

The general superintendent consulted his folder again before continuing.

"Mr. Creighton Logan is to replace McFate. Mr. Logan has a reputation as a tough police officer who doesn't mind using his fists. What this all means, 89, is that there has been installed, in Lawrence County, a determined law enforcement contingent that is going to begin slapping the Black Hand. What's more, they have the press, the court and the voters behind them."

Tearce sat back in his chair and looked at Saville. The latter slumped in his chair with his legs crossed. He made no attempt to sit up.

"This is why we brought y'all here," Mr. Saville said. "We wanted to make ya aware of the change that's comin', but what y'all told us complicates things some. If the situation in Hillsville gets nasty, the new authorities are gonna' come down hard. Y'all could find yourself between a hammer and an anvil."

"Do you understand the implications of this, 89?" Tearce asked.

"Yes, sir. I've been between a hammer and an anvil since I arrived in Hillsville. But will the information I supplied about Rocco Racca help?"

The two men shared another of those knowing looks. Finally, Mr. Tearce spoke up. "Rocco's statements, to date, only indicate a strong suspicion, 89. They will not win a conviction in court."

The general superintendent took on the look of a hungry fox. "Listen, we're doing everything we can to keep the case open, but without a timely confession, I don't know."

"Problem's the newly elected governor," Mr. Saville drawled. "The man's got the idea he's throw'n good money after bad. Governor Pennypacker had hired us to find the game warden's killer, after all. Not conduct an investigation into this little ol' society of yours."

"But surely the governor can see that wiping out the Black Hand would be to his benefit?"

"I'm sure the governor understands the implications," Mr. Tearce said dryly. "We have reports the governor received a couple Black Hand letters threatening his person. But the truth of the matter is: it's going to take something pretty powerful to get the state legislature to take on the Black Hand, although I understand the new State Constabulary is itching for the job."

"We might have the mechanism we need if the quarries shut down." Saville added. "The steel mills need limestone, and steel is power."

"The bottom line, 89," Mr. Tearce urged, "is that you need to exploit your advantage with Rocco. If he trusts you, take advantage of it."

"Trust will only go so far, sir, and I have already pushed it to the limits. Rocco Racca is no fool. But given time, I believe he will confide in me."

"Time is running out, 89, and it's running out on all fronts."

Two days later, Dominick caught the morning train from Pittsburgh to New Castle. At Lawrence Junction two other society members boarded. One was from New Castle and one from Youngstown. To loosen their tongues, he shared sips of whiskey from a quarter flask he carried. They had successfully whisked two men away who were wanted for robbery. He made a mental note of where they were hiding to include in his reports. These men had come to report to Boggiano, and he accompanied them to the headman's house.

As they drew near a familiar form appeared on the porch. Joe had the sleeves of his shirt rolled up despite the freezing temperature.

"Ho, Dominick. Welcome home, I trust you had a good Christmas?"

He was glad to see the boisterous headman smiling, but then Joe's mood could change like the wind. Joe looked at the other two men and his smile disappeared behind thick lips and furled brow. Both men wilted under that stare.

"I hope you men have something good to report," he growled.

"Si, signore," one mumbled.

Suddenly, the smile was back. "Good! Let's get out of this cold, no?"

Inside, the room was uncomfortably hot from a stove glowing dull red.

"Excuse us a moment, Dominick," Joe said. "Have a seat while I discuss business with these two." Joe ushered them through the curtains into the kitchen area. Now and then he could hear Joe's rumbling voice proclaim, "Good! Good!"

Before long they came back out with glasses of wine. Joe was carrying a bottle and an extra glass. He splashed some pale liquid into the glass and handed it to Dominick.

When he took a sip, Joe raised a bushy eyebrow. "What do you think? A bit sweet, no?"

"Sweeter than I care for normally, but it is different. What is it?"

Joe nodded his baldhead. "Some of Ignazio's wine. A gift. Too sweet for me, but my wife loves the stuff. Ignazio calls it watermelon wine. Claims he learned to make it from a negro servant in Louisiana."

"Servant? Ignazio Sebastianelli?"

"Si, the old fool has an interesting history I hear." Joe paused for a moment watching Dominick intently before continuing. "Is not bad for a gift, no?"

Suddenly he realized what Joe was hinting at. Blushing, Dominick opened his satchel and pulled out a flashlight. He opened the back, slid two batteries into the tube, and turned it on before handing it to Joe. "Merry Christmas, signore."

The barrel-chested headman looked very serious when he took the light from Dominick. Touching it gently, as though it were magic, Joe turned the light over carefully, switching it on and off a couple of times before nodding vigorously. "Very good. I have heard about these electric torches, but I have never seen one before. Grazie!"

The Ciampanelli's house was warm and cheery. Dominick saved Rosa's gift for last. She blushed when he handed her a gold necklace with a little heart that opened.

"When you are old enough to have a boy friend, you can wear his picture next to your heart," he told her. He didn't notice her parent's share knowing looks.

After gifts were exchanged, Mrs. Ciampanelli went out to the kitchen to warm some leftovers for his supper. After eating he told the Ciampanelli's he was ordered to leave.

It was Mary who broke the stunned silence. "But you're our big brother. I don't want you to leave."

"What if something happens to you again?" Rosa asked. "Who will take care of you?" He could tell she was struggling to fight back the tears.

He forced a smile. "I'm only moving down the street. I'll still be close enough to hear you and Grace arguing."

Grace smiled. "Now I can have my own room back."

"Grace!" her father snapped. "Kindly show some manners." He turned to Dominick. "I know this wasn't your doing, son. But you can still keep in touch."

"Si, I would hope to," Dominick replied. "I...I wonder if I could have a word with you privately, signore?"

Casimo nodded his head slowly. "Somehow I thought there would be more." He glanced at his wife.

"Come on, girls, you can help me clean this mess and do the supper dishes."

"Mamma, may I go to my room?" Rosa asked weakly.

"Of course, child." Everyone could see Rosa was losing the fight with her tears.

"Mamma, that's not fair!" Mary exclaimed.

"Come along now. We must leave the men to their little chat."

When the room was empty, he offered Casimo a cigar. The latter shook his head and fetched a tin can, partly filled with paper, which he kept behind his chair to use as a spittoon during inclement weather. He bit off a sizeable hunk of dark tobacco from a plug he carried in his overall pocket, and then looked intently at Dominick. "What's on your mind, boy?"

He told him about Boggiano's plan to force all the men in the settlements to join The Society of Honor.

Casimo listened without a word, only occasionally spitting into the can with a grunt.

"Boggiano realizes you won't join the society, signore. That is why he ordered me to move out. When I asked if you were still under my protection, Joe got mad. Finally, he agreed not to bother you, or your family, so long as you don't interfere."

Casimo's face was a mask of emotion, dark emotion. "What do you expect me to do? I can't just stand still and allow him to brutalize my friends and countrymen!"

"I was afraid you would say that, husband."

They turned to see Mrs. Ciampanelli standing in the entry to the kitchen, the backs of her hands planted firmly against the sides of her hips.

"Mamma, what are you...?"

"I have a right to know what is going on when it affects my family. I knew Dominick's moving out was leading up to no-good." She looked at the young man. "My husband will do as you ask," she said firmly.

Casimo stood up. "Please allow my wife and I to talk in private."

"Si, signore." Dominick got up and moved toward his room. "I'll pack my things."

"Don't you dare move, young man!" Mrs. Ciampanelli snapped.

"Mamma, this..."

"There is nothing to discuss!" she declared flatly. "What do you think will become of us if something happens to you? Dominick stuck his neck out to give you a chance. You must either accept it or we must move away. There are no other choices."

"You know I can't move from here. Mr. Duff promised the foreman's job come spring."

"Then you will mind your own business, Casimo Ciampanelli. I won't have you butchered by these pigs!"

"I'll pack my bags then, signore," Dominick said.

Casimo nodded, his massive jaws giving the chew a hard working over.

Three days later, on New Year's Eve, Rocco Racca and his wife came to see Dominick in a sleigh driven by Frank Martino. The sun glittered off ten inches of newly fallen snow. They were crowded in the one-horse sleigh and wrapped tightly in blankets against the cold.

"We must go over to my father-in-law's house," Rocco shouted.

"We want you to come over and have dinner with us," his wife added.

Dominick laughed. "Si, I'll get my coat and meet you at Signore Soccisano's house. There is no more room in the sleigh."

When Dominick arrived at Gino Soccisano's house he was surprised at the variety of food, including fish caught through the ice in a pond nearby. Two men, that Sam had brought in to work at the quarry, were playing a guitar and tambourines. A couple was dancing the tarantella, their bodies undulating with the music and clapping.

Someone nudged his arm, and when Dominick turned around Frank Martino was holding two glasses of wine.

Frank wrinkled his nose. "Not near as good as mine."

Rocco joined them. "What we need is some beer," he grumbled.

"If you find someone to go for it, I'll buy the beer for all of us," Dominick offered.

Rocco nodded approval. "Fine, you buy it, and we'll get Docato Trevino to run for it."

Two hours later the beer ran out. Dominick was playing a game of morra, or throwing fingers, with one of the new laborers when Rocco interrupted.

"Dominick, we are going to leave. We want you to come with us. Perhaps we'll go to the opera house in New Castle. I hear they're having a dance tonight."

"Si, I'll go with you, but we all can't ride in that sleigh."

"Tell you what, compare!" Frank Martino swayed over to them. "Let Rocco and his signora take the sleigh. We'll catch the trolley. I'm getting to old to freeze in a sleigh."

They waited for Rocco at a bar room beside the opera. When Rocco came in they weren't feeling much pain. The former headman eyed them suspiciously, then bought a bottle of whiskey to take to the dance. "Doesn't look like you'll need any of this," he grumbled.

"Well, in that case we'll get our own," Frank snapped. He staggered toward the bar and returned with his own bottle.

They went to two more saloons, drinking and singing with other members of the Society before Rocco led them to the opera house. In the lower level the seats had been removed and tables set up. A small Italian band was playing in the orchestra pit. With the scenery removed the stage made a fair-sized dance floor and several couples were already taking advantage of the music. As they took a table, Rocco led his wife onto the stage for a dance.

"Jus' think'n," Frank slurred.

"Bout what," Dominick asked.

"Bout how good it's...bout how good it is to be Talian."

"You mean Italian, don't you?"

"Better then bein' Irish!"

Both men giggled in the manner of drunks sharing a special secret.

"What are you men giggling about," Mrs. Racca asked. Her face was flushed after dancing a fast number with her husband.

"Uh, jus' a man's joke, madam," Dominick replied sheepishly.

Mrs. Racca snorted, before taking her seat at the table.

Suddenly, Dominick noticed Rocco stiffen. The young man followed the outlaw's gaze. His sight was a little blurry. He wasn't sure if there were two or four policemen strutting toward them.

The place grew quiet. The band, which had started a lively piece, suddenly switched to a mellow number as if to soothe the crowd.

Then Frank slumped forward, his head hitting the table and knocking one of the bottles over with a crash. Rocco cursed and set the bottle up before it could roll onto the floor. Frank was out cold. Rocco took a seat beside his wife as the policemen approached their table swinging long-handled Billy clubs. One of the officers pointed a club at Frank slumped across the table. "Is this man causing a disturbance?"

Dominick couldn't be sure if there were two or three uniforms in front of him. Or, was the third man not wearing a uniform? The man was big, he was sure of that. He heard Rocco speaking.

"No, signore, he justa has'a too much to drink is'a all. He don'a bother no one."

One of the uniforms turned to a broad chested, curly haired man in a suit coat. "That's the man who killed the game warden at Hillsville, but they can't do noth'n to him on account of there ain't no proof."

Dominick lurched to his feet. "What do you know about that!"

The policeman shrugged his shoulders. "Everyone knows it."

"Well, I don't!"

"Oh, no?" The policeman chuckled. "I'll bet you don't."

Rocco tugged on Dominick's hand. "Sit down, Prugitore. Don't be a fool!"

Dominick didn't notice the big man's gaze suddenly fall on him at the mention of his name. He was too drunk to notice much of anything. He wrenched his hand free of Rocco's grasp. "I say we take these men out and cut their faces!" he proclaimed in Italian.

Rocco slammed his fist on the table. "They know nothing. Now sit down!"

"No!" Dominick shouted, lurching toward the policeman. He slipped into English without realizing it. "I say we put him out of the way, tonight!" Something told him it was important to let Rocco know he was firmly on his side.

Suddenly there was a blurry movement in front of him and he caught the brief glimpse of a meaty fist just before it slammed into his face. Sparks and pain shattered through him like shards of broken glass. Then he hit the floor.

Rocco and several others jumped to their feet. Rocco's wife began crying and clutching at Rocco's arm.

The big man never changed his expression. He just stared into one face after another with disgust. "Drag him outside," he said.

The stranger pulled a small white card from his coat pocket and laid it in front of the former headman. He kept one finger on it momentarily, almost daring Rocco to touch it. The band had stopped playing and Mrs. Racca seemed to be holding her breath.

"Creighton Logan," the man said quietly. "County detective. You would do me a favor by interfering, Rocco. Then I could throw your dago ass in jail and save the county a lot of trouble."

The two men stared at one another for a long moment. Then Logan turned to follow the policemen out the door.

On the street, Logan directed the policemen to carry Dominick into an alley. Scooping up a handful of snow, Logan rubbed it in his face. The sudden cold yanked Dominick back into a world of pain. His right eye was swollen shut. He rolled over and spewed out some of the whiskey he'd consumed. When the spasms stopped he tried to stand, but couldn't seem to get his legs working. He felt a firm hand grab his arm and lift him to his feet. A thick voice ordered the patrolmen to go about their business. He still was having trouble focusing.

"Wh..who are you?"

"Is your name Prugitore, Dominick Prugitore?"

"Si...I mean yes."

"Then we've got to talk. Come on, I'll help you." The man picked up another handful of snow and slapped it against his eye.

"Ow!" He tried to brush the hand away.

"Hold that snow on your eye. It'll keep the swelling down."

"Where are you taking me?"

"To my office."

In a small room at the back of the courthouse, Logan handed Dominick a cup of steaming black coffee. He was still queasy, but thinking clearer now thanks to the pain, and the snow, and the coffee.

"Did you have to hit me so hard?"

"I'm an opportunist, Mr. Prugitore. I had to get you alone where we could talk, and you presented the opportunity. You will be charged with causing a public disturbance; to protect your cover, of course."

"Of course," he replied dryly. "But why am I so important?"

"Don't get cocky. You were about to attack us, or don't you remember?"

"No, I don't."

"Mr. Young will be here in a bit. He'll explain everything to you."

"Mr. Young? The new district attorney? You mean he's coming here to talk with me on New Year's eve?"

"Yep. So you see? You're an important part of what we're planning."

Dominick touched his swollen eye and winced before stepping outside to grab another handful of snow.

Charles H. Young, was only a couple of years older than Dominick. Of medium height and slim, he possessed an aristocratic nose that presided over a generous mouth and prominent chin. He wore his hair parted precisely in the middle and trimmed well above his ears. Small round spectacles and a white linen collar added to his distinguished appearance. After hanging his topcoat and scarf on a coat tree by the door, Mr. Young nodded to his new detective before holding out a slim hand to Dominick.

As Dominick stood melted snow ran down his arm and made little puddles on the wooden floor.

Mr. Young flashed a hard look at Logan. "What happened here, Craig?"

"I'm afraid your detective is a bit quick with his fists," Dominick cut in. He flung the remaining snow onto the floor and wiped his hand on the seat of his pants before taking the district attorney's hand. "Dominick Prugitore at your service, sir."

"Would you like me to call a doctor to look at that eye, Dominick?"

"No sir. My head will be worse than the eye by morning."

The DA smiled. "Well then, I suggest we get started. Mr. Logan seems to think we need to put you in jail to protect your cover, but I suppose we could dispense with that if you wish."

"My friends will come looking for me tomorrow. They'll grow suspicious if I'm not where I should be."

"I'm sure you know best about that sort of thing, but I do apologize for the roughness. I chose Craig because of his expertise with those fists, I'm afraid. You see, we're determined to break the Black Hand in this region once and for all."

"That's a comfort, sir," Dominick said.

"But that isn't what we wanted to talk to you about, Domin...er, 89. I suppose, I should get accustomed to using your code name," he mused.

The DA frowned slightly before continuing. "The Black Hand preys upon its own people. We're hoping to organize a group of honest Italians to stand against these criminals."

Dominick sadly shook his head. "I'm afraid you don't understand our people, Mr. Young. They are from the old country. There the government has always been the enemy."

"If they will testify against the criminals who rob and extort their hard earned money, we'll provide police protection."

"My people have lived for generations under corrupt governments, sir. The Mafia's justice, brutal though it is, is something they accept because it's impartial. Therefore, it is fair in their eyes. They know very well that betrayal carries a sentence of death."

Mr. Young looked surprised. "The Mafia? This is America. We wiped that blight out sixteen years ago down in New Orleans."

"I used to think so, too," Dominick replied.

"Well whoever they are, surely you can see your people must begin to fight back, or they will never be free." The DA paused and gestured toward Dominick with his hand. "You know your people. Tell them we are ready to help."

"I can't do that, sir."

"Why not?"

"I'm supposed to be one of the bad guys, remember? If I start playing the role of a double agent, I'm going to be found out. If that happens I'm dead."

"But surely you know some people you can trust?"

"In my job, I can't afford to trust anyone. Not even you."

Mr. Young looked perplexed for a moment. "I see," he said softly.

"No, sir, I don't think you do. I walk a razor's edge every day. I have nightmares every night. These are the most suspicious people I have ever known. And I have enemies in the Society, sir. Bad enemies! You don't have any idea what it's like. I've seen friends murdered, blown to bits right in front of me!" He shivered and shook his head. "No sir, you don't have any idea what it's like."

A long silence followed. Finally Dominick cleared his throat. "There is one person who may help you though."

Both of the other men looked at him hopefully.

"Father DeMita, sir. The Catholic priest in New Castle. He is terribly saddened by the plight of his people. Perhaps, you could convince him to help in some way."

Mr. Young slowly nodded before standing. "Well thank you, 89. We'll try Father DeMita." After they shook hands again, the young attorney rubbed the side of his nose thoughtfully. "Is there a...er...more conventional way we can contact you in the future?"

"Through the Pinkerton's. They have ways of reaching me."

Over the next couple of weeks Dominick traveled with Sam Bennett. They collected dues and fines levied on society members. He learned that Joe Boggiano held a far larger territory than the Italian settlements at Hillsville. Joe was feared and respected by headmen all the way into Pittsburgh.

Their deadly methods slammed graphically home the day Dominick and Sam visited Vincent Scibilia, the headman in South Sharon,

Pennsylvania. Vin wasn't submitting Boggiano's cut in new membership fees. They met in a little Italian restaurant downtown.

"So," Vin said, handing a stack of silver dollars to Sam, "Boggiano thinks I'm holding out, eh?"

Sam held up his hands. "The word gets around, signore. I think it would be advisable to keep Signore Boggiano on your side."

Vin appeared to be in his mid-forties. He was a powerful man, a blacksmith by trade. Vin nodded thoughtfully. "Of course, but it isn't true. Boggiano always gets his share of memberships."

Then he smiled a bit too broadly for Dominick's liking. "Just to show there are no hard feelings, I want you to come to a little initiation we have planned for this evening. I'll meet you at the bar across from the cigar shop. Seven o'clock. Ciao!"

With that Vin sauntered out of the restaurant.

"What do you suppose Scibilia has on his mind?" Dominick asked.

"I don't know, but I wish I had a gun or a knife," Sam replied slowly.

Vin was waiting for them at the bar. He led them down a narrow side street toward a brick and wooden structure that was sorely in need of repairs. Two solemn looking young men were leaning against a rusted metal railing that opened into a basement entry. Vin stopped them just out of hearing of the others, his face intent. "You understand that the Omerta is evoked here. You must never speak of what you see."

Sam and Dominick glanced at one another before slowly nodding their heads.

Vin studied them carefully for a moment, then led them toward the entry. The two men straightened as he approached.

"No one else is to enter until we are finished," he commanded roughly. "You must give warning if the polizia come."

Vin led them down a flight of rickety wooden steps before opening a rough plank door. Pale light and the reek of kerosene lanterns spilled into the night.

As they entered an expectant hush fell over a group of about twenty men. The cellar was musty, and cobwebs hung thick from hewed beams overhead. Near the middle of the room mounds of fresh dirt stood piled beside two long holes dug into the earthen floor.

"Is everything in readiness?" Vin asked in a hushed voice that somehow made the circumstances even more ominous.

There was a shifting in the crowd, which slowly parted to reveal two men, stripped to the waist, bare footed, with dirt caked to their pants and sweating bodies. One of them, a man of about fifty, stood quietly with his hands tied behind his back. The other, only a kid in his late teens, stood trembling as two men tied cords about his wrists. Wetness stained the front of his dirty trousers. Some of those around him pointed and laughed. Tears ran freely down the boy's face. When they were both tightly bound, Vin took a position between the holes and motioned for the prisoners to be brought to the edge.

The older man walked slowly with his head down, but the boy stiffened, whimpering. Rough hands shoved him forward until his legs buckled and he fell into the dirt, whining pitifully. Two men grabbed the boy, one under each arm, and dragged him forward. The lad was left kneeling on the brink of one of the holes, sobbing uncontrollably. The second man was also forced to kneel on the edge of a hole. Two men stood poised behind each of them, knifes in hand.

Vin cleared his throat. "Listen to me carefully," he intoned, "that you may live and not die. Both of you have been chosen to undergo the rite of assassination. Both of you have entered this country illegally. You have no families here." Vin paused letting those statements sink in.

The lad was still whining and sobbing, and Dominick doubted he even heard what Vin said. Unconsciously he touched the side of his neck that had felt the bite of Siciliano's blade.

"No!" The boy wailed. "I kill no one! Mother of Mercy, have pity."

Vin nodded grimly to the men standing behind the two victims. A man to the right of each grabbed them by the hair and pulled their heads backward, laying a keen edged blade along the side of their jugular. The men to their left grabbed a shoulder and poised the tip of a long butcher knife just under their fifth rib.

"Nooooo!" The boy screeched. He was sobbing so violently that the man holding the knife at his throat had to ease the blade off slightly to keep from slitting the vein accidentally. The older man was sweating profusely.

"Listen to me!" Vin shouted. "Answer correctly and you will live. I will only ask once."

"Mercy! Please, mercy, I beg you." the boy blurted between sobs.

Dominick uttered an oath and took a step forward. He felt a hand grip his arm.

"Stay," Sam hissed. "Interfere, and you will take his place."

Dominick gave Sam a hard look before knocking his hand roughly off his arm.

Vin looked at the boy with disgust before proceeding. "Do you swear by the name of the Blessed Virgin, the Holy Mother of God, to obey the orders of assassination given by The Society of Honor?"

"Si," the older man mumbled through clenched teeth. The boy just continued sobbing, tears running freely down his face.

"Answer or die!" Vin demanded roughly.

"Mercy," the lad whimpered.

The two men behind him raised questioning looks at Vincent.

"Answer to the oath!" Vin demanded again.

"Noooo!" The boy wailed.

Dominick's heart stopped. Vin nodded briefly. The long bladed butcher knife slid easily into the boy's side. A spray of aortal blood splattered as the second knife slit his throat. Then they shoved the kicking boy into the hole. Dominick could hear his death struggles gurgle up from the darkness. Suddenly he was on his knees wrenching.

On the trip back to Hillsville, Dominick was quiet and moody despite Sam's attempts to cheer him. He couldn't believe his friend's hardness. They had seen a boy murdered, and Sam shrugged it off as though it were business as usual. When they reached Sam's house, he grabbed Dominick's arm before opening the gate by the tracks.

"Remember what Vin said. We must tell no one what we saw."

Dominick knew he couldn't write about this murder in his reports. If the police suddenly arrived at the building and found the body, it would lead directly to him. He also knew he couldn't let his feelings interfere with his work. He was upset with Sam's callous attitude about the murder, but forced himself to push it aside. When Boggiano ordered him to report to Sam's place later that week for more schooling, he went willingly.

It was late February when Dominick again visited with Rocco Racca. They met at Frank Martino's new restaurant. The two men sat at a table in the small bar adjoining the restaurant itself. Frank was tending bar and waiting on customers.

Rocco pointed to Dominick's bandaged hand before raising a questioning eyebrow.

Dominick shrugged, then leaned forward talking quietly. "We train once a week with the stiletto."

Rocco nodded in understanding.

"So, how are things with you?" Dominick asked.

Rocco took a sip of his beer, pausing to look moodily into the mug before answering. "I've been called to appear at court in three more days."

"So you got a new trial then?"

Rocco shook his head. "The appeal was denied. This is for sentencing."

"What are you going to do?"

"So what are a few more months in jail, eh? I've been there before." He paused to light a cigar, passing one to Dominick. "Besides, when it is over I will be free."

"But how do you know you will only get a few months in jail?"

Rocco pursed his lips. "We have taken some precautions to insure this."

Dominick looked around to be sure no one was listening before leaning even closer to the former Black Hand chieftain. "You must be careful, compare. They still think you had something to do with the Houk murder."

Surprisingly Rocco leaned back in his chair and casually blew a smoke ring into the air before smiling. "You remember what the policeman said at the dance on New Year's Eve? They can't prove nothing."

Dominick shook his head. "I'm afraid I only remember bits and pieces, compare."

"Si, you were very foolish. Still, you were a magnificent fool. On New Year's Eve you finally convinced my wife. The other day she said to me, 'Rocco' she said, 'Dominick is the best friend you have.'"

Rocco raised his mug in a toast. "Here is to friendship."

Dominick raised his in reply.

On Monday, March 1st, Dominick sat in the back of the courtroom with Rocco's wife, accompanied by Susan Martino. Rocco was sitting in front of the courtroom with his attorney at a table opposite District Attorney Young. The latter had just completed a resume of the case.

Judge Porter, a thick jowled man in his early fifties, nodded to the tipstaff standing near the bench.

"The defendant will rise." The man intoned in a voice that sounded hollow in the large room.

Rocco looked at his attorney who motioned for him to stand up. When Rocco stood, Judge Porter leaned forward.

"Rocco Racca, you have been found guilty of larceny by bailee by a jury of your peers. This court hereby sentences you to serve one-year imprisonment at the Western Penitentiary in Pittsburgh. The sentence is to commence immediately."

Susan gasped, while Dominick interpreted for Mrs. Racca. When she heard her husband's fate, Rocco's wife began to sob. Susan put an arm around her as the judge continued to speak.

"I do not consider you a good citizen. I want you to understand that when threatening letters are sent to officers for the purpose of deterring them from their duty, that is a very serious matter. American officers pay no attention to communications from the Black Hand or any other such society."

When he was finished the judge motioned for the sheriff's deputy to take Rocco away. Meanwhile, emboldened by their success in sending Rocco to prison Mr. Young and Creighton Logan sought the support of Italians in New Castle where the seventh ward was under siege by the Black Hand. For the past several months wealthy Italians in this section endured a siege of blackmail and extortion by members of the Society. Using threatening letters the Society had collected hundreds of dollars. Rumors reported that the New Castle Priest, Father DeMita, was organizing honest Italians to oppose the Black Hand.

One day, late in March, Dominick stopped by the post office and was surprised to see another coded letter from his supposed mother in Philadelphia. The content of the missive was simple. He was to report to Pittsburgh at once. The governor had closed the investigation into the murder of Seeley Houk.

That evening, Dominick felt hollowness creep into his stomach as he sat on the Ciampanelli's porch step talking to Rosa.

"I know you are not one of them," Rosa said softly. She had been crying after he told the Ciampanelli's he was leaving Hillsville. "I think you are a detective or something."

Dominick's head snapped around.

"You must never tell that to anyone, Sis. If you keep this secret, perhaps I may get a chance to come back."

"I won't tell," she said softly. "This will be our secret, like the little glade in the woods." Tears started running again.

Dominick suppressed an urge to put his arm around her.

"Somehow I always felt safe knowing you were around," she continued. "Now, I don't know what to do."

"What do you mean?"

She shook her head sharply as if to shake loose her weepy emotions. "It's just that things are getting worse. Papa said they cut the face of a worker at the Johnson quarry, and another man got beat up pretty bad. Men are quitting, and families are moving away. I...I don't know!"

"You'll be alright, Sis. They haven't bothered your papa have they?""

"N...No, but papa keeps talking about starting a White Hand Association like the priest started in New Castle."

He reached out and touched her arm. "You and your mother must not let him get involved. Boggiano promised your papa wouldn't be bothered so long as he didn't interfere."

A haunted look came into Rosa's eyes when she looked at his hand resting on her arm. "I...I wish you wouldn't call me that."

He moved his hand away. He found he really didn't want to. "Call you what?"

"Sis," she said, standing up suddenly. She smoothed her skirt before looking determinedly into his eyes. "I'm not your sister." She walked to the door before pausing. "Good bye, Dominick."

Chapter 17

The screeching of the double-trucked wheels faded into the soft humming of traction motors as the interurban trolley slowed to a stop at Kennedy's Crossing. A series of warm spring days had caused maple saplings covering the bluffs along the river to break into a blanket of red. Here and there slender branches of pussy willows offered a fuzzy white contrast to the over stimulated maples and green spring grass.

The somber young man stepping off the trolley looked out of place among the gaiety bursting around him. He wore a black suit coat over a stiffly starched shirt with a silk collar and black bow tie. The young man set his satchel on a weathered bench beside the tracks and paused to pick flecks of lint from his coat sleeves. His face was a study in sharp angles neatly set off by a thick handlebar mustache. It was a face that forgot how to smile.

Behind him the humming of traction motors suddenly increased in pitch, and the screeching of steel on steel signaled the heavy electric car was once again bearing its passengers through the Italian settlements. He looked up when horse's hooves rattled the wooden planking of the bridge.

Another young man wearing a loose collarless shirt pulled the old wagon to a stop beside the bench. The two men stared at one another. There were no smiles, no words of greeting. The stranger tossed his satchel in the wagon and climbed onto the seat beside the driver.

A cluck and flick of the reigns got the old mare moving up the bluff toward Hillsville, her head swaying slowly back and forth with the effort.

"How's Carmine?" the stranger asked finally.

Toni flashed him a hard look. "Why do you ask?"

"She married the wrong man, you know."

"She doesn't think so, cousin."

Eyes like dark pools stared unemotionally back at Toni for several moments. "Where do you stand with the Society these days, Toni?"

"That's none of your business."

"You know it broke your father's heart when you jointed those cut-throats, don't you?"

"You keep papa out of this, Nick! Besides, you know nothing about the Society."

"They killed my father, Toni."

"Your father was found dead in the stock yards at Pittsburgh. Nobody knows who killed him."

"I know! They killed him for not paying their bloody protection money." The dark pools continued to stare at Toni. "Your father asked me to help start a White Hand Society like they have in New Castle. What I want to know: are you going to stand with your family, or your cutthroat friends?"

Toni's face paled. "You're crazy, Nick! You and papa both. What you are going to do is get yourselves killed."

Nick Tergilli turned away and lit a cigarette. The rest of the trip passed in strained silence.

After Toni put the horse in the barn, he found Nick and his father talking quietly in the hotel's kitchen.

"I've talked to District Attorney Young and Detective Logan," Nick was saying. "They promised police protection to anyone who testified against members of The Society of Honor."

"This is crazy talk!" Toni exclaimed. "This is Hillsville. We don't have polizia here."

"They promised to send the State Constabulary if we need them," Nick replied dryly.

"Need them?" Toni stalked over to Nick waving his hands in the air before bending almost nose to nose with his cousin. "Need them?"

He whirled to face the sternness of his father. "Papa, listen to me. By then, you and a lot of other good people will be dead. I beg you, Papa. Leave this alone!"

The slap rang among the copper kettles hanging over the stove. Tears welled freely from Toni's surprised eyes and trickled down a cheek that burned hot over the red print of his father's hand.

"I never thought my own son would be without honor," the old man hissed.

Toni blinked to stop the tears. "Fine," he whispered, "but I'm taking Carmine and the children out of here. I won't see them harmed to satisfy your sense of pride."

Frank Santi followed his son into the lobby. "Where will you go, Toni? Answer me that."

"There are plenty of places to rent in Hillsville, Papa," Toni replied as he started up the stairs.

"And just what do you expect to do for money?"

"The quarries need help these days," Toni flung back over his shoulder.

"Why don't you listen to me for once. Quit this society."

Toni paused on the landing to look back at his father. "Papa, you don't understand. I took a blood oath. I can never quit, and I can never go against them. To do so would mark me for death."

"Then you would go against your own family?"

"Never, Papa," he said softly. "Somehow, I will stay out of it."

"You can't stay out of it!" his father yelled as Toni bounced up the stairs two at a time.

Three weeks later Joe Boggiano summoned Toni. When he walked into Boggiano's parlor the barrel-chested headman was pacing the floor. Sam Bennett and Jim Rossi were seated on a worn sofa, looking unusually grave. Toni nodded solemnly at Sam and Jim before speaking to Joe.

"Good evening, signore."

Joe stopped pacing and whirled on the curly haired young man before him. "What's going on, huh?" He thrust a thick finger at Toni's face. "You tell me, Toni."

"I'm sorry, signore. No disrespect, but I don't understand."

Boggiano's face turned a darker shade of red until Sam interrupted, "He probably doesn't understand, Joe. Toni moved his family out of his father's hotel a couple of weeks ago."

Joe puckered his lips. "So then! Tell me why you left your father's house, huh?"

Joe, rocking back and forth on the balls of his feet, stared intently into Toni's face.

When he spoke there was a cautious edge in his voice. "It is my cousin, signore. Nick Tergilli."

Boggiano whirled waving his arms at Bennett and Rossi. "Tergilli! Tergilli! I am not liking this name so much." Then he faced Toni. "So what about this Nick Tergilli?"

"Before I married Carmine, we both courted her. Nick has never forgotten that she chose me instead of him. I moved out to avoid trouble."

The headman stared at him for a long moment before nodding his baldhead. "So you don't know what is going on, huh?"

"No, signore."

Joe's fist flew up in front of Toni's nose so fast he blinked. "Well, I'll tell you what's going on! Your father and this Nick Tergilli are trying to make trouble. That's what! They're trying to get people to tell the polizia when my men collect dues or solicit new members."

"Please, signore, my father is an old man."

Boggiano planted his fists back on his hips and leaned into Toni's face. "Yes, but old, toothless lions still have claws."

Toni opened his mouth to speak, but Joe pressed a thick finger against his nose to silence him. Leaving his finger pressing against Toni's nose he turned to Jim Rossi. "This Tergilli is the problem. I want you to approach Signore Tergilli. I want you to invite him to join The Society of Honor."

"He won't do that, signore," Toni whispered.

Without turning around, Boggiano impatiently pushed on Toni's nose flattening it painfully against his face. "Should Tergilli join we will have a leash on him. If not, we'll send Vito to deal with him."

Nick Tergilli did not join The Society of Honor, and he was very careful not to travel alone. Twice Joe sent boys with messages requesting Nick meet with him. He refused. Moreover, through the efforts of Nick and Toni's father, The White Hand Society in Hillsville began to attract a small but faithful following. They met at the hotel once a week to discuss strategy and urged their fellow countrymen not to join The Society of Honor.

Boggiano sent Vito and Mario to the quarries on payday to collect dues, even from people who were not members. Usually the workers were so terrified they paid without question. Some of those who refused were beaten. One man, who continued to refuse, got his face cut. More families fled, and now the quarries were down to less then half their normal production of limestone.

Nick countered by arranging for the worker's wives to collect their husband's pay. The deep inbred respect Italians have for their women prevented Boggiano's men from accosting them. Frank Santi and Nick Tergilli wandered through the crowd gathered at the pay office encouraging those who were fearful of retaliation. But Boggiano suddenly found he was fighting a war on several fronts.

The small gathering of solemn-faced men fidgeted nervously in Joe Boggiano's parlor. They were all men of rank within the Society. Joe paced the floor, huffing like a bull in rut.

He stopped suddenly and smashed his fist into the palm of his hand. "I am not going to stand by and watch this society come apart! First, we have this so-called White Hand Society in New Castle. Now it's in Hillsville!"

Joe stopped and glared at the men sitting around the room. "Right in our own back yard!" His voice dropped into a growl. "I consider that a slap in the face."

A throaty rumble rolled out of a shadow by the door. "I can handle the two problems in Hillsville—whenever you say."

Joe turned slowly toward the voice and nodded. "Patience, Vito. We have some bigger problems to handle first, no?"

Suddenly Joe started pacing the floor again. "Two weeks ago I sent Sam Zellos and Sandy Talanio into South Sharon to help reorganize the Society there. They were to invite some of the wealthy merchants to join The Society of Honor." Joe stopped and shook his fist at the ceiling. "Last night Sandy and Sam were playing cards at Guy Potello's house when a group of men slipped up in the dark and opened fire with shotguns and revolvers through the window. Sam was killed.

Sandy is in the hospital, but I'm told he is not going to make it. One of the Potello brothers is wounded. The polizia are looking for the assassins, but they don't know who they are. I do!"

A meaty finger pointed at Jim Rossi. "I want you to take some men over to Sharon. Take some guns and some dynamite from the quarry." Joe's finger joined their comrades in a tight fist. "I want you to shoot those pigs the same way they shot our men. If that isn't possible blow them into peaces! You hear me?"

"Si, signore," Jim replied, nodding his head rapidly.

"But this is not all," Joe continued. "Yesterday that hot-shot county detective dragged Absardio Sabino out of his home in handcuffs. Absardio is in jail tonight because that dog, Leo Mizio, went to the Polizia and accused him of blackmail."

Again Joe slammed a fist into his palm. "To think that they have the nerve to fight against The Society of Honor! We must teach them respect, no?" Boggiano pointed his finger at Vito. "I want you to pick some men to teach this pig of a landlord respect. He must withdraw his complaint against Absardio or die! Capeesh?"

"Si," Vito growled.

Boggiano turned from Siciliano and pointed a thick finger at Londo Racca. "You get around, Londo. You talk to a lot of people, no?"

Londo shrugged.

"OK, I want you to put the word out that this unauthorized blackmail is to stop." Boggiano shook his finger at Londo. "I mean this, Londo! The next person who writes one of those so-called Black Hand letters without my permission gets his face cut."

Joe stopped and made a disgusting face and flipped his fingers in the air as though trying to rid them of something distasteful. "Letters written in blood. Bah!" He made a thrusting motion with his hand. "Letters with pictures of stilettos!" Suddenly he threw both arms in the air. "...and bursting bombs!" He paused to point a thick finger at Londo again. "You tell them, Londo." He brought the finger to his face and drew it across his cheek. "I mean it!"

"Romon Cerini started it," Londo said flatly, "by trying to blackmail D'Alessio after he fled to Buffalo. I heard he got over a thousand dollars out of that fat pig."

"Well, by the Blessed Virgin, it stops now!" Boggiano roared.

The room grew quiet as the men shifted uncomfortably under the scrutiny of the angry headman. Finally, Sam Bennett cleared his throat. "There is another problem, signore."

Joe Boggiano looked blankly at Sam a moment. "Well, Benedetti? Are you going to tell us, or make us beg, huh?"

Sam squirmed for a moment before continuing. "Pannizzo's been captured."

All of the men turned to face Sam as Boggiano took a step in his direction—fists balled at his sides. "But we hid him on a farm. How can this be?"

Sam shrugged, "The word is one of our own people turned him in to the polizia. Probably someone who's been listening to Tergilli."

"You find that Judas pig! You hear me, Benedetti? You find that Judas pig and kill him!" Joe's face was black with rage.

Sam looked up at Joe. "Si, signore. I hear you, but our people move from farm to farm depending on where work is available."

"I don't care! You and Vito find that Judas-pig and kill him. Take some men who speak a little American and talk to the farmers. Talk to all the farmers if you have to, but you find him, understand?"

"Si," Sam said meekly.

Joe turned around slowly, sweeping the room with his hand. There was a calculated smile on his face. "After we teach these people respect, Nick Tergilli's little flock will be pissing in their pants." Joe looked pointedly at Vito. "Then we will deal with him and still find time to teach old man Santi a little respect, too, eh?"

. . .

Jim Bolino smiled to himself as he strolled along the dirt road that led back to his shanty near Briarhill. Jim wasn't worried. He sent his wife and five children over to Youngstown to visit her cousin until things quieted down. And things looked better now that the American's were taking a hand in fighting The Society of Honor. He chuckled as he remembered the way Sam Benedetti and his men ran leaping through the field as farmer Mort fired his shotgun at them. The Amerian newspaper had quoted District Attorney Young telling people to defend themselves if roving bands of Italians came prowling around. Country folks, especially, were taking it seriously.

Jim worked part-time for Mort Fraizer helping to plant potatoes. Mort didn't know one of the men working for him was wanted for murder. He just hired cheap labor during planting and harvest time and it didn't matter who they were. But it mattered to Jim. He belonged to The White Hand Society.

It was well after dark when Jim arrived at his shanty. As he reached for the door someone grabbed his hair and slammed him painfully against the wall. Jim groped at the man's arm, but strong fingers smashed his wrist against the wall while a steel blade pinned his hand in place. His scream cut off when another hand slammed into his chin clamping his mouth shut. The last thing he saw was Sam Bennett staring at him. Then he heard Siciliano's bubbling purr just before Vito yanked the knife from his hand and brought it slashing across his neck.

. . .

Leonardo and Angela Serafini had always worked late after their store closed for the day. There were shelves to stock, and Angela prided herself on a clean store. They had worked hard for the past eighteen years building a successful business. It wasn't easy. But, they had almost saved enough to return to Italy and live in comfort. Now The Society of Honor demanded more of their hard-earned dollars. So Leonardo had joined South Sharon's newly formed White Hand Society. Against Angela's wishes he had joined in the attack against members of the Black Hand. Two days ago the head of the White Hand was gunned down in his own home. Tonight they worked with the shades drawn and jumped at every noise.

Angela was just sweeping the last pile of dirt into a dustpan when she noticed shadows outside the window. Suddenly the window shattered and something bounced off the meat counter and rolled across the floor by her feet. It was a bundle of orange sticks taped to a brick with a short sputtering fuze. Angela began to scream. As Leonardo raced toward his wife the place erupted in a blast of fire and smoke. The Serafini's would not return to the old country.

. . .

In New Castle, Leo Mizio was having a good time. Four Italian men had invited him to join their table in the barroom of Hotel New Castle where Leo did most of his drinking these days. They had been laughing and talking about the old country most of the evening. Leo hadn't had such a good time since the American newspapers carried the story about him turning in Absardio Sabino.

Absardio had approached Leo's mother while she was attending a funeral and told her that unless Leo paid the money he demanded the Society was going to have her son killed. That's when Leo, and his brother Angelo, got in touch with The White Hand Society through Father DeMita. Since then, he had received two threatening letters from

The Society of Honor demanding that he withdraw the charges against Absardio Sabino.

Leo hadn't seen these men before, but they seemed like a merry bunch. Now the friendliest one in the group asked him to show them where an acquaintance lived in the Fifth Ward. Leo and Angelo owned two apartment buildings there, so he readily agreed. The route took him right past his house, and he could easily direct them from there.

They started off singing songs from the old country as they made their way up the street. When they arrived at the front of Leo's house, he invited them in for a final drink. They refused, and suddenly their demeanor changed.

"We have some important business to discuss with you," a man said.

The other men were nervously glancing every which way.

"What is your business?" he demanded.

A voice behind him declared gruffly, "you'll find out soon enough."

Suddenly, Leo realized these men weren't his friends. He screamed for his brother at the top of his voice.

One of the men dropped his hand into a coat pocket as though he were grabbing a weapon. Leo was faster. A .32 cal. revolver popped out of his pocket, and Leo spun around in a circle jamming the barrel against every nose closest to him. With round eyes and hands waving in the air, they began backing away. A knife dropped, clattering across the brick pavement.

Leo could hear his brother, Angelo, running down the lane. Now three of the men turned and began running. Leo didn't see the fourth man trying to open a razor behind his back, but he heard the man groan when Angelo slammed into him. The instrument bounced under Leo's legs drawing his attention momentarily. When Leo saw the open razor lying on the street, a red rage gripped his soul. The fleeing men suddenly began high stepping down the street pursued by short jabbing tongues of flame and the roaring of Leo's pistol.

"Leo! It's OK! I've got this one!" Angelo shouted.

He spun around to see a painful grimace on the face of the man his brother held in an arm lock. Suddenly, Leo Mizio was shaking all over.

"Put the gun away, Leo," his brother said. We'll take this one inside and call the polizia."

The episode made headlines in The New Castle News, but the skirmishes didn't end there.

In Hillsville, members of The White Hand Society were threatened with knives and razors. More families quietly packed their meager belongings and moved away. Production at both quarries was at an all time low.

Nick Tergilli and Frank Santi were under siege. No one came to the meetings anymore, and they feared to leave the hotel. The two men sat at a table in the kitchen examining the second letter Frank received from The Black Hand in as many weeks.

Frank Santi stroked a wrinkled hand over the white stubble on his face. It sounded like two pieces of sandpaper rubbing together. "My wife and daughter must not learn of this," he whispered.

Nick slowly nodded. He had taken the first letter to District Attorney Young in New Castle and demanded action. The letter, written in Italian, had demanded Frank pay $1000 to correct wrongs done to The Society of Honor and to receive what it called the hand of friendship. The last sentence was written in blood. "Lose no time, otherwise death!" There was no signature, only a few crosses also scribbled in blood. Nick read the letter to District Attorney Young before demanding the arrest of Joe Boggiano.

The D.A. tapped a long elegant finger against his chin before answering. "We can't pick Joe Boggiano up without proof, and there is nothing in this letter that implicates him."

"But, surely you could arrest Boggiano on suspicion," Nick suggested.

The D.A. patiently shook his head. "We could only hold him forty-eight hours without proof. Then we would be obliged to let him go."

When Nick asked for police protection, District Attorney Young sadly shook his head. "I'm sorry," he said. Then, noting the fear in Nick Tergilli's face, he added. "Listen Nick, I shouldn't even tell you this, but help is on the way. That is all I can say. You're just going to have to trust me for now."

That was five days ago. Now they received the second letter that was even more explicit. If Frank didn't come up with $1500, he and his family were going to be blown up along with the hotel.

Frank's eyebrows furled over his hooked nose as he slammed his hand down on the open letter.

"I'll tell you what we are going to do." Frank whispered. "Many of the Society men frequent Signora Firilli's store. We will ask her to give them a message for Boggiano. We will tell that pig-of-a-man we have shown these letters to the American polizia. We will tell him we are working with them, and that if anything should happen to us the American's will come here in force."

Nick frowned. "That could be dangerous, uncle."

"Bah!" Frank snorted. "Everything we have been doing is dangerous." He tapped the letter on the table with his finger. "This is dangerous. Doing nothing is more dangerous!"

"Perhaps you are right, uncle. But we must be careful. Maybe, we should send someone to Signora Firilli first to see if she will accept this message for Boggiano."

"Si," Frank agreed. "We will send my daughter. At least they're not hurting women so far."

Signora Firilli replied that she would discuss this with her husband. The next evening a boy came with a note. Signora Firilli was asking that they bring the message in person. That way, she wrote, Frank could explain exactly what he wanted her to convey so there wouldn't be a misunderstanding. She suggested they come about mid-morning when there were fewer customers to bother with.

Frank and Nick found two of the four tables in Signora Firilli's store piled full of merchandise waiting to be placed on shelves. Two men in work clothes and covered with lime dust, sat at the third table sipping a glass of wine. The other table sat in front of a row of wooden pegs fastened to the wall near the door. A dusty jacket hung on one peg and an equally dusty hat on another. With the jingling of the bell, Mrs. Firilli plowed through the heavy drapes hanging across the entry to her kitchen. Her face lit into a smile when she saw Nick and Frank standing by the door.

"Why, Signore Santi!" she exclaimed. "So good of you to come by."

Frank bowed stiffly from the waist. "Signora Firilli," he gestured toward Nick. "This is Signore Tergilli."

"Pleased to meet you, young man," she said pleasantly. "Now why don't you sit down? I'll bring some wine while Signore Santi fills me in on the latest gossip from the hotel?"

Nick's serious face showed concern. "But, Signora Firilli, we must talk with you together."

"Don't be foolish, young man. I have known Signore Santi for many years. He is perfectly capable of handling an old woman by himself. Now you just sit down while I bring some wine. I don't need both of you confusing these old ears. Signore Santi will do perfectly well. Won't you, Frank?"

Frank shrugged. "Si, I guess it will be best if only one of us does the speaking."

With that Mrs. Firilli slipped her arm through Frank's and began towing him toward her kitchen. A minute later she swept back through the curtain with a glass of wine.

"Don't worry," she said, "he'll be out just as soon as I get it all wrote down."

As she turned to leave, the two dusty men stood up and clanked a coin down on the table.

"Grazie, signores," she said to them. "Give a care up at that quarry. We don't need any more accidents."

"Si, signora. We'll be careful."

The men made their way over to the pegs behind Nick and began fumbling for their garments. Nick, never took his worried eyes off the curtain. He heard the rustle of clothing, and smelled the sweet reek of lime dust just before an explosion of pain and white light went off in his head. Then blackness engulfed him.

One of the men grabbed the slim youth before he slumped unto the floor. The other man slipped the leather wrapped sap into his pocket as his partner swung Nick over his shoulder like a sack of potatoes. While one man carried Nick out the door the other gulped down the glass of wine, pulled the chair back from the table slightly, then followed his partner outside.

More than a half-hour passed before Mrs. Firilli finally understood the message she was to convey to Joe Boggiano. She carefully wrote down every word, and even then she seemed to have a hard time understanding exactly what Frank wanted her to say. Now Nick was gone.

"Oh, not to worry, signore," Mrs. Firilli declared. "See? He finished his wine and probably went back to the hotel."

"Si," Frank replied uncertainly, "but this is not like him."

When Frank Santi left, Mrs. Firilli frowned at the closed door. "Messages," she mumbled. "He'll get a message."

Nick Tergilli awoke to a searing pain in his head. The slightest movement sent jagged bolts of lighting tearing through his skull and almost made him pass out again. His stomach kept threatening to expel his breakfast, and he fought to control it. The struggle was lethal. A fowl tasting rag was stuffed in his mouth. A bandanna that ran through his teeth like a horse's bit held the rag. With his hands bound behind his back and his feet tied together Nick couldn't stand. He was lying on a muddy floor in someone's dark and musty basement. Nick could only see the faint outline of a barrel by his head and what appeared to be the bottom of a pair of steps.

Nick lay still for a long time listening to someone walking on the floor above and a rat scurrying around nearby. Eventually he could wiggle around some without lighting bolts ripping through his skull, but his head still thumped terribly.

He must have passed out again because the red fire was still behind his eyes when Nick felt strong hands jerk him to his feet. With grunts and curses the men began to drag him up the stairs into a stream of yellow light. Nick's shins banged against the rough edges of steps as he struggled to make his legs work. When they thrust the young man into a room full of people he nearly collapsed. Joe Boggiano sat on a chair directly in front of Nick. Vito Siciliano stood behind Boggiano like a leering carnivore. Sam Bennett, Jim Rossi, Londo Racca, and Mario Nardozi were there among others.

"Cut him loose," Boggiano ordered.

Fingers fumbled at the knot behind his head and then the bandanna was off. When they cut his hands free Nick nearly gagged as he pulled the filthy rag out of his mouth. The men laughed.

"So! The great Nick Tergilli," Boggiano sneered. He swept his hand outward in a welcoming gesture. "So we finally get to meet, no?"

Nick's voice came out in choking gasps. His mouth was dry and raw, and his tongue didn't seem to work properly. "Ki...kidnapped me," he managed finally.

Joe Boggiano rose slowly and took a step toward Nick. "Kidnapped you? Those are strong words for someone who doesn't even have the honor to answer my requests for a meeting." His voice was mockingly pleasant. "We extend to you the honor of joining our society, but you don't even show enough respect to answer. Later, we invite you to sit down and discuss our differences." Now his voice began to harden. "Again you show no respect!"

Joe's face began clouding over. His voice dropped into a deep rumble. "What am I supposed to do, huh? Am I supposed to come crawling on my belly to a dog such as you?"

Boggiano's meaty hand came crashing down across Nick's face knocking him to the floor. Blood flowed from a split lip. Then Joe bent over and spit into Nick's face.

When Boggiano stood he gestured to the men who had brought Nick into the room. "Get the slobbering idiot on his feet."

When they dragged Nick to his feet, Boggiano's deep rumbling filled the room. "You dare challenge The Society of Honor?"

Nick held his head up and stared boldly into Boggiano's enraged face. "I am prepared to die, signore. Do what you must."

Boggiano's harsh laughter was frightening. Joe turned to face the others standing behind him. "So, he thinks we intend to kill him does he?"

There was a smattering of chuckles as though all this were only a cruel joke. Boggiano whirled, facing Nick once again. This time his voice was low, threatening. "You may very well wish to die before this is over, Tergilli." Joe took a step closer to Nick and put his face very close to his. "But if you die, it will happen because you choose to do so."

Suddenly Joe sat down in his chair with a flourish. He studied Nick a moment before speaking again. "Just to show that we are honorable men, I am going to give you one last chance. Take the oaths of The Society of Honor this night and," he shrugged slightly, "maybe pay a small fine, say five hundred dollars, and we'll let you go."

Nick stiffened. A hard, determined look settled on his face. "I would never dishonor myself, and my father's name, by joining with you murdering dogs."

Surprisingly Boggiano just sat there slowly nodding his head. "I thought so," he said finally. "I thought so."

Joe waved his arm. "Show this dog what the Society thinks of those who don't show respect."

The men lined up in front of Nick. One by one they brought their open palms across his face with a sickening smack, then spit squarely into his face. Amazingly he was still on his feet when they were done. Blood poured freely from a laceration above his eye and from a broken nose. One eye had nearly swollen shut. An ear was raw and bleeding. Spittle stained with tobacco juice and mingled with blood dripped from his chin.

"Take him outside and strip off his clothes," Boggiano ordered.

Rough hands pushed and shoved Nick into the cool night air. The smell of freshly cut grass blended with the rich odor of freshly turned earth in a nearby garden. Suddenly they were pulling at his clothes, popping buttons and tearing his shirt. Nick tried to struggle, but a fist smashed into the back of his head, and he fell to his knees. Another fist slammed into his face knocking him backwards. He came to a few minutes later lying naked on the grass with something warm splashing across his body and the reek of urine steaming in the cool air. Nick struggled to get up until someone kicked him hard in the ribs. Hot, searing pain shot through his side. He lay still gasping for breath and spitting out the salty liquid running into his mouth and nose. Then the men turned away buttoning their pants.

"Bring the buckets," Joe rumbled. "We'll give this dog a taste of justice he'll not be forgetting soon!"

They plopped two buckets of filth from the nearby outhouse down beside the naked man. Nick tried to move again, but the pain in his side caused him to moan and he lay back. The men laughed harshly. Two men, using work gloves and a broom, scooped out handfuls of slimly, stinking filth and began to rub it all over the stricken man. They paid particular attention to his head, rubbing it into his hair, and shoving the foul stuff into his ears, nose and mouth. Nick began to gag and his stomach turned over trying to expel the horrible stuff from his mouth and throat. He managed to roll onto his good side before passing out again.

"Drag this worthless piece of shit into Hillsville," Joe said, "and let him lie on the street for everyone to see."

Chapter 18

The charge of dynamite blew out most of the windows at Frank Santi's hotel and ripped a large smoking hole in the porch roof.

Toni Santi paced the lobby. "Where is Nick, Papa?"

His father sat staring at the floor. "I sent him home yesterday," he muttered.

"This is all his fault," Toni exclaimed. "If he hadn't come here, this would never have happened."

Toni's father slowly raised his head. "No," he declared suddenly. "You are wrong again, Toni. Nick was trying to do a good thing. He was trying to help people fight back against a monster called The Society of Honor. Some honor, huh? They strike in the night like thieves!"

Frank nodded toward the ceiling and what was beyond. A tinkling of glass and the voices of women drifted down from above. "They strike without honor against women and children."

Frank began trembling. He squeezed his eyes shut for a moment. Two tears broke loose anyway and ran down the prickly furrows of his cheeks.

"If the coward who threw it had been more accurate, your sister would have been blown to pieces!" The old man's voice dropped to nearly a whisper. "Nina heard the dynamite hit her windowsill and roll down the roof." Then Frank looked pointedly into his son's stricken face. "The blast knocked her to the floor. Had she been in front of the window...," Toni's father shook his head, unable to speak the words.

Tears welled in Toni's eyes. "I'm sorry, Papa," he said softly. "I'm so sorry."

Frank took a few cautious steps toward his weeping son and put his arms around him. "That's OK, Toni. I forgive you. Nina got cut with glass fragments but she will be okay."

After a few moments Toni pushed his father to arms length. A fire glowed in his eyes. "They must pay, Papa!"

"No! This ends now. No more, Toni. Promise me! No more."

"But they attacked my family."

Frank looked into his son's face. "Just let it end, Toni. Do not challenge them. You hear me? Just let it end and have nothing more to do with them."

Toni allowed his head to drop. "I want to see Nina, Papa." He got shakily to his feet and started up the stairs.

The next day Detective Logan stopped at the hotel with an Italian interpreter. Nick Tergilli had not gone straight home. He stopped to see District Attorney Young and told him what happened. Detective Logan said Nick planned to bring charges against Boggiano and some of the others if Frank Santi would back him. But when Frank learned nothing would be done about the bombing without witnesses, Toni's father had enough.

That evening Toni found Joe Boggiano at Rossi's saloon. Joe, Sam Bennett, and Jim were sitting at one of the tables, a half-empty bottle of wine in front of them. Toni approached the table with long, purposeful strides. Sam Bennett lurched to his feet, dropping a hand into his jacket pocket. The hard look on Toni's face softened somewhat.

"So, compare, you would gun down a friend would you? You have changed, Sam," he said sadly. "These men have corrupted you."

Sam's mouth remained a thin flat line.

Toni turned his gaze on Boggiano who regarded him with a glimmer of amusement. "You attacked my family, signore!"

Joe Boggiano shrugged. "I heard there was some sort of accident at your father's hotel, but what does that have to do with me, huh?"

Toni's fist curled into tight balls. "You pig! You almost killed my sister."

Joe turned his palms up and gestured toward the chair in front of Toni. "I understand your concern. It was unfortunate. Come, sit down and have some wine with us, no?"

Toni gripped the back of the chair till his knuckles cracked. "I would sooner drink with the devil!" Suddenly he spat on the table. "That is what I think of your rotten society."

Boggiano bounced to his feet knocking his chair over.

"Oh? Maybe you would like to beat me up the way you did my cousin? Or maybe my old friend, Sam, here," Toni allowed his hand to sweep in the latter's direction, "would rather shoot me. Well go ahead. The polizia are watching you closely, signore. Do you know that?"

Boggiano didn't move. His clenched fists rested on the table as if frozen.

Toni hurried on, "I'll bet you thought my cousin would be too ashamed to say anything about what you did to him, but Nick went to the polizia. He is going to have you arrested. You are going to prison, signore!" Casting a defiant glance at Sam, Toni stalked out the door.

A week passed. Then word flashed through the settlements that Joe Boggiano left for Italy. People flocked to Boggiano's house to see for themselves. They found the place deserted. Rumors claimed he took ten thousand dollars in gold collected over the years through The Society of Honor. Rocco Racca was in prison, and Joe Boggiano had left. The people were jubilant. But it was a quiet, if not troubled, joy as people waited nervously to see what new terror would follow.

The chording of a guitar roused Toni Santi from his bed one warm summer night as a wedding party spilled into the street beside the apartment he and Carmine had rented. He returned earlier in the evening from Pittsburgh where he had met with Nick Tergilli. Traveling in the humidity had tired him, but now, in the cool of the evening, the young man grabbed his mandolin and went outside. Toni joined the guitar player and together they provided music for the wedding party as they sang and danced in the street. Sitting on an old nail keg, Toni felt a rough hand shove his shoulder causing his fingers to strike a wrong chord. He looked up to see Mario Nardozi swaying over him.

Mario pushed an unsteady finger at Toni's face. "You are a traitor to our society," he stammered. "Come on! Fight me if you dare."

Tony glared at the younger man, "Get out of here, Nardozi!"

He watched Mario slink away as Carmine came over to him holding their youngest son, still in diapers. Giuseppe, now five, was asleep in the apartment. People danced in the dusty street and pinned money on the bride's dress as one acquaintance after another twirled her around and around.

Suddenly, Carmine let out a delighted squeal. "Dominick!" She began dancing up and down on her toes like a little girl.

Toni looked up to see Dominick Prugitore coming toward them through the crowd, a broad smile stretching the pock marks on his normally serious face. As Dominick drew near he gave Carmine and the baby a friendly hug before kissing his friend's wife on the cheek.

Smiling, Toni stood up and embraced his friend. "Compare, what brings you back to this murder hole?"

Dominick shrugged. "My business in Pittsburgh was finished. Besides, there isn't such good work in the city."

"When did you get in?"

"Just a little while ago. I'm on my way over to tell Sam I'm back. I hear he's in charge now."

The change in Toni's demeanor was almost frightening. Toni spat on the ground. "That Judas-pig! Have you heard what they did to my family?"

Dominick nodded, but Toni proceeded to tell him about the bombing of his father's hotel anyway. "They almost killed Nina in the blast. So I confronted that dog Boggiano and told him my cousin and I would see him in jail." Toni smiled. "Now he's left for good. Scared I guess."

"Toni, no!" Carmine wailed. "You promised your father you would let it go." She raised a hand to her mouth, trying hard not to cry.

"No, Carmine. I let papa believe what he wanted, but I never promised. Do you think I could let something like this pass?"

Dominick felt a chill. He knew his friend could still be in trouble. "Compare, we must talk with Sam."

"Baugh! Sam's as bad as the rest. He was there when I confronted Boggiano. Sam had a gun in his pocket. He would have shot me if Boggiano said to."

"Sam is your friend, compare. He could not do such a thing."

Toni sadly shook his head. "Sam has changed, Dominick. Now I must ask you the same question my cousin, Nick, asked me. Where do you stand? Wwith the no-good society or your friends?"

Dominick stood speechless. Sorrow, fear, anger, all the familiar, ugly emotions poured through him again. He had been back in Hillsville less than an hour, and already he was caught in the middle. The young detective steeled himself to give the answer he knew would alienate him from Toni. It was Carmine who spared him.

"You men wait a minute," she demanded. They watched her say a few words to another woman before handing her the baby. Carmine marched back to them with a determined stride to stand defiantly in front of her husband.

"Toni, you sit yourself down on that keg and play us a tune. Dominick and I are going to dance." She grabbed Dominick by the arm, then stood on her toes to give her husband a quick kiss. "I've heard enough of this foolishness for one night."

Soon the sweet chords of Toni's mandolin picked up a fast number that the guitar player quickly followed. Dominick twirled Carmine through the crowd and the dust. He felt relieved for the moment but knew he would have to answer the question Toni asked sooner or later. Probably sooner, and the thought saddened him. He looked over Carmine's bouncing head at his friend sitting on the keg, concentrating on the instrument in his hands. Mario Nardozi was standing behind him. Suddenly, something didn't seem right. Everyone was watching the dancers milling in the street. He saw something flash in Mario's hand as it arced above Toni's head, but he couldn't stop dancing. It was as though his legs were moving automatically, while his mind watched in horrible fascination as the hand dropped toward his friend's neck. "No!" he screamed.

His shout froze Carmine in wide-eyed fear. Dominick's legs finally stopped their crazy movement as he gathered them to run, but it was too late. He watched as the knife sank into Toni's neck.

The bite of steel caused Toni to whirl, breaking his attacker's hold on the hilt. He looked into the wide eyes of Mario who began to stagger backwards before he turned and started running. Toni leaped to his feet and flipped his beloved mandolin over his back in one fluid motion. He could feel the steel in his neck and glancing down focused on the black, bloody handle sticking up toward his ear. In a fit of rage he grabbed the handle and yanked the blade from his neck. Arterial blood spurted into the air, splattering the horrified guitar player beside him. In long legged strides, he began to overtake Mario who was fleeing toward the church and Kennedy's Crossing. Toni overtook the drunken assassin at the edge of town and, grabbing Mario by the shoulder, plunged the knife twice into the boy's armpit. Then he collapsed. Mario broke free, staggering into the woods below the church as Dominick and a group of men came running up.

Dominick jerked to a stop when he saw Toni lying on the broken mandolin, blood spurting from his neck. Kneeling beside his friend, he tried to stanch the flow of blood with a bandanna as others gathered around.

Someone tore off his shirt and thrust it into Dominick's hands. He tied the blood soaked bandanna in place over the wound with several layers of shirt, but blood still seeped through. Suddenly he heard a strangled scream as Carmine threw herself over her husband's body, wailing loudly.

"Do...don't take me home." Toni gasped amid a wheezing spray of red. "Don't want...frighten children."

Gnarled hands pulled Carmine away from her husband. "Come, daughter, he needs air."

Dominick looked up into the tortured face of Frank Santi as he held his daughter-in-law in a consoling embrace.

Toni died long before faint streaks of red began silhouetting the hills east of New Castle. Bloody Hillsville, Dominick thought as he stared out of District Attorney Young's kitchen window at the brilliant sunrise. Perhaps the American newspapers dubbed it right.

"Does that shirt fit all right?" District Attorney Young asked as he set steaming cups of black coffee down in front of Dominick and Detective Logan.

"Scusi? Oh, yes. Thank you, sir." His blood soaked shirt lay by the kitchen door.

"Toni was your friend, I understand," Mr. Young said.

"Si," he answered. Then his voice grew sterner. "So was Sam Bennett."

The district attorney and the county detective chanced a worried glance at each other. Earlier, Dominick had told them about the encounter between Toni, Boggiano and Sam Bennett.

"Perhaps, there is an opportunity here," Mr. Young offered.

Dominick shook his head. "Sam is not a leader, but he's no fool. He may even try to bring Romon Cerini back to take over." He shook his head again. "I just don't know. I've been away while important things have been happening. I wouldn't be here now except for the steel mills in Pittsburgh."

The other men nodded. They knew The United States Steel Corporation had hired the Pinkerton's to destroy The Black Hand Society. The steel mills needed limestone in large quantities, and the situation in Hillsville had damaged the quarry's production. They knew too, that the Pinkerton's were supposed to cooperate with the local authorities this time. The two county men glanced at each other again, and Creighton Logan gave a barely perceptional nod to the district attorney.

"Listen, Dominick, I'm going to share some information that must not leave this room. We have already sent extradition papers to Buffalo for the arrest of Cerini. That should pull the rug out from under Sam Bennett. If you remain his friend, perhaps Sam could be led into a trap that will catch the whole gang.

Dominick slowly nodded. "I think it's worth a try." He paused and gave each of the others a searching stare. "But you must remember, I am only useful if I remain undercover. If you do or say anything that could compromise my position, I will be dead."

They sat under a heavy silence for a moment before Dominick rose, extending his hand. "Thank you for the loan of the shirt, Mr. Young. Perhaps, I should get back to Hillsville." He paused to recover his bloody shirt from the floor before stepping into the early quiet of a Sunday morning.

Chapter 19

A large piece of limestone bias clanked off an iron rail of the Pennsylvania line as Dominick lined up another piece of crushed stone with the toe of his boot and sent it bouncing down the row of ties. Already the morning air hung heavy with humidity. He had spent Sunday settling into the little room at Nick Sparaio's house, while trying to convince himself Sam Bennett didn't have anything to do with their friend's murder.

He could see Sam's little house looming through the haze in the distance. He noticed with no little apprehension that the fence wore a new coat of paint. How dare he prosper, he wondered, after what happened to Toni.

The screen door clattered when he rapped on its wooden frame. Then Sam appeared in the doorway. He just stood there, mouth tight, staring at Dominick through the screen.

"Hello, Sam."

Still Sam stood there.

"I understand you are in charge now, compare. I thought, I'd better report in."

Sam's eyes tightened slightly.

"Toni's dead, Sam. He died yesterday morning."

Sam's lips compressed into a bloodless line.

Suddenly Maria was there. "Dominick!" she cried. When Maria glanced at her husband, her smiling face changed to an expression of concern. "Sam? Aren't you going to let your friend in?"

Sam pushed the screen door open a crack with his left hand. When Dominick opened the door he could see Sam's other hand was clutching something inside the pocket of his trousers.

Dominick bent to kiss Maria on the cheek, ignoring Sam for the moment. "You're as beautiful as ever I see."

Maria flashed another smile before casting a worried glance at her husband.

Dominick extended his hand. "Sam, are you all right?"

Sam blinked before withdrawing the hand from his pocket to grip his friend's. His hand felt clammy and trembled slightly.

A half-apologetic smile curled up one side of Sam's face. "Looks as though we have a guest for dinner," he declared, pulling Dominick into an embrace. "I'm glad you're back, compare," he choked, hugging him like a brother.

They spent the time before dinner getting reacquainted. Sam wanted to know what he did while he was away. Dominick lied. He was getting good at it.

After dinner the two men, smoking wrinkled little cigars, strolled down a path to the river. There, where the water gurgled quietly, their conversation turned serious.

"I don't know what I'm going to do," Sam began. "One day Boggiano sends for me. When I get there, he and Rossi are loading the last of Joe's things onto a wagon. Vito is there, too. Joe: he just climbs in and picks up the reins. Then he says, 'Sam, you're in charge.' Just like that!"

"So you are the capo now?"

Sam grunted. "Capo of what?" He paused to toss a stone at the river. "Boggiano took all the money. I don't know if Vito will work for me or not."

"We don't need Siciliano," Dominick said.

"I don't know. Everything is such a mess, and there's the White Hand and all. Without Vito, I don't know if we can keep up the collections."

"Why did Boggiano leave?" Dominick watched the water part to accept another stone Sam tossed into river. The ripples quickly caught in the fast current and swirled away.

"Rossi told me there was a warrant out for Joe. Had something to do with Nick Tergilli and ...well, that whole thing was one awful mess."

Dominick, noticed Sam avoided mentioning Toni. "You still have Jim Rossi. What about the others?"

"I don't know if they'll work for me. Jim will vouch for what Joe said that day, but it's not like receiving a blessing from the Dons."

Suddenly, an idea that had been playing at the edges of Dominick's mind began to crystallize.

"Dominick," Sam said slowly, "I'm going to need a lieutenant. Someone I can trust." His eyes flickered sideways at Dominick then scurried away. "Will you do it? Will you be my second in command?"

"I have to know one thing first, compare," he said slowly, his voice deepening with emotion. "Did you have anything to do with Toni's murder?"

The eyes faltered, blinked. Then Sam stood up, nervously brushing off the seat of his trousers. Dominick noticed a heavy bulge in his trouser pocket.

"No," Sam said flatly, "I didn't know anything about it."

Your lying. Dominick thought. He shrugged. "OK," he said tensely, getting up. "I had to know, Sam. I had to ask."

"You'll do it then?"

"Si," Dominick said. "Count on me."

Turning back to the house, he put his arm around Sam's shoulder. "Seems to me," he said, "you need conformation from the Dons. Write to them. Suggest a meeting like we had last summer when we had that trouble between Rocco and Romon. Ask for advice. They'll have to put someone in charge, and I'm sure they would bless Boggiano's appointment."

By the time they got back to the house, Sam was nodding. "You will write these letters for me, compare?"

"Si," Dominick replied, his mind racing ahead. He needed to get in touch with Superintendent Dimuro right away.

They met at Toni Capazzi's room in Youngstown. It was the third meeting over as many weeks in as many different places. District Attorney Young and County Detective Logan were present, as was another man Dominick had never met before. He was a tall, stern looking man of about thirty who carried himself with the bearing of a military officer. Things were moving so fast it was unsettling.

"Gentlemen," Mr. Young said. "This is Lieutenant Campbell of the Pennsylvania Constabulary." There were nods and handshakes all around.

"The lieutenant is responsible for establishing a detachment of troopers in Hillsville after. …ah…our little business is finished there," the District Attorney continued, smiling.

Dominick cast a concerned look at Superintendent Dimuro.

"Dominick," Dimuro said, "would you fill us in on the latest developments in Hillsville, please."

A hush fell over the room.

"Well," Dominick replied, "Don Cardi from Pittsburgh will not be present for the meeting. The Don is getting old, and he's not well enough to travel. I suspect he will send someone in his place."

He waited until groans of disappointment settled before continuing.

"Likewise Don Filasto from New York sent his regrets. However two of his lieutenants have already arrived in Hillsville. They are helping Sam collect dues from delinquent members."

"Who are these men?" Dimuro asked, notepad in hand.

"One is Nicolo Leraci, the other's name is Pete Novello. They're from New Jersey." He looked at Superintendent Dimuro. "I've included a description of them in my reports."

Frank Dimuro nodded. "Go on."

"As far as I know Don Sochetti will be there in person to run the meeting. Luca Caruzzi will probably accompany him. The meeting will be held this Sunday, probably in the woods behind the Peanut settlement where it was held last year."

"Good!" Lieutenant Campbell exclaimed. "That's where we'll take 'em."

Dominick flashed a worried look at Dimuro.

"I'm afraid that wouldn't be advisable, gentlemen," the superintendent declared.

The lieutenant slammed a hand on his knee. "Nonsense! My troopers are mounted. They'll go through those woods like fleas over a hound's back!"

"Your men won't get within five miles of Hillsville before the suspects were long gone," Dominick stated flatly. "But there is another reason why it wouldn't work, Lieutenant. The meeting site is on the steep bluffs above the railroad. The only level access is a narrow path that leads in from the Peanut settlement. Your men, if they could reach that point without being detected, would be obliged to ride in single file. That could be a problem considering Vito Siciliano will have his men surrounding the area, all of them armed to the teeth."

"I'm sorry, Lieutenant," Mr. Young interrupted. "I know your people want in on this, but we simply can't afford a detachment of uniformed police to be seen in the area."

Noticing the disappointment on the lieutenant's face, Mr. Young continued in a softer tone. "Your role will be most important, Lieutenant. You will insure the peace, thereby giving those foreigners who have been victimized by the Black Hand the courage to testify."

"And I can assure you they won't," Dominick injected, "unless the government does something to protect them."

"All right," Lieutenant Campbell answered reluctantly, "but how do you propose to catch the leaders?"

"On Saturday, they'll be playing cards at either Mrs. Firilli's store or Jim Rossi's saloon," Dominick replied. "I will find out exactly where and let Mr. Young know."

"Which brings us to the reason we called this meeting," District Attorney Young added. "The Pinkertons and I have a plan that just might snare the whole nest."

Chapter 20

Dominick was worried. Despite the tight cloak of security surrounding their plans, The New Castle News had reported on Friday that warrants for members of the Black Hand had been issued. Worse, the paper also reported that a dozen Pinkerton detectives were in the city. Angry voices greeted the young detective as he pulled open the screen door at Rossi's saloon. A small group of men had gathered here. They stopped talking when they heard the creak of the door's spring.

"Dominick!" Jim hurried around the table they were gathered at. "You must talk sense into this man." He pointed at Sam, who was standing rigidly, arms folded across his chest, lips pressed into a tight stubborn line. "Look at the American newspaper." Jim's hand waved at an open copy of the paper spread out on the table. "I only understand, maybe, one word out of three. But something is wrong. We must stop the meeting!"

"I read the papers, Jim. How could they have warrants for our guests when the polizia don't even know who they are?"

"Someone must have told the Americans!" Jim shouted back.

Dominick shrugged. "So? What makes you think they are coming here?" He glanced at Sam. "What do you say, compare? Do you think we should stop the meeting?"

Sam Bennett only offered a slow shake of his head.

Jim threw his hands in the air. "I tell you," he said shaking a finger, "Something is not smelling so good here. Two weeks ago the Johnson Quarry told their workers the women couldn't present their husband's load-slips for payment anymore. Now this. I say we warn Don Sochetti and the others."

Nick Sparaio, never one for many words, began nodding his head.

Dominick walked to the table and pulled out a chair. Settling into the seat, he casually folded one leg over the other. "Let me tell you what will happen if this meeting is called off," he said quietly. "Look around the room." He gestured casually with his arm. "Go ahead, look around. I see six people out of how many society men left in Hillsville? Twenty? Maybe more? Without a leader sanctioned by the Dons our society will continue to break up. The White Hand Society will grow."

He nodded at Rossi. "Do you think people will continue to come here to drink?"

He gestured at Nick Sparaio. "You bought Rocco Racca's store. They only pay your outrageous prices out of respect for the Society."

"So, why do you think the quarry felt comfortable enough to require the men to submit their own load-slips again? It is because they believe we are weak." He shrugged and rolled his arm over gesturing slightly toward Sam. "But, with a headman blessed by the Dons the people will know they must answer for what they do here. That is the real strength of The Society of Honor."

"What of the polizia?" Jim insisted. "What if they come here?"

"Our people know how to scramble out of the way. As for Don Sochetti, and the others? What is illegal about playing cards and drinking wine?"

"Suppose they come during the meeting?"

Dominick glanced at Sam with a raised eyebrow.

"Vito will be here tonight." Sam replied. "He will have enough men surrounding the area to give warning."

Sam glanced at Dominick before letting his gaze flicker across the other men. "One more thing. Dominick is going to be my lieutenant," he declared quickly.

Clearing his throat, Sam continued in a voice that trembled only slightly. "Dominick, I want you to take Santo here," he gestured toward a man with a nose that slanted crazily toward one side of his face, "and go to the quarry office."

Then he pointed at a skinny looking young man who always wore a smirking grin under a pair of sparkling brown eyes. "Take Luigi, too."

Luigi Scavello had a reputation as a brawler.

"Collect dues and five dollars fine from members who didn't show up at this meeting. We will show them Sam Benedetti is not to be trifled with."

The pay station for the Johnson Quarry sat on a little knoll next to the company's limestone crusher. It was a long, one-story building partitioned into three rooms. The pay station occupied the front with accounting offices in the middle and a storeroom in the rear. On the side facing the stone crusher a narrow corridor led to a heavy door bolted on the inside. In the center of the door was an eight by ten-inch opening protected with iron bars. Through this little window the workers received their pay. For security reasons, a company man stood outside to check the worker's pay stubs for errors, admitting them one at a time into the pay window. This afternoon a stranger stood beside the entry to the pay station.

A group of fifty or more workers gathered around the long wooden building. Mostly, they came straight from the quarry. They talked in small groups or sprawled among patches of withered grass coated with lime dust. Here and there a few groups of women alternated between talking and casting angry stares at Dominick's men. Even Santo, despite his hard looks, hunched his heavy shoulders under those stares.

In groups of two or three the workers approached the man beside the entry and handed over their pay slips. The man carefully studied each slip before running his finger down a wrinkled sheet of paper he carried inside his coat pocket. Sometimes the finger stopped and the man would look up reassuringly at the worker before declaring in Italian, "There seems to be some mistake. Come with me, and we'll take care of it."

The man would then lead the worker around the building to a back door. The man knocked loudly on the heavy door until a small peephole screeched open from inside. Peering at a pair of eyes and a nose framed in the hole, the man said in a voice loud enough for anyone nearby to hear, "There is something wrong with this man's slip. Fix it up." Whereupon the door would open partially, and the worker waved inside before the door slammed shut again. A slight shuffling sound sometimes followed the Pinkerton detective back into the sunshine.

By five o'clock seven men, known to be active in the Black Hand, had disappeared inside the pay shanty. Each time the detective strolled casually back to his place at the front of the building, Dominick feared other members of the Society would become suspicious. He breathed a sigh of relief when they continued talking with their fellow workers without seeming to notice.

He allowed Santo and Luigi to roam about collecting dues from members who weren't on the detective's list. They came back with more promises than coin, however. Sometime later some of the women began inquiring after their husbands. Dominick felt the tension slowly building among those still waiting for their pay.

One woman sat on the slope above the track with two dirty children clinging to a skirt pieced together from rags. Signora Terini was visibly pregnant. Her husband, an old man, gambled terribly. They said she slept on the floor with only a sack full of straw for a pillow. Her husband was inside with the detectives. While this was going on an engine backed a single boxcar onto the switch beside the crusher, not fifty paces from where they stood. The boxcar's double doors were tightly closed, but Dominick noticed they were not locked. The young detective nervously brushed at the strand of hair hanging over his forehead. By six o'clock eleven men had disappeared inside the back of the pay shanty.

Suddenly the doors of the boxcar were thrown open, and a body of armed men jumped out, led by Young and Logan. When Lieutenant Campbell and a contingent of uniformed troopers leaped from the car, Santo and Luigi turned and started to run past Dominick. Without thinking, he turned as if to run, then seemed to slip and fall directly in front of the two men. They fell together in a heap, legs and elbows thrashing wildly, before being sorted out and handcuffed by Detective Logan and the others. Dominick had the breath knocked out of him. Creighton Logan hauled him roughly to his feet.

"Well!" The burley detective demanded.

"Two." He managed to gasp, but it sounded more like "Whew".

"Give him a moment to catch his breath," Mr. Young said.

"The dagos are running, sir. We've got to get them before their bosses are warned."

"Two," Dominick finally managed between gasps. "Number two."

The county detective dropped his hold on Dominick's arm and motioned to a group of seven armed men, including Lieutenant Campbell and two of his troopers. Soon they were trotting quickly toward a settlement nearly a mile away.

Mr. Young motioned a young constable to him and pointed toward Dominick, "Take this man down to the building with the others," he ordered. After consulting with the Pinkerton detective who had the list of names, he formed several groups of policemen and detectives, sending them in search of those who were missing. Finally, in company with two deputies, the DA marched to the rear of the paymaster's building to wait.

Dominick sat handcuffed on the floor. With his back resting against the wall of the little storeroom he watched Toni Capazzi and Frank Dimuro methodically searching two prisoners. A double-edged stiletto and a straight razor joined a small pile of pocketknives on a table. These latest prisoners brought the total apprehended to eighteen. Time seemed to drag. Suddenly, Sam Bennett and Nick Sparaio stumbled into the room having been shoved through the doorway by Logan. Unlike the other prisioners, Bennett and Sparaio were already handcuffed.

"You needn't bother searching them," the county detective stated flatly. "We already have." He dangled a small chrome plated revolver from a finger thrust through the trigger guard. "Look what that little bugger had in his pocket," he added, nodding toward Sam.

"Where are the others?" the district attorney asked sharply.

Logan glanced at the prisoners sitting against the wall, then motioned toward the door with a perfunctory nod of his head. Tightening his lips, the DA followed him outside.

Dimuro and Capazzi started searching Sam and Nick as soon as the door closed. When they were finished, Toni told them to join the others by the wall. Dominick clumsily got to his feet as Sam and Nick ambled over. Nick only looked at his shoes. He seemed badly shaken. Dominick raised his eyebrows questioningly when Sam reached him. The latter shrugged and looked grim. Sam had a puffy, purple bulge under his left eye.

When the district attorney and county detective came back inside they gathered the confiscated weapons into a burlap sack and examined the list of names copied down by Superintendent Dimuro. Perhaps another half-hour passed before Lieutenant Campbell and his troopers returned. Another short conference was held outside. When the DA stepped back into the room he nodded at Dimuro, "Let's get them back to New Castle, shall we?"

With that, most of the officers filed outside. Those remaining began handcuffing the prisoners together in pairs. Speaking in Italian, Dimuro announced roughly, "We're going outside. You will walk directly to the boxcar and climb inside. Anyone who speaks will be clubbed down. If you try to run away you will be shot. Capeesh?"

The men nodded somberly.

"OK, on your feet! Line up at the door. When I tell you to move, don't stop until you are inside the car."

As they shuffled toward the line forming at the door, the heart-rending cries of women and children tore at Dominick's soul. He knew the families of these men were watching their only providers being marched away. Some of them would be reduced to begging, or worse. Amid piercing shrieks from loving mothers and the touching cries of "Papa, Papa!" the line stumbled to a halt.

The prisoners had been marching between a double file of heavily armed men with faces that reflected grim determination, excitement and fear. As the surging crowd of women and children reached the file of officers the men roughly pushed them back. That was what caused the prisoners to halt. Now Dominick could hear angry shouts from some of the Italian men who hadn't fled.

A rough hand shoved him against Nick Sparaio. "Move! Or I'll club you down."

"Keep going," Dominick shouted in Italian.

With tears etching furrows through the lime dust clinging to their cheeks the prisoners slowly stumbled forward.. Dominick caught a flurry of dirty rags out of the corner of his eye just as he started climbing into the boxcar. Rough hands grabbed his shoulder, rolling him across the wooden floor of the car and causing the heavy steel cuffs to bite into his flesh. Getting slowly to his feet, he watched Signora Terini fall to her knees on the stones along the track. Then her wails of anguish turned into a frenzied attempt at self-destruction as her husband's form entered the car. The train's conductor and another man grabbed the woman's arms to stop her from flailing at her swollen abdomen. Finally she fainted and lay still. The two men carried her to the top of the hill where several Italian women waved them away and began dousing cold water on the woman's face.

Dominick was relieved when the chugging engine drowned out her pathetic wails. The car was run into Lowellville over the Pennsylvania line, then across the river to the Pittsburgh & Lake Erie tracks. It was nine o'clock before their engine pulled them into the New Castle depot.

Within the hour the prisoners were roused from their cells and marched to the office of an alderman for arraignment. Thirteen were charged with conspiracy to rob. The rest, including Dominick, were charged with suspicion.

Except for Sam and Nick, the rest of the gang at Jim Rossi's saloon had escaped out the back. Sam told Dominick that he and Nick were supposed to delay the officers at the front of the building until the others made good their escape. That was how Sam earned his black eye. When Detective Logan saw him standing on the porch of the saloon with his hand in his pocket, as though he may be clutching a pistol, Logan leaped up the single step and punched Sam in the face. The blow knocked Sam to the floor, and while Logan snapped the handcuffs on, Nick just dropped to his knees begging for mercy. Meanwhile, the confusion allowed the rest to escape. Rossi led Don Sochetti, and the emissaries from New York and Pittsburgh, through the woods toward Youngstown.

Gently fingering his swollen eye, Sam smiled when he finished telling the story. "At least the Dons owe me a favor now. When we get out they will have to support me. It is a matter of honor."

Dominick shook his head gravely. "We're not going anywhere soon."

Sam looked around quickly then lowered his voice before leaning closer. "Don Sochetti told me he would send Luca Caruzzi here tomorrow to find an attorney. He'll get us out."

"And Siciliano?"

"Vito was supposed to come into Hillsville this evening to get everything ready for tomorrow. I doubt he will go near the place now."

That night Dominick wondered how he could get a note to Dimuro warning him that Caruzzi was coming to New Castle in the morning. Luca's saloon was across the state line. If the authorities could arrest him here it would save a lot of trouble and maybe some bloodshed.

He slept fitfully that night, listening to the snores and weeping in the cellblock. When sleep did come he dreamed of Rosa. He awoke with desire burning in his loins.

After breakfast the next morning the prisoners were taken one at a time for questioning. When Dominick was led into the sheriff's office, Dimuro was there along with Logan and District Attorney Young. They were all smiling when he entered the room.

Both of the county officials shook his hand. "You did a fine piece of work," Mr. Young said warmly. "We netted a big catch of fish."

Dominick sadly shook his head. "Like most fish stories, I'm afraid the big ones got away."

When he told them his information about Luca, the county detective grabbed his hat then turned toward Dominick. "How does Caruzzi normally travel?" he asked.

"He'll come by trolley."

"Make sure you get some help, Craig," the district attorney said as Logan started out the door.

"Unfortunately we lost Sochetti and the one from Pittsburgh," Young continued. "But, I'll wire the authorities in New York. Maybe they'll pick up the two from there and hold them for us." He didn't sound very confident.

Dimuro shifted his bulk from the corner of a desk and offered Dominick a cigar. After holding a match until the lad got the thing billowing, Frank looked at the district attorny. "I'll wire our Philadelphia office. Maybe we can put some of our people to watching the trains going into New York. Perhaps they can pluck them off the train as it passes through New Jersey. The people there owe us some favors. They'll hold them for us."

"There is one other problem, sir." Dominick said softly.

Both men paused to look at him.

"Vito Siciliano is probably hiding in Youngstown. But you can bet before the trials start, he'll sneak back into Hillsville and try to keep your witnesses from testifying."

The district attorney smiled thinly. "I think we have that covered, Dominick. A detachment of state troopers will be moving into Hillsville this week. They should be able to keep the peace while giving everyone there some confidence in American authority."

"I don't know, sir. Vito can slither around like a snake."

"Your assignment will continue in Hillsville," Dimuro said. "You'll have to hire on at one of the quarries for cover, but I want you to keep an eye out for Vito, or anyone else who may be trying to intimidate witnesses. We've worked too hard convincing people to sign complaints against these hoodlums. I'll not have it spoiled now."

Luca found himself in the New Castle jail before lunch, and the Lowellville headman was in a rage. When the cell door clanged shut, Luca whirled whipping his coat at the iron bars and causing the deputy to leap backwards with wide eyes. "You worthless dogs!" Luca raged, turning on the five men locked inside with him. "You Hillsville pigs just wouldn't quit, would you?" Luca stood in the middle of the cell with his hands on his hips glaring at everyone. "Now they're arresting our people in Youngstown!"

Then the burly saloon owner's eyes fell on Dominick and Sam sitting together on the edge of a bunk. In two strides he was looming over them.

"Hello, Luca," Dominick said. "Good to see you again."

Caruzzi gave him a hard glare before flipping his hand in the air. "Ah, Dominick. At least your friend Rocco Racca was only a fool!"

Then he reached down and grabbed the front of Sam's shirt lifting him easily off the bunk and hauling him up so they were nose to nose. Sam's toes were barely touching the concrete floor. To his credit Sam kept his mouth tightly compressed in a thin line.

"You, Benedetti." Luca growled into his face. "That greedy, no-good pig whose boots you licked is the one who started this…Boggiano!" He spat the name out, spraying Sam's face with spittle in the process.

There were shouts from the hall now, and the pounding of running shoes. Luca released Sam suddenly. He staggered back against the bunk and began straightening his rumpled shirt.

Caruzzi's attention diverted to Logan and a small group of deputies gathering around the cell door.

Dominick squeezed by Luca's bulk. "It's all right!" he shouted. "No one is hurt."

Suddenly Caruzzi's meaty hand clamped onto his shoulder, jerking him backwards. Luca shook a ham-sized fist at the county detective. "Some time we gonna' meet alone, Signore Big Shot! Then we will see how tough you are, no?"

"Anytime you want, you dago pimp!" came the reply.

"Oh yeah! Well how about right now, huh?" He began rolling his sleeves up. "Come on! Open the door, you gutless dog."

Logan grabbed a ring of keys from one of the deputies and started fitting it into the lock.

"That will be quite enough, Craig!" The voice was thin but cracked like a whip. District Attorney Young ambled slowly down the hallway; hands behind his back like a captain pacing the bridge of his ship. It was a ship in the midst of a storm. "Go back to the office. All of you."

Logan, his eyes locked with Caruzzi's like crossed swords, slowly pulled the key from the lock. After the others left, Mr. Young stood staring into the cell for several moments. Then he turned and walked back toward the office, polished shoes echoing through the hallway as though he were marching through the dusty vault of a tomb.

That evening Dominick and several others charged with suspicion were released. He and Nick Sparaio rode back to Hillsville on the electric car. They found the Italian settlements under a gloom of despondency. The dirt streets were strangely deserted. No violin or guitar music drifted from the tumbled down shanties. No children's laughter could be heard in the streets. When they arrived at Nick's store his wife told them they were sold out of satchels and trunks.

"All the Society people are running," she said softly.

The next morning Dominick walked to the Johnson Quarry to see about getting a job.

"We don't want no truck with the likes of you," a goose necked, bald-headed man told him at the company office when he recognized him as one of those arrested the previous Friday. He waved toward the door. "Best get on outa' here if ya know what's good fer ya."

On his way through town another strange sight greeted him. A double file of mounted state troopers, wearing gray uniforms and bobby helmets, pistols and Billy clubs slapping at their sides, rode into town straight-backed, hard-faced and deadly serious. Lieutenant Campbell turned the troop of constabulary toward Frank Santi's hotel. After they clattered by and the dust began to settle, a curious chirping directed Dominick's attention toward his elbow. Ignazio Sebastianelli, covered with limestone dust, his thin grey hair splayed wildly in all directions, stood beside him wagging a crinkled old face.

"Beginning to look more and more like the old country around here," Ignazio said. "Now we'll see if these Americans are as bad as the king's men back home, no?" Then, chirping like a strangling bird, he ambled off.

Dominick watched him go. A mysterious old man to whom even hard-bitten assassins paid social calls on dark nights. Shaking his head in wonder he made his way over to the Peanut quarry. If he could get a job there perhaps Casimo would consent to a visit— provided Rosa's father would even talk to him now.

Chapter 21

The quarry scarred the bluff above the river as though a giant plowshare had ripped a furrow along its crest. Spoil piles spilled down the gentle slope, disappearing into a thick belt of brush and briars before the grade careened more steeply toward the tracks of the Pennsy's main line. Dominick watched a thickset man sitting with his shoulders slumped beside an ugly wood and tin structure that housed the quarry's stone crusher. Here a dirty white powder covered the ground like soiled snow. It was lunchtime, and only the rhythmic breathing of the steam shovel's boiler could be heard in the distance where it waited to remove topsoil for a new salient angling off the main cut.

During the week he had been in the quarry Dominick noticed other Italians avoided Casimo Ciampanelli as though he carried the plague. Usually Casimo went home to eat his noon meal, but today he sat ignoring his lunch packed in a small wicker basket. When Dominick sat down beside him and silently opened his bag, Casimo glanced over before projecting a stream of tobacco juice toward a rock some fifteen feet down slope. Dominick watched brown liquid splatter over the stone and smiled despite his nervousness.

"I noticed you were eating alone, signore."

"Thanks to you, young man."

"Me? What have I to do with it?"

Casimo gave him a long look. "Boggiano's henchmen harassed every Italian here to join the society. Everyone but me!" He stabbed his chest with a greasy finger for emphasis.

"I only wanted to protect your family, signore."

"I hear you were thrown in jail with the others."

"Si, signore." Dominick rolled the top of his bag shut. He didn't feel much like eating after all.

"Rosa told me what you are really up to," Casimo said quietly.

A sudden pang of fear rolled Dominick's stomach over. "B..But she promised."

"She was trying to defend your honor." When he saw the worry on Dominick's face, he added softly, "She told no one else."

After a few awkward moments, Casimo got stiffly to his feet and launched another dark stream of juice at the rock. "Time to get back to work I guess."

Dominick remained seated. "Thank you for telling me, signore."

Rosa's father grunted, then nodded slowly. "Why don't you come over for dinner on Sunday? I'd have you sooner, but it wouldn't do to spring you on everybody without a little warning. You know how women are."

"Are you sure, signore?"

With a grunt Casimo turned and walked slowly back to the crusher.

On Friday, Dominick took fruit to Sam and the others in the New Castle jail. He found their spirits were up, except for Luca Caruzzi who stalked about his cell growling at anyone who's gaze fell on him for more than a heartbeat.

"Would you keep an eye on Maria?" Sam asked quietly. "See if she needs anything?"

"Si, compare."

"If I go to prison I am afraid for her."

He nodded. "Does anyone need an interpreter?"

Sam shook his head. "Don Sochetti is providing attorneys and interpreters from Youngstown."

"Why? There are enough attorneys in New Castle."

Sam shrugged. "The Don is upset because the Americans are finding Italians to testify against us. Haven't you read the papers? They are arresting someone almost every day. Nicolo Leraci and Pete Novello were arrested in New Jersey. They are even arresting our people in Youngstown, and Buffalo. Don Sochetti is afraid this will go too far, and he wants to stop it."

"But how can he stop what has already begun?"

Sam gave a tight-mouthed smile. "If there are no witnesses..." he shrugged.

"That will cause more trouble."

Sam's face darkened. "I'm not going to prison." He slammed his fist into an open palm for emphasis. "I'm not!"

Dominick wasn't sure if the witnesses in the Black Hand cases were marked for assassination or if the Youngstown people would simply try to frighten them. He thought about trying to find District Attorney Young. Instead, he wrote a report and mailed it to Pinkerton headquarters before he left New Castle.

On Sunday, he bought a nickel's worth of fresh flowers from Signora Firilli. He felt as nervous as a fox on a razor's edge. When Casimo answered the door he quickly thrust the flowers into his calloused hands.

Rosa's father looked askance at the colorful bouquet. "Are these for me?"

"Ahh, they are for the ladies, signore."

The smells of roasting chicken and fresh baked bread swirled around the big man. Feminine laughter and the rattle of dishes drifted from the kitchen.

Stepping aside, Casimo held a bemused look on his face.

As Dominick stepped inside he was nearly bowled over by a mass of arms, legs and pigtails, packaged in a plain cotton dress.

"Dominick! Dominick!" Mary squealed, hugging him around the waist.

"Don't you think some dignity might be in order, young lady?" Casimo asked sternly.

"But, Papa. This is my big brother, Dominick."

"Dignity isn't something you put on a shelf when it doesn't suit, Mary."

Dominick got down on one knee to give her a proper hug. When he stood up Rosa was there. She had changed. A blossoming young lady stood quietly in front of him, smiling shyly.

"Hello, Rosa," he said softly.

Taking his hand in both of hers she squeezed it briefly before letting go. "We're glad to see you, Dominick."

"Humph!" Casimo grunted, catching a narrow eyed glare from Rosa. "Here," he said, thrusting the fist full of flowers at her. "I believe he would prefer if you took care of these."

"And you're just in time for dinner," Mrs. Ciampanelli declared, gilding in from the kitchen with a golden brown chicken on a large platter. Her oldest daughter, looking as stern as a court judge, followed her into the room with two bowls. One piled high with steaming mashed patatoes.

After dinner, when Mrs. Ciampanelli and the girls were once again banging pots and pans in the kitchen, Casimo pushed his chair back. "Come," he offered, "let's walk this meal off."

They walked into the July sun allowing the heat to soak into their bones. Soon a sheen of sweat glistened on their faces as Casimo led him toward the back edge of the village where the path led into the woods. Here a new cluster of small shanties balanced along the edge of the bluff with a cart path serving as a street between them. A middle-aged man was hoeing a small garden beside the path.

"Buongiorno, Signore Pundinelli," Casimo offered in passing.

"Signore," the other man said flatly without as much as a nod of his head.

Casimo's face stiffened. When they were far enough away from the man hoeing his garden, he growled at Dominick. "You see what I must suffer. There is no more respect." He shook his head sadly. "I fear I must leave this place. Perhaps we can start over again somewhere else."

Dominick glanced at the older man walking beside him. He could almost feel the man's shame and embarrassment. The anger. "I..I'm sorry, signore. But I knew you wouldn't bend, and I was afraid Boggiano would have you killed."

"Sometimes, that is the price of honor." He spat. "I mean true honor, boy. Not that twisted version the society is always talking about."

"Si, but at least you are still alive to take care of your family, or move elsewhere if you wish. There is honor in that, too."

"Humph! Signora Ciampanelli tells me this all the time."

"She is a wise woman, signore."

They walked on in silence before veering to the left on a smaller trail that Dominick knew led toward a small flat with a stand of taller trees.

Reaching the flat, Casimo sat with his back to a tree beside a little spring that bubbled out of the nearby hillside. Dominick hunkered down beside him and began throwing small stones at a blob-topped beer bottle. He didn't know how to break the silence.

"Rosa cares for you more than for a brother, I think."

The bold statement took him in mid-throw causing him to lose his balance and fall over onto his side. He slowly rose to his feet brushing dead leaves and dirt from his clothes with as much dignity as he could muster. Casimo was glaring with a flat stare that should have pinned him to the nearest tree.

"So, I'll ask you again. Where do you stand with regard to my Rosa?"

Dominick's eyes focused on where his hands were busy brushing at a particularly stubborn leaf. "I..I don't know, signore." He forced himself to look levelly at Rosa's father. "I'm afraid my feelings are confused. I have always thought of her as a sister, but I've been away and..." He threw his arms in the air. "Well, she's changed."

"Children have the misfortune of growing up. She is becoming a young lady."

"Si, signore. I've noticed."

"Humph!" Casimo casually fired a stream of tobacco juice at the amber beer bottle.

Dominick watched in fascination as the syrupy liquid splattered over the brown glass.

"Until you sort it out, young man, I expect you to adhere to the amenities of our people. One of her sisters or an adult will be present when you're together. I'll not have any more dishonor falling on my family."

Dominick stuttered with shock. "I..I would never to anything to dishonor your family, signore!"

"Si, but just keep in mind what we talked about this day."

A week and a half passed in which Dominick avoided the Ciampanelli's. He was confused about his feelings for Rosa. Beyond that, Dimuro ordered him to stay in close touch with the prisoners in the New Castle jail. They were the best source of information on what the society intended to do about the witnesses, and Dominick knew the struggle was far from over. He also realized he must keep his wits about him. He couldn't afford to become deeply involved with a personal agenda. A mistake on his part could still cost people their lives.

Representatives of the Society, ostensibly in the employ of Youngstown attorneys, haunted the Italian settlements in Hillsville and badgered witnesses in New Castle. To their credit the Italian witnesses didn't falter. Bolstered by the detachment of state troopers stationed in Hillsville and the New Castle police, they testified at preliminary hearings against those who had gripped their lives with terror only weeks before.

Meanwhile, authorities throughout Pennsylvania and surrounding states probed and prodded The Society of Honor. A gunfight exploded near Punxsutawney when state troopers surrounded a house allegedly occupied by fugitive members of the Society. And in Pittsburgh, a running gun battle erupted through the city's stockyards when members of The White Hand Society decided to take matters into their own hands.

In early August, Romon Cerini arrived in chains at the New Castle jail. Later, Vincent Scibilia, the feared headman in Sharon, was arrested, and Transit Company Detective Ruben Mehard delivered Jim Rossi who had been arrested in Wilkes-Barre.

As District Attorney Young was busy preparing Black Hand cases scheduled for the Grand Jury in September, Dominick became increasing uneasy with each visit to the county jail.

Instead of seeming cowed by the steadfastness of the witnesses, the prisoners acted more detached, almost cocky. Sam, however, was in a melancholy mood when Dominick visited him near the end of August. He gripped the bars on his cell until his knuckles turned white. "Maria? How is she?"

"She waits for you, compare," Dominick, answered softly.

"Tell her to be ready," he whispered. "I'll send for her when I'm safe."

"What do you mean, Sam?"

"I..I can't say exactly." He shot a careful glance back into the cell.

Luca Caruzzi was pacing up and down as usual. Romon Cerini sat on the edge of a bunk glaring at them with the eyes of a crouching panther.

"Listen to me, Sam." Dominick struggled to keep his voice in a whisper. "There is no way you can get out of here."

"There is always the skylight, compare," Sam snapped.

"If you get caught you'll go to prison for sure."

"I'll go to prison anyway," he hissed. "I am learning to read the American papers. All you see is Black Hand this and Black Hand that!"

"If you get caught trying to escape, you'll go to prison and they'll throw away the key," Dominick replied coldly. "Listen," he said, leaning closer to the bars, "perhaps it would be better to plead guilty. So what if you spend a few months in prison? When you get out you will be a free man. Look at Rocco Racca. In a few months he'll be free again."

Dominick wanted Sam to go to prison for Toni. And, he realized suddenly, he resented Sam for his callused feelings when that boy died in Sharon under Scibilia's hand.

Later he walked over to the courthouse. Only a couple of farmers roamed the marble tiled halls, and they soon disappeared into the office for the recorder of deeds. Dominick knew he was taking a chance, but he knew the matter was urgent enough to risk it. He made his way quickly to the back where District Attorney Young's office was. Photographs of the Italian prisoners were pinned to the wall. They all seemed to be staring at him accusingly. Dominick focused on Sam, blank eyed and tight-mouthed. A slip of paper was pinned beside the photograph. "Robbery—Black Hand."

"Well, this is a surprise."

He turned to see District Attorney Young leaning against the doorframe regarding him with interest over the brim of his wire-rimmed glasses. "I need to talk with you privately for a few minutes. It's important."

Mr. Young motioned toward the little room.

After Dominick repeated Sam's story about the possibility of a jailbreak, he paused. "There is something else, sir."

The vision of a body tumbling into a grave in the basement of a warehouse swam through his mind. He knew he had to exorcise that ghost if he could.

"There is a warehouse in Sharon where Vincent Scibilia held meetings and conducted initiations for assassins. There are bodies buried there of men who refused to take the oaths."

The DA looked grim. "May God help us," he said solemnly. "Are you sure?"

"Yes, sir. I met an Italian from Sharon who claims Vin Scibilia talked of it once, but I don't know where it is." He still had to protect his cover. Besides, he didn't want to get into trouble for not reporting it to the Pinkertons.

"Surely you must be mistaken. People don't just...surely not in America!"

"I tried to tell you before, the organization you call the Black Hand is what we call The Society of Honor. It is centuries old and dominates others through fear and terror. The Society's blood-oaths are enforced through assassins and murder. I know. I had to take those oaths. Someday, I may pay for them."

As summer rolled into September, he visited the Ciampanelli's several times. He wanted to be friends with Rosa, and the fact that she clearly wanted more frightened him. Dominick realized he could never settle down. He could only become like Toni Capazzi, living in cheap hotels or rented rooms.

Sheriff Waddington's increased security at the jail curtailed further talk of a jailbreak. A search was made of a warehouse in Sharon but to no avail. Then the trials began.

Dominick sat near the back of the courtroom interpreting for the defendant's wives. The first defendant tried was Jim Rossi who was charged with two counts of robbery by menace. Nicolo Tricine, a worker at the Johnson quarry, testified how Jim demanded money from him and forced him to join The Society of Honor. Suddenly, in mid-sentence, Nicolo hesitated, turned chalk white, and began shaking.

"Go on," the DA urged.

But the witness did not go on. Trembling visibly, he stared blankly at one of the interpreters sitting beside Jim.

Roused by the silence, Mr. Young glanced up from his papers spread on the polished table before him. "Please tell the court to whom you paid the money, Mr. Tricine."

"I..I don't know."

A murmur rose in the courtroom that brought the judge's anvil down with a sharp rap. The defense attorney and interpreter sitting with Jim Rossi were smiling.

Mr. Young was on his feet. "Mr. Tricine, you look frightened. Is anything the matter?"

The witness shook his head frantically. Words seemed to snag on something inside Nicola's mouth.

Frank Dimuro had positioned himself at the front of the gallery so he could keep an eye on the defense table. Now he moved quickly across the front of the courtroom and tapped Mr. Young on the shoulder. When Young leaned toward him, Dimuro whispered in his ear. The DA cast a deadly expression at the Italian interpreter and watched with satisfaction as the oily smile vanished from the man's face. Then he faced the judge.

"Your Honor, may we approach the bench?"

The defense counsel got to his feet. "I must object, Your Honor. The prosecution is trying to delay. Obviously this witness has nothing to testify against my client."

"Your Honor, I have found the reason for the trepidation on the part of the witness."

"Very well, Mr. Young, you may approach the bench."

Both attorneys started forward as Mr. Young motioned for Dimuro to accompany him. Speaking in a low voice, the DA began. "Your Honor, Mr. Dimuro is with the Pinkerton National Detective Agency. He just told me that he saw the defendant's interpreter flash the witness a Black Hand death sign."

"That's preposterous! Your Honor, I must object to such a ridiculous statement." The defense attorney pointed to Dimuro. "Obviously, this man is overtaken with the recent publicity about the so called Black Hand and mistook a simple gesture."

Judge Porter looked to Dimuro. "This is a serious charge, Mr. Dimuro. Could you be mistaken?"

"No, sir. Mr. Lento looked directly at the witness and gave a clear and deliberate sign that I recognize for the death sign of the Italian Mafia."

Judge Porter raised his eyebrows. "The Mafia, Mr. Dimuro?"

"Yes, Your Honor. The press calls them the Black Hand, in Italy it is called The Society of Honor, in Sicily the Mafia."

"If it pleases the court," Mr. Young added hastily, "Mr. Dimuro is able to demonstrate the sign."

"That may be, Mr. Young, but first I would hear his qualifications with respect to the subject at hand. Well, Mr. Dimuro?"

"Your Honor, my first assignment with the Pinkerton's was an undercover assignment that placed me in the Louisiana State Penitentiary with certain leaders of the Mafia from New Orleans. I learned their signs from very close association with them."

"I see. This court will recognize you for an expert in such matters then, Mr. Dimuro. Please demonstrate."

Frank placed his thumbs under his chin and extended the forefinger of each hand toward his eyes, curling the fingers down swiftly toward his chin. "That is the exact signal Mr. Lento gave to the witness, Your Honor. It is interpreted by members of the Society, and understood by other Italians, as marked for death."

"Your Honor, this is preposterous! I…"

Judge Porter held up his hand. The judge was looking at Nicolo Tricine, trembling and wringing his hands. "Your objections have been noted by the court and overruled, counselor." The judge glanced at the district attorney. "I suggest we recess to give you a chance to regroup, Mr. Young."

"Yes, Your Honor. But this has frightened the other witnesses as well. I may require a few days to overcome the damage."

"Very well, please take your seats gentlemen."

Judge Porter addressed the court. "The court will recess until Monday. I will see the counsel for the defense and his interpreter in my chambers immediately."

When the Black Hand trials proceeded the court appointed its own interpreters and they moved ahead without further interference. Each session brought fresh testimony against the former leaders of the Society. Accounts of robbery, threats, blackmail and brutality were carried in graphic detail by the local newspapers. By late September all of the prisoners on trial were showing signs of nervous frustration. Pressure continued to build until Nick Tergilli took the stand.

Nick had just pointed out Sam Bennett and Jim Rossi as two that were present during his ordeal in Hillsville, when Jim suddenly jumped to his feet screaming hoarsely. "Mr. Young! Mr. Young! Me plead guilty, me plead guilty!" Then pale and weeping he started toward the bench. "Me plead guilty," he said again placing his hands on the bench in front of the Judge.

Scarcely had Jim started toward the judge's bench when the others, including Romon Cerini, hurried forward crying out in Italian that they wanted to plead guilty.

Confusion reigned as the defendant's attorneys tried to shove their clients back to their seats, scolding them to be quiet. Italians in the visitor's gallery jumped up and began talking excitedly. Judge Porter heaved to his feet, his face a thundercloud of indignation. The judge repeatedly slammed his gavel on the bench so hard those clamoring around him fell back. When order was restored, Judge Porter glared at the crowd as though daring someone, anyone, to utter a sound. Then he turned toward the jury's box.

"The jury will retire," he said tightly.

Their attorneys counseled each of the prisoners individually in a back room. When they finally came back out most agreed to continue with the trial, except for Sam Bennett and Jim Rossi who pled guilty. For the next two weeks the courtroom battle continued. In the end, the jury returned a guilty verdict in each case. Nearly another month passed while arrangements for disposition of the pending sentences were made. On October 10th, the courtroom erupted once again.

Twenty-three prisoners, under an escort of sheriff's deputies, were marched into a courtroom jammed with family and friends. Women clutched babes to their breasts, while children nervously clung to their mother's skirts. Eyes were red from weeping. Somewhere in the room a muffled sob and then a wail broke the silence. When order was restored, the prisoners were called before the bench one by one.

Luca Caruzzi was first. He approached with arms crossed over his chest.

Looking sternly down from the bench, Judge Porter asked, "Have you anything to say before sentence is passed?"

Luca's head nodded. "I am not guilty, Judge!"

Without emotion, Judge Porter announced. "Prisoner is hereby sentenced to five years in the Western Penitentiary."

Luca turned on his heel and stalked back to his seat.

Romon Cerini approached the bench trembling and nervous. "I am not worried about myself, Judge," he declared. "It is for my wife and child that I worry." Then his face hardened. "I have never received money from Signore D'Alessio!" He fired one finger into the air. "But when I get out, then we shall see what will happen."

"Your sentence just went to ten years, Mr. Cerini. No citizen of this country need live under such threats. Is that understood!"

"I didn't mean that as a threat, Judge."

"I believe you did, Mr. Cerini. The sentence stands."

As Vin Scibilia was called for sentencing one of his children began to cry until the mother quickly hushed it. Sitting in stunned silence, a babe tugging at her breast, she watched as her husband received five years. Placing his head in trembling hands, Vincent Scibilia wept bitterly as he took his seat.

In the back of the courtroom, Dominick remembered a young man tumbling into a bloody grave. Five years wasn't enough, but it would have to do.

Jim Rossi crashed to his knees in front of the bench, tears streaming down his cheeks. "Please, Judge, I have a soft heart. I would not even kill a chicken!" Holding his hands clasped together he raised them in supplication. "This was all Boggiano's fault. He made me do these things. I beg you, be merciful!"

Judge Porter motioned for Sheriff Waddington and a deputy to lift the weeping prisoner to his feet. Even with a man under each arm they had a hard time. It was as though Jim was unable to support himself, and he slumped between them shaking and weeping.

"Mr. Rossi, you ask the court for mercy. Yet, you showed no mercy to Nick Tergilli. Nor did you show mercy to those from whom you extorted their hard-earned dollars. I sentence you to five years in the Western Penitentiary at Pittsburgh."

Sam Bennett took his four years, nine months without blinking, lips pressed into a thin determined line.

Mrs. Terini's husband was sentenced to time served with an additional two months in the county jail. Finally, five young men were let go with time served.

The following day, after bitter farewells with loved ones, seventeen prisoners, shackled together by twos, were marched under heavy guard to the train station. On the return trip, a lone prisoner sat quietly between two guards. Rocco Racca was returning to New Castle to stand trial for robbery.

Chapter 22

They sat on elegantly carved chairs, straight backed, but upholstered with a paisley print that matched the wallpaper above highly varnished oak wainscoting. The chairs, placed along the walls, sat facing a broad oak desk covered with green felt and overlaid with a thick sheet of glass. The man in the leather chair behind the desk was tall and slim with short-cropped sandy hair and hazel eyes.

J.J. Goodwin, General Superintendent of the Pittsburgh district, surveyed the three men facing him. Elmer Cafee was hunting lint specks on his pant legs as though they may be lice.

Mr. Goodwin cleared his throat, and Cafee's baldhead popped up as if expecting a revelation from God. "I want to thank each of you for coming in early on such a frosty morning."

Heads nodded.

"What I am about to say is not to go beyond this room. Is that understood?"

A chorus of, "Yes, sir's," followed.

"Good. District Attorney Young has received information that Fred Carnetti is in Syracuse, New York and that Rolando Saverino may be in the Albany area. They are hesitant to notify the local police and have asked for our help.

Mr. Goodwin looked at the pockmarked young man beside Superintendent Dimuro. "89, I understand you can positively identify these men?"

"Yes, sir."

Dimuro leaned forward in his chair. "Jim, I don't like where this is going. If either of these men recognize him, he'll be dead."

"Well then, Frank? Perhaps a disguise?"

"Sir, why not use our own people in Buffalo?"

Mr. Goodwin smiled slightly. "They don't have anyone who speaks Italian."

"Then allow me to send Toni Capizzi along for back up."

"I'm sorry, Frank. Lawrence County isn't paying enough to cover the extra expense."

Dimuro exhaled deeply. From the look on his face he wasn't at all satisfied.

"I can handle the assignment, sir," Dominick said evenly.

"Good. That's settled then." Mr. Goodwin studied the younger man a moment before continuing. "If you find them let us know where they may be apprehended. That is all you have to do."

"Yes, sir."

Mr. Goodwin turned to the little bald-headed man perched on the edge of his seat as if at attention. "Elmer, I want you to scan all of 89's reports for anything concerning Rocco Racca and the Houk murder. Pour over newspaper accounts of the incident, and provide me with a plan to conduct a full overt investigation into the matter. I want to know who should be interviewed and for what reason."

"May I inquire if you plan to reopen the Houk investigation then?"

"At this time, I don't know. But I would like to recapture that state contract if at all possible. That won't happen, though, unless we can find some evidence that point solidly to his killer. Hard to tell what the Duff investigation will turn up, but it may present an opportunity. I want to be ready."

Goodwin paused and looked at Cafee. The little man seemed poised on the edge of his chair as though ready to leap off a starting line.

In late January Fred Carnetti finally joined Rocco Racca in the New Castle jail. Meanwhile, Dominick wandered the Italian haunts of Albany in search of Rolando Saverino.

Interviewed by District Attorney Young and Detective Logan, Fred Carnetti refused to admit anything about the murder of Squire Duff. At his arraignment, however, Fred finally realized he was charged with murdering the old man. A few days later, Carnetti asked for a meeting with the district attorney. What he had to say was startling.

Through an interpreter, Fred claimed he and two others had been drinking heavily when they decided to go hunting birds in the vicinity of the Duff farm. Rolando Saverino and another man were carrying shotguns. Attracted by the gunfire, the squire came over and ordered them off his property. When Rolando shot at more birds, the old man came back and started chasing them. Fred was too drunk to run, so when the old man came too close Saverino turned and shot him.

Fred Carnetti, however, didn't stop there.

Fred claimed that in March of that year he ran into Saverino carrying a shotgun along the railroad tracks below the Peanut Quarry. Saverino said he was looking for the game policeman. Fred asked why, and Saverino replied he was going to kill him. Fred said he thought Rolando was joking, so he continued walking with him. Soon they saw a tall American with a mustache coming towards them. The man was wearing a long overcoat and slouch hat.

Carnetti said that Saverino shot the man in the chest and when he fell to the ground Saverino shot him in the face. Fred said he became frightened and ran away, but claimed that Rolando bragged that he later dragged the body into the river.

Despite going over the story several times, District Attorney Young could not trip Carnetti up. The DA had little choice but to take Carnetti's story seriously. That was when word came from the Pinkerton's that Rolando Saverino had been located in Albany. Saverino arrived in late January, and Mr. Goodwin was called to assist in the interview with the man now accused of murdering Squire Duff and Seeley Houk.

Mr. Goodwin found the atmosphere in the District Attorney's office glum. As soon as he arrived, Mr. Young whisked the Pinkerton detective into his private office and shut the door.

"I take it the interview isn't going well," Mr. Goodwin said.

Young sat down heavily in his chair. "You take it right. Sometime past, Saverino has benefited by passing through the hands of a clever interrogator I'm afraid."

"I see. Well, fill me in on what details you do have, and I'll give it a try."

The interrogation lasted two hours. Rolando Saverino squirmed, lied, stuttered, wrung his hands, and then fell into a standard answer for almost everything. He couldn't remember.

Smiling, Mr. Goodwin rose to his feet. "Why don't we take Rolando out to Hillsville? I'm sure we can find enough people who will confirm he was there in 1906. Then we can have him arraigned and be done with it."

Rolando glanced from Mr. Young to Superintendent Goodwin. He didn't appear nearly so sure of himself.

They loaded Saverino onto a trolley and disembarked in Edinburg. There they rented a livery and drove to the Duff farm. Walter Duff confirmed that Rolando had worked on the steam shovel in the Peanut Quarry until he disappeared after his father was killed.

Leaving Saverino with the sheriff and Walter Duff, the others drove into Hillsville in search of people who knew the prisoner. They returned with six witnesses, including Nick Sparaio and Dominick, who had returned to Hillsville just before Rolando was arrested by the New York authorities. All of them greeted Saverino warmly and, much to the prisoner's consternation, declared they last saw him in Hillsville at the time of the Duff murder. Saverino declared they must all be crazy.

When they returned to New Castle, County Detective Logan brought Fred Carnetti from the jail. Carnetti greeted Saverino openly enough, then sat down and calmly told everyone how Saverino shot Squire Duff and Seeley Houk.

"You are crazy." Saverino growled in Italian. "Anyone watching your face would know you are lying."

Carnetti only shrugged.

After they led the two prisoners away, Superintendent Goodwin turned to Mr. Young. "Has Carnetti been quartered with Rocco Racca?"

"No. Carnetti occupies a cell in the women's section. We've been striving to keep them apart." Then Mr. Young smiled apologetically. "However, prisoners do find ways to communicate."

"Then it is possible that Rocco put Carnetti up to blaming the Houk murder on Saverino to shift suspicion from himself."

Mr. Young stood up and stretched. "Possible," he muttered through his knuckles, trying to suppress a yawn. "But I can't discover any cracks in his story."

Superintendent Goodwin reached for his coat and hat on the rack beside the door. "It's nearly midnight, and it's been a long day. I suggest you come down to Pittsburgh tomorrow, and we'll see if we can talk with Romon Cerini. Carnetti claimed Saverino took the shotguns to Romon's house after the shooting of Squire Duff." He paused and rubbed his chin thoughtfully. "Perhaps, we can gain something by talking to Cerini now that he's in prison."

Two days later Mr. Goodwin visited Frank Dimuro in his office. Dimuro watched the tall, slim man walk slowly around the room carefully studying the photographs pinned to the walls. When he finished, Mr. Goodwin turned to look at the man sitting behind what looked more like a battlefield than a desk.

"They're all Italians?"

Dimuro's bushy eyebrows raised slightly. "This is the agency's Italian section after all."

Mr. Goodwin's serious expression never changed. "You knew we were dealing with the Mafia all along didn't you, Frank?"

Frank Dimuro slowly plucked the wrinkled stub of a cigar from his mouth and ground it into a heavy ashtray on his desk. "No one wanted to hear about it, Jim."

"Just how bad is it?"

"I think the Mafia is going to be one of the biggest internal threats this country will ever face. So far they've concentrated on their countrymen, but that will change after they become more comfortable here. More Americanized."

"I see," Mr. Goodwin mumbled, his thoughts obviously turning elsewhere.

Dimuro sank back into his chair to study his boss. "But that's not why you're here, Jim," he said after a moment. "The meeting with Cerini didn't go well?"

Mr. Goodwin shook his head. "He wasn't very cooperative; especially about the Houk murder. I don't understand. Romon Cerini has no love for Rocco Racca. He has everything to gain by cooperating and everything to lose if he doesn't."

Dimuro smiled slightly. "You're not Italian, Jim."

"What does that have to do with it?" Goodwin sounded exasperated.

Frank allowed a grin to spread across his broad face. "Everything. Italians seldom trust anyone who is not from the old country. Besides there is still the Omerta."

"The what?"

"The Code of Silence. Society people must take a blood oath never to reveal secrets. Even though Cerini dislikes Racca, Rocco is still a member in the Society. Romon is honor bound to keep the oath."

"Maybe he would talk to you."

"Perhaps, but first we must give him a way to save his honor and, maybe, his life."

"What do you have in mind, Frank?"

"I've been thinking about this for some time." Dimuro got up and scooped some papers off a chair. "Have a seat, Jim, and I'll tell you what I propose."

A week later Rocco Racca found himself in Sheriff Waddington's office with District Attorney Young, County Detective Logan and the court interpreter.

"Your attorney has offered to enter a plea to the charge of robbery, provided you agree to leave Pennsylvania and never return." Mr. Young declared.

"Si, Si. That is a good arrangement. I will never come back here again."

"Well, I have a problem with it, Rocco. You haven't been very cooperative with our efforts to solve the Duff and Houk murders."

Rocco held his hands out, palms up. "But, signore...I meana', Mr. Young. I don't know nothing about these murders."

"So you say."

"But why would I lie about such a thing?"

"You were the headman of the Society when Houk was killed. I believe you do know something."

Rocco's eyes fell to the floor for a moment. "Si," he said softly. "I was the presidente of the St. Lucy...ah how youa' say? Yes! Beneficia Society."

"Enough, Rocco. I'll accept no plea." Mr. Young turned to Logan. "Please take him back to his cell, Craig."

Rocco jumped to his feet. "Per favore! Whata' you want me to do?"

The district attorney looked at Rocco with interest for a moment before sadly shaking his head. "No. I don't think you can be trusted."

"Please, Mr. Young. I wanta' to help. Tell me what to do."

Mr. Young shook his head again. "I don't know, Craig. What do you think?"

"Be good to get a confession from Saverino, sir. Perhaps, Rocco could help us with that."

"Si! I help, yes? No one should shoot a helpless old man like that."

Mr. Young cast a stern expression at the former headman. "You must understand that I can't promise you anything regarding this plea offer. It is really up to the judge, after all. But a little cooperation on your part might help."

"Si, I help."

The two American's turned to each other, seeming to ignore the prisoner. "Well, Craig?" Mr. Young asked again.

"I don't know, sir. Maybe Saverino would talk to Rocco here, especially if he thinks they're alone."

"Si! Si!" Rocco injected himself into the conversation with his best broken English. "Rolando, he talk to me. Especially if we speaka' Italiano. He knows Americanos no'a speak Italian." He shrugged shrewdly. "Maybe you puta' court interpreter where she can listen, huh?"

Rolando Saverino, found himself escorted to Rocco's cell just a few days before his trial. A heavy blanket hung over the bars of the neighboring cell so that no one could see inside.

Rocco was sitting on the edge of his cot staring at Rolando until the cell door clanged shut and the guard's footsteps faded away. "Come, Rolando." Rocco gestured toward an empty cot facing him. "Sit, and we will talk."

Rolando pointed at the blanket hanging behind the bars in the adjoining cell. "What is going on there?" he growled suspiciously.

Rocco shrugged causally. "They are fixing the masonry around the window. The blanket helps in keeping away the dust." He waved his hands in a broad gesture. "But the noise goes on all day long." Rocco gestured to the cot again. "Please, sit."

"What is it you wish to talk to me about, signore?"

"I want to help you, Rolando. But..." Rocco shrugged. "Fred tells me you keep denying what you did. This is not good. He tells me they already proved you lied."

Rolando's face reddened. "Carnetti tells lies about me. You know I didn't kill the game policeman."

Rocco glanced worriedly at the blanket behind Saverino. "I don't want to talk about the game policeman. We will only talk about old man Duff. You must tell the truth to Mr. Young. The judge will go easier on you then, I think."

Rolando jutted out his chin. "I will tell everything at the trial."

Rocco shook his head as though he were dealing with a stubborn little boy. "Listen to me. I have been in jail many times. I know about these things. If you tell them before the trial you may save your neck." He wagged a finger in Rolando's face. "If not, they will probably hang you for one or both of those murders."

Rolando jumped to his feet, anger clouding his face. "Yes, I killed old man Duff. You know that." He pointed a trembling finger at Rocco. "But you must tell the truth about the Houk murder."

"No! I told you I do not want to talk about that." He walked quickly to the cell door. "Guard! Where is the guard?"

Rolando walked over to the older man. "I think I will wait until the trial. Then I will tell all I know about both murders."

They could hear footsteps approaching from down the hall.

"You would break the Omerta?" Rocco hissed between clenched teeth.

"I will not hang for what you did." Rolando snapped.

Rocco started to reach for the younger man when the guard came into view. "You fellows done so soon?" the man asked, jingling the ring of keys from his belt.

That afternoon, Harry Penlenii told Young and Goodwin what he overheard from Rocco and Rolando's conversation as he sat behind the blanket in the adjoining cell. "I was a good policeman in the old country," he told the district attorney. "Now will you speak to the police chief about me?"

Mr. Young nodded his head. "You did well, Mr. Penlenii. However, we may need you to testify in court."

"Si..I mean, yes sir. I will do that, sir."

Mr. Young opened the door to his office. "Good. Thank you very much for your help."

As Mr. Young closed the door behind the former Italian policeman, Mr. Goodwin let out a low whistle. "We sure got more than we expected."

Mr. Young nodded gravely. "Yes, but still not enough to charge Rocco with the murder of Houk."

"Yes," Mr. Goodwin agreed, "But perhaps it is enough to convince the state to reopen the Houk investigation.

When Mr. Young revealed to Saverino that Rocco Racca had tricked him, he flew into a rage before collapsing on the floor and convulsing in the throes of a grand mal seizure. Two days later he entered a plea of guilty to the Duff murder, and Sheriff Waddington intercepted a letter from Rolando to Sam Bennett. In the letter, Rolando urged Sam and the other prisoners to tell the truth about the Houk murder because Rocco Racca had broken the Omerta. District Attorney Young had Dimuro interpret and copy the letter before forwarding it to Bennett.

Two weeks later, Elmer Cafee wandered through the quarries and shanties of Hillsville. Cafee focused his investigation on the English-speaking people in the region, which began to reveal some interesting things. He found most of the folks living in Hillsville believed that Rocco Racca killed Houk. He also learned that Rocco's brother-in-law, Gus Mazzocco, packed up his family and suddenly left about the time Houk was killed. Several people claimed they frequently saw Gus Mazzocco and Rocco Racca hunting with shotguns along the railroad tracks in the vicinity where the game warden was killed. Then Elmer Cafee stumbled upon the best lead of his investigation. He learned a young Italian girl may have witnessed the murder.

Chapter 23

The girls walked slowly down the trail enjoying the afternoon sun and the tingle of new spring grass on their bare feet. Brown leather shoes, tied together with the laces, dangled around their necks. The older girl carried a bundle of well-worn books over her shoulder, bound together by an old leather belt.

"Ow!" Mary screeched, hopping about suddenly on one foot.

"Don't be such a baby," Rosa chided. Then she, too, screeched as a pebble jabbed into her tender sole.

An equally bare-footed boy ran up to them shouting Rosa's name. He stopped suddenly and bent over with his hands on his knees, chest heaving.

"Leo, what's the matter?" Rosa asked.

"There is a detective at your house asking for you," the lad blurted between breaths.

A smile began to spread across Rosa's cheeks.

"H..He's bald and wears glasses...and...and he looks like a chicken hawk!"

The smile vanished.

The boy straightened when his chest stopped pounding like a hammer. He looked intently at Rosa. "Your mamma said to take your time coming home, and maybe the man will go away. My brother ran to get your papa."

Rosa cast a worried glance down the trail toward the settlement. Then she grabbed Leo by the shoulders and spun him around. "Go back! Tell mamma we'll wait here until you come back for us."

The boy trotted off.

"Rosa, I'm scared. Why would a detective want to talk to you?"

"I don't know, Mary. Let's just sit in the grass and work on your arithmetic until Leo comes back."

"Yuck!"

More than an hour passed before the girls saw their father striding towards them. Casimo hugged both his daughters warmly before patting Mary on the head. "Trot ahead and tell mamma we're coming right behind. Tell her we are very hungry, yes?"

Mary pulled on her shoes, and trotted off down the path.

"Papa?" Rosa asked. "What did this detective want, do you think?"

"I was hoping you would tell me, girl."

"I don't know, Papa. Maybe he had a message from Dominick."

Casimo reached out and gathered the books into his large hands. "I don't think so. The men at the quarry say this detective is asking questions about the murder of the game policeman." His eyes narrowed when he saw his daughter involuntarily clutch her stomach. "Are you all right, Rosa?"

She nodded, but her eyes were large and moist.

"If you know something about this, perhaps I can help."

Rosa shook her head, still clutching her stomach.

"Come along then, but I want you to stay in the house and out of sight until we know what this man wants. Capeesh?"

"Si, Papa." She managed weakly.

Casimo kept the girls out of school for the rest of the week. The neighbor's children brought their homework assignments and reported that the detective had stopped by the school asking for Rosa. On Friday, he came to the house with a scar-faced detective who spoke Italian. Signora Ciampanelli told him her daughters were out of town visiting relatives. The Italian detective was polite enough, but the bald-headed American left in a fury. Meanwhile, Rosa fretted over Dominick and told her parents she hoped he would know what the American detective wanted from her.

•••

Dominick hunched his shoulders against a gust of wind whipping spirals of dust from the brick paved street and causing a sheet of newspaper to twist and dance in the air. A delivery truck clattered by spooking a livery horse tethered to an iron stanchion at the curb. The young man made his way toward a small group of men huddled under an awning snapping wildly over the front of a men's clothing store.

"A fine spring day, is it not?" Dominick announced when he joined them.

"A change in the weather," Pasquale Agastino answered soberly. "It is going to rain, I think."

As though in response to his statement, a crash of thunder rattled the store window. The horse at the curb skittered backwards, snapping the tethered reins and rolling the wagon into a red-faced man loading a keg of nails. The man heaved himself off the brick pavement as large drops of rain began pounding against the dusty street with enough fury to drown his curses.

"We were just discussing where to go for a drink," Pietro Vartolla declared, raising his voice enough to be heard over the demonic cadence of the rain and the whipping canvas.

Dominick nodded. "I was waiting for them to call Rolando Saverino's case in court, but it will be a while yet." He motioned toward the street now veiled under slanting sheets of rain. "There is a bar in the Cloud Hotel."

"Si," Jim Calucci said. "Would you do the honor of joining us there?"

A sizzling flash tore the air above the street, drowning the horse's scream under a rolling crescendo of thunder.

"We are going to get wet crossing the street," Nick Sparaio grumbled.

"We are getting wet now!" Pasquale yelled at him. "If we run fast enough maybe we will only get wet on the outside."

"We can't keep our dignity while running like dogs," Pietro declared.

"Si," Nick answered. "We will cross the street with honor." Backs straight, they stepped proudly into the sheeting rain.

Dripping little puddles over a black and white tiled floor in the hotel's lobby they marched past the raised brow of a pinched nosed clerk and, with heads erect, entered the dark, smoky bar.

After the older men each bought a round of drinks, Dominick ordered a round and motioned toward an archway flanked by heavy velvet curtains. "Signores, there is a billiard room back there. Perhaps, we may talk privately."

"But I don't play this American game," Nick Sparaio grumbled.

"We will have a cigar and talk," Dominick replied. "But, Nick, this is not an American game, it is an Italian game."

"Si," Jim Calucci chuckled. "Besides, the American's don't like our fine cigars. We should have the room to ourselves for a while, no?"

Laughing, they filed between the curtains. The men settled into comfortable wooden chairs in a corner of the room. Dominick pulled a chair around to face them so they formed a loose circle.

"Saverino has admitted to the killing of Squire Duff," Dominick said, "but the judge won't accept his plea because he wants a jury to hear the case."

"How do you know this?" Jim Calucci asked.

"Rolando is my friend," Dominick replied evenly. "But he is plenty worried. I can tell you that."

Pietro Vartolla wrapped one thin leg over the other and slowly exhaled a stream of smoke through his long tapered nose. "Tell me, Dominick. Did he admit to the Houk murder?"

Dominick shook his head in reply.

Pietro studied his cigar for a moment, rolling it around in his fingers. "Well," he said slowly, "Rolando would be a fool if he did. They are trying to put that murder on him, but he doesn't know anything about it."

"Who is trying to put the murder on him?" Dominick asked.

Pietro shrugged. "I will tell you this. Saverino doesn't know anything about the Houk murder, but they are trying to put it on him so no one else will get in trouble."

Dominick noticed that Nick Sparaio was nodding his head.

"Si, that may be, but they don't have a motive for someone killing Houk." That was a lie, but Dominick hoped it would keep them talking about the murder.

"The game policeman killed Rocco's dog," Nick blurted.

The glares of the two older men froze Nick's face into marble.

"I don't care about any of that," Dominick said. "But, what are you going to do if the district attorney asks you about it on the witness stand?"

Pietro looked astonished. "I know nothing! We only came here to testify that Saverino was in Hillsville during the time Duff was killed... same as you," he added menacingly.

Pasquale Agastino tugged a watch from a pocket hidden under the spacious roll of his belly. "Perhaps we should go to the courthouse now. We don't want to get into trouble with Signore Young, no?"

Outside, tendrils of vapor rose from the brick pavement as a shaft of sunlight chased the storm across the hills south of town. However, the seating of a jury for the case was the only thing accomplished at court that afternoon. After a brief adjournment, Saverino's attorney was given a continuance until June.

After the others left for Hillsville, Dominick went to a secluded neighborhood. A familiar squarish shape leaned against a lightpost beside a corner grocery serving a block of row homes. Thunder grumbled in the distance.

"Were you waiting long, signore?" Dominick asked walking up behind his boss.

"Long enough to wonder if you were coming," Dimuro growled. Shoving away from the streetlight, Frank jerked his head toward a board sidewalk. "Come on. I don't want to attract attention."

"Cigar, signore?"

"No! The smell of those things will give us away for a mile or more." He cast the young man a hard look. "What's the matter with you? Did you forget how to speak English already?"

Taken back by Dimuro's gruff mood, Dominick simply fell into place beside him as they clomped across the hollow sounding boards.

"I want you to write a letter to Sam Bennett," Dimuro said after a while. "Convince him that you have been working diligently to secure a pardon. Make it plain that since he didn't cooperate with Mr. Young and the Pinkerton detective, his cause is useless. Tell him everything depends upon a favorable recommendation from the district attorney. Understand?"

"No, sir."

Dimuro gave him a frustrated look. "Listen, in a few days Mr. Young and I are going to pay your friend another visit. This time I would hope to find him in a more cooperative mood."

"Yes, sir. But he isn't my friend. He had Toni Santi killed, or at least allowed it to happen. Sam is as bad as the others."

Dimuro grunted. "I'm going to turn at the next street. If you go two more blocks and turn left it will take you back to the Cloud Hotel."

Another rumble of thunder rolled with a quickening breeze, closer this time.

"Try to stay out of the rain, Dominick. You smell like a wet dog."

Dominick smiled. "Better then smelling like a dead dog."

"Yeah," Frank plucked a badly chewed American cigar out of his coat pocket and stuck it in his mouth. "Get out to Hillsville in the morning and keep an eye on things. Cafee is loose up there, and somehow that bothers me."

When they reached the corner, Frank reached up and squeezed Dominick's shoulder. "Take care of yourself, boy. I got a bad feeling about things for some reason."

. . .

"Rosa?" The teacher's voice carried clearly over the tumult of children enjoying the morning's recess.

Rosa detached herself from two other girls.

"Would you come inside for a moment please?" Miss Simpson stood on the limestone steps of a weather beaten pile of boards that made up the one-room school in Hillsville. Stepping aside, she held open the door as Rosa bounded up the steps and entered the familiar room with its rows of worn wooden desks. Once inside the girl stiffened. Lounging on the top of her desk was a bald-headed man, glaring at her over the top of wire-rimmed spectacles.

Rosa turned frightened eyes on her teacher.

Miss Simpson hurried to wrap a reassuring arm around her. "Don't worry, Rosa. This is Mr. Cafee of the Pinkerton National Detective Agency. He just wants to ask you a few questions. And I promise to stay right here, okay?"

Superintendent Cafee slid off the desk. "Really, Miss Simpson, there is no need for you to stay. I would prefer to speak with the young lady alone."

"As I have already explained, Mr. Cafee," she replied icily, "it wouldn't be proper." Glancing tenderly at the frightened girl she added more softly. "These children are so frightened of anyone in authority."

"Frightened my foot!" Cafee's nasal voice pitched to a higher octave. "These people are simply adept at avoiding the law. Why, this girl's family has been hiding her for nearly three weeks!"

"I suggest you get on with your business, sir. Before the rest of the children come back from recess."

Cafee, towering a whole inch above the women, bent to glare over the rims of his glasses at Rosa. "Very well! I understand, Miss Ciampanelli, that you witnessed the murder of Game Warden Seeley Houk."

Miss Simpson gasped.

"Is this true?" Cafee demanded.

Rosa frantically shook her head. Tears began streaming down her cheeks.

"Oh come now, young lady. You might as well admit it. If you'll remember, you already told Mrs. Young all about it when you went there to purchase milk."

Rosa's head swiveled back and forth much faster.

"Now, you listen to me! Either you tell the truth or I swear—I'll have you subpoenaed into court."

"No!" Rosa screamed into the face leering over her, splashing it with tears and spittle.

As Cafee jerked backwards, Rosa peeled away from Miss Simpson and darted through the door.

Recovering quickly, Miss Simpson whirled on the little man who was busy wiping his face with a handkerchief. "I'll thank you to leave my school, sir! And your employers shall be notified of your discourtesy!" When she hurried after her frightened pupil, Rosa was nowhere to be found.

...

Returning from the post office late that afternoon, Dominick noticed a crowd of people gathered in the street in front of the Ciampanelli house. He had just received a letter from Sam Bennett thanking him for the interest he had supposedly taken on his behalf. Sam assured him he was cooperating with the authorities, especially Dictrict Attorney Young. He pointed out, however, that Dominick must hurry to get him out because Cerini and the others were growing suspicious. "Prison is bitter," he wrote in closing.

Life is bitter for Toni Santi's widow and children, Dominick thought as he slipped the envelope into his pocket before hurrying toward the Ciampanelli's house. Anxiety began to well up as he drew closer. The young man could see worry and concern on the faces gathered there. Suddenly, fear stabbed at his heart when he heard Signora Ciampanelli call Rosa's name with a shrieking wail.

Shoving his way through the crowd, he didn't go far before Mary ran up to him in tears.

"Dominick! Dominick! You have to help us find her."

He knelt and coaxed Mary into explaining what happened.

"Papa and some of the men from the quarry are still looking for her," she paused to fight the sobs. "She's been gone all afternoon!"

"I'll find her, Mary. But stay here. I think your mamma needs you just now."

Dominick eased his way through the crowd of women and children until he came to the path behind the little settlement. Just before the trail began to dip sharply toward the tracks below, he stopped. Here a smaller path branched to the left, and he took it without further hesitation. Soon he could make out the tops of mature trees towering over the red brush and tangles of green briar.

The little glade appeared empty at first. Then he noticed a bit of blue calico behind a tree, followed by the whirl of a slender arm as the girl tossed a pebble into the small brook leaking out of the hillside.

"I wonder if the princess of this glade would allow me to enter?" he said.

Rosa's face appeared from behind the tree. He could tell she had been crying. There was the flash of a smile, a flurry of movement, then she flattened herself against him, hugging him tightly. The tears started again.

Dominick was all too aware of her budding body pressing against him, but he held her until the crying slowed. Then he gently unwrapped her arms. "What happened, Rosa?"

She shook her head, unable to talk. Finally she wiped her leaky eyes with a slender wrist.

He fumbled a red bandanna from his pocket and handed it to her.

When she finished, she gave him a remorseful glance. "I was such a baby," she managed before burying her face in the bandanna again.

After a while she took a deep breath before looking evenly at him. "That's the worst part. You must think I'm terrible."

He shook his head. "No, Rosa, I don't. But could you tell me why Detective Cafee thinks you know something about the murder of the game policeman?"

She squinted her eyes tight and stomped her foot angrily on the ground. Her fists clenched. "I don't want to cry anymore," she managed through clenched teeth.

He reached out and pulled her close. She snuggled her face into his chest until the trembling stopped.

"Rosa, I've known for some time you saw something. I've tried to hide it, tried to protect you, but I need to know what it is if I am to help you now."

She shook her head before pushing away. She looked so pathetic it wrenched his heart. "I can't talk about it," she managed at last. "I just can't!"

They heard someone crashing through the brush along the narrow path before they heard Casimo's booming voice. "Dominick! Is she all right?"

"Papa!" Rosa ran to her father. "Papa, I was so afraid. So ashamed." She was crying uncontrollably again.

"Rosa, I want you to tell me what this man wants."

"I can't, Papa. I just can't."

Casimo looked questioningly over his daughter's head.

Dominick shrugged and shook his head in return.

"Come on then. We're going home. Your mamma is frantic with worry." Then he shot Dominick an angry frown. "I will find this detective. And when I do..."

"Please, signore," Dominick interrupted. "Let me handle Detective Cafee. I promise he won't bother Rosa again."

Casimo shook a meaty fist. "If he comes near my home again, he will not walk away on his own, I think."

That evening Dominick took the electric car into New Castle to call Dimuro. He was ordered to a conference at Pinkerton headquarters in the morning. He would catch what sleep he could on the night train to Pittsburgh.

When he let himself into Dimuro's office through the back door, he found his boss and Toni Capizzi waiting. Dimuro waved them into chairs with an impatient flick of his cigar.

"I have a meeting with Goodwin and Cafee inside the hour. Cafee claims he found an eye-witness to the Houk murder."

Dominick jumped to his feet. "Sir, you can't let..."

"Sit!" Frank roared around his cigar. Then in a softer voice, "Please allow me to finish."

He ground his cigar roughly into the ashtray.

"You stayed with the Ciampanelli family while you were sick. What did you find out?" When the lad didn't answer right away he barked, "Well?"

Dominick blinked. "I'm sorry, but I really don't have much. The girl saw something that frightens her terribly, but she won't talk about it, not even to her parents."

"Could it have something to do with the Houk murder?"

"Maybe, but she's just a young girl. We can't involve her in this. There are still those who are loyal to the Society in Hillsville. They could hurt her, or worse."

"Dominick is right, boss." Toni offered. "My informants tell me Siciliano is making frequent trips from Youngstown to Hillsville. He is still the Society's enforcer, you know."

"Well, I guess we'll have to hear what Cafee has to say then. Unless he knows for sure that the girl saw something important, I don't think we'll need her."

"Have the prison interviews been going well then?" Dominick asked.

"Ah, more or less. Bennett is trying to help us now. At first, he thought Cerini may have killed Houk. But now he claims that Rocco Racca and his brother-in-law shot him. Sam claims this information comes from Cerini, who still has a dislike for Rocco. I'm going over to the prison later this week to interview Cerini and some of the other society members. Now that they believe Rocco is helping the police, I think they will talk. Unless they agree to testify though, we won't have a case."

Frank pulled a gold watch from his vest pocket. "I need to get next door." He yanked the chewed up cigar out of his mouth and stabbed it in the direction of the other two men. "Be here when I get back."

When Dimuro stomped back into his office, he slumped heavily into the chair behind his desk. Dominick leaned forward in anticipation. "Well, sir?"

The older man shook his head before running a hand over his slick hair. "Cafee doesn't have much. It all boiled down to some woman claiming a girl from the Peanut settlement said she saw a terrible thing happen about the time Rocco's brother-in-law moved away."

"That's it? That's all he has?"

"Yes, but Cafee learned that Gus Mazzocco moved away right after Houk disappeared. This girl bought milk from the informant, and the Ciampanelli's were one of her customers. Rosa fits the bill."

"But that doesn't mean she witnessed Houk's murder."

Frank raised his eyebrows and studied Dominick curiously for a moment. Finally he said, "No, but I got a feeling this girl knows something important."

"You can bet on one thing, boss."

"What's that, Capizzi?"

"Because of Cafee, just about everyone in Hillsville thinks the girl knows something about the murder. That will draw Siciliano like flies to an outhouse."

Dominick jumped to his feet. "Toni's right! We can't involve Rosa in this thing."

Superintendent Dimuro held up his hand. "Cafee's been told to stay away from the Ciampanelli's." His brow knitted together as he looked directly at Dominick. "Apparently someone else knows about this girl, too," he added coldly.

Dominick suddenly remembered Rubin Mehard's warning about a young Italian girl supposedly knowing something about Houk's murder. A flush of fear passed through him. Had Dimuro learned he deliberately withheld information?

"Cafee was severely reprimanded about his conduct at the school," Frank added. "He'll obey orders this time, I think."

"I just hope it's not too late, sir."

"You'll just have to keep an eye on her as best you can." Then his voice hardened somewhat. "But if you learn anything new make sure you report it this time, capeesh?"

...

Superintendent Dimuro paced the small drab office inside the Western Penitentiary while District Attorney Young sat on the edge of the warden's desk with one knee folded over its partner.

"You may as well relax, Frank. They'll bring him when they're good and ready."

"We've been waiting for over an hour," the older man growled. He stopped and shook his head. "I don't like prisons. I nearly died in one down in New Orleans during an assignment a while back."

He fixed dark brown eyes on the thin young man facing him. "They're terrible places: damp, cold and filthy. No wonder Cerini's got tuberculosis."

"You don't think we should put criminals in plush hotels do you?"

"Of course not! Still, there ought to be some better controls over the environment here. Cerini may not live to testify against Rocco Racca."

"Let's see if he has something to testify about first, shall we?"

As if in answer to the district attorney's question the door opened and a thin man appeared dressed in faded black and dirty white stripes. Behind him marched Warden Gerard Thompson. The prisoner shuffled over to a chair and slumped down, obviously sick. Cerini held a crumpled rag in his hand, which he used to muffle coughing spasms rising from deep in his chest.

"Sorry for the delay," the warden said, "but it's after visiting hours, and we've had to count noses. I'm stretching the rules allowing you to talk to this man as it is."

"Thank you, warden, we appreciate your cooperation," Dimuro replied. Then he turned to the prisoner who was eyeing him intently.

"The rules require us to speak English if possible. Do you comprehend enough to understand everything that is said to you?"

"No, signore. I would prefer to speak in our native tongue."

"Very well." Frank pulled a chair around facing the prisoner and sat down. "I am here to talk to you about the murder of the game warden."

Romon Cerini looked at Dimuro for a long time. "I know nothing about it," he said finally.

Seeing that the prisoner was not going to speak further, Frank took a note from his pocket that was sent to him by Sam Bennett. He handed it to Cerini. The note stated that Romon knew all about the murder of the game warden.

Romon's dark eyes darted across the crumpled paper and his mouth tightened into a thin line. Then he thrust the note back at Frank as a fit of coughing racked his thin body. When it was over he stated in a gravelly voice. "I never was a spy, and would not give any man away that was on the level." Then, still staring at Dimuro, he sat back and slowly crossed his legs.

"As I explained to you previously, Rocco Racca has already broken the Omerta and worked as a spy for District Attorney Young."

Romon glanced at the district attorney who was still sitting on the edge of the desk, then back to Frank. When he did, the Pinkerton man made a hand sign. It was a sign of the Society that meant he could speak safely.

Romon raised an eyebrow then nodded slowly.

Chapter 24

Three men shuffled awkwardly down the main street of New Castle under the watchful eyes of Lawrence County officials. The jingling of leg irons and handcuffs turned the heads of curious pedestrians and drew a wake of young boys skipping along behind. When they reached the office of Alderman Green, the men filed inside, and the doors closed firmly against a crowd gathering in the street.

Rocco Racca sat quietly with his attorney as the prosecution paraded a line of witnesses declaring the defendant lived in Hillsville during the spring of 1906. Docato Trevino told about the shooting of Rocco's dog, and several witnesses testified that Rocco bragged he would get even with the game warden. However, it was the prisoners from the Western Penitentiary who decided the issue. Especially Romon Cerini and Luca Caruzzi, who both testified that Rocco told them he and his brother-in-law killed Seeley Houk and dumped his body in the Mahoning River. Alderman Green bound the case over to the Grand Jury but despite the district attorney's pleas for a swift hearing, Rocco's trial was delayed until September.

That evening Dominick sat in the poorly furnished room of the Cloud Hotel. He was falling into a dark mood when a knock on the door jarred him from a host of bad memories. The past three years in Hillsville had been a nightmare. Maybe, he thought, it was going to end now.

Without a word of greeting, District Attorney Young slipped inside when Dominick opened the door. Dimuro followed on the DA's heals the superintendent's head swiveling back and forth, scanning the hallway, as he backed inside the room.

"What took you so long," Frank growled when Dominick closed the door. "Anyone could have seen us come in here." His thick fingers throttled a brown paper sack.

The district attorney's slim hand held a surprisingly firm grip. A bemused half-smile hung under those wire-rimmed spectacles. "And how are you, Dominick?" he asked warmly.

"Fine, sir."

"The older man took a seat in the only chair available, pulling a bottle of red wine from the wrinkled sack. I don't suppose you have any glasses in this flea-bag hotel?"

Dominick shook his head and then smiled. "I don't have a corkscrew either."

"These young pups aren't very well prepared," Frank commented to the DA as he pulled a corkscrew from his pocket.

Mr. Young smiled conspiratorially and produced a glass from his coat pocket. "The judge always keeps a water glass on the shelf under his bench."

Frank raised an eyebrow.

"I'm sure his Honor would understand a little libation this evening."

"I'm not sure a celebration is in order," Dominick said. "We have three months before Rocco's trial. Siciliano and the others can still wreck havoc among the witnesses."

"That's true, young man," Dimuro growled, "but we're a lot further along than when a certain rookie detective got this crazy idea about avenging his friend."

"Dominick's right, Frank," Mr. Young said, holding the glass out for the older man to fill. "Cerini is the best witness, but he has tuberculosis. He might not even live until September."

"Yes," Dominick added, "and Sam Bennett didn't look well either."

The district attorney took a sip of wine before passing the glass to Dominick. "Sheriff Waddington said he was complaining of a headache and fever. I suggested he report Sam's condition to the warden when they get back to the prison. Although, he doesn't offer direct testimony: merely collaborates the other two's stories."

Dimuro took the glass, twirling the red liquid under his nose. "Gentlemen, need I remind you this is to be a celebration. You're going to spoil the wine with all this despondent talk." He tossed the remainder into his mouth, then refilled the glass and passed it to the DA.

"I would like to know how you got those men to testify in the first place," Dominick said. "I can hardly believe they broke their vow of silence."

"Seems your boss knows a good deal more about the Mafia than he lets on," Mr. Young said. "Romon Cerini wasn't cooperating at all until Frank flashed him a hand sign. Later, when they brought Caruzzi down, Luca was just as stubborn until Cerini flashed him the same sign. I still don't understand what happened."

"Of course you don't, Charles," Frank declared smoothly. "You're not Italian."

"Well," the DA declared. "Do you want to clue me in?"

"Actually," Frank began, "it all has to do with honor."

"How can such men profess a sense of honor?"

"You see," Dominick chipped in, "it takes an Italian to understand Italians."

"Precisely," Frank replied. "To the Italian, personal honor is everything; even if one is a crook. In this case, society men are honor bound never to talk to the law about one of their own. And, although Romon knew Rocco had already broken the Omerta, he was afraid the man was still protected by its codes."

Frank paused to refill the glass.

"When I showed him the Society's sign, indicating that he could talk freely, Romon was off the hook. Later, when he actually realized we wanted him to testify, Cerini refused unless the others also agreed. So we brought Luca Caruzzi down, and he clammed up for the same reasons Cerini did. That's why Romon flashed him the same sign, which had the same results for the same reasons."

The DA shook his head. "That sounds incredible!"

"Yes it does, to the outsider." Dimuro shrugged. "But that is our way. Unfortunately, these people have perfected the old saying about honor among thieves."

"Yes, but Jim Rossi and some of the others didn't buy it."

"That's true, but one of them is Rocco's brother and Jim Rossi was a godfather to Rocco's child. What can you expect? Sam Bennett, on the other hand, was already in too deep. Thanks to Number 89 here,

Sam had already committed himself by providing the information we needed to break this case."

"Well, just remember the case isn't broken until we get a conviction. We need to find more witnesses. Preferably, someone more credible than a bunch of prisoners."

Superintendent Dimuro studied the wine bottle for a moment, his thick eyebrows gnarled over his nose, then looked intently at Dominick. "What about the Ciampanelli girl?" he asked quietly.

Dominick jolted erect. "We agreed not to involve her in this."

"We agreed to no such thing, young man."

"She's just a girl."

"Dominick," Mr. Young injected quietly, "if this young lady does know something and could be persuaded to testify, we could ask to have one of the troopers quartered at her house."

Dominick shook his head in frustration. "A trooper can't be with her every minute. Vito Siciliano is a professional assassin. He could kill her some night when she goes to the outhouse."

"Just the same." Dimuro rumbled. "Your assignment is to find out if she does know anything about the Houk murder. Then we can decide what to do, if anything."

Dominick opened his mouth to protest but clacked it shut when Frank held up a warning finger.

"The alternative is to turn Cafee loose again. I believe it would be better if that didn't happen."

He was reluctant, at first, to see Rosa. Although he felt as though he was betraying her, Dominick realized he had no choice. Cafee's blundering about was sure to bring Siciliano. That fact acted as a ladle stirring the seething pot of his emotions. He knew he was attracted to the girl. When they walked together in the evenings, with Mary skipping along beside, she had a way of casually allowing her hip to sway into him. It drove him crazy. She didn't seem to notice. Yet he was sure she knew what she was doing, and that made her seem older than her fifteen years. That, and her serious conversations. Rosa wanted children. She dreamed of raising a family in a real house. Dominick even found he dared dream of such things, but kept them to himself. Her bubbly personality and positive attitude was a balm to his soul. And Dominick was basking in it, allowing her to soothe the emotional scars of Hillsville. He found himself becoming addicted to her gentle voice and the fragrance of wild flowers that seemed to drift mysteriously from her hair. But time was running out.

The pressure for Dominick to conclude his assignment had doubled since Sam Bennett died of typhoid fever late in June. Since then the young detective had been given a deadline. In September, Cafee would continue his investigations in Hillsville.

September was only a few days away.

The summer had been an eventful one. Rolando Saverino began serving twenty years in the Western Penitentiary for the murder of Squire Duff, and Mario Nardozi died on the New Castle gallows for the murder of Toni Santi. Unfortunately, the rope didn't snap Mario's neck as it should. He spun slowly around, kicking, and struggling, and choking. Death, when it came, was evidenced by a wet stain spreading down the front of his woolen trousers as the limp body rotated to the sound of creaking rope. Mario was only nineteen.

Dominick moodily contemplated these things as he and Rosa sat on the porch stoop listening to the noises of katydids in the August night. Rosa sat beside him with her elbows propped on her knees. Her small oval face resting in cupped hands as she studied him intently.

"A penny for your thoughts," she said softly.

Dominick roused himself with an effort. "I was just thinking about all the people who suffered or died since I came here."

"Isn't that why you were sent here? To try and stop it?"

He looked at her a moment before answering. "Seeley Houk was a friend of mine. Everything started with him."

Rosa let her arms fall into her lap. Her dark brown eyes widened slightly. "The game policeman was a friend of yours?"

"Seeley was the first American who treated me with respect. I asked to come here. They said I was too young. So I pleaded with them until I convinced them I was their best chance. I wanted to catch this murderer and make him pay for killing my friend."

He turned away. "I had no idea, Rosa. No idea what it would bring."

She scooted closer, reaching up to gently touch his arm. "This bald-headed detective, he works for you?"

"No. He works for the same people I do." The young man's face became even more serious. "They think you know something about this murder, Rosa. They asked me to find out what it is."

He hurried when she began to tremble.

"They gave me until September. Then they will send the bald detective again. I'm afraid your father will hurt him. Your papa will go to jail if he does."

Tears began to leak down Rosa's cheeks. She turned away, hugging her arms around herself as she stared into the blackness. "I..I..." she began in a hoarse whisper.

"Rosa, you..."

She waved a hand to quiet him. "It was in the spring... two years ago. I saw the game policeman go by our house and turn toward the Peanut quarry. Since the rain had stopped I decided to go for a walk. Mamma knows I have a hard time when I have to stay inside for long. When I started down the path toward our secret place the rain started again. When I turned toward home I heard someone coming. I got scared and hid. It was Rocco Rocca and Gus Mazzocco, Rocco's brother-in-law. They were carrying guns and talking angrily. I waited for a while, thinking I should go back home. I was afraid. Then I heard someone else coming down the trail. This man was quieter and I barely had time to hide again." She paused and wiped her eyes with a bare arm. "I should have gone home then."

Rosa cried softly for a moment, and Dominick handed her his handkerchief. She took it without comment, dabbing her eyes. "But I didn't. I had the feeling something awful was going to happen. Something seemed to pull me along behind them. I could barely see the tracks below when a gunshot made me jump. I hid beside some brush. Then I saw the game policeman looking into the woods where the shot seemed to come from. He had a pistol in his hand. I heard him crashing through the brush along the tracks, climbing into the woods. I heard more gunshots. Signore Mazzocco yelled, 'He's down. We got him.' I could hear men moving, someone groaning. There was another loud shot." She paused and looked determinedly at Dominick. "Then I ran back up the hill."

"Do you think you could tell this to the district attorney?" he asked quietly.

"I don't know, Dominick. I'm scared."

"Maybe you should tell your papa. Let's hear what he has to say."

Rosa slowly nodded her head.

Mary came skipping around the side of the house. One look at Rosa and her smile died. "What's the matter, Rosa? Why are you crying?"

"I'm okay, Mary." She smiled faintly. "Where is Papa?"

"He's in the kitchen helping Mamma and Grace scald tomatoes."

"Do us a favor, Mary," Dominick asked. "Go ask your papa to come out here for a few minutes."

"Si, Dominick," she said brightly, bouncing onto the porch and letting the screen door slam behind her as she trotted through the house.

Casimo's face hardened into flint by the time Rosa finished repeating her story. He cast an icy glare at Dominick. "You would risk her life just to satisfy your desire for revenge!"

"No, signore. But if I say she knows nothing about the Houk murder, I don't think they will believe me. They will send the bald-headed detective. I fear his questions will draw Siciliano to Rosa. If we tell them the truth they will protect her."

"How will they protect her from a dog like Siciliano?"

"They will keep it a secret until the day of Rocco's trial. If you wish, they will station one of the mounted policemen at your house."

"These mounted policemen are all young," Casimo stated. "Americans don't respect our ways or our women."

"How about a middle aged Italian with an ugly scar on his face?"

Rosa's eyes widened. She put her hand to her mouth. "You mean the one who traveled with the bald-headed detective?"

"Si, he is a good friend of mine. His name is Toni Capizzi. Toni is tough and very good with a pistola."

Casimo grunted. "I will think on this."

"Signore," he said carefully, "if the polizia do not catch Siciliano by the time the trial is over, you will have to move away from here."

Casimo nodded solemnly then turned to Rosa. "Perhaps, Dominick is right. You and Mary were born in this country. Here things are different from the old way. Here the government protects its people. Perhaps, you should do as he asks and talk to this district attorney." He put his arm lovingly around Rosa. "Come, daughter. We will think on it this night."

Dominick watched them go into the house. He should have felt better. But he didn't. He wasn't sure the government did such a fine job protecting its people.

Chapter 25

"All Rise!"

A stout man of middle years strode through the doorway behind the judge's bench.

"Oyez! Oyez! Oyez! All persons bound to appear before the court this day draw near and give attention and all shall be heard! The Honorable William E. Porter, presiding. God save the Commonwealth and this honorable court!"

"Please be seated." The judge's deep voice resounded through the courtroom.

Sitting quietly in the back row, Dominick shifted his gaze to the defendant's table. There, dejected and worn and flanked by two attorneys, sat Rocco Racca. Dominick thought about all he had suffered just to bring the Black Hand Chieftain to this point. Now he just wanted it finished.

The DA's voice drew Dominick's attention to the witness stand.

"Do you know who owned the dog you saw the game warden shoot?" Mr. Young asked.

"Yes sir, Rocco Racca."

"For the record, Mr. List, would you point Rocco Racca out for the court?"

"Yes sir, He's the fellow sitting by..."

Dominick was finding it hard to concentrate. He was worried about Rosa. Toni had been staying at the Ciampanelli's for the past three weeks. This afternoon he was supposed to escort Rosa and her father into New Castle to testify. Her testimony should seal the case. But there had been no word of Siciliano, and that was what worried him most.

"The witness may step down." The judge said.

The district attorney came slowly to his feet. "Your honor, the Commonwealth will call Docato Trevino as its next witness. I would like to remind the court that both parties in this case have agreed with Mr. Dimuro's suggestion as to the swearing of Italian witnesses."

"I am aware of this, Mr. Young. I assume you have the implement in question?"

"Yes, your honor, I do."

Mr. Young pulled a brass crucifix from his coat pocket and handed it to the tipstaff.

"You will hand the crucifix to the Italian witnesses instead of the open bible when you swear them in, Mr. Johnson."

"Yes, your honor," Mr. Johnson replied, looking at the implement in his hand as though it might bite him.

Docato Trevino glanced from the tipstaff, to the judge, to Mr. Young. When the tipstaff placed the crucifix in his hands, Docato kissed it before crossing himself. The court interpreter repeated the oath intoned by the tipstaff while the lad shifted his head quickly between them.

"Si," Docato responded to the interpreter, handing the crucifix back to Mr. Johnson who appeared a little confused as what to do with it. Docato then completed his testimony with very little stuttering. After Docato finished his cross-examination the court recessed for lunch.

After lunch Dominick waited at the trolley stop for Toni, Rosa and her father. When the Youngstown car arrived, they weren't on it. A feeling that something was wrong began to nag him.

Shoving the feeling aside, he slowly made his way back to the courthouse. When Dominick couldn't find them in the courtroom his anxiety intensified.

. . .

By ten o'clock, Toni Capizzi was reading the latest article about Rocco Racca's trial in the New Castle News and enjoying his fourth cup of coffee. Life had been good these past three weeks, waiting for the trial to begin. Toni and Casimo played scopa almost every night, and the big quarry worker was uncommonly good at taking his cigars. A steady rapping on the front door interrupted Toni's reprieve.

Mary rushed by him. "Billy DeGarmo," Mary declared, opening the door to reveal a boy about her own age with unruly black hair. "What are you doing here?"

"Buongiorno, Mary," the boy replied, bright eyes and toothy grin revealing a youthful fondness for the girl. "Is Signore Capizzi around?"

"Si, he is here."

"Please tell him to come to the quarry's office right away."

With a rattle, Toni lay the newspaper down and stood up. Mary stood aside when the lean detective reached the doorway.

"I am Signore Capizzi, young man. What is this about?"

The boy's eyes turned into brown saucers as they fastened on Toni's revolver tucked into a worn, brown holster under his arm. "They sent me to tell you to come to the Johnson quarry. That you must make a phone call to New Castle."

"Who told you this?" Toni asked roughly.

The boy's cheeks colored. "Th..the men at the quarry, signore."

"Billy works in the quarry office sometimes," Mrs. Ciampanelli said, gliding in behind Toni.

"I see. And did they tell you who I'm supposed to call?"

"Si. A Superintendent Demmo I believe it was."

"Dimuro? Could it have been Superintendent Dimuro?"

The boy's face brightened. "Si, signore. That's it."

"Grazie, I'll be along shortly."

"But, signore. They said you are to come right away."

Toni waved the boy away before turning to Mrs. Ciampanelli. "I don't like this. Why would the boss call me now? He knows we're going to New Castle this afternoon."

"You men! You always try to make something with nothing. Maybe they don't need my Rosa anymore. She shouldn't be involved with this business. This is men's business." She flipped a hand angrily in the air before waving at the shoulder holster under his arm. "You men with your big guns! This is not the thing little girls should have to do."

Toni sighed. They had been over this discussion almost every day since he had been here. He didn't want to argue the point again. The woman was as unmovable as the mountains of Sicily.

"Well don't let the girl go outside until I get back," Toni replied moving toward his coat and hat.

...

When the court reconvened, Romon Cerini took the stand with calm and deadly assurance. Romon took his oath on the crucifix without emotion. He stated Rocco told him he hurt his back placing stones over the body of the game policeman after Rocco and his brother-in-law ambushed Houk in the woods above the tracks.

Shortly after the defense attorneys began their cross-examination the doors opened. Dominick turned to the rustle of skirts expecting to see Rosa. Instead, Mrs. Cerini and her children came into the courtroom escorted by a Pinkerton detective.

Where could Toni and Rosa be? He wondered. His anxiety began rising again. Then Romon's little boy started crying softly.

...

Rosa stood quietly by the doorway to the kitchen as Toni left to make his phone call. She had been quiet and moody for the past several days. When her mother turned toward the kitchen Rosa asked when her father was coming home.

"Don't be afraid, child. He should be here anytime now."

"I'm not afraid, Mamma. But it's so nice out. Just let me walk up the quarry path to meet papa. We can walk home together."

"Signore Capizzi said you should stay in the house until he gets back."

"I would like some fresh air. Besides, I need to go to the shed."

Traces of a storm began edging around Signora Ciampanelli's mouth. "OK, Rosa. But stay in the yard. Capeesh?"

. . .

Romon was half way back to his seat after finishing his testimony when he heard his little boy calling to him. Stopping in mid-stride he looked pleadingly at the judge. The judge rapped his anvil on the bench and declared a fifteen minute recess.

During the interlude, Dominick noticed an elderly man hand Dimuro a note. The Pinkerton superintendent followed him out of the courtroom talking excitedly. For the hundredth time he wondered where Rosa was. Frank Dimuro did not return when the court reconvened.

They called Luca Caruzzi next and he began testifying along the same lines as Cerini, relating Rocco's confession to him about the murder of Seeley Houk.

Somewhere in the middle of Luca's testimony, the same elderly man who brought the note to Dimuro tapped Dominick on the shoulder.

"Excuse me, sir, but Mr. Dimuro asks that you go to the district attorney's office at once."

Worry began to crystallize into a burning fear in the pit of his stomach. "Why? What's wrong?"

.   .   .

The Ciampanelli's back yard was mostly garden, now spaded and mulched with straw for the winter. The outhouse crouched against a wall of brush and spindly trees that made up the woods between settlements. As she stepped out of the little shed a sinewy arm clamped around her waist. The girl managed to leak out a squeal before a callused hand slammed painfully over her mouth.

"Quickly!" A voice growled. "This way, before her papa comes."

Rosa tried to kick, but another man grabbed her legs. Briars tore at her clothes and cut her skin as they carried the girl toward the railroad. When they reached a small clearing, the man holding her legs dropped them. Then the hand over Rosa's mouth turned into a clamp as fingers pinched her lips painfully together and jerked her head around. Through tears of rage and fear Rosa stared into a face cruel beyond description. Then a rush of putrid breath filled her nostrils, a blend of whiskey, tobacco, and rotten teeth. Suddenly Rosa's mouth filled with bile. Vomit squirted between the ugly man's fingers, spraying his face.

Bent over the man's arm, she emptied her stomach. Curses and blows struck the back of her head. She felt fingers in her hair and realized her captor was cleaning his hand. She kept retching even after there was nothing left to bring up.

"Gag the bitch!"

They stuffed a dirty handkerchief in her mouth and tied it in place with a second.

"Grab her arms and hold her on the ground," the ugly man said. His guttural voice sounding more like a growling dog.

She tried to struggle again, but they were too strong. The youngest grabbed Rosa's arms and hair, yanking her down. She fell, a rock digging painfully into her back. The other, an unshaven man nearly her father's age, sat on her legs and began fumbling her skirts up over her waist. Then she felt rough, callused hands rip off her underclothes. She tossed her head back and forth, trying to scream through the filthy gag.

When she saw the ugly man's maleness, Rosa's throat went raw trying to scream. She felt weak. Tears blurred her vision.

"Get out of the way, Saverio! Just hold her legs until I'm ready."

She thought of Dominick and cold determination set in. As the older man started to slide off her legs Rosa managed to kick him hard in the face. He cursed, then crashed his fist into the small of her thigh. Her leg went numb.

"Wench!" he cursed, wiping blood from a cracked lip.

"Better hurry, Vito." The boy holding her arms declared. "She's a lively one."

The older man held Rosa's good leg as Vito Siciliano knelt in front of her. She felt him fumbling roughly between her legs. Then pain ripped into her middle as the ugly man moved and grunted over her. Suddenly his eyes bulged, and a stream of tobacco stained saliva drooled onto her face. Somewhere between the older man and the boy she passed out.

Rosa was jolted awake by stinging slaps that rocked her head back and forth.

"There you are now, my little doll baby," the growling man said.

The young man who had held her arms quickly buttoned his fly. There was numbness in her groin, and it seemed very wet down there. She slowly realized the gag was gone, but something else was wrong. Something cold and sharp seemed to be caught at the edge of her mouth. Rosa's eyes focused on a scarred hand with dirty fingernails holding a knife at her mouth where her lips joined.

"Don't move, baby doll, and keep your mouth open." The voice seemed to be purring now, but it was like the purring of a lion teasing its prey.

The leering face hung at the edge of her vision, just above the knife.

"I thought if we could get that traitor out of your house, you might do something stupid. But now, I have a little present for Dominick Prugitore, eh?"

Suddenly the hand moved and a burning pain shot across her face. Rosa tried to scream but no sound came. Blood poured into her mouth. She rolled over and started coughing to clear her throat.

"Come on, Vito!" The youth pleaded. "Let's get out of here."

.   .   .

When Dominick reached the DA's office he found Toni and Dimuro talking quietly. They stopped abruptly when he walked into the room.

"Toni!" Dominick exclaimed. "What are you doing here?"

They just stared at him.

"Where is Rosa?"

"Best sit down, Dominick," Dimuro said quietly.

Dominick gave Toni a smoldering look. "You were supposed to protect her."

"It wasn't his fault," Dimuro put in.

Dominick threw his hands in the air. "Will somebody tell me what happened?"

"She was cut," Toni said, running his finger along the scar on his face.

Dominick looked at him blankly.

"She's alive, Dominick," Dimuro declared.

He took a half step backwards, toward the door. "Where is she?"

"You can't go to her. She's in the woman's ward at the hospital. She lost a lot of blood."

"They just stitched her cheek back together," Toni added. "It was an especially brutal cut."

"Siciliano!"

"We don't know that for sure," Dimuro said.

"I do!" With that Dominick spun on his heel and started for the door.

"Get back here!" Dimuro shouted.

As Dominick disappeared around the corner, Dimuro motioned for Toni to go after him. "Get that young fool," he sputtered.

Toni trotted out the door, but when he rounded the corner there was a loud smack. Superintendent Dimuro watched Toni fall against the doorway and slump to the floor. When Dimuro reached him, Toni was holding his eye and shaking his head.

Dominick hovered over them as Frank tried to help Toni to his feet. "I owed you that one, Toni," he said coldly. Then he turned and began running down the hallway.

Chapter 26

"Why do you want this man so bad?" asked a suspicious, middle-aged man wearing the working bibs of a laborer.

They were in an unlicensed bar that occupied the cellar of a rundown tenement. Yellowish brown cigar smoke eddied around coal oil lamps sitting on a few derelict tables. The place smelled of stale beer and vomit.

"Because I'm going to kill him."

Picking up his beer, Dominick wove through groups seated in rickety looking chairs toward a secluded table where several men were playing cards. He noticed that almost everyone in the room avoided this table giving it only occasional, if fearful, glances.

Dominick surveyed the men seated there. One man, stick thin, with a contemptuous leer hanging under a bristling mustache, seemed in control.

"Mi scusi, signore," Dominick said. "I'm looking for someone, and..."

Without looking up the skinny man shot a finger into the air signaling silence. He reminded Dominick of a skinny caricature of Joe Boggiano.

"I said, I'm looking for someone, you pompous fool."

A sudden hush fell as the man's eyes snapped up in surprise. The other men stared expectantly at their leader.

"You arrogant pig! The least you could do is display a semblance of courtesy when someone speaks to you." Scorn flickered like lighting along the edge of his voice.

With a look cold enough to turn a nun's heart to stone, the man pointed a bony finger. "You're dead!"

He flipped his hand at a thick-chested brute with powerful shoulders sitting across the table from him. The man had his back to Dominick. "Take care of this dog for me, Geno," he said casually.

As Geno began rising, a calculated smile spread over the skinny man's face.

Dominick spun, slamming his elbow into the temple of a man sitting quietly behind him and grabbing the top of the chair as its occupant tumbled to the floor. Putting his whole body into the effort, Dominick swung the chair upward in an arc smashing Geno in the face and knocking him to the floor. Blood spurted from a deep gash over his eye.

The man sitting next to Geno lunged to his feet. Dominick caught the glint of steel in his right hand as the man whirled toward him. Dropping the broken chair, Dominick stepped in quickly striking the man in the face with his fist. Then, using a trick Toni had taught him, he grabbed the back of the hand holding a long bladed knife before twisting it viciously around and backwards. The knife popped out of the man's fist as though it possessed a life of its own and clattered onto the table. Dominick continued twisting the man's wrist, causing him to fall on his back where Geno was frantically trying to kick his way clear of the struggle. Dominick savagely kicked the man in the mouth, causing a fountain of blood to squirt through lips pierced with broken teeth.

Now the skinny man across the table lurched to his feet in a rage, leaning his torso against the table's edge in front of him. Dominick grabbed the knife, brought it over his head and down with a fluid motion of his arm. He laughed as the man jerked his pelvis backwards trying to move his manhood away from the flying steel. The knife thunked into the table's edge, vibrating lewdly in front of the skinny man's groin.

Slowly Dominick pointed a finger at the table's leader. "You tell Don Sochetti, I want Vito Siciliano's ass. You got that?"

Dominick turned on his heel and stalked up the stairs into a frosty October night. Dimly he realized he should feel some emotion: elation, remorse, something. Sadly, the young man remembered when the coldness entered his soul.

The first time he tried to see Rosa she was still in a bed in the women's ward. The second time he managed to get by the cold-eyed nurse while she was talking to a doctor. Dominick could see Rosa through an open door. She was sitting up in a chair, her pretty face wrapped in bandages. Her mother was talking to her, but Rosa wasn't responding. She just sat, staring blankly at nothing.

"What do you think you're doing?"

The nurse's voice caused Dominick's head to snap around. She was standing beside him with her arms folded determinedly under her breasts.

"I...uh, just want to see how Rosa is doing."

"She is doing as well as can be expected." She reached up and grabbed his elbow. "Now come along, she may not see male visitors just now."

Dominick pulled his arm away. "But why? I don't understand."

The woman made a clicking sound with her tongue. "Men usually don't understand rape." she snapped.

Something sharp pierced Dominick's heart. The bouquet of flowers he bought for Rosa spilled across the floor as they dropped from limp hands.

Suddenly the nurse's face softened. "I..I'm sorry. You didn't know."

She bent down and scooped up the flowers before grabbing him by the arm once again. Gently, but firmly, she began leading the young man away from the door.

"The men who did this raped her," she said quietly. "After something like this happens some girls manage to get on with life. Most..."She paused and looked carefully at Dominick. "...are never the same."

She patted Dominick on the shoulder. "I'll see she gets these pretty flowers."

Now, Dominick only wanted to kill the man responsible. With a purposeful stride he started for the next street with its collection of smelly dives.

The morning was growing late when Dominick awoke to a persistent knocking.

"Signore! Signore!" The boarding mistress called excitedly from the hallway. "You have a visitor."

Dominick shook himself awake. His head hurt, and his mouth felt like he had eaten mud.

Then panic struck. Capizzi must have found him. Two nights ago, a man running a basement dive told him a scar-faced man had been asking for someone who fit his description.

"Scusi, signora. Does this man have a scar on his face?"

"Why no, signore. He is wearing a uniform though."

"Polizia then?"

"No, no, signore! Is not that kind of uniform, I think."

"Thank you, signora. Please tell him I will be down shortly."

Walking into the parlor, he was surprised to see a distinguished looking gentleman wearing the suit of an automan.

"Good morning, signore," the man exclaimed with a short bow. "Don Sochetti asks the favor of your presence and to do him the honor of being his guest for dinner."

For a long moment Dominick stood speechless. "Dinner?" he asked finally.

"Si, signore." The man made a broad gesture with his open hand toward the door. "The motorcar is waiting outside."

"Motorcar?"

"Si, signore. A 1907 Oakland is a fine car."

The chauffeur deftly squared his high brimmed hat and opened the door. "If you will permit me, signore?" Then noticing Dominick's hesitation he added quietly, "Don Sochetti said you will be under his protection for the day."

They drove several blocks deeper into the Italian section, the driver applying liberal doses of the harsh sounding horn to hustle pedestrians and horse drawn carts out of the way. When they arrived at a section that held a subtle blend of Italian and Jewish cultures the car stopped in front of a two-tone green door.

The car's door opened suddenly and Dominick looked down into the tanned and leathery face of the automan.

"Don Sochetti awaits you inside, signore. I'll be here to drive you home when you and the Don are finished talking."

"Grazie."

The restaurant was fairly dark inside, but Dominick could make out the slim form of a man sitting alone in a corner booth. Dominick had met Don Sochetti only briefly, just before the raid in Hillsville. Suddenly, he realized Don Sochetti had to know he was the spy who broke up the Society of Honor. He smiled at the vision of the Don running like a rabbit through the briars around Hillsville.

"Good morning, Don Sochetti."

The Don stared at him a moment, his face an impassive mask, before motioning him into the seat across the table.

A waiter appeared and addressed the Don. "May I take your order, signore?"

"Bring my guest a glass, eh."

An open bottle of white wine sat on the table.

"I would recommend the fish," the Don said casually. "It's Friday after all."

"What is that to men like us, signore?"

Don Sochetti frowned. "We still have a soul, Prugitore. No matter what our deeds."

The waiter reappeared with a wineglass, setting it down carefully in front of Dominick without looking at him, then waited patiently for their order.

Don Sochetti ordered fish. Dominick ordered veal and a bottle of red wine.

They ate their meal in detached silence. When they were finished the Don pushed his plate aside and poured a second glass of wine. "I suppose you know Rocco Racca was convicted of the murder of the game policeman," he began.

"I read the American papers, signore."

"Si, so you do. He is going to hang you know." Don Sochetti made a distasteful face. "The stupid fool had to bring up that unfortunate affair with Marsicano's wife when he took the stand. The Americans are rather self-righteous, I'm afraid."

"Si," Dominick replied, "that, and his lies about his prison record in the old country, discredited his testimony. The Americans are also rather strict about lying under oath."

"So are we." The Don's voice took on a chill.

Dominick made a sign with his hand, asking for permission to talk freely. Don Sochetti nodded, eyes gleaming like black ice.

"I work for the Pinkerton National Detective Agency..."

"Do you? The Don interrupted, I have the impression you are running from them, no?"

"No."

"Oh? Then why is that traitor Dimuro and the scar-faced detective looking for you?"

Dominick felt a pang of guilt. Then coldness filled his heart. Dimuro had forced him to push the issue with Rosa, and now...

"Well, no matter," Don Sochetti continued. "You have broken the Omerta. You do know what that means, do you not?"

"Si. But as I started to say, I was a detective before I joined the Society. I only joined because I was ordered to."

"But join you did. And take the oath you did. Unfortunately, there is this matter of honor—this matter of the girl."

Dominick raised a questioning eyebrow. "What more can you possibly do to her, signore?"

"That's just it, Prugitore. We didn't do anything to her. Siciliano acted on his own. In fact, we decided to let Rocco Racca answer for his murder of the game policeman. Rocco was very stupid. Because of him...," he paused, "...and because of you, The Society of Honor must go to sleep for a while."

"Good! Then my labors have not been in vain."

Don Sochetti paused to sip some wine, peering intently at Dominick over the rim of his glass. "You have managed to cost myself and the other Dons a good deal of money," he said, setting the wine glass down carefully. "It is a shame. You had the potential to be a Don some day."

He shrugged.

"As it is, the Society is faced with an interesting dilemma. You must die, of course. However, there is this vendetta of yours with Siciliano. This is a thing the Society cannot ignore. So, I must ask you Prugitore, will you agree to fight a duel with Siciliano? A duel to the death under the rules of The Society of Honor?"

Dominick leaned forward eagerly. "Si," he hissed. There was a hungry, intense look on his face. A look of such hate, that Don Sochetti shivered despite himself.

The Don took another sip of wine. "Then here is what you shall do. I will give you three weeks to prepare." He shrugged his slim shoulders again. "No, I will do better than that. You must go back to Hillsville. Go to Ignazio Sebastianelli. Ignazio will help you get ready for this duel. He will be expecting you."

Now it was Dominick's turn to look shaken. "Ignazio Sebastianelli? How can that crazy old man help me fight a duel?"

Don Sochetti lifted his chin slightly. "Signore Sebastianelli was the best knifeman in all Sicily."

"But why..?"

"Who knows? Some men get tired of killing. Some say there was a woman. But whatever the reason, Signore Sebastianelli disappeared from Sicily many years ago. They say he killed only for just cause." Don Sochetti looked scornful. "We discovered him in Hillsville, but decided to respect an old man's wishes for privacy. Now, perhaps, it is time to enlist his services once again."

The Don pushed his wineglass aside, folding one slim hand carefully over the other. "But in the end you will die anyway, I think." His voice turned into a harsh whisper. "Vito is too good with a knife. Perhaps, he is as good as Signore Sebastianelli was in his prime. So you see? You will pay for your treachery while the Society will have solved this problem of honor."

Dominick leaned forward as well, deliberately folding his hands on the table, his fingertips brushing those of Don Sochetti. "But suppose I kill the pig. What then?" His voice was barely above a whisper, yet hard as flint.

"Then we shall see," the Don replied evenly.

"Si, we shall see. But if it was your order to cut the girl; I will be coming for you next, Sochetti!"

Dominick started to slide out of the booth when the Don's slim hand clamped down on his arm with surprising force.

"Three weeks, Prugitore."

.　.　.

Panting and sweating despite a chilly October drizzle, Dominick rose to his feet after completing yet another demanding set of calisthenics.

"Good! Good! Now run around the quarry again, but try to pick up the time a little, silly boy."

Dominick, flushed, tired and sore, looked angrily at the old man. "But why? You haven't shown me anything with the knife yet, just that silly form you make me do over and over again."

"Are you so anxious to die, silly boy?"

Lunging quickly, Ignazio slammed his fist into Dominick's ribs with enough force to double him over. Then, chirping like a bird, the old man stepped back leaving Dominick on his knees clutching his side and gasping for breath.

"You think you will end this fight...," Ignazio snapped his finger, "... quick like that?" He snorted loudly. "Siciliano is a tough, hardened fighter. If you live long enough, the fight could go on for fifteen minutes, maybe more."

The old man stepped close again grasping Dominick by the hair, lifting his head.

"To fight like this takes endurance." Continuing to lift, Ignazio forced Dominick to stand erect. "Now run! Run for your life, silly boy."

That evening they sat at Ignazio's small, homemade table enjoying a quiet meal. Cool rainwater, gathered in a barrel under a corner of the shanty's tin roof, washed down their meager provision. When Ignazio finished eating, he pushed his chair back and studied the young man who was sopping up the leavings on his plate with a thick slice of coarse bread. Already, hardened muscles were beginning to show some definition on his lean frame.

Dominick looked up when Ignazio, emitting that curious bird-like chirping, stood and walked toward his small board-framed bed. Squatting down, the old man pulled a flat-lidded trunk from underneath. Opening the trunk and shuffling through some clothing, he removed a small, slim box. Ignazio inserted a small key into the lock, then holding his hand over the lid as though reluctant to open it, sat down facing the young man.

"The form you complain about is necessary." Glancing at the box under his bony hand, the old man's thin eyebrows gnarled. "Something to help you become one with the knife. You must not concentrate on what you are doing, so much as allowing it to flow out of you...from in here." The old man tapped his chest. You understand?"

"No."

"You will."

Sighing heavily, Ignazio shoved the box toward the eager young man. Inside a pair of slim stilettos lay poised in slotted brackets. Their oiled blades gleamed in the light of the kerosene lamp. Dominick could tell at a glance they were honed to a razor's edge. Each was fitted with a slightly bowed hilt covered with strips of intricately woven leather.

"I am sorry, signore," Dominick said quietly. "Sorry you had to get involved in this."

"They are slayers of evil, these blades," Ignazio replied softly. "Go on, pick them up. But be careful! They bite."

Dominick held one in each hand, studying them.

"They are perfectly balanced and can be thrown accurately," Ignazio went on. "But only a fool would throw his weapon away. Designed for stabbing, their edges can weaken your opponent by bleeding him. In the old country this was common. Here, the Society doesn't permit slashing for fear of the American polizia. Still, there are ways. I will teach you. Vito will try to bleed you if the fight drags on. Tomorrow you will do the form with the knives instead of a stick." He shrugged one thin shoulder. "If you do well, perhaps, we will begin sparring."

"Sparring? You mean we are going to fight one another with real knives?"

"Si, how can you learn to fight without fighting?"

Dominick worked the form until he could flow through each move with perfect balance, slashing or stabbing with speed and power. When he mastered that form Ignazio started him on a more difficult one. They worked from dawn until dark, stopping to take a meager meal at noon. Between forms Dominick did calisthenics and ran a torturous path around the quarry. By the middle of the third week they were spending more and more time trying to cut each other. Dominick's arms and torso were criss-crossed with small cuts that burned under the sweat of his workouts. A few deeper slices were wrapped with blood stained strips of cloth. Ignazio had just received his first cut on a forearm.

"You must learn to ignore the bite of steel," he said as they circled one another in a semi-crouch. "Some men even savor it."

Dominick could see old scars running down Ignazio's bony ribs and along his skinny arms where the sinews snapped and danced under his leathery hide. The old man never even looked at the cut. Blood flowed freely down his arm and, when it began to cover his knife hand, Ignazio deftly flipped the weapon into the other.

"You must learn to fight with both hands," the old man was saying. Suddenly he feinted left. Dominick swung to counter the blow and felt the burn of steel across his ribs as Ignazio spun past his right side.

"You must also learn to tell the difference between a feint and an attack. Come. This is enough for now. We must bathe your wounds. There is so little time, and so much you must know."

Dominick asked about different ways to hold the knife and about switching them from hand to hand.

"Don't try being fancy, silly boy. You do not have the experience. Keep it simple. Most importantly do not allow Vito to lure you into a trap. He will try. If you keep out of his reach long enough he will grow weary, maybe over-confident. You will get a chance if you can stay alive long enough. But don't let him lure you in. You will know when it is time to lunge."

Ignazio opened a jar of home canned pears, and they sat in the sun enjoying the sugar rich juice as much as the fruit. Ignazio looked at Dominick a moment as the young man fished the last slice of fruit from the jar.

"What I fear the most," the old man said finally, "is that Vito will taunt you into doing something stupid."

Dominick nodded around the last mouthful of pear juice. "Don't worry, I'm ready for that. He tried before."

"He will tell you," Ignazio said slowly, "how much he enjoyed the girl."

Dominick choked. Jumping to his feet he threw the jar at a rock. Shards of blue-green glass few in all directions.

"Vito will taunt you in the most lewd terms, perhaps even claiming she enjoyed it." The old man shook his head. "If you react, you will die."

Ignazio stood slowly to his feet facing the enraged young man. "Tell me, is that how you plan to avenge the girl? By dying foolishly? Perhaps, you feel you failed her because this happened. So you plan to punish yourself."

"No! You have it all wrong, old man!"

"Do I?" Ignazio came close, placing his grizzled face next to Dominick's. "I tell you this. If you die, the girl will die."

Dominick backed away, shaking his head.

Ignazio followed him, staying close. "No? She will blame herself, silly boy. With what she suffered she thinks she is no longer worthy of you. She will not be able to live with the burden of your death. You must fight to live!"

Dominick's face contorted into a sculpture of anguish. Then the tears came. They came slowly at first. Then a torrent. His slumping shoulders began to shake as a wail finally broke from deep in his soul. Ignazio's arms pulled him in, and he clung to the old man sobbing and crying like a child. They stood like that for a long time as Dominick sobbed out his anguish, his fear, his rage. Afterward they sat down in the lime dust.

After a final sob, Dominick shook himself. "I have brought dishonor to the people I cared the most about. Maybe I deserve to die."

"No," Ignazio said, shaking his head. "Bad things happen. The question is, what are you going to do about the girl when this is over?"

"I don't know, compare. First, I must concentrate on being here when it is done, no?"

"Good!" The old man exclaimed getting to his feet. "Now let's see if you can learn to throw these things."

The night before the fight, Ignazio fitted a piece of leather into the side of Dominick's boot. "Keep the extra knife there," he said. "You can bet Vito will have an extra blade somewhere."

They met in one of Ignazio's clearings where he netted birds during the summer. The clearing was protected by thick brambles and red brush, so the chance of being surprised by the American authorities was minimal. By ten o'clock the sun had burned off the silvery frost.

Ignazio fretted and fussed over Dominick all morning. The old man insisted they make Vito and the others wait at least fifteen minutes before they arrived.

"This is part of the strategy," Ignazio explained. "It will anger him before we even get there." He shook a finger at Dominick. "Just remember to stay aloof no matter what he says or does. This will confuse him. Capeesh?"

"Si, signore. You have been telling me this for days now."

"See that you listen to crazy Ignazio, no?"

As they wove their way down the narrow path, a man holding a double-barreled shotgun suddenly rose from a patch of red brush alongside the trail. "You're late," the man grumbled. "Vito's been howling like a scalded pig for the past five minutes."

Ignazio emitted that curious chirping. Then rounding a bend they were suddenly in the clearing.

Dominick recognized Nick Sparaio and a few others who were all that remained of the Hillsville Society of Honor. Across the clearing, Vito was rebuttoning his shirt. Glaring and snarling at Ignazio and Dominick he began undoing it again. Dominick also recognized the skinny man from the bar. The big man was there as well. Both grinned wolfishly at him. The skinny man held one of those short-barreled wolf guns the Sicilians favored so much.

"So the traitor has decided to come after all," Vito yelled. "Or did the old man have to soothe your tears and prod you with a knife to get you here, eh?"

Dominick turned his back and peeled off his jacket, before slowly unbuttoning his shirt.

Vito stopped removing his shirt and took a couple of steps toward the center of the clearing. A long bladed stiletto was thrust into his belt. "Don't you turn your back on me, boy. You hear me!"

One of the men with Vito came up behind him and said something Dominick couldn't hear. Then he began pulling the shirt from Vito's back.

Vito sneered. "Maybe you don't want to look at the man who took your little girl's virginity, huh? Is that it?"

Dominick's hand paused and trembled for a moment on the next to last button of his shirt. He breathed deeply before continuing.

"I'll tell you, she's a little doll baby. She liked it, too, even when the others took her. Too bad she's not so pretty now."

Dominick swallowed and held his eyes tight shut, but tears leaked out anyway as he peeled off his shirt. He could hear the old man chirping behind him.

Ignazio was standing with his legs apart, grinning like a maniac. Sparks danced in his eyes. Slowly the old man pulled the dagger Dominick was to use from his belt and held it up with the gleaming tip pointed at Vito.

Vito sneered. "I am not going to fight you. There is no honor in killing a crazy old man."

Ignazio's voice crackled. "You are without honor. You are too low even to be called a dog. You are nothing but a pig."

Ignazio drew the blade slowly across his forearm. Blood ran onto the knife as Ignazio wiped both sides of the blade over the wound.

"I wash this knife in honorable blood so it can't be dishonored by the taint of a pig's foul blood."

Vito began to tremble with rage. "Stop your curses, old man. Give the boy the knife so I can kill him and be done with this foolishness."

"Un momento!" The skinny man with the shotgun shouted, stepping out to where Vito was standing. "We must first go over the rules."

With a roar Vito turned and shoved the man backwards. "No rules!"

Ignazio smiled. "So be it. There will be no rules in this fight." The old man turned, winking at Dominick, as he handed him the stiletto. "Bleed him first. Then kill the pig!"

Dominick took the knife and strode purposefully toward the center of the clearing. The heaviness of it felt strangely comforting in his hand.

Vito crouched, easily tossing his blade from hand to hand. Then he stood up suddenly and began to laugh.

"Look at him," Vito roared. "Look at the cuts and welts. Am I a dog? Must I face a boy who let an old man do this to him?"

"Not a dog." Ignazio called from the clearing's edge. "A pig!"

Vito growled and spat before settling into a semi-crouch once again. Still flipping his knife from hand to hand, he called to Dominick. "Just come to me, boy. I will kill you quickly and not torture you like that crazy old man did."

Without missing a stride, Dominick glided smoothly into a crouch pointing the tip of the stiletto at Vito's chest and holding his other hand out for balance. Staying just outside of the taller man's reach, Dominick began to circle left. Vito snarled and followed him around awkwardly. Dominick wondered if Vito was used to an opponent circling right instead of left, or was he simply trying to trick him into doing something stupid. Vito's knife was in his left hand. It was time to find out!

Suddenly extending his wrist into a fencer's grip on his stiletto, Dominick made a thrust at the right side of Vito's abdomen. With amazing agility, Vito's right hand came down to block and grab Dominick's knife arm as he spun into a counter attack of his own. Quickly Dominick checked his lunge and allowed his blade to slide around Vito's wrist. He felt it grate along bone, but as he spun away he also felt the burning sting of Vito's blade sliding along a rib, laying a long and bloody gash on his side. Numbly Dominick realized he had almost taken a fatal thrust aimed for his lung. Dimly he heard the words "Silly boy!" drift across the clearing. Then Dominick noticed Vito's hand covered with blood and dangling limply.

Vito's face contorted with rage. Suddenly, with an assortment of whirling slashes, Vito charged. With amazing speed a slash turned into a lunge, then a lunge into a series of circular slashes forcing Dominick ever backward in a series of right or left obliques. With their arms and torsos glistened with sweat and blood, the clash of steel rang across the clearing as they blocked one thrust after another.

Dominick fought for each breath. His arms and legs ached. His motions grew sluggish. He was cut in several places, the knife becoming slippery from blood and sweat. Now it was all he could do to block Vito's powerful thrusts. Suddenly, a searing flash of white fire exploded across his forehead, and down over his eye. Then he felt his knife wrenched from his hand as Vito's body whirled by.

I'm a dead man, he thought. Dominick braced himself for the fatal lunge as he tried to wipe blood from his good eye with an equally bloody arm. A long moment slipped by. Then Dominick's vision cleared enough to see his opponent swaying. The bloody hilt of his stiletto protruded from Vito's ribs. The leering face contorted then Vito's arm rose and dropped suddenly.

Lurching to the side Dominick felt something strike his left shoulder, knocking him to his knees. He looked down to see the hilt of Vito's stiletto sticking just under his collarbone. As though in slow motion, he watched Vito pull the blade free from his ribs emitting a spray of bright red blood as the assassin staggered toward him. Dominick grabbed the hilt of the dagger sticking in his shoulder. Shards of pain ripped through his arm as he tried to pull the knife free, but the blade, embedded in his collar bone, was wedged tight. Vito was almost on him when he remembered the knife in his boot. His hand clasped the hilt as Vito's boot struck him in the chest, pinning him to the ground. Another bolt of searing pain nearly caused him to pass out. Dimly he saw a bloody blade thrusting at him, saw frothy pink blood foaming from Vito's mouth. Then Rosa's face, wrapped in bandages, swam before him. With a final surge of strength Dominick struck upwards with all his might. He felt the blade sink into soft tissue, heard Vito scream before Dominick gave the blade a vicious twist. Again the hilt yanked free of his hand as Vito tumbled backwards, the stiletto protruding obscenely from a bloody mess in his groin. Dominick watched as the assassin rolled from side to side, his legs kicking spasmodically before stiffening suddenly. Then he lay still.

Suddenly Ignazio was at his side. "Get him to my place, quickly. We must stop this bleeding if we are to save his life."

"I don't think so."

Dominick heard the heavy hammers of the skinny man's shotgun being cocked.

"Don Sochetti said this man is to die. So I think you will let him lay until this happens, no?"

"No!"

Now Dominick could hear pistol hammers being cocked.

"This is not Youngstown! Now go, or there will be much more bloodshed here, I think!" The voice was Nick Sparaio's.

"Don Sochetti will not allow this!" The skinny man sputtered.

"Away with Don Sochetti. This is Hillsville, and that boy...," Nick motioned toward Dominick, "...is a Hillsville boy!"

Dominick heard the heavy hammers of the shotgun being eased back into place, then felt himself being lifted. The last thing he heard, before falling into darkness, was a sound like the chirping of birds.

Chapter 27

In the exercise yard trustees and deputies could be seen scurrying through the predawn light. Now and then one of the hurrying figures would steal a glance at the ominous platform standing shrouded in shadows next to a wall that separated the jail from the courthouse.

In a cell on the second tier, two men sat eating an exceptionally large breakfast. One of the men, a Negro, watched the other from under heavy lids. Rocco Racca was wolfing down large portions of ham, eggs and fried potatoes. Finally, he looked up and waved a hand at Fred Leech's plate.

"What's the matter with you? You no like ham?"

Fred's dark face seemed to break in half. Both halves separated by a wide band of yellow ivory that seemed to float in waves of dark wrinkles flowing back to the man's ears.

"Man, help yo self."

Rocco grunted, then speared the half-eaten slab of ham off Fred's plate and began sawing at it with a dull butter knife. When he finished, Rocco stared at his companion for a moment. "You been gooda' company last night, Fred. Grazie."

Footsteps in the corridor interrupted their conversation. The sheriff's deputy appeared first and unlocked the cell. Behind him was Father Maturo of Hillsville and Peter Capito the undertaker.

Father Maturo took Rocco aside and, sitting beside him on the bunk, quietly asked, "Are you ready to meet your maker, Rocco?"

"Forgive me, Father, for I have sinned."

Father Maturo nodded before handing the condemned man a crucifix and donning his white linen amice.

Rocco crossed himself and kissed the crucifix several times before speaking quietly to the priest in Italian. When he was finished the priest pulled a small vile of oil from his robe, then praying in Latin, wet his thumb before beginning a ritual dating back to the burial of Christ. When the condemned man's last rights were completed, the priest rose.

"You may now go to your destiny knowing you will be welcome in Heaven," Father Maturo proclaimed.

Rocco gathered the edge of the priest's robe between his fingers, kissing it lightly. Grazie, Father."

Rising, Rocco removed a picture of Mario Nardozi from his coat pocket and handed it to the undertaker. "Mario and I will have shared the same fate, so put this in my coffin when it is over. You must also place the coffin at the church so my people can say good-bye."

The undertaker nodded then stood up to remove a tape from his coat pocket.

Rocco stood quietly as the undertaker began his measurements.

It was mid-morning before Sheriff John Waddington and Deputy Sheriff Frank Waddington arrived with a physician in tow. Frank was carrying a long leather thong with which to bind the prisoner's hands.

"It's about time you got here," Rocco said cheerfully. "Me no like waiting. It should have been over fifteen minutes ago."

"How are you feeling?" the doctor asked.

"Good enough to die," Rocco replied.

The doctor stepped back, red-faced.

As Waddington stepped forward with the leather thong, Rocco grabbed his shoulders. "Gooda'-bye, Frank. You treat me good all the time I am here." With that he reached up on his tiptoes and kissed the deputy sheriff on the cheek.

Next, Rocco went over and kissed the sheriff and his guard. Then turning to face the black man, who was left to cheer him during the night, Rocco kissed Fred full on the mouth. Startled, Fred wiped his lips on his sleeve as Rocco bent to kiss the priest's hand. Then, still smiling, Rocco thrust his hands behind him before turning his back to Waddington. The deputy sheriff bound his hands, then gently turned him toward the cell door. Rocco marched out of the cellblock and down the stairs into a yard crowded with spectators.

The hushed crowd parted to form a corridor leading to the gallows. The prisoner marched quickly through the crowd and, without the slightest hesitation, mounted the steps of the scaffold. Placing Rocco's feet directly over the trap doors, Waddington turned the prisoner to face the crowd before whispering something in Rocco's ear.

Looking calmly over the people gathered there, Rocco declared with a firm voice. "I am to be hanged an innocent man! But I pardon everybody, Cerini, the sheriff, all of the people who had anything to do with my trial." He paused and nodded. "Gooda'-bye!"

Moving quickly, Frank Waddington adjusted the hood before placing the noose over Rocco's head, taking care to position the heavy knot just under his right ear. Then, receiving a quiet nod from his son, Sheriff Waddington pulled the lever that released the trap. With the sound of a pistol shot the doors broke open under Rocco's feet. At precisely four and a half feet, the rope snapped taut with the twang of a broken guitar string. Rocco's body spasmed once as the sheriff was urging the crowd of spectators to depart quietly. Only twelve men of the sheriff's jury, selected to officially witness the execution, mostly doctors, newspapermen and officers, were permitted to remain.

After a few minutes the body was slowly lowered to the ground, and the doctors proclaimed Rocco Racca officially dead. The state had avenged the death of Game Protector Seeley Houk.

The next morning, September 27th, 1909, a pink sunrise dawned into a cloudless day. By nine o'clock, almost the entire population of the Hillsville district had gathered at the little church above Kennedy's Crossing. After a brief service by Father Maturo, long lines of people marched around an open casket placed outside the church. Expressions varied from solemn to a glow of satisfaction. Four men, however, stood apart from the gathering.

"These people don't know if they should cry or laugh," Toni observed.

"Perhaps they just want to make sure he's really dead, Toni," Dimuro answered. "He was a bad man."

Dominick shook his head. An ugly, red scar slanted down over his forehead and disappeared under a patch covering his left eye. "He was more than that. He was a haunted man with a distorted sense of honor."

"Well, at least we broke up The Society of Honor," Toni replied. "I hope it has received a death blow."

Three heads shook in unison.

"I am afraid we only put it to sleep for awhile," Dominick replied.

"Si," Dimuro echoed. "When it awakens it will be Americanized."

Dominick looked fondly down at the old man standing beside him. "I have been away many months. Tell me, signore. Where have the Ciampanelli's gone, and how is the girl?"

"They moved away this summer. Place called Renovo. Signore Ciampanelli got a job in a railroad shop there. They say it's the second largest car shop on the Pennsylvania line."

"And...?" Dominick insisted.

"I don't know about the girl."

"Well, if her father's working for the railroad they'll be all right," Toni commented.

Dominick nodded, then let loose a brown syrupy streak of tobacco juice and watched in satisfaction as it splattered over a clump of withered grass some ten feet from where he was standing. "Be safe there anyway, I guess."

Ignazio wagged his head causing his thin hair to splay about even more. "I don't know," he said slowly. "They say there are a lot of white sheets in that town."

Dominick looked at him aghast. "White sheets? You mean the Ku Klux Klan?"

All of them were looking with interest at the old man now.

"Signore, that organization is down south. It was organized to keep the Negroes in line."

"Silly boy!" Ignazio scolded. "The white sheets are also in the north. Here they are organized to keep us in line."

Dimuro laid a thick hand on Dominick's shoulder. "It's true," he said sadly.

"Si," Ignazio added. "Mike Polito was here from North Bend, which is near this Renovo. He said they burn crosses and hold parades."

The old man sighed heavily before drawing a small white envelope from his coat pocket. Looking intently at Dominick he held it out to the young man. "I found this on my table when they left. It is addressed to you."

Dominick recognized the dainty script on the envelope. With a trembling hand he took the envelope from the old man. "Scusi," he said hoarsely before strolling off a few paces to open the letter.

> *Dearest Dominick,*
>
> *You will never know how much you mean to me. I only regret that I have failed you so terribly. I know I will never be worthy of you. Not now. But I hope you will find a special girl some day that will take care of you the way you deserve. I heard about what you did. It was very brave. I just wanted to thank you, because I know you suffered for me. Please do not try to find me. It would break my heart if you saw me now.*
>
> *Rosa.*

Dominick waited until his one good eye was dry before stuffing the envelope into his pocket. Without a word he started down the hill toward Kennedy's Crossing.

"Hey!" Dimuro hollered. "Where do you think you're going?"

"To pack my bags," Dominick yelled back.

Dimuro looked pointedly at Toni.

"Oh no you don't, boss. I'm not going to run after him. He's become quite a scrapper, in case you haven't noticed."

Dimuro jammed his knuckles into the sides of his hips. "Well, I can't send a detective to check on this Ku Klux Klan business without sending someone to back him up. Now can I?"

Toni's face broke into a crooked grin. "No sir! You sure can't."

THE END

About the Author

Jack Weaver is a retired wildlife conservation officer serving thirty-one years with the Pa. Game Commission. Jack served twenty-two years in various field assignments, two years with the Division of Law Enforcement in Harrisburg, and retired as a Information and Education Supervisor for the agency's Northeast Region. During his tenure with the Game Commission, Jack also wrote numerous articles for the Pennsylvania Game News and served as a firearms and defensive tactics instructor. Jack is a third degree black belt instructor in Tang Soo Do Karate. The author resides with his wife Caroline near Howard, PA. The couple ride their Goldwing trike with Mended Wings, the Centre County Chapter of the Christian Motorcyclist Association.